AN OUTCAST AND AN ALLY

AN OUTCAST AND AN ALLY

CAITLIN LOCHNER

Swoon READS

NEW YORK

A Swoon Reads Book
An imprint of Feiwel and Friends and Macmillan Publishing Group, LLC
120 Broadway, New York, NY 10271

Our books may be purchased in bulk for promotional, educational,
or business use. Please contact your local bookseller or the Macmillan Corporate
and Premium Sales Department at (800) 221-7945 ext. 5442 or by email
at MacmillanSpecialMarkets@macmillan.com.

Library of Congress Cataloging-in-Publication Data is available.
ISBN 978-1-250-25664-5 (hardcover) / ISBN 978-1-250-25665-2 (ebook)

Book design by Katie Klimowicz

First edition, 2020

1 3 5 7 9 10 8 6 4 2

swoonreads.com

To Kristin Dodson, without whom I never would've made it this far.
You constantly encourage me and inspire me to do better—
and make me laugh so much it should be illegal. I love you.
Also I promise I'm laughing with you, not at you.

1

LAI

BRIGHT YELLOW CAUTION tape surrounds the warehouses, almost glowing in the moonlight. Caution tape, and more than a fair number of guards. They patrol the long, low concrete structures. There aren't many windows, but there *are* a few gaping holes from the rebels' attack almost a week ago. More than doable as break-in entrances. If the High Council didn't have so many other matters to take care of, they probably would've ordered the openings boarded up. But between the rebel Nytes' declaration of war, public panic at the rebels' infiltration of the sector and successful attack here, and my team's "betrayal" and subsequent escape from prison two days ago, they've had a few other things going on. Still. The rebels must've attacked this place for a reason. They wouldn't have gone out of their way to pull such a risky operation if it didn't somehow further their goal of wiping out all the ungifted. And the Council wouldn't have set so many guards here if there wasn't something to hide.

Even though the attack is long finished, I almost imagine I can see smoke curling up from the ash-stained buildings. That I hear screams in the distance as the civilians who were working here suddenly found themselves face-to-face with death.

I shake my head. Not helping.

Behind me in the underbrush concealing us, Erik cocks his head in question. I wave it off.

The team should've had enough time by now to get to their respective positions. I reach out with my gift to check on everyone's thoughts.

Everyone ready? I ask telepathically.

Yeah. From Erik, both of us hiding across from the main warehouse building. We'll be the ones who go in. With my extensive history of sneaking around and breaking into places and his useful gift of telekinesis, it was decided we had the best chances of success.

Roger. From Jay, stationed by the back of the warehouses, his gift already sweeping over the buildings to sense and track the people inside. Our eyes.

Can we just start already? From Al, over by the front entrance. **Why do I always have to be the distraction?**

Because you're good at it.

Disgruntled, half-formed thoughts come back to me in reply.

Before the rebels ambushed our team almost a week ago, I might've smiled. As it is, I hold back my irritation that she can't just suck it up and follow the plan we all agreed on without complaining.

Okay. Let's go.

I've barely sent the thought to everyone when a flash suddenly splits the night. Flames engulf the wooden bits of the front gate. Guards all over the grounds shout and race toward the entrance. Their swords and badges shine in the light of the fire.

"That *idiot*," I hiss. "What are we going to do if the guards call for backup? Not to mention anyone in the area will be able to see an inferno like that. I told her to start a *small* fire—what part of that is so hard to understand?"

"Guess we better get in and out fast, then," Erik says. He's already standing, shadows cast by the trees and shrubs around us flickering over his pale face. His messy blond hair looks duller in the night, his bright green eyes uncharacteristically serious.

I sigh, but there's no point continuing my rant. He's right.

We make a run for the nearest opening in the building—a jagged, gaping thing that looks intent on swallowing us whole. All the guards outside have swarmed to the fire by the front, so there's no one to stop us.

Be careful. There are two guards not far inside the first corridor, to the left. They're moving fast. Alarmed. Probably trying to figure out what's happening outside.

Got it. Thanks, Jay.

I pass the message on to Erik and he nods. As soon as we're inside, we duck underneath a table with two of its legs broken off one side; it leans precariously against the wall, forming enough of a gap for us to hide in.

It's only thanks to Jay's warning that we don't run straight into that pair of guards. My gift can't pinpoint the location of thoughts. And as dark as it had been outside, the hazy moonlight and guards' flashlights had provided some light. Inside, it's unexpectedly, totally dark. The electricity is probably down from the rebel attack. But there are no temporary lights set up, no signs of brightness from the guards—nothing to indicate their presence.

Erik and I sit in still silence as they hurry through the hall. I can barely see the edge of their night-vision goggles as they pass. So. The Council is trying to give its men the home advantage by intentionally leaving this place in the dark. Smart—except the Councilors forget they're dealing with Nytes.

Once the guards are gone, Erik and I slip out of our hiding space and down the hall to the left, the way they came from. Even though my eyes have somewhat adjusted to the dark, it's still hard not to run into anything. Rubble litters the floor, along with broken bits of furniture, scattered files and papers, shattered glass. It crunches under our boots, and I cringe at the noise. Jay guides us through the building and out of the way of the guards.

We've just reached the safe room, the most likely place anything important would be kept, when Jay's thoughts burst in. **They've extinguished the fire. Johann's started another, but they've caught on that someone is doing this intentionally. They're looking for her—and doubling back into the building to search for intruders.**

Shit. *Got it.*

"We have to hurry," I whisper to Erik. "They're coming."

Erik waves his hand, and the bent metal door propped against the doorframe in front of us lifts into the air as easily as a piece of paper and sets itself back down out of our way. "Good thing we're here."

"Close your eyes." I reach for my necklace and touch one of the power crystals hanging from it. Syon's power crystal is small and electric-yellow, no bigger than my thumbnail. When I draw out his gift from it, light immediately floods the safe room, blinding if you didn't have your eyes closed to the initial intensity of it. As soon as the light calms down, I open my eyes.

Before us is a space no bigger than our old bedrooms back in the military. The walls are solid metal, dented and scorched in multiple places. Cracks streak the linoleum floor. A few overturned filing cabinets are the only furniture, but whatever contents they might've once held have clearly been emptied out. The drawers hang open at awkward angles, the locks snapped clean off. Erik lifts them into the air with his gift anyway, shakes them, but nothing falls out. There's nothing else here.

Erik looks at me. "Lai."

"No," I say. "This can't be it. There *has* to be something."

"Lai, whatever was here, the rebels have it now."

"*No.* They must have left something behind. Why else would the Council be guarding this place?"

"How should I know? Maybe they're just trying to keep people out for their own good. This place is a wreck."

Three guards headed your way. You need to get out of there, now.

I bite my lip.

Erik catches it. "Message from Jay?"

"Three guards incoming."

"Then we need to go."

"But—"

"Lai." His voice is sharp. "There's nothing here."

"The rebels stole whatever was in this room, but what if there's something else the Council is hiding out here?"

"You're the one who stole the blueprints of this place. You said yourself there were no other secured rooms in these buildings."

"But what if—"

Lai. Go. Now.

I choke back my aggravation. With heavy feet, I turn to the empty doorframe. "Let's go."

Erik and I make it about five steps before shouts of discovery ricochet through the hall. No use for stealth now. We run.

Our boots pound over rocks and glass, the noise echoed by the guards pursuing us.

Jay, how many behind us?

Four for now, but more converging on your location.

The words have barely entered my head when a blaring alarm rings through the building.

"Great," Erik mutters. "Just what we needed."

"Better look alive," I say as two guards rush in front of us from an intersecting hallway. I pull a black metal cylinder from my belt and click the button on its side. Metal pieces unfold from inside it and snap into place until I'm holding a double-headed spear. I don't slow down, just keep running until I'm right in front of one of the guards. She thrusts her sword forward, but I duck to the side, grab her wrist, and twist it until she drops her weapon. A knee to her gut, and she's on the ground clutching her stomach. The other guard swings an axe toward me, but before it gets anywhere close, he's flying back through the air. He crashes against the wall with a *whoosh* of lost breath.

Erik rolls his wrist easily as he runs past me. "No sweat."

I roll my eyes as I fall in beside him. "Must be nice to have such an overpowered gift."

"You would know."

We keep running, stopping only when guards stand in our way, and only long enough to dispatch them.

You're going to be surrounded soon. You have to get out of the building.

That would be ideal—the only problem is finding an exit.

Why find one?

I pause, almost taking a fist to the face before I use my spear shaft to sweep the legs out from under the guard in front of me.

"Erik, you wanna make us a way out?" I ask.

Erik glances at me as he dodges back from a guard's sword swing. He grins. "I can't believe I didn't think of that."

We switch places as he runs a little farther ahead and I take on the guard. The guard's sword comes down on my spear shaft. I tilt the shaft so his blade slides down it and he loses his balance. He backsteps, but I rush in at his side. His sword swings up to block, but I strike his knuckles with my shaft and the weapon drops from his grip with a clatter. A kick to his stomach and he's down. After facing the rebel Nytes, fighting a bunch of Etioles feels like beating up children. As if they could hope to match a Nyte's enhanced speed and strength.

When I look for Erik, I find him standing ahead with a bunch of broken furniture pieces and beams hovering in the air. With one shove of his hands, the clump of parts thrusts through the concrete wall all at once. A groan like an earthquake rocks the hall as dust showers down. The guards pursuing us freeze as the building shudders.

"C'mon!" Erik shouts as he races through his makeshift exit. Like I need telling—I'm already sprinting after him as fast as my feet will take me.

We break out into the cool night air and keep running. Shouts surge up around us into the night, along with an ominous creaking, but we don't stop. A few guards break off to try to detain us, but Erik deals with them with a wave of his hand. As soon as we've jumped the gate, Jay and Al are there waiting for us. We don't say anything as we disappear into the maze of streets beyond the warehouse grounds' perimeter.

We manage to make it back to the safehouse without incident. Our hideout is a tiny apartment, one just like every other in the area: rickety, old, and barely standing. The inside is sparsely furnished, with just one main room, a kitchenette in the back, and a small bathroom. A landlord in the Order owns it and lets members use it as needed, whether it be for secret meetups outside our home base, screenings of new members, or anything else. Like when some of us need a place to hide.

"So that was a waste of time," Al says as soon as we're inside. She throws her jacket into her self-chosen corner of the room with more anger than the thing deserves. Without it, the scars on her muscular arms catch the dim light, faint streaks against her dark brown skin. She runs a hand over her close-shaven black hair.

"And just whose fault is that?" I twist the door's lock with a *snap*. "What part of *small fire* didn't you understand? We could've had more time to investigate if you hadn't been so obvious. But *no*, you just *had* to make it huge and flashy like always and blow the fact that we were there."

"Oh, what, so it's my fault the place was empty?" Al spins on her heel to come back and stand right in my face. She lifts her chin. "My fault the rebels stole whatever *was* there? My fault your stupid plan was pointless?"

"Like you had a better plan in mind?"

"Stop," Jay says. He sets a hand on each of our shoulders. Al jerks away. "We're all disappointed, tired, and stressed. It's been a hard couple of days and an even harder week. We need to stick together at a time like this, not blame each other."

Jay's usually tidy black hair is a ruffled mess. His thoughts drag with exhaustion, but even so, he's trying to keep everyone together. I want to smooth his hair down, take off his glasses, look him in his gentle brown eyes, and tell him it'll be okay, we'll be okay. But I can't. I don't say empty words.

"Whatever," Al says. She's already heading for her corner. There's only one mattress in the place, and tonight is Erik's turn to use it.

Erik himself is staring off into space. An unsettling new habit he's picked up since our prison break.

I'd been worried about Erik after the High Council turned on us and declared us traitors, and while he's mostly gone back to his old sarcastic self, my anxiety increases by the day. How long until he decides staying in the sector that betrayed him isn't worth it? How long until he gets tired of our rapidly disintegrating team? How long until he wants to know about his past badly enough to return to the rebels?

Stop that, I tell myself. Erik isn't going anywhere. He's our friend.

"Look, the warehouses were a bust," Al says, still with her back to us. "That's finished. We can't just sit around doing nothing, so we need to pick a new direction. A more useful one."

"Such as?" Erik asks.

But Al doesn't have anything to offer. She knows she's right—we all do—but no next step comes to mind. Well. Not to Al's or Erik's mind.

I feel Jay watching me. **Don't you think this is a good time to tell them about the Order?**

Jay's gaze is steady when I meet his eyes, but that just makes me look away again.

I still haven't told Al and Erik about the secret organization seeking peace between gifted and ungifted that I helped found with several old friends. I need to. They're already suspicious about me *just happening* to know a place for us to hide out. But I don't want to. The four of us can barely hold a conversation for more than ten seconds without it dissolving into a fight anymore.

Our peace coalition of gifted and ungifted is sacred to me. I don't want to bring two impulsive, mistrustful people—one who could decide to go to the rebels and another who indirectly caused the death of Paul, one of my oldest friends—to the Order just because we have nowhere else to go. But I also know it's our only option. I won't abandon my team, and there's no other place for all of us. I just don't want to face it yet.

"How many times have we had this conversation already?" Erik asks when no one says anything aloud. "Isn't that *why* we decided to investigate the warehouses? We have nowhere to go, we're notoriously wanted criminals, and there's nothing we can do to fight against the rebels without drawing attention to ourselves and getting caught by the military. We're stuck."

"Everything's going to be fine," Jay says softly but firmly, in that way only he can, with words only he could say without anyone getting angry or arguing over them. "We just need a little time. Once the rebels make their next move, the military will have to shift their focus from finding us to countering them."

He doesn't mention the Order. He doesn't say if Erik and Al wait just a little longer, we'll be able to go somewhere we can actually work toward making a difference. Even though he doesn't understand my hesitation, he doesn't interfere with my decision.

That consideration is so like him. A well of gratitude surges in my chest and I send the telepathic message, *Thank you*. He smiles slightly but says nothing aloud.

"How long are we going to have to wait?" Al mutters. She sits with a thump and props her chin up on her fist, but her impatience from before has already blown away. Now she only looks tired. "The longer we just sit around here, the more damage the rebels can do."

"I know," Jay says. "Believe me, I know. But if we move too rashly, we're just going to make more trouble for ourselves—and then we won't be able to do anything at all. We'll come up with something. We always do."

Silence greets his words, and I can't decide if it's one of uneasiness or agreement. Either way, no one's really satisfied.

"Lai's in charge of breakfast, right?" Erik asks without looking at anyone. "Be sure not to burn anything this time."

"Hey, that was once, and it was a mistake anyone could've made," I say.

"Pretty sure you're the only one who's caught the food on fire, though," Al mutters.

"Learning curve."

She rolls her eyes.

Erik goes to the single mattress, pretty much signaling the end of the night's conversation. "I'm going for a walk in the morning. I'll pick up food on the way."

"Be careful," Jay says.

Erik waves a hand vaguely over his shoulder in response. He's already lying facedown on the mattress. His thoughts are preoccupied with a multitude of things, and I don't know whether or not I should say something to him. It feels like I should, but I have no idea what I could say.

Not that it matters. In another few moments, he's out. He used his gift so much tonight, it's little wonder he's exhausted. I'll have to think of something before he comes back from his walk in the morning and then try talking to him. I don't like this feeling of growing distance.

I feel Jay's eyes on me again, but I can't bring myself to look at him. **You can't avoid this forever, Lai. Putting it off is only hurting us. I'm sorry.**

Again, I don't reply to Jay's thoughts. I know he's right. I know I need to do *something*. And the longer I put off telling Al and Erik about the Order, the angrier they'll be when I finally do. But when I think about actually sitting them down and telling them everything, and then taking them to the Order, I can't help but feel a little sick. Paul's face flashes before my eyes—when we go back, I'll have to face Regail Hall without his presence. His death is going to be so much more real.

I push down a threatening wave of grief and guilt—and anger. If Al hadn't separated from us during that ambush to chase after her brother, we could've escaped. Paul would still be alive. And I can't forgive her for that yet.

How am I supposed to share the most important thing in my life, something I would die for in a heartbeat, with someone who's barely here mentally and someone whose actions led to the death of one of my oldest friends?

2
ERIK

BETWEEN BEING STUCK with people who're driving me up the wall and annoying thoughts about the rebels, I don't know which is gonna cave my head in first. Gods, what I wouldn't give to go somewhere quiet and be alone. Just for a while.

Go where? a voice scoffs in the back of my head. *You're a wanted criminal, idiot.*

A criminal even though I stuck around. A criminal even though I turned down the chance to join the rebels and find out more about the past I have no memories of. A criminal for choosing the "right" thing.

Screw this.

I stride through the streets like I'm any other normal Etiole and no one looks at me twice. So much for being wanted. So long as I don't act guilty, no one'll think I am. But I make the mistake of looking down a side alley and seeing some kid getting beaten up by a few middle-aged guys. From the ground, his arms make a weak shield as the men shower him with kicks. I wonder if he's actually a Nyte or if the men just think he is. Not like it matters.

I flick my fingers and the men go flying back through the air. The kid blinks at them. Then he runs for it. I don't go after him to ask if he's okay. Being the hero isn't really my thing. But after that, I keep my hat—found in this mystery apartment we've been staying in—drawn lower over my eyes.

This is why I hate going out into the city. At least in the military Nytes were left alone. Not treated as equals, but not beaten up. Not only because the army knew the gifted were saving their asses, but because anyone who tried to gang up on a trained gifted soldier was just going to end up in the infirmary. But out here in the city, the sector's attitude toward Nytes has just gotten worse thanks to the rebel gifted.

The streets are quiet. After the rebels attacked the sector and declared war, it's like people finally realized they were an actual threat. Took them long enough. Groups stand in doorways and talk quietly. Forced laughs mix with the shouts of the vendors going about their business. Eyes shift back and forth, searching. Everyone under the age of twenty keeps their head down. I guess even the ungifted kids have something to fear, since there are no obvious physical differences between Nytes and Etioles. It must be so hard for them, having to be afraid they'll be accused of being gifted. I try not to think of the kid I saw taking all those kicks.

I weave through the thin crowds easily. Every time I turn a corner, my eyes automatically search for the easiest exit from whatever road I'm on. A side alley between two towering, ugly apartment buildings. An open gate to a shopping center. The walkways that cross back and forth overhead cast shadows down here—definitely helpful for hiding. The sky and dome beyond them are invisible through the spiderwebbing paths.

"What are we going to do if they attack the dome?" I overhear someone whisper. "If the glass breaks, the air Outside will kill us all."

"Don't worry, it'll be fine," someone answers. I'm a good enough liar to recognize doubt when I hear it. "It'd take more than some rebel demons to break the dome. Besides, we have the military and High Council to protect us. They'd never let anything like that happen."

Now there's a good joke. I try not to laugh as I keep moving. The military and the High Council are going to protect everyone? They couldn't protect a piece of paper if their lives depended on it.

Why did I think it was such a good idea to stay with the military for so long? Sure, they're the ones who found me injured Outside the sector's gates and took me in despite my total amnesia, but I knew they were shady. After their information database couldn't tell me anything about my past, I should've left. I could've made something work on my own. I never would've ended up in this situation.

But then I never would've met my team. Would that've been a good thing or not? I want to think I'd be better off without the lot of them, but I know that's just because we've been fraying since the ambush. It's only thanks to them that I started paying attention to the present instead of just blindly chasing after my past. If I hadn't met my teammates, how would I have felt when I found out I used to be a rebel? Would I have just been happy to have clues, a place to go back to? Would there've been any of this dread?

One thing's for sure—only clue to my past or not, I don't want to go back to being a rebel. I've seen what they do to innocent people. I'm no pinnacle of morality, but even I can't accept their violence.

There's nowhere I actually want to go—I just needed to finally get some space from everyone—so I let my feet lead me down a side street lined with makeshift stalls. Some beat-up sign says it's a craft fair, this weekend only. There're a bunch of shops selling jewelry and paintings, but some sell bigger wares like furniture, too. Spindly tables sit next to elegant wooden chairs. A wooden footrest carved in the shape of a rosebush sticks out like a gaudy sore thumb. I stop to get a better look at a chair with birds etched along the backing. When I run my fingers over the detailed carvings, an itch to create stings my hands.

Man, I miss Central's woodshop. Everything else about being in the military might have sucked, but at least I had that. I wonder what they did with all my stuff after we were arrested. Did they throw away the furniture I made? Sell it? Burn it? What about my sketchbooks? I don't really care about the furniture, but I poured my soul into those drawings. Now they're probably at the bottom of a trash can somewhere.

Great. Just great.

A hand on my shoulder nearly gives me a heart attack. I spin around to find a kid, maybe around fourteen years old, behind me. He's pretty small, with bronze-colored skin, unruly black hair, and intense brown eyes staring at me from out of a small, angular face.

Ice trickles down my spine. I know this kid. He was one of the rebel leaders at the ambush they set up to kill us.

Do I run? Punch him in the face? That'd give me a good head start. But his hands shoot up, palms out, and he says, "I'm not here to fight. I just want to talk."

"Talk." I take a step back. "Right." Stalls run up and down the whole street, blocking some of the alley entrances, but there was an opening a few yards back. I can cause a distraction with my gift and make a run for it.

The kid reads me easily. "It'd be better for both of us if you don't cause a scene. Just hear me out."

"That's rich coming from one of the rebels who tried to kill me and my teammates not that long ago." I flex my hands, reaching for my gift. But then I remember this guy probably has some kind of neutralization power crystal. I won't be able to use my telekinesis on him. Could he stop me from using my gift at all?

The kid grabs his elbow. It's the same thing Jay does when he gets nervous. "I know. I know you have no reason to trust me. I know the last time you saw me, we were on opposite sides of a battle. But I had to see you again." His eyes focus on the chair behind me. "I couldn't just leave things like that. I wanted to talk—one last time. Please."

A likely story. Gods, I go out on my own for the first time since before the ambush and a rebel leader finds me in less than twenty minutes. Just my luck.

But . . . ever since I got back to Sector Eight, I've been dealing with the fact that I'm shit out of luck when it comes to learning more about my past. And now someone who probably knew me says he wants to talk. This could be my chance. My *only* chance. Even if he is a rebel.

I'm still trying to decide what to do when the kid speaks again. His eyes stay on the chair. "Pretend we're looking at the market together. We look too suspicious just standing here." He heads to the next stall before I can answer.

Ugh. This is such a pain.

When I catch up to him, he's pretending to admire a necklace. He holds it up to the light, runs the chain through his fingers as he talks quietly. "My name is Cal. We were best friends. You taught me how to fight and saved me more times than I can count. When you went missing, I searched everywhere for you. But when I finally found you, it was already . . ."

"Let me guess," I say, "you're here to convince me to come back to the rebels."

He shakes his head, surprising me. "No. If this is the decision you've made, then I won't try to force you to come back. I just wanted to talk to you again."

When the stall vendor comes over and starts talking to us, the kid humors her, asking about the necklace, the materials, how much time it took to make, the price, before he sets it back down on the blanket-covered display stand and keeps walking. I follow.

"I don't remember you," I say.

"I know."

"All I know about you is that you ambushed me and my team at that fake negotiations meeting."

His back is to me, but I swear I see him flinch. "I know."

I wait for him to justify himself, but he doesn't. He doesn't try to say that he never thought I'd refuse to come back to the rebels or that he'd be forced to fight me. He doesn't make any excuses, and that makes me like him a bit more. Not that I like him at all. He's an enemy. *Not* a friend.

I sigh and make it obvious I'm not happy about any of this.

The kid—Cal—stops at another stall, this one selling hanging chimes. Streamers tied to silver, tinkling cylinders blow gently in the wind. The vendor is nowhere in sight.

"Fine," I say. "What did you want to talk about?"

I don't think my voice has lost any of its hostility, but Cal brightens. "I thought I could tell you about your past. Or, at least, what I know of it. I could answer questions you have about your time with us." He hesitates, then adds all in a rush, "I know you don't remember me, but I remember you. To me, you're still my best friend, and I want to help you."

His burst of sincerity catches me off guard. His eyes are shining, almost desperate, and I get the feeling he's being honest.

No, what if that's just what he wants me to think? Or what if he's using his gift to manipulate my emotions or what I'm seeing? Nytes with unknown gifts can't be trusted, and *especially* not a rebel Nyte—and *especially especially* not a higher-up rebel Nyte. No matter how earnest he seems, it doesn't mean anything when I don't know him.

"Did Ellis send you?" I ask. What if this is just a trap she set up to get to me?

Cal hesitates. Shakes his head. "She doesn't know I'm here. I shouldn't be. It's too risky now that there's war." He looks at me, expression caught somewhere between misery and desperation. "But I *had* to see you. And help you out if I could. This is the last chance I'll get."

His intensity makes me hesitate. Is this really a trick? Were we actually close? I'd thought about former friends in a vague, offhand way before, but I guess I never thought that I *had* to have had them and that they must've been worried when I disappeared.

Something in my chest twists. Damn it all.

I flick one of the thicker wind chimes. A low, dull sound rings out. "You'll really answer my questions?"

"As best I can."

My shoulders tense. I can ask anything I want. About the people who were important to me, what I was doing with the rebels, what I'd been doing before all that. I can't trust whatever he says. But I can't stop my heart from pounding with excitement, either.

I open my mouth to ask how and why I joined the rebels, but the words that come out are, "Do I have any family?"

No, wait. I didn't want to ask that—it wasn't even something I'd known I was thinking about. And it makes me sound weak in front of this rebel.

The lines around Cal's eyes soften. I wish I could take the words back. "I don't really know the details—you never wanted to talk about it—but I know you and your parents didn't . . . get along," he says. "You had a younger brother, but you told me he's dead. You never mentioned how or when."

"Oh." The single exhalation is a betrayal. Don't show anything. Definitely don't show anything that could be taken for weakness. Maybe the real reason he's here is to find something to hold over me by feeding me fake answers. I can't trust him. I have to treat everything he says as a lie until I have actual proof.

But my heart still hits the bottom of my stomach.

I try to get rid of whatever expression is on my face. The vendor rushes over from another stall, apologizing for not noticing us sooner, and we have to fake casual small talk. I imagine hurling the chimes to the ground, the awful noise they'd make as they hit the concrete, the streamers flecked with dirt. I just want to ask my next question already.

When we're finally able to move on without looking suspicious, I say, "How'd I end up with the rebels? What was I trying to do with them?"

A frown turns the corners of Cal's mouth. "I don't know. You and Sara founded our group, but you never told me how you guys met or decided to start it. I know you hated the Etioles, though."

Ellis had said something like that at the ambush, too, but the thought that I helped form the rebels still makes me sick. "Yeah? And why'd I hate the Etioles?"

"You never told me the reason, but it was pretty obvious you did. You never showed them any mercy. You couldn't wait to see the day we'd killed them all."

My stomach turns, but I keep my face neutral. What could've

made me that hateful? Maybe it's a good thing I never told Cal the reason. I don't think I want to know.

When Cal looks like he's about to stop at another stall, I grab his shoulder and keep him walking down the street. He glances at me but doesn't say anything.

"You don't actually seem to have a whole lot of answers, you know." I drop my hand from him.

"It's not my fault you never talked about yourself," Cal says. "I said I'd answer your questions the best I could. If you want someone to blame for the lack of answers, blame your past self for being so closed off." He crosses his arms, lifts his chin. The display of backbone ups my respect for him a little.

"Fine," I say. "Then my time with the rebels." But I hesitate. Do I really want to know about that? It's bad enough knowing I really did want to wipe out all the Etioles for some reason. Supposedly. What worse things could I find out?

No. Don't forget that I can't trust him or anything he says. I don't know what he's playing at yet.

"You said we were friends," I say. "How'd we meet?"

Cal ducks his head, but I still catch the edge of his smile. Is he . . . happy I asked about him? "You saved me," he says. "I was being attacked by a group of Etioles in Sector Eight. If you hadn't stepped in, they probably would've killed me. You even treated my injuries."

Now *that* doesn't sound like me. My policy has always been to keep my head down. Subtly saving someone with my gift and not having to take responsibility for it is one thing. But actually showing myself? No way. Just how different was I before? Then again, that's one thing about my past self that might've been better than the me now.

Cal's eyes fall to the ground. The murmured conversation of vendors, friends, and families hums around us as we keep walking. "You invited me to come with you, Sara, and Joan. I didn't have anything else, so I said yes. We did everything together after that. Well—mostly. You made a lot of solo infiltration trips into Sector Eight. But other than that, anywhere one of us went, the other went, too."

"Except for when I disappeared?" I ask dryly.

He looks miserable when he says, "It was just a routine raid. We'd done dozens before—that time shouldn't have been any different. But the military knew we were coming. They were ready when our team came."

Now that sparks my interest. "What do you mean?"

"The military ambushed us. They separated our team and hit hard with more soldiers than the five of us could handle. There was no choice but to run and try to regroup after. I thought—I thought for sure that you out of all of us had made it out, that you'd already retreated—if I'd known you hadn't—that you'd—"

Cal's ragged voice cuts off as his breath hitches. Something inside me I don't recognize wants to hug him.

"Hey," I say. "It wasn't your fault. At a time like that, you have to protect yourself, right? Even if you'd stayed, I might've still ended up here and you would've gotten yourself killed for nothing." My voice is softer than I expected. Why am I trying to comfort a rebel—and one who just tried to kill me last week? But there's something nagging at me in the back of my head, something that says, *I don't want to see this person upset.*

I don't want to listen to it. Whatever kind of relationship we had before, he's a stranger now. And an enemy. The whole thing makes me uncomfortable, so before Cal can reply, I say, "But then wouldn't the military have known I was a rebel? They said they found me injured Outside. They couldn't *not* have known I was an enemy. Why would they take me in?"

"Erik, no matter what, you can't trust the military. I don't know why they took you or what they had planned, but they knew exactly who you were. They were only using you." Cal's eyes are hard, his guilt and grief from a few seconds ago totally gone. The coldness in them chills my lungs. But no matter how much he looks and acts like a normal kid, he's a high-ranking rebel. There has to be a reason for it. I can't forget that.

It feels wrong that his words ring so true, though. Why would the military knowingly take in a rebel unless they had something planned? And then there's my amnesia. Lai thinks a Nyte is responsible for that, someone whose gift can affect memories. Could the military have gotten someone to erase my memories so I'd join them? But *why?* I haven't exactly done anything important for them since joining up. It doesn't make any sense.

Cal abruptly stops in the middle of the street. I tense, reflexively reaching for the compressed weapon in my pocket, but he isn't even looking at me. He holds out a hand to thin air—the same gesture Lai sometimes makes—with a concentrated expression like he's listening to someone talk. Then he says, eyes still staring straight ahead, "I have to go. Sara is calling me."

The rebels' leader. My gut twists as I remember her sharp eyes cutting through me like the edge of a saw blade at that ambush.

Cal faces me again. "Erik, I've always thought of you like an older brother. You taught me so much, and you were always there for me. I miss you more than you can imagine. But I want you to be happy, whether you return to us or not. Be cautious. Choose what you do from here on out carefully." He half-laughs to himself. "Well, you always choose everything carefully, so I guess that's not saying much. But be safe."

I can only stare at him. No one's ever talked to me with such open care before. How can he be so earnest? He shouldn't have even risked coming here. We're enemies. Whatever we might have been before is over now.

Maybe for you, a voice whispers in the back of my head. *You don't remember being friends. But he still does.*

"Thank you," I manage to say without sounding weird. I think. "For everything."

He smiles, but his eyes are tipped in sadness. "Yeah. Of course." He holds out his hand to me. "You know, if you ever want to come back, you'll always be welcome. I hope you do. I have a lot I'd love to talk about with you."

I hesitate, but only for a moment, before taking his hand. "Yeah. Me too."

I hate how much I mean that.

It's getting dark by the time I return to our hideout. I didn't mean to stay out all day, but after my talk with Cal, I couldn't bring myself to go back. Especially not when there's an irritatingly nosy mind reader I'm going to have to deal with. At least I picked up some more food and supplies for everyone, so it's not like they can complain.

I can't stop thinking about Cal. He said we were close, and despite myself, with the way he acted, I mostly believe him. That means he'd know a lot about me, right? Well, obviously not from before I joined the rebels—but what other kind of info does he have? What else could I learn from him?

But more daunting is seeing how much he really did seem to care about me. His concern felt real. He came all this way, risked discovery in enemy territory, just to talk to me—to answer my questions. So he could *help* me. He didn't even want anything in return. When has anyone done something like that for me? I've never felt that kind of care even from my teammates.

No. It doesn't matter. Cal's a rebel.

So? a voice that's louder than it should be asks in the back of my head. *You think the sector's in the right? They chased you out even after you stayed loyal to them, and then they made you a wanted criminal. Wouldn't you have been better off going to the rebels? Wouldn't you be better off?*

Stop it. That rebel is just getting to me.

But the more I think about it, the more I wonder what I'm still doing here. The military and sector obviously don't give a damn about me. Why should I care about them? Why should I fight for them?

Not that I'm fighting right now anyway. I just hide in a cramped apartment all day with a team that's barely keeping it together. We can't go anywhere; we can't do anything. What am I doing? What am I supposed to do?

Right or wrong doesn't feel so important anymore. I just want to do more than survive.

I'm so lost in my thoughts I don't notice Lai leaning against a building near our apartment until she says, "Erik. We need to talk."

My head snaps up. She knows. Of course she knows. She told us before that she can't turn her gift off—that she's always hearing the thoughts of everyone around her whether she wants to or not. The best she can do is try to tune it all out. But even without that, she doesn't really have any sense of privacy, even for her so-called friends.

"It's not 'so-called,'" Lai says stiffly. "You *are* my friend. You all are."

"And that's why you don't feel any kind of need to leave our thoughts alone?" I shove my hands in my pockets. The bag of food constricts around my wrist.

She doesn't argue. She just jerks her chin toward our hideout. "The others are waiting. But I wanted to ask you first whether you want to keep that rebel's visit a secret or not."

My hands clench into fists. I'm glad they're in my pockets so she can't see. "I'd think the answer to that would be obvious."

She shrugs. "You're not a very obvious person. More roundabout, I'd say." She kicks off the side of the building she's been leaning against and heads for the apartment. "But if you want it secret, I'll keep it secret."

I follow after her more slowly. "You're not worried about it?"

She glances back over her shoulder at me. "Should I be?"

With Jay or Johann or anyone else, I'd lie. Well, maybe not Jay. His gift senses lies, so that'd be pointless. But with Lai, maybe because we're both so similar or maybe because she can just read my thoughts and hear the truth anyway, I don't feel like I need to hide myself. "I don't know."

She nods but doesn't say anything. We don't talk as we climb the stairs to the tiny apartment door and Lai knocks three times, waits a breath, then knocks twice. The same knock comes from the other side before Jay opens the door.

He steps back to let us in. "No trouble, I take it?"

"None," I say. It's just a crappy, temporary apartment, but being back hits me with a wave of relief. It's the closest thing to "safe" I've got. Having my teammates around me again helps. Yeah, they bicker constantly, but damn, can we hold our own together. "It sounds like the Etioles are finally worried about the rebels."

"About time," Johann says with a snort. She stops sharpening the blades of her halberd to stand up. "Maybe if they hadn't been so carefree about them to begin with, things wouldn't have gotten this bad."

"Yeah, 'cause I'm sure all the normal citizens' opinions affect what the military can do so much." I try not to roll my eyes. "It doesn't matter what the people who aren't in charge think."

Johann's about to reply, but Jay steps between us and takes the bag of food from me. "Now that we're all here again, we need to talk." He and Lai share a look that makes my shoulders tense.

"Talk? About what?" I ask. Was Lai just bluffing earlier when she said she'd keep Cal's visit a secret? But then why go out of her way to ask me about it?

She catches my eye and shakes her head slightly. "There's something I need to tell all of you." She waves a hand at the floor.

Now Johann and I share a glance. We only sit on the floor to talk when we're strategizing. Whatever Lai wants to say, it must have to do with our next plan of attack. Or she's worried we'll get angry enough to attack her and she wants to slow us down. And by us, I mean Johann.

But we all sit in our loose ring on the floor, and even Johann doesn't ask questions. It'll be faster to just let Lai get on with it.

"You asked me when we first got to this apartment how I knew about this place," Lai starts, and stops, which is so *not* like her I almost ask if she's okay. Her hands twist in her lap. "I said it was a friend's place. That they'd be okay with us using it." No one says anything. We all knew she was telling the truth, because for whatever reason she obstinately refuses to outright lie, but we also knew that it wasn't the whole truth, either. There was no point arguing it, so we didn't. Just like there's no point saying anything now. But the silence looks like it's getting under Lai's skin. I try to bite back a smirk. Serves her right. "It *is* a friend's place—well, more like a colleague's, but—well, we belong to the same group. An organization called the Amaryllis Order, which seeks peace between the gifted and ungifted."

"Amaryllis Order?" Johann repeats. Her eyes narrow, searching Lai's face. "Never heard of it."

"No," Lai says, "you wouldn't have. We've worked very hard to stay secret."

"Wow, that sounds right up your alley," I say.

Lai glares at me, but there's none of her usual venom in it. "If the Council found out about us, they'd try to destroy us—or say we're part of the rebels or something else ludicrous. They don't want the gifted and ungifted getting along. If the gifted weren't backed into a corner with nowhere else to go, not as many of us would join the military—which would be disadvantageous for them. Hence the Order's secrecy. At least until we're strong enough to hold our own against both them and whatever the rebels might try if they take an interest in us."

"Why would the rebels have any interest in your upstart group?" Johann asks. For once, she's asked a good question. I can't imagine the rebels, who have their hands full with a war, would even notice some small ragtag group calling for peace. It's a little late for that anyway.

Lai's lips tighten. "Because the leader of the rebels helped found the Order, back when we were . . . friends."

Friends. Ha. Lai already told us all about how she and Sara Ellis, leader of the rebels, used to pal around with some other guy named Luke. They were all soldiers in the military together. Apparently they were inseparable—until two and a half, three years ago, when Luke killed himself and Ellis stormed off on her own to start the rebels. But that war-hungry rebel leader helping start some peace group between the gifted and ungifted? I can't imagine it. If I didn't know Lai doesn't lie, I'd call her out on something so ridiculous.

"Look, I know how it sounds," Lai says. I'm probably not the only one with doubt in my thoughts. "But she was different before the rebels. I don't think she ever really believed peace would come between Nytes and Etioles, just like I didn't, but we followed Luke and gave it our best shot. She might not take any interest in us at all now—I just don't know. But that's not a chance we can afford to take." She waits to see if any of us will say anything. When we don't, she goes on. "We've grown a lot stronger since the time Ellis was a part of us. We're enough of a force to *do* something now. Something real. We just have to be careful about it. And careful who we tell about us." Her dark blue eyes flick to each of our faces. "I'm sorry I didn't tell you sooner. The Order means everything to me. All that I've done for the last three years, I've done for them. I didn't want to do anything that could jeopardize our group, or my friends."

"And you thought telling us might do that?" Johann asks. "What did you think we were going to do—go scream about it all over the sector?"

Of course Johann would get angry. But expecting Lai not to keep secrets is like expecting Etioles to suddenly get along with Nytes. I'm just happy she decided to tell us at all. Because where there's some secret group that gave us this apartment to hide in, there's a place to go. To be safe. To *do* something again.

"It was just a precaution," Lai says stiffly. Her back straightens, and it's obvious she's having a hard time holding back her own anger. I swear, these two will go off on each other for anything these days.

I look to Jay to, I don't know, share some kind of exasperation, but his expression is carefully neutral. Something about the way he's sitting—lowered chin, eyes sharp, shoulders drawn in—makes me realize he hasn't said anything.

"You knew about the Order, didn't you?" I ask.

Lai and Johann both put their anger on hold to look at me, then Jay.

But Jay isn't like the rest of us. He doesn't get defensive, doesn't try to hide. He meets my eyes. "Yes. Lai told me a few weeks ago."

Johann explodes to her feet. I resist the urge to yank her arm to get her to sit back down. It's not like I want her temper turned on me. "So you told Kitahara about all this, but not the rest of us? You thought we were, what, less trustworthy?"

"You and Erik were both keeping important information secret," Lai says. "That does tend to make one less trustworthy."

Fire sparks from Johann's fists—literally. "I can't believe after all this time, you would—"

"Trust you with the thing that's most important to me?" Lai says. "Yes, thank you, I'm glad you appreciate the gesture."

Before Johann can drag this out any longer, I say, "I can't imagine you'd suddenly tell us about the Order without a reason. We've been here for a few days. Why now? Because our investigation at the warehouses failed?"

Lai's eyes drop, but only for a second. "Partly, yes. We need a new plan. Something that lets us move forward."

"So you want us all to go to the Order," I guess.

"Yes. Well, no." She glances quickly at me, then away again. Her being so on edge creeps me out. "I want most of us to go to the Order."

A stunned silence fills the room.

"You want to leave one of us behind?" I have a bad feeling I know who she's got in mind.

"No, not leave behind," Lai says with a shake of her head so furious I actually believe her. She finally looks at me directly. "Erik. Before you lost your memories, you were a rebel."

The tips of my fingers freeze. "Thanks for the reminder. I *was*. Emphasis on the past tense there."

"But what if you went back?" she presses. "I bet they would accept you. They'd probably be glad to have their friend back."

"You're suggesting Erik return to the rebels?" Jay demands. It's not exactly every day you hear Jay lose his cool, and him getting angry for me makes me kind of happy. It also makes me relieved to hear he wasn't in on this crazy idea. "You can't be serious."

Lai holds up a finger. "If Erik went back, he'd have the chance to learn more about his past. Right now, we don't have any idea how to get his memories back—but he could at least talk to the people who used to know him and who could give him clues. More clues than he'll get by just sticking around here." She holds up a second finger. "And he could act as a spy for the Order and tell us what the rebels are up to."

I don't know what throws me off more. The blunt truth about the dead end I've hit for finding out about the past I can't remember coming from someone else's mouth, or the idea that Lai wants me to risk my neck spying on the people who apparently used to be my friends. Cal comes to mind. The way he looked up at me, how happy he was when I asked about our past friendship. Something like anger boils in my blood. She's seriously saying I should go back just so I can help her stupid Order? Despite everything that would mean for me?

Luckily Jay speaks before I can. I don't know what I would've said, but it wouldn't have been good. "Lai, that's insanely dangerous. If the rebels caught Erik, he'd be killed—and that's assuming they'd even accept him back in the first place. We need to stick together if we want to stop this war, not separate for suicide missions."

"We have nothing on the rebels right now," Lai says. She lifts her chin that way she does when she's digging in her heels about something. Which is almost everything. "We don't know where their bases are, their numbers, the weaponry at their disposal, what they're planning—we don't even know what they stole from those warehouses. For all we know, it could be a weapon dangerous enough to destroy the entire sector in one go. We have a shot at getting a pair of eyes and ears inside not only their troops but their core of leaders." Lai looks at me again, and this time, she keeps her eyes locked on mine. She has to know what a mess my thoughts are, but she doesn't show it. "Ellis said you used to be her right-hand man. I know her; she can't stand losing those close to her. She'll want things between you to go back to how they used to be. Which means she'll keep you close by and well informed, as you would have been before. And she'll tell you everything you want to know about your past because she'll *want* you to remember."

When I don't say anything, she says quietly, "I know how it sounds. I know it's incredibly risky—and selfish of me to even ask. But this could be a chance to turn the war before it's even really begun. It gives us an in, and it gives Erik a chance to learn more about his past. That's what you want, isn't it?"

That last question is for me, but now I'm the one who can't look at her. Because even though it *is* ridiculous, risky, and way too thin a plan, and even though I'm mad at her for trying to use me for her own purposes, I can't deny the flare of hope that jumped up my throat when she suggested it. I'd already been thinking about the rebels and my options when I came back tonight—and Lai knew it. She's giving me a way to get what I want without betraying our team or the innocent people the rebels are out to kill.

But there's no hiding anything from a mind reader; I don't have to look at her or speak for her to know exactly what's going through my head. And from the way Jay pulls back, I get the feeling he's sensed something in me with his gift that's giving him a pretty good idea of where I stand right now, too. Johann just watches me without saying anything, and even though she doesn't have a gift that lets her into other people's heads or hearts, I realize she knows this is probably what I want, too. I'd have thought she'd be the first one to shoot down this plan, if only because she argues against everything Lai suggests these days, but she hasn't said anything.

Now, Johann turns her back on all of us. "Just do what you want. I'm making dinner."

Jay almost looks like he'll go after her, but he just shakes his head. His glasses slide down his nose. "How would Erik even get to them when we have no idea where they are?"

"I'm sure he can come up with something."

I frown. Underneath a pile of worn clothes in the corner I've been sleeping in sits the sketchbook Ellis gave me at that ambush. And inside it, a way to get in touch with the rebel leader. But I never told anyone about that. Damn mind reader.

Even though I doubt Jay knows about the sketchbook, he picks up on Lai's hint. "This is a terrible plan," he says.

"I know," Lai says.

"Hey, I haven't agreed to anything yet," I say. The words sound hollow even to me. The looks Jay and Lai give me are halfway between pity and saying, *Really?* I throw my hands up. "Okay, fine, *yes*, I'm in. Happy now?"

Jay closes his eyes. He's always taken his position as our leader seriously—and even I'll admit he's done a good job of it. I can't really imagine him letting me walk alone straight into the enemy's lair. He's a good guy like that. But when he opens his eyes, I know he's not going to say what he wants to. "We'll take tomorrow to prepare. Erik, collect whatever supplies you need before you head out—don't forget anything, because I doubt you'll be able to come back. The rest of us will get ready to head to the Order. We'll depart at midnight. You can take the day to think it over, make sure you're certain of this. If you change your mind, you'll of course be able to come with us. There's no shame in refusing to go through with something this dangerous." His eyes cut to Lai, but she pretends not to see.

"Yeah," I say. "Sure. Cool." But we all know I'm not going to change my mind.

3
JAY

I DISLIKE THE idea of Erik parting from us. We should stick together now more than ever. However, I can't, or perhaps won't, argue the matter with him. Last night he was a tumultuous current of violet anxiety and orange-red resolve. A worrisome mix, to say the least. But there was not a single shade of doubt.

I awake at dawn for no immediately discernible reason. However, it doesn't take long to realize Lai isn't in the apartment. I close my eyes and allow the internal grid in my head to unravel itself. The landscape of the area around me takes shape in a three-dimensional map; fluctuating shapes in various shades move through buildings and the streets below, or else remain still in the neutral shades of sleep. I search for one particular presence, and the grid focuses in on an area not far from here. A café? Lai is there, along with someone I recognize from the Order. Seung. A catch-up meeting, then.

Erik and Johann's slow, steady breaths fill the space around me in a comforting hum. I allow myself a few heartbeats to lie there on the hard wooden floor, listening, taking strength from their presence. I won't be able to for much longer. When I open my eyes, dust motes dance through the dim, gray, watery light of daybreak filtering in through the single window. I take a deep breath. Then I rock to my feet, wash my face, and make for the café.

Most of the sector has yet to awaken this early. The warm scent of baking bread drifts through the streets. A few early risers stride past me, but they each appear duly determined to head for wherever they're going and stop for nothing else. They pay me no mind, and I try very hard not to act like they should. I'm a normal citizen. Certainly not a Nyte and ex-soldier wanted for treason.

Something like acid sweeps up my stomach and throat. How many years did I loyally work for the military? How many years did we all? Yet they forced us to go to "peace negotiations" with the rebels, something we all knew was a trap, then branded us traitors when we barely made it back alive from said trap. I'd always known they were less than perfect, especially in regard to their treatment of Nytes. But I never thought they were so openly despicable. Backstabbing, lying, manipulative—

It takes several heartbeats for my anger to run its course and fade to the background. By that time, I've made it to the café where Lai and Seung are meeting. It's on the sixth floor of a skyscraper housing various shops, and because I want to minimize my chances of being seen and recognized, I take the stairs rather than the elevator.

The café is surprisingly large, tucked into a corner between a clothing shop and a stationery store. Gray stone tables of an intricate design that I'm certain Erik would appreciate line the floor in neat rows. A counter to the far side sits underneath a large menu board displaying various coffees, teas, and alcohols. The barista looks up expectantly as I walk in. I hesitate before stepping up to order a black coffee. It would be rude to come and take up space without purchasing anything.

We're lucky Lai and Erik both stored their salaries outside of our military-issued bank accounts. Lai because she didn't want her transactions with the Order to be tracked, and Erik because he trusts no one. Thanks to that, we're not without funds now.

The barista hands me my coffee with no more suspicion than any other teenager might warrant. The loose, light civilian clothes I've been wearing the past few days still feel like a stranger's skin, but they've camouflaged me well. I thank him before heading to a table in the back corner, where Lai and Seung sit with papers splayed between them.

Seung's head snaps up at my approach, sending her short, dark hair flying, but Lai waves away her concern without looking up, and it doesn't take long for Seung to recognize me. She, Syon, and the Wood twins, Peter and Paul, all joined us when we headed out to meet the rebel leaders. They wanted to protect Lai even though she insisted they stay in Sector Eight. It's probably only because of them that we all managed to get out alive. Well. Almost all of us.

My stomach wrenches at the memory of Lai grieving over Paul's body.

My mug clatters against the stone tabletop. "I hope you're well, Seung."

"As well as could be expected," Seung says. It's my first time seeing her out of combat gear. A white blouse with long, loose sleeves covers her golden-brown skin. A necklace with power crystals strung around it, not unlike the one Lai always wears, circles her neck. Her light brown eyes follow me as I seat myself at their table.

Lai still hasn't looked up. Her fingers trace a line on one of the documents Seung must have brought. I can see the gears turning behind her dark blue eyes. Her pale skin looks paler than usual with the dark jacket she's wearing. She absently tucks a long strand of brown hair behind her ear, and I notice the pair of red-framed glasses she's wearing. I've never seen her wear glasses before. The lenses are obviously fake—or perhaps it's only obvious to me as someone who wears prescription glasses—but she looks cute in them. I resist the urge to pull them off and kiss her.

I wait until Lai is ready to speak. Once she's finished her mental calculations, she jots down a note on the paper and turns to me with a smile. A tired smile, but a smile nonetheless. "I wasn't expecting you to be up this early."

"I could say the same of you," I say. I glance at Seung, who's as skilled at murderous glares as Johann—though there's something about Seung's that is more subtle and refined. "I hope I'm not interrupting."

"If you were, I would've asked you not to come when I heard your thoughts headed our way," Lai says.

"If you knew he was coming, you could've mentioned it," Seung says. She folds her hands together on the table.

"Don't mind Fiona, she's always looking for an excuse to be grumpy," Lai fake-whispers to me loudly enough for Seung to hear.

Seung rolls her eyes. "In any case, we were just finishing up. I need to get back to Regail Hall. Ever since the rebels declared war, we've had more than enough work on our hands." Sharp white guilt cuts through Lai's presence. "I look forward to you rejoining us soon."

Lai murmurs agreement.

Seung gathers all the papers on the table and slips them into her bag. She stands, and with a nod to each of us, she leaves the café without another word. It feels much emptier with her gone.

I turn my attention back to Lai, but she's frowning out the window, looking down over the twisting streets below that are only now beginning to fill.

I reach over to push her glasses up her nose. "These are new."

She blinks and laughs as she pulls my hand from her face. She doesn't let go of it. "It's part of the disguise. Like it?"

The disguise in question consists of a black jacket that looks chosen more for style than function—something I've never seen Lai wear—a scarlet blouse, and a high-waisted black skirt. Her hair is down, yet another rarity, and bits of it are tied into braids that pull around to the back of her head. Her usual cord of power crystals hangs around her neck, but a bracelet dangles from her wrist where I'm used to seeing her MMA, a high-functioning, military-issued "watch" used for communicating, tracking, signaling, and other tasks. And of course the fake glasses.

"People are less likely to suspect a fashionably dressed young girl of being an ex-soldier," Lai says with a wink. "It doesn't really fit the image, you know? Besides, it's fun to dress like this when I can." She stretches her arms out in front of her with a yawn and tips her coffee mug to see if there's anything left inside.

"You look pretty," I say, because it's what I think and I don't know what else to say. Trust Lai to have a double motive even for getting dressed.

She laughs and turns her empty mug around. "Thanks."

"I mean it."

"I know."

It takes a heartbeat for me to register the pink of her presence and yet another to realize there's a reason she isn't looking at me directly. I smile and take her mug. "I'll get you a refill."

"Oh—thank you. Um, it's the house blend with milk and three packs of sugar."

"Three? Isn't that a bit excessive?"

"I need something to make me happy in this world."

I laugh and yellow pleasure fills her presence.

By the time I return with her refill, Lai's focus has drifted off again. I set the coffee in front of her. She flashes me a grateful smile as her fingers wrap around the mug.

"What news did Seung have?" I ask.

"The Order is restless," Lai says. "Many members want us to enter the war ourselves, fight the rebels. Especially with Paul's death at their hands." Her eyes drop momentarily, but before I can attempt to offer any words of comfort, she says, "The idea's ridiculous. The Order is a peace organization. We never intended to do any kind of fighting other than self-defense—we're not even equipped for it. We'd be wiped off the map. And just how are we supposed to spread the message of peace if we put ourselves in the middle of a war? Yet Fiona and a lot of the others are pushing for it." Her frown deepens as she takes a sip of her coffee.

Lai protects the Order more fiercely than she does her own life. If she thinks an action could even potentially endanger the Order, she won't take it. But she isn't the only one who dictates what the Order does. As far as I know, she's a Helper and seen as a leader—but the real leader of the Order is a woman named Walker. I wonder what she wants the Order's future actions to be. After all, her decision is likely to be the final one. Hers and that of her two seconds-in-command, Seung and Clemente.

A few more patrons have started to trickle into the café. I watch a well-dressed businesswoman enter and order at the counter.

I understand Lai's side. However, I also understand where Seung and the others are coming from. The Order has an extensive intelligence network, methods of operating secretly, and several members with strengths that could greatly aid in stopping the war—whether physically or politically. They could even have a spy amid the rebels' leaders if all goes well with Erik. The Order is certainly a force to be reckoned with. And joining the war could be a chance for them to be heard. If the Order helped take down the rebels, people might be more inclined to listen to what they have to say about peace between the gifted and ungifted. Is staying secret, protecting themselves in hiding, truly the best route for the Order to take?

I say none of this aloud because it's not my place to, but Lai's presence swirls with violet anxiety. Neither of us mentions what I'm thinking.

4
AL

OUTSIDE THE APARTMENT'S one window, the night is black as coal. The four of us stand together with bags over our shoulders, and I don't know who I can't stand more. There's the obvious option of Lai, liar that she is, who only *just* told us about her huge secret peace organization or whatever. But then there's Mendel, being an idiot and going over to the rebels even though he could get himself killed. And even Kitahara, who usually makes it hard to hate anything about him, was in on all this Order crap from the get-go. I'm teamed up with a bunch of liars and backstabbers and I only just figured it out.

Lai and Kitahara both glance at me, but I don't care. So what if they know what I'm thinking or feeling? Why shouldn't they? Unlike the rest of them, I'm not so stuffed full of secrets you could throw a knife blindfolded and hit one of them.

Lai's voice in my head makes me grit my teeth. *This is the last time we'll all be together for—who knows how long? Maybe ever. Don't you think you could at least* pretend *you care?*

Why should I? I think back.

Lai doesn't reply, but it's obvious by her face she's not happy.

A spark of satisfaction lights in my chest. It doesn't last, though.

When I look around at my teammates' faces, a weight presses down on my throat. I remind myself of my anger and all the perfectly good reasons I have to be angry at each of them, but the feeling doesn't go away.

"You're sure about this?" Lai asks.

"Aren't you the one who suggested it in the first place?" Mendel asks.

"There's no changing your mind once you're back with them," Lai says. "You know that, don't you?"

Mendel hesitates, but not for long. "I'm sure. Look, there's no point beating around the bush. I want to know about my past more than anything. You all know that. This is the best shot I've got without actually turning traitor, and I'm going to take it. If I don't go, I'm always going to wonder. I'd regret *not* going more than I would going."

Kitahara sighs. If Mendel was lying, I'm guessing he would've sensed it with his gift. I wonder if the sigh means he's telling the truth or not.

"So I guess this is it," Mendel says. He kicks at a loose floorboard.

"Just for now," Lai says. "We'll meet again."

"If we're lucky," I mutter.

Lai shoots me a glare that I ignore.

"We will," Kitahara says. "I know it." His voice is strong, unwavering. We all look to him. He has a way of talking that just makes you *want* to believe what he says. It's sure as hell more comforting than when Lai said it.

"Be careful," Lai says to Mendel. She presses something into his hand. When he tucks it into his pocket, I catch a glimpse of a small, bright green crystal. "Use that to get in touch with me whenever you need to. It's too risky to give you access to all of my gift—it's difficult to control and you don't have time to practice—so you'll only be able to use it to communicate with me telepathically. Make sure no one finds out about it. Remember everything I told you about Ellis, her gift, her way of planning. If you feel that you're in danger at any point or like you've been discovered, get out. Above all else, you have to live."

"I got it, I got it," Mendel says. He leans back against the wall, trying to look casual, probably, but his shaking hands give him away. His nerves dampen my anger. "Get in, learn about my past, send on intel about the rebels, end the war, get out. Easy."

Lai's lips press together. "Just watch your back. And don't take any unnecessary risks."

"Yeah, because that's so my shtick," Mendel says. "I'm the one who lays low, remember? I've got this."

"I know," Lai says. She sounds so sure it surprises me. Where do you get that kind of confidence for a plan this crazy? "If I didn't think you could do it, I wouldn't have asked you to. I just . . ."

"Worry," Kitahara supplies.

Lai's frown deepens. Mendel laughs, but he stops abruptly when she says, "Yes. I'm worried."

"Don't be." Mendel pretends to shudder. "It's weird and I don't like it."

Lai shoves him and he laughs again.

"Watch yourself out there," Kitahara says. He holds out a hand to Mendel, which seems way overformal, but that's the major. Ex-major.

Mendel shakes his hand anyway. "I will."

Then Mendel is looking at me, and I don't know what I'm supposed to do. What I *want* to do is tell him what a reckless idiot he is and that if he gets himself killed, it'll be his own fault. But Lai's words still ring in my head. *This is the last time we'll all be together for—who knows how long? Maybe ever.*

"You better come back to us all in one piece," I say. "It won't be any fun kicking your ass in training if you're missing an arm or leg."

Mendel cracks a grin. "Just for your entertainment purposes, I'll try to keep everything attached."

"Good."

We all keep standing around, but there's nothing else to say. Lai heads for the door first. Everyone follows. And then we're down the stairs and Mendel breaks off from our group with a wave and I'm trying not to look back after him. This whole team thing really does suck.

Lai leads the way through the sector's cramped streets. We pass through Market, the stalls all shuttered, and into the rich streets with clean new skyscrapers that make me feel like we stick out like fireworks in the dead of night, before ending up in the warehouse district. No one's around. Eventually we get to an old abandoned-looking warehouse that Lai calls Regail Hall. The windows are boarded up, and graffiti and torn flyers cover the red-brick walls. I don't really get how a beat-up place like this could be the Order's home base, but Lai doesn't stop for questions. She unlocks the door and goes straight in. My irritation returns. I hate how she just keeps walking and assumes we'll follow her. I hate even more that her assumption's right.

The inside is dark. I snap my fingers and flames flicker above them. All around us are stacks and stacks of crates. Nothing else. Definitely not anything that makes it look like anyone ever comes here. Lai heads for a stack of crates in the back that looks just like every other stack and moves them over to reveal a trapdoor in the ground. Okay. I guess that's better.

She pulls a key out of her pocket, unlocks it, and jumps straight down. Kitahara gestures for me to go ahead. "There's a ladder if you'd like."

If Lai doesn't need a ladder, then neither do I.

The drop is shorter than I expected. Lai stands ahead of me in a tunnel that goes on so far I can't see the end. Lanterns line both sides of the gray-stone tunnel. The flames are warm and welcoming, but something about them feels off. They're not natural fires.

Kitahara lands behind me. He pulls a cord and the trapdoor slams shut. Something clicks. An auto-lock, probably.

"Underground tunnels?" I wasn't expecting something this . . . huge. There are tons of tunnel networks beneath Sector Eight back from when humanity nearly wiped itself out through nuclear warfare hundreds of years ago. The smarter people built the domed sectors that could resist the radiation and added tunnels for underground farms and—I don't know. Extra space, I guess. Not many records are left from that time. Just enough that we have laws to prevent nuclear warfare from happening again, laws that ban guns, missiles, bombs, stuff like that. There are only a few things all the sectors agree on, but one of them is taking out anyone who tries to bring back the weapons of old. Entire sectors have been wiped out for it before.

But only the military and underground farm corporations have control over the tunnels. How could they not know about this system? How did Lai's group even find these tunnels?

"An old friend found them with his gift," Lai says. I hate it when she responds to my thoughts instead of what I said. "It took a while, but eventually we were able to save up and buy the warehouse above us. It's the only building with a way into this network—plus it makes a good place for storing extra supplies."

She waits, but when I don't ask anything else, she keeps walking.

I grudgingly follow, Kitahara right behind me. We pass a bunch of entrances into side tunnels, but we stay in the main one. Eventually the tunnel turns into a real hallway, more cleanly carved out, and we start seeing more people. Everyone waves to Lai when they see her. A few stop to ask her questions I don't understand. But there's a sort of restless energy to all the people we meet. By Lai and Kitahara's tensed shoulders, I know they can feel it, too. Their gifts probably make it worse.

"Just how many people are in the Order?" I ask when we finally ditch yet another person who stopped Lai.

"A thousand and some," Lai says. "Although we're always gaining new members." She sounds distracted as we start walking again. I don't even know where we're heading in this huge maze.

Maybe if I wasn't so surprised by the Order, I'd want to punch Lai. Except I still want to punch her. Over a thousand people, based in an underground tunnel network the military doesn't know about? How could she hide something this big? Just what the hell am I to her?

I watch her trade looks with Kitahara, and I know they're communicating telepathically. That just pisses me off even more. Or maybe it hurts. They're the only two of our team who've managed to keep up their good relationship after the rebel ambush, and now that Mendel's gone, I'm the only one on the outs. Some team. I'm just being dragged along for the ride.

Kitahara glances at me and falls back so we're walking together. I lift an eyebrow and he smiles. "I'm glad you're here with us," he says. "I always feel better when you're around."

"You don't have to force yourself to include me." He probably just read my emotions with his gift and felt obligated to cheer me up. But I don't need his pity.

"You can take it however you like, but I do mean it." He meets my eyes when he says it—something Lai *and* Mendel haven't done that much since the ambush. "There's obviously your physical strength, but I'm glad you're so honest and straightforward, too." He lowers his voice as Lai stops ahead of us to talk to another stranger. "I like both Lai and Erik very much. However, sometimes their calculating way of seeing the world exhausts me. I start to feel confused. Doubtful. But with you, I know you're sincerely speaking your mind. I don't have to worry about if you have some hidden agenda or test." He sighs, and his exhaustion from the last week, which he usually keeps locked up so well, bleeds through the cracks in his leader mask. "It's nice having a friend who's completely honest with me."

A friend. I don't think Kitahara's ever actually called me that before. It's not like we've talked a whole lot before this past week. I didn't know much about him—still don't, really. But I'm pretty sure he's being honest, and the fact that he's confiding in me at all makes me unexpectedly happy. Plus, in this new place, one teammate short, with another looking more and more untrustworthy, it'd be nice to have a friend right about now. And Kitahara's not a bad option.

"Well, I think our friendship needs some work," I say as I hold up a closed fist, "but it's something I'm willing to develop, Jay."

He blinks in surprise. Then a smile slowly spreads across his face, and he bumps my fist with his. "Sounds like a deal, Al."

"Hey, you two coming?" Lai calls from ahead of us. I hadn't realized she'd started moving again. Jay and I catch up to her, but I take my time, making her wait. She rolls her eyes and keeps walking.

We finally reach a giant fork that splits into five hallways. Two people are waiting for us.

One of them I recognize as Fiona Seung. The other is a stranger—and an Etiole. The ungifted woman is covered in bright yellow and orange clothing with intricate embroidery. A bright red scarf is wrapped around her head, but a few strands of brown-black hair a little darker than her skin poke out around her ears. It's obvious from her clothes she's from another sector, but I have no idea which one. The lines around her eyes crinkle when she smiles at us.

"Kitahara, you're needed," Seung says as soon as we stop in front of them.

"It's good to see you again, too," Lai mutters.

Seung ignores her. "The members we've assigned to start the underground farm need help, and you're our expert on the subject. Amal will take you. She's also working on the project."

"Before you go, I wanted to introduce our friend," Lai says to the woman. Amal. She gestures to me. "This is—"

"Alary Johann," I say as I hold a hand out to Amal. Lai and Jay look at me with raised eyebrows, and I remember they've never heard my real full name before. A pang of guilt hits me—a feeling I do *not* like. But I can't help feeling like a hypocrite for getting mad at Lai for keeping her secrets when I have some of my own. Or did. Now that I'm free from the military, I don't have to pretend to be a boy anymore. "I go by Al. Nice to meet you."

"It's a pleasure to meet you, Al," Amal says. If she picks up on any of the friction in our group, she doesn't show it. "Welcome to our home. I apologize for having to leave so soon, and I look forward to getting to know you, but I need to borrow your friend for a bit."

"Yeah, no problem." The sound of *friend* rings nicely in my ears after the talk Jay and I just had. It still lands pretty false, but we'll get there. At least with Jay, I feel like I can trust him. He's hard to read, but patient and earnest. I can work with that. Besides, now that we've talked, I actually *want* to get to know him better.

Jay glances at me and Lai before reluctantly following Amal down one of the hallways. He probably thinks the two of us will be at each other's throats as soon as he's gone. He might not be wrong.

"We're holding a core group meeting in an hour," Seung says before Jay and Amal are even out of sight. "We'll catch you up on everything. We need your input on a number of matters, so it will likely take some time."

"Got it," Lai says. Suddenly, she looks a lot more tired. I don't know what all she has to give her "input" on, but if the number of people who stopped us on our way here is anything to go by, she'll probably be in that meeting for the rest of her life. "I'm just going to show Al around a bit and then I'll head over."

"I'll let the others know."

"Thanks."

Seung nods, then heads off down one of the hallways.

Lai turns to me. "I'll give you the grand tour, then. Just stop me if you have any questions."

For the next half hour, she leads me through the confusing maze of underground tunnels as she explains more about the Amaryllis Order and their goal of establishing peace between the gifted and ungifted and how they're trying to do that, but honestly, I barely listen. I'm too distracted by the place and trying to remember where to go for food and the bathroom. Besides, the main point is they want peace, right? It's not like the details have anything to do with me.

Lai sighs the sigh that means she's trying to hold back her anger. "Could you at least try to care?"

"Is there a reason I should?" I ask. "You kept something this huge a secret from me for so long, dumped it on me all at once, and now you expect me to be impressed or something? You should've just taken us here from the beginning—so why didn't you?"

"Because I knew better than to trust you with this," Lai snarls. It's not like her to get so angry so fast. "You're mad at me for not telling you about the Order, but then when I *try* to tell you about it, you won't even listen. You don't get it, do you? How important all this is to me or how different it is now without Paul here—" She clamps her mouth shut and turns her back on me. "Look, just don't get in anyone's way while you're here."

Guilt rings through my chest. Paul isn't here because I went back to try to kill my brother at that ambush—which I failed to do, and then Paul was killed when he and the others came to help me instead of retreating.

No, I remind myself, *I didn't ask any of them to come back for me. Their decision, their fault.* But even as I think it, I know it's not true. If it'd been Lai or Jay or Mendel, I would've stayed, too. It isn't fair for me to blame anyone else. It was my fault. And it wasn't even worth anything in the end.

I follow Lai through the tunnels. Neither of us says anything, and I don't know if I want either of us to. The silence sucks, but I know I'll only get angry again if we try to talk.

We end in a small bedroom. There's just a cot in the corner, and a dresser and desk. Everything looks like it's about a good kick away from collapsing into a pile of tinder.

"You can stay here," Lai says. Her back is still to me, and I wonder if she's dealing with the same problem of speaking without letting her emotions explode out. "If you need anything, I'll be in the room next door, and Jay will be on the other side. It'll take a while to get used to this place and remember how to get around, but you've got time."

"Right," I say. "And now?"

"Now nothing." She crosses her arms, still facing away from me.

"I've got business to take care of. Jay is helping with the startup of our new underground farm, and I don't know how long he'll be, so just stay here and don't cause any trouble."

"You expect me to just sit around and wait until you come get me?" My fury sets my words on fire.

She finally turns around to look at me. "I don't have time to show you around any more than this—especially when you were hardly paying attention to begin with. You can't go anywhere without getting lost, and we don't have the people to spare to babysit you. I said not to get in the way, didn't I? I didn't have to bring you here, so stop acting upset when I'm giving you a safe place to go and all I ask in return is that you don't be a nuisance."

"Oh, so I should be *thankful* to you, is that it?" The fire that had been in my words before runs wild through my blood. It nearly bursts to the surface, but I hold back my gift. "Thankful you didn't abandon me, thankful you're telling me to just sit around and wait for nothing, thankful you're finally letting me in on something this big after hiding it for so long? You really are a conceited piece of work."

"I never claimed to be otherwise. If you don't like it, you can get out."

I don't say anything. I'm having a hard enough time holding back my gift—and trying not to storm out of this room and never come back. Because she is right about one thing: I don't have anywhere else to go. I don't know how much I could get away with without actually pushing her far enough to kick me out. And if that happened, I'd be as good as dead.

"I'll come back in a few hours with lunch," Lai says. She brushes past me on her way to the door. "Don't do anything reckless until then."

"Isn't that *your* thing?" I ask.

She slams the door shut behind her. Good riddance.

But almost as soon as she's gone, my anger burns out into unhappiness. I miss training with Lai and laughing with her over stupid things and being able to say whatever I wanted. I miss knowing I could trust her with my back and feeling invincible when we fought together. Why did things turn out like this? Why do I have to question every single little thing she does? Why does it feel like she never trusted me with anything even once? Even after I told her about my past and the fact I was a girl pretending to be a boy for years, she didn't tell me anything. Not about her gift of telepathy, not about her past with the leader of the rebels, not about this place—nothing.

Then it turns out Mendel's been hiding his memory loss and was a former rebel. And even though I'm excited to become better friends with Jay, the truth is that he was in on at least some of this Order stuff all along—even if he was just keeping it secret for Lai's sake, he was still hiding it.

I slam the door back open and storm into the hall. Like hell I'm just going to sit here waiting for Lai to order me around. I'm *no one's* dog.

I rush through the halls in an angry haze. It takes a while for me to realize I haven't been keeping track of where I'm going. When I look back at all the twisting tunnels, I know I'm screwed. Shit. Why's this place gotta be so confusing?

Whatever. It doesn't matter.

I keep going forward, taking a random path whenever I reach splits. I pass all sorts of rooms, and when I feel like it, I poke my head inside to see what's there. Storerooms, bedrooms, what look like meeting rooms. At one point, I pass an entrance that lets out into a cavernous hall with nothing but a stage set in the back and a continuous ramp circling the rounded walls of the room. A lot of people rush through the multiple entrances of the huge hall or huddle together to talk inside it. It's too many strangers, and I don't want to get stopped by anyone or have to talk, so I keep going down the hallway until the huge room is far behind me.

The more I walk, the better I feel. It's not as good as walking in fresh air, but it does the job.

I don't stop again until I hear the dull clanging of metal against metal. I recognize the sound instantly. Sparring.

Funny. I thought this was supposed to be a peace coalition.

I follow the sound through the tunnels, careful to keep quiet in case I'm not supposed to be here. Just because I decided to wander around doesn't mean I want to get caught.

There's no door that leads into what's obviously a training room—just a hole in the shape of a doorway. I sneak a look around the edge of it. Inside, dozens of people are sparring with each other. With dulled weapons, with sticks, with just their fists. A couple of people stand around watching the matches and calling out advice or instructions, but they're way outnumbered by the people training— and they don't even sound like they're sure of what they're saying.

It's nothing like when I'd watch soldiers spar in Central. Back in the military, there was this sort of synchronicity everyone had. Even if someone wasn't the best fighter, they were good enough to last. They'd be dead on the field otherwise. People knew what they were doing. And if they didn't know, they were good enough to improvise. There weren't people who fell after one hit. There weren't people who hesitated. There wasn't anyone who didn't fight like their life depended on it—because it always did.

I sigh. What are these people even doing? What's the point of sparring if you're going to do it this badly?

A man falls over backward—not because of a strike from his opponent, but because he trips over his own feet.

That's it. I stride into the training room. I don't know why I'm so annoyed watching them, but I don't have to keep quietly spying on them as they suck.

"You need to fix your stance," I say as the man who fell gets back up. He and his partner turn to me with startled looks. "You fell because your feet are too far apart. You can't balance like that in a fight. Look, like this."

I sink into a crouch, my feet shoulder-width apart, fists raised in front of me. I nod for him to do the same.

He glances at his partner and hesitates, but the woman shrugs and copies me. After a few seconds, the man does the same.

"Good," I say. "Be careful where you put your weight. You're leaning too far forward." I move his shoulders back and rap his lower back. "Keep it straight." After I adjust the woman's stance, I say, "There. Now try it again."

The man lunges forward with a punch that almost makes me groan. The woman dodges it easily, but the way she moves is so stiff that if he'd been fast enough to throw another hit, she would've taken it.

"Stop. You have to lead with your arm, not with your fist. That's where your actual strength is." I make sure they're both watching as I demonstrate with a few punches. "See? My arm controls the direction and force. I'm not just flinging my fist out hoping it'll hit something." I jerk my chin at the woman. "And when you dodge, you can't hesitate about it. You don't have time to think in a real fight—you *move*, and you try to do it as naturally and smoothly as walking. Try it again."

I keep running them through the practice, stopping them to give advice when I need to. Honestly, though, what they need are drills. They don't even know the basics, and they're trying to fight. It's like trying to drive a byc when you don't know the controls. This is as good as pointless. Just who's teaching them?

A bunch of the people sparring around us start to come over and practice with the original pair as I go through demonstrations. Eventually, I stop the matches altogether and do actually start drilling them. Proper stance, ways to punch, effective ways to dodge. More and more people begin to drift over until one of the "teachers" stomps over with his face screwed up.

"What are you doing?" he asks. "We're practicing *fighting* here, in case you hadn't noticed."

"I noticed," I say. "Your practice needed improvement."

His face turns red. "Who are you? Who authorized you as an instructor?"

The giant group I've accumulated stops practicing their punches. I don't need Jay's gift to pick up on their unease as they probably realize they've never seen me before. Shit. I was trying *not* to get caught wandering around on my own, and instead I openly give myself away. Great job, Al.

I'm about to tell him I'm a new member who couldn't just stand aside watching such a pathetic display when someone says from behind me, "I did."

Everyone turns to the speaker. He's a man in maybe his mid-twenties, with midnight-black skin and a close-shaven head. He's huge and muscular—probably solid in a fight. He watches me curiously from where he leans against the wall by the entranceway. My heart pounds, but he just smiles.

"T-Trist, sir," the teacher says. He fumbles to get the words out, but the newcomer doesn't seem to notice.

"I thought we could use assistance," the stranger says. "We still need much work, do we not? I asked our new friend to observe and help. She is a very skilled fighter, you see." He beckons me over to join him, still smiling. "Excuse us while I ask her thoughts."

"Of course, sir. Very well, sir." The teacher glances at all the people still watching. "Well? What are you waiting for? Get back to practicing what the new instructor has taught you."

I don't usually follow strangers, but this one did just save me and it's not like I want to stick around here, so I go with the new guy. We don't go far. Once we're in the hall, far enough away from the training room to be out of earshot, he stops.

"You are Al, correct?" he says. "I do not believe we've met before. I am Tristao Clemente—but please, call me Trist."

I keep my eyes trained on his hands in case he makes any sudden moves. "How do you know who I am?"

"Ah, Lai has told us much about you," Clemente says. "Determined, strong, just." His smile grows a little wider. "Headstrong and willful. But a good friend and teammate."

Lai said all that about me? The praise—or mostly praise—makes my chest feel light. Until I remember our last conversation and how she slammed the door on her way out. My heart sinks even lower than before. All those things she said must've been before Paul's death. Before we ended up in this mess. Of course.

"Yeah, well, she hasn't mentioned you to me at all," I say. "Or anything about this place, in fact."

"She protects the Order as if it were her own life," Clemente says. There's a knowing look in his eye like he can see inside my head, which makes me scowl. "She means well by keeping everything secret. But she is very prickly now, yes? Last time we lost someone, she pulled away from us then, too. It is her way. Please forgive her that."

"What do you mean?"

"Some years ago, we lost a good friend." For the first time, the light in his eyes dims. He looks to the ground, but only for a few seconds. "To Lai, he was a very important friend. After he died, she was mean for some time. When she feels pain, she lashes out." His fire returns a little, and he winks at me like we're sharing some important secret. "But do not tell her I said so. She will become angry—actually angry." And then he laughs.

I watch him closely. I can't decide what to make of him. He seems well intentioned enough, I guess. And he did save my skin back there in the training room. But why's he telling me all this about Lai? Why's he trying to cover for her?

"You guys must be pretty good friends," I finally say. "She's lucky to have you."

"And she you," Clemente says. When I start to protest, he says, "Maybe she has not told you, but she loves her friendship with you. I have talked with her since you started fighting. I can tell she is not happy like this. I hope you two will fix your friendship soon, but Lai is stubborn. It might take time."

I don't know how to answer. I don't even know this guy, and he's vouching for my friendship—or what remains of it—with Lai. He talks about it so easily. Like Lai wasn't keeping a million secrets from me. Like she didn't betray my trust a thousand times over. Like I didn't cause the death of her friend.

I don't know what he wants me to say.

Clemente shakes his head. "But this is not the reason I wanted to talk with you."

"You wanted to talk with me?" Now my confusion gives way to curiosity. What could he possibly want with me of all people?

"Yes," Clemente says. "Lai has said you are maybe the strongest fighter in Central. So I wanted to ask—would you help the Order with its training?"

Pushing aside my sudden happiness at the fact that Lai, a hell of a fighter herself, said I might be the strongest in Central, I say, "Wait, what?"

Clemente gestures with one hand to the training room behind us. "You can see, can you not? We have started teaching our members to fight recently, but we are weak. Undisciplined. Inexperienced. Those of us who know how to fight are busy running the Order. We cannot take the time to train other members." Now he gestures to me. "But you? You are skilled. You know how to win. If you are willing, would you help us?"

"What does the Order even need trained fighters for? Aren't you guys a peace group?"

"Ah," Clemente says softly. "That we are. But if we wish for peace, we may need to join the war. If the military cannot defeat the rebels, maybe we can help. But only if we have capable fighters."

The idea of it is absurd. Me, teaching a bunch of strangers how to fight? From the basics, no less. It sounds like a pain.

But when I think of the sorry excuse for fighters I saw just a few minutes ago, I get what Clemente's saying. If the Order *does* plan on joining this war, they're not going to survive like that. They might as well be dead already unless someone who knows what they're doing helps them. And as much as I hate to admit it, a part of me was weirdly happy training those guys. Satisfied in a way I haven't felt in a long time.

I've spent the last week on the run and stuck in a dead-end chase to find info that's already long gone. I've been lied to, stabbed in the back, and told to just wait around and not get in the way.

A spark ignites in my chest as the idea of training these wannabe fighters grows on me. I could actually be doing something and helping people—and not because Lai told me to. By my own choice.

I meet Clemente's eyes. "I'll do it."

Clemente fills me in on the details of how the training works now, I offer my suggestions for changes, and we agree to meet up tomorrow and start with everyone. He offers to show me the way to my room, but I'm not ready to go back yet, and the thought of being there when Lai returns is irritating, so I turn him down and keep wandering around.

After probably an hour of walking, I think I'm actually kind of starting to get the hang of this place. Things aren't really as random as they seem, and when I run my hands over the walls, I feel symbols and arrows etched into them. They must be some kind of coded directions. I can't figure out the symbols' exact meanings, but I'm able to remember them and follow them to their destinations. Three swirls, a triangle, and a square lead to some kind of market. Two circles, two squares, and a triangle to an infirmary. A square, two swirls, and a circle take me to a big room with a bunch of tables.

It's like a puzzle. I'm sure Jay'll have a field day figuring this place out, but I get bored of it quickly. What I want isn't to memorize my way around this place. I want to *do* something. I want to get out there and show the rebels and the Council and everyone else what's what. I want to stop being on the run. I want to find my brother and kill him for sure this time.

I stop at what looks like a dead end and sit on my heels. I don't know how to get back. I don't really care that I don't know, but it's annoying that I don't, if only because it's like proving Lai was right. And I can't think of anything more irritating right now.

But the halls are suffocatingly quiet. It makes me want to break something just to hear the noise. The silence feels the same as when I walked into my childhood living room to find blood splattered across the walls and my brother hunched over the bodies of our parents. The instant my entire reality was quietly ripped into shreds.

I bury my face in my arms. Idiot. It's been nine years already. Why are you getting this upset over something that happened so long ago? Besides, I'm going to kill my brother and get justice for our parents and closure for myself. I just have to keep pushing forward. Then everything will be right again. Then everything will be okay.

Footsteps echo down the hall. I look up to see Lai standing behind me. Her eyes are beyond tired in the dim light as she holds a hand out to me. "Let's go back, Al."

5

ERIK

SAYING GOODBYE TO everyone was harder than I thought it'd be. I figured I'd be glad to finally escape our dead-end situation, cramped apartment, and the constant tension of the team, but as soon as I'm on my own, I wish I was back with them. I'm getting soft.

It doesn't take long to find a deserted side street that'll do the job. I don't exactly want anyone catching me doing what I'm about to do— not that I think anyone would be strolling by at this hour. But just in case.

I adjust the backpack slung over my shoulder, weighed down by a couple sketchbooks, a few sets of clothes, and some of the leftover food. I tell myself it's because the weight lies unevenly, but honestly, I'm just procrastinating. I was all for going back to the rebels when we were just talking about it, but now that the moment is actually here, my hands shake with nerves. Once I do this, there's no backing out. A one-way ticket if ever there was one.

But waiting around here isn't going to change anything. I made my choice.

I pull a silver chain out of my pocket. A pure black crystal glitters on the end of it.

At our meeting with the rebels, Ellis said to "look close to home" for a way to contact her. I didn't give it a whole lot of thought at the time. But a few nights ago, when I was flipping through my old sketchbook she gave me at that meeting, I found this necklace taped into the back. There was no note, no explanation, but I knew what it was immediately. Ellis's power crystal.

I couldn't bring myself to tell the others about it—not that my silence stopped Lai from digging around in my thoughts and finding out. She probably knew as soon as I found it. Then again, she did do me a favor by telling me all about Ellis's gift of controlling shadows. Ellis can travel through them, send shadow butterflies as messengers that only their intended receiver can see and hear, and use those same butterflies to observe people through their shadows. But that last one can only happen with the knowledge and permission of the person being watched.

My fingers close around her power crystal. Deep breaths. It'll be fine. I can do this.

Power crystals don't work unless you're touching them and you *want* to use their power. One out of two down, but it takes a couple more calming breaths before I manage to call out to the power—not exactly sure what'll happen when I do.

The shadows around me shift and surge, and it takes all my willpower not to step back out of their way as they detach from the ground and walls to engulf me. I expect to feel pain or be unable to breathe, like if a wave of water crashed over me, but I don't feel anything. When I blink, I'm in a dimly lit room that is definitely not some back alley of Sector Eight.

Another few blinks and the room starts to come into focus around me. Or maybe my eyes just adjust to the half-light. It looks like an office. There's one door and a window that's pitch black on the other side. Mismatched furniture takes up most of the space. The air smells damp and heavy with—what, incense? I realize the room is so dark because the only light is from the candles scattered around it. Wax drips down them to pool in shallow bowls set on the dark wooden furniture. Mahogany? I stare at the main desk. The design, the feel of it . . .

"Do you remember, Erik?" a voice asks behind me. I whip around. No one was in the room a few seconds ago, but now, Ellis stands between me and the door. Behind her is Cal, along with the pale-eyed girl with the ice gift and the vicious rebel I fought on our team's second mission. Joan and Devin, I think. "You made all the furniture in this room."

It takes everything in me not to back away. My heart races like crazy. This is really happening. I'm here with the rebels.

I force my face and voice to be calm. "I can't say I remember, but I do recognize my own work when I see it."

Disappointment falls over Ellis's face, but it's quickly replaced by excitement as she claps her hands together. "So, you decided to come back? I knew you would."

Cal looks just as happy as Ellis—maybe even more—but Joan watches me with narrowed eyes. Devin outright scowls.

"It's hardly surprising after we dealt Sector Two such thorough losses," Joan says. Her pale blue eyes gleam in the candlelight. A single braid of dark brown hair hangs over one shoulder, but pieces stick out like she made it in a hurry. When I look at her more closely, I realize the edges of her eyes are red. Her dark tan skin seems to have taken on a more sickly hue since the last time I saw her, too. Or maybe it's just the candlelight.

She turns to Ellis. "Are you sure we can trust him? Seems to me like he's just running to us with his tail between his legs now that the military's turned on him."

"For once, I agree with her," Devin snarls. "He's just a coward. We don't need him."

My irritation flicks on, and that emotion I don't hide. "I'm sorry my timing isn't exactly trustworthy to you, but it's not like I've had a whole lot of time to think things over since you nearly killed me and my teammates. Things have been a little busy."

"I didn't realize one needed time to know where their loyalties lie," Joan says.

"Oh, Joan, you're starting to sound like Devin," Ellis teases. Devin's eyes flick to her like he doesn't know whether to take that as an insult or a compliment. Joan scowls darkly at the comparison. I can't blame her. From what I remember of Devin, he's crazy for violence. Not someone any sane person would want to be compared to.

Ellis turns to face me again. Long blond hair tumbles past her shoulders, over plain black clothes that seem to be the color of choice around here. They're stark against her pale skin. "He was lied to for months by the military, and then we suddenly sprung the truth on him. I'm sure it took time to process."

"I'm sure being branded a traitor didn't hurt, either," Joan mutters.

Cal doesn't look like he even heard their conversation. He grins from ear to ear. "You really decided to come back to us, Erik?"

"I wouldn't have come here with all my stuff otherwise," I say. Joan and Devin are throwing me off, but as distrustful of me as they are, neither of them actually seems suspicious of me being a spy. That, at least, calms my racing heart a little.

"Excellent!" Ellis says with another clap of her hands. "Oh, it's so good to have you back, Erik! You have no idea how much we've missed you."

Her excitement catches me off guard. It feels weirdly genuine. Is she just that good at faking, or is it real? Is it possible we all really were good friends? That they cared about me—that I cared about them? I mean, a part of me must have known we were, with all the effort they put into seeing me and trying to convince me to come back. But it's still hard to wrap my head around.

That's why I'm here, I remind myself. I'm going to learn the truth for myself. I'm finally going to find what I've been searching for these past several months.

I must not be hiding my surprise at Ellis's reaction that well, because her smile wavers. "Well, you don't remember us, of course. Not yet. But don't worry, Erik. We'll remind you."

"Yeah!" Cal agrees with shining eyes. He reaches me in three steps and clasps my hands in his. Despite our pretty good talk in the sector, I have to force myself not to flinch from the physical contact. "We can talk as much as we want now that you're here. And we can work together again to take down the sectors! No one will be able to beat us with our team back together."

My breath trips over the guilt stuck in my lungs. I try to hide it, but Ellis's eyes narrow.

"Erik," she says slowly. Carefully, like she's trying not to spook a wild Feral, the vicious creatures that roam Outside. "You do know that coming back includes fighting with us, right?"

Thank the gods. She thinks I'm nervous about fighting the sector—not that I'm here as a spy. And I need to keep it that way. "Of course," I say. "You think I'd come back just to sit around and chat?"

Ellis watches me carefully. Shadows flicker over her face from the candles, giving her an almost sinister look that doesn't match the warring sympathy in her eyes. "Well, we can deal with that later," she says eventually. "For now, there's something I need you to do for me."

I swallow, hard. She doesn't know. She doesn't suspect. Everything is fine. "Yeah?"

She holds out her hand, palm up. The shadows in the room shift again, and when I blink, a black butterfly is sitting in her hand. The edges are hazy like I'm looking at it through water. When Devin sees it, he smirks. Joan's face remains neutral while Cal frowns.

"I trust you, Erik," Ellis says in a voice that sounds more like she *wants* to believe that. "But I need to take precautions. You understand, don't you?"

I nod, not trusting myself to speak.

"I'm going to put my butterfly in your shadow to keep an eye on you, make sure you're not doing anything to betray us. It's nothing bad—like I said, just a precaution—and it won't hurt. I just need your permission, or my butterfly won't be able to enter your shadow."

Lai warned me Ellis would probably ask to monitor me as a test of loyalty—but it's still unnerving. Knowing about it beforehand doesn't make it any easier to say the words I know I need to. Once I agree, she'll be able to see my every movement, hear anything I say. If I make even one mistake in getting info back to Lai and the others, Ellis will know what I'm up to. I'll be as good as dead. But I can't say no, or I might as well stab myself with my own sword right now.

"Yeah, sure thing." My voice sounds steady. I think. "Do what you have to."

Ellis smiles. Her teeth don't show like they did before. She doesn't move, but the butterfly takes off from her hand and flies straight for me. It lands on a section of my shadow falling across an armchair. It melts into it, but I don't feel anything. My body doesn't feel any different from before, either.

"That it?" I look at my hands, but there's no change. "I thought I'd feel . . . something."

Ellis laughs, and her apparent happiness from before finally returns. I try not to let out a sigh of relief. "Everyone always thinks that."

Devin's smirk is gone. Now he's just glaring at me from under lowered eyebrows. "Are you sure about this, Sara? I don't like it. I don't trust him as far as I could throw him."

"You can throw pretty far," Ellis muses. Devin's scowl deepens. "I'm sure, Devin. If Erik does anything suspicious, I'll know about it right away." Her eyes cut to me. She's still smiling, but there's an edge to it now. My heart misses a beat. "And I'm sure Erik knows what would happen if we found any reason to distrust him."

I shrug and try to make the gesture look as careless as always. My heart pounds like crazy. "Why would I do something that stupid? Besides, it's not like anyone back in the sector has my loyalties. Not anymore."

"Good," Ellis says. The edge falls away. "You've finally come back to us. Why don't we catch up?"

Devin is still scowling, but I can't read Joan's expression. Cal is practically bouncing in place. "I'll go make some tea," he says. His excitement hasn't dimmed since I got here, even though I haven't returned his enthusiasm at all. I was expecting more of Joan and Devin's reactions, not this . . . happiness. When Ellis isn't trying to intimidate me, she seems just as excited as Cal—like she's greeting an old, long-lost friend. Which I guess she is.

The rebels are supposed to be heartless killers who want to wipe out all the ungifted from the world. But even though that's the goal of the war *they* waged, they just feel like normal people. Without the adrenaline and mercilessness of the battlefield, it's hard to really see them as the enemy. Especially when they're clapping in excitement and saying they'll make tea for you.

But still, Ellis's sharp smile won't leave my head. I need to be careful. No matter how down-to-earth these people seem, they *are* the enemy. I can't forget that—as soon as I do, it could cost me my life.

Once we've finished tea—still weird—Ellis takes me on a tour through the rebels' home base. Cal and the others split off to go do whatever it is rebel leaders do. I thought I'd be glad to have fewer people around, but as soon as they're gone, I realize how much worse it is to be alone with Ellis.

After she leads me into the hallway, down a few flights of stairs, and out of the building, I realize why everything is so damn dark. We're underground. Way above us, an earthen sky looms. It's not as high as the dome of a sector, but it's still up there. The cavern is wide and tall enough that the place doesn't feel claustrophobic. A city of low, ramshackle "buildings" thrown together from sheets of wood and metal spreads out around us as far as I can see.

"Wow," I say. "I didn't know places like this existed Outside."

"I doubt anyone in the sectors does," Ellis says. She doesn't stop walking, so I keep trailing her as my eyes try to suck everything in. Not because I think it'll be helpful for Lai or whatever, but because I want to see it all. "The Etioles don't explore Outside. Even if they found a place like this, what good would it do them? They can't even go Outside without safety equipment—it'd be too much of a hassle for them to try and settle in." She taps the side of her nose. "Nytes, on the other hand? The air Outside doesn't affect us."

"Makes sense," I say. There's no electricity. Flashlights and candles light up everything. As we pass a collection of rubble and blankets that's serving as someone's shelter, I realize the only real building in the whole area is the one Ellis and I just left. The homes are leaning wooden planks, or cobbled together with busted pieces of plastic and metal, or sometimes just blankets laid out on the ground around piles of things. Personal belongings. Small heaps of food.

I glance back over my shoulder. The sole building rises above everything else, a grand old thing with a steepled roof and elegant balconies.

"What's with the building?" I ask. "You guys didn't build that yourselves, did you?"

"It was already here when we found this place," Ellis says. "When *you and I* found this place."

A mystery if I've ever heard one—how *did* anyone find this place, anyway?—but I don't push for more. With all the other questions I have, it isn't exactly at the top of my list. And I don't like the way she emphasized it being the two of us who found this place. It also makes me realize my mistake; I shouldn't refer to the rebels as if I'm not a part of them.

I try to ignore my twisting stomach. "Okay, so, the building is like the central meeting point for all of us?"

"Something like that," Ellis says. She steps over an abandoned teddy bear lying in what passes for a street. Empty paths twist through the messily assembled homes, but so far, none of them seem to lead anywhere in particular. "We call it the main office—and we use it for a lot of things. The room we just met in is where we make and discuss our plans. And by we, I mean me, Joan, Devin, Cal, and Gabriel— and you, in the past."

"Gabriel?" I've never heard the name before. When I think back to the ambush, I don't remember seeing a fifth person, either. The thought that we've been missing an enemy general isn't a great one.

"You'll meet him eventually," Ellis says with a dismissive wave of her hand. "His health isn't the best, so he doesn't get out much. But the main office is also where all the people I just mentioned stay. We have an infirmary and several multipurpose rooms—storage, smaller meeting rooms, stuff like that."

A few people poke their heads out of the makeshift homes as we pass. Whispers follow. I catch Ellis's name, obviously, but I hear mine a lot, too. It makes the hair on the back of my neck rise—and I always thought that was just some dumb expression.

Some of them smile with recognition, and a bunch say hi, but no one tries to actually talk to us. They're all young, most of them around fourteen, I'd guess. Of course. Everyone here is a Nyte, so obviously everyone is younger than twenty—but it still throws me off to see kids who can't be older than six or seven running around tossing balls back and forth.

I wonder if I knew any of these people in the past. I wonder if everyone already knows I lost my memories and if that's why they're not saying more than hello even though they look like they want to talk. Which is another surprising thing. When they see Ellis, they don't act like they've seen some terrifying leader who rules with an iron fist but like they've seen their guardian. Their eyes light up. They call out greetings to her like they would to any other person on the street. A few little kids run up to her and wrap their arms around her legs until she laughs and gently pries them off.

The feeling of camaraderie is so thick I almost choke on it. Whenever I thought of the rebels before, I always imagined them as desperate—clinging to anything that might let them live and attack the sector. But the people I see are different from that. The farther we go into the underground city, the busier it gets. Kids run around screaming obnoxiously but happily. Some of the older Nytes keep an eye on them, protective older siblings, while others stroll down the streets running errands as if all this was totally normal. Picking up food at the distribution center Ellis points out to me? All right. Chatting with anyone you happen to run into on the way? Cool. Living in the dark underground? Sure, why not.

They don't seem like bloodthirsty killers. They're just going about their lives. Yeah, sure, without most luxuries that living in the sector gets you, but there's no sense of danger here. They're all in this together, and you can tell from the feeling in the air. Everyone here is just . . . normal.

When we reach the end of what I'd guess is the main street, Ellis stops and spins around to face me. She's been dropping so many names and so much info on places we pass that it's all spinning in my head. "So?" She holds her hands clasped behind her back, arms extended straight behind her. It's the same exact thing Lai does when she's messing around. "What do you think? Not bad for only having two years behind us, right?"

"Not bad is an understatement," I say, and I mean it. "This place is incredible. I still can't believe you managed to find such a perfect place for all this."

"Well, *we* couldn't have done it without the help of our fellow gifted," Ellis says. "This place isn't the only one of its kind, either. The other underground caverns are much smaller, but they make the perfect locations for bases."

"Why even bother having bases aboveground, then?" I ask, thinking of my first mission with the team, when we took out a rebel base. The memory unexpectedly hurts. It's only been a few hours, but I'm surprised by how much I miss them. Or maybe I just miss the feeling that I could trust them with my back. Now, I'm surrounded by people I have to watch my every word around. "Wouldn't it be safer to just do everything below? How do you even have the supplies to build bases aboveground, anyway?"

"Not everything *can* be done belowground," Ellis says. "Besides, if we always have our people coming up and down for everything, it'd only be a matter of time before the military caught on. We do everything of import down below, and the aboveground bases act as transition points for less critical matters. That way, even if they're taken down, it won't be a huge loss to us. And we don't build the bases up above—they already existed, just like these caverns. We just fix them up a bit and take them for ourselves."

Great to know how much effect our mission had. "How do you just *find* abandoned bases? And wouldn't one of the sectors have claimed them?"

"It's the same with these caverns and the broken sector we set up our ambush in," Ellis says. "Sorry about that, by the way. But they're places that used to be occupied before people up and abandoned them for whatever reason. Probably from before the nuclear war. And sure, the military could try to occupy them—but they're so far out of the way of the sectors themselves, it would be too much trouble to keep them. What Etiole wants to wear that stupid protective suit and go all the way to the middle of nowhere to guard a base that has no strategic value to the sector? It's not worth it for them."

It makes sense as she says it, but I'd never thought too deeply about all that before. Who cared how the rebels set up their bases? Where the buildings came from? My only job was to empty them out, and I only did that because the military told me to and I had nowhere to stay other than with them. Maybe it's time I started asking more questions.

"I've been wondering this for a while," I say, thinking back to the team, "but what were you guys doing at those old warehouses in Sector Eight? Why attack them? It doesn't seem like a strategic place to strike. There're rumors you stole something, maybe a weapon, but . . ."

Ellis looks at me evenly. The expression reminds me so much of Lai my skin crawls. "I think it'd be best," she says slowly, "if we don't discuss that just yet. But what we took wasn't a weapon. It was information."

"Information?"

She shakes her head. "It's not important for now. When it becomes relevant, I'll let you know."

Her tone doesn't really leave room for argument. Even though my curiosity is only stronger now, I need to switch topics before I make her suspicious. "Well, anyway, you guys really do have a great system set up here."

"We have to if we're going to take down the sectors." Ellis's nose wrinkles like she just smelled a pile of crap. "Nytes are stronger, but the sectors have more people, more resources, and more firmly established structural organization. We need to use everything we have in the most efficient way possible if we're going to win." Her eyes suddenly harden. For the first time since I came here, she looks like the rebel leader I met in that broken sector. Ruthless. Proud. Wild. "And we *will* win."

I'm saved from having to reply when someone says, "I see the rumors are true."

Ellis and I both turn to see a tall black guy with short, curly dark brown hair walking toward us. He looks like he could be nineteen or twenty, probably one of the oldest people here. He walks with a cane, his back slightly hunched, his mouth turned down at the corners in a mildly concerned frown.

The crazed fervor disappears from Ellis's eyes as she smiles and waves to the new guy. "Gabriel! Glad to see you up and about again. How are you feeling?"

"Like a byc just plowed into me," he says dryly. He stops in front of us and takes a second to catch his breath before straightening. His dark brown eyes look me up and down, lips pursed in thought. "You really came back, Erik?"

"I don't remember anything," I say reflexively, somehow filled with the need to defend myself even though this guy probably already knows that and he didn't mention my memories or past whatsoever. But how's he think I'm supposed to answer a question like that?

Well, at least now I can solve the mystery of the last rebel leader.

"I know," he says. Obviously. "I'm just a little surprised."

"Why's that?"

He laughs. "You've always been skeptical of everything and everyone. I didn't think you'd take a shot on us having told you the truth. At least not so quickly."

"Yeah, well, the Council wasn't exactly doing me any favors branding me a traitor. Figured I might as well take my chances here."

He cracks a grin. "Well, glad you did. It's good to have you back."

"I mean, I haven't really done anything but ask questions and be clueless, but thanks."

He laughs again and I abruptly find myself wishing he would keep laughing. But then he says, "Sorry, I haven't introduced myself yet. The name's Gabriel."

"Erik," I say. Ellis explained on her tour how all the Nytes here have dropped their last names in defiance of the sectors that use them to track you. Ellis being the exception, since she wants to announce her betrayal loud and clear. "But you already knew that, I imagine."

"But of course."

"Gabriel has the ability to neutralize other Nytes' gifts," Ellis says. "We'd have a much harder time on our hands without him."

My heart almost stops. *This* is the person responsible for all those neutralization power crystals that gave us so much trouble? Of course someone with such a useful gift would be one of the rebel leaders. I should've thought of that before. But somehow I thought he'd be . . . different. Not hunched over a cane looking like a good wind would blow him over. Not that there is wind down here.

"You'd still manage," Gabriel says. I'm probably imagining it, but I think there's sadness in his voice, in the way his smile comes more slowly than it did before.

"But at a much higher cost," Ellis says. "The more gifted lives we can save, the better." She beams at the both of us. "Sorry to take my leave here, but I have a meeting planned with Joan. Why don't you two catch up—or become better acquainted, I suppose."

She goes on her way with a smile and a wave to us. After she leaves, she doesn't look back.

It isn't until she's gone that I realize I have absolutely no clue what I'm supposed to say to this guy. I don't remember him. He remembers me. I don't know what kind of relationship we had. Were we friends? Barely more than acquaintances? I hate this new state of not knowing where I stand with anyone I meet—especially when *everyone* I meet seems to know me.

"When did you get back?" Gabriel asks. He gestures down the main street with his cane, and we head down it. I have to slow my pace a lot to match him.

"Just a few hours ago," I say. "Still getting caught up."

"I'm sure it'll take you some time to adjust, but you'll be fine. You always are."

I glance at his cane as he takes another painstaking step forward.

"Do you always use that?" I ask. "Seems like it'd be hard to maneuver with in a war." If he's the one with the neutralization gift, he *had* to have been at that ambush a week ago, right? How the hell did he get around?

"Blunt as always," Gabriel says, which makes me realize how rude my question was. I start to take it back, but he shakes his head. "No, don't worry about it. Of course you'd want to know. I don't usually need the cane, but I've been expending my gift so much lately that it's been taking a toll on my body." He clicks his tongue. "Whoever decided some Nytes' gifts were limitless didn't do enough research. My limit might be far and away past normal, but it can still cause huge backlash."

"Especially when you've spread it to so many people through power crystals, I take it?"

His mouth becomes a thin line. We stop on the side of the street as Gabriel looks out over all the people—all the kids—going about their lives around us. A group of children play with old dolls while two teenagers chat and keep an eye on them. A boy walks past us with a loaf of stale-looking bread and an apple in his hands. A little girl chases a boy down the length of the street, the boy squealing when the girl catches him with a triumphant shout.

"Why did you come back, Erik?" Gabriel asks.

The question is so abrupt I don't know how to answer right away. Obviously I can't say to spy on the rebels and defeat them from the inside. But an outright lie seems like a bad idea, too. Especially with how little I know about everyone here and how well they know me. Plus, there's Ellis's butterfly in my shadow now. A constant spy of my own.

"I wanted to learn about my past." I stare straight ahead. "I've been looking for months, but I don't know anything except that I used to be a rebel. I thought if I came here, I could find out more about myself. Family, friends, goals—stuff like that."

"You'd go so far as to betray the sector for that?"

"When has the sector ever shown me kindness?" I ask. "I don't owe them anything." The defensiveness comes right away, but so does the guilt. I know I'm not betraying them. Not really. But it still feels wrong to be here—and to know I might've ended up here eventually even without Lai's offer.

"And your old team?" Gabriel watches the two kids as they start chasing each other again. I have no idea what he's thinking. "I was there at the ambush. I saw you all fight together. I didn't think you'd turn your back on them."

"I didn't . . ." But I don't know how to finish that sentence. At least not without giving myself away. But for the same reason I was semi-honest earlier, I try to be semi-honest now. I can't afford for any of my lies to be seen through. "I actually talked with them about it before I left. They didn't like it, but they didn't try to stop me, either. I . . . really don't want to fight them. I didn't want to leave them. But I couldn't go the rest of my life without knowing. I didn't know if I'd ever get another chance like this."

My semi-honesty got a lot more honest than I meant it to, so I snap my jaw shut. Does saying I don't want to fight my old team count as disloyalty to the rebels? Is there any chance this guy will use my desperation to find out about my past against me? Idiot. How could you reveal so much? Any bigger slips than that and I'll be dead before the day is over.

But when Gabriel looks at me, his expression isn't calculating—it's thoughtful, like I just shared an interesting theory that he needs some time to think over before he agrees or disagrees with it.

"I see," he says. "I don't think I'll be able to help you with your past—we weren't close. But if there's anything you need, just let me know. I'll try to help you as best I can."

It's weird that he doesn't mention my team again or the fact that I actually told them I was coming back to the rebels, but I'm not complaining. Better to get off this subject.

"So, how long've you been with the rebels?" I ask.

"About a year now."

"And you joined because you want to see all the Etioles dead like everyone else, I'm guessing."

His eyes narrow. "Something like that."

So nothing like that at all. Interesting. I almost ask more, but if I start asking personal questions, he might do the same. And I definitely don't want to invite that.

Instead, I ask about how the rebels have changed since he first joined. He asks if there's anything specific I want to know about them nowadays. I ask what a normal day in this place looks like for him. He tells me about the lack of food and clean clothes. But all the way back to the main office, I wonder why he didn't ask more about my team.

6
LAI

THE ORDER HAS been moving nonstop—and so have I, trying to keep up with it all. Rumors of the Order planning to join the war have spread through our members like Al's all-consuming flames. Trist, Fiona, and I decide to postpone the full-member meeting until we and the captains have had a chance to talk to our members in smaller groups and feel out what everyone's thoughts are. I can't imagine the chaos that would ensue if we tried to talk to the whole Order at once about this. We need to get everyone near the same page before we try to rally morale.

The fact that there's division among our core leaders about whether or not the Order should join the war isn't helping. No matter how many times I push that the Order is a peace organization, Fiona pushes right back that the sector needs us if the rebels are to be stopped. Trist, Peter, and Syon are basically neutral. Syon points out pros and cons on both sides while Peter stares off into the distance and Trist tries to stop me and Fiona from ripping each other's throats out. I wish Paul was here. He was always a good voice of reason—and I think we would've been on the same side with this. His absence is like a constant blade lodged between my ribs. But he's not here, and our discussions always end in a standoff.

Everywhere I go, I'm met with questions and arguments and distress.

"Is it true the Order's going to war? This is just a rumor, isn't it, Cathwell?"

"How are we supposed to win against the rebels when even the military can't?"

"We aren't equipped for war—we're just going to get slaughtered!"

I've never seen our members so anxious or quick to snap. But given the situation, how could they not be? And yet, for all our members who seem at their wits' end, double that number are gearing up for war, wanting to know more, how they can assist, when we'll make our move.

"You just let me know if there's anything I can do to help."

"I think my brother's mother-in-law deals with weapons—I might be able to get them to help us out."

"Hey, hey, Lai, do you mind if I get a research team together? I bet we could make improvements to weapons and Outside gear—I'm not a fighter, but I want to help."

The reluctance and fear, I had expected. The willingness to fight? It blindsides me. And makes me realize that I've been so focused on the idea of "peace" for so long that I hadn't even noticed most of our members' growing anxiety to *do* something. Something to help against the rebels. Something to move toward real peace instead of just talking about it and creating it within our own little society.

Somewhere along the line, the Order grew up. Without me. Now, I feel myself desperate to catch up before it leaves me behind and moves on to bigger and better things.

"Opinion is mixed but leaning toward a positive reception of joining the war," Fiona says. We've convened in our usual meeting room for what we've all agreed will be our final decision on the Order joining the war. We can't keep putting it off. All our core leaders are seated around the table, and today I invited Jay as well. We could use a new perspective. Al is currently training our members in self-defense. I wanted to invite her, too, but I was afraid our friction would sidetrack the discussion. Besides, I know where she would stand. But the Order wasn't created for war. Its message has always been nonviolence. Even if everyone *is* willing to fight.

"They're too optimistic," Peter mutters. "They don't realize what war actually involves."

Peter's barely spoken since our return from the ambush and the funeral for his brother. I can hear the weight of that loss in his words. I want to say something to him, but every time I look at him, I think of his twin and can't find the words.

"The Order isn't a private army," I say. "Our members aren't trained, we don't have enough equipment—it would be suicide. And we're a *peace* organization. How are we supposed to spread that kind of message if we're killing others?"

"We don't have to attack directly," Fiona says. Her hands press palm down against the table. "I'm not saying we face the rebels head-on. But what about quick strikes? Disrupting their raids with small teams?"

"It's too dangerous," I say. "And now that we no longer have eyes in the military, we have no idea what they might be up to. They'll definitely notice if we start attacking the rebels. We can't risk catching their attention and becoming the enemy of both the rebels *and* the sector."

"What if we got the military on our side?"

All five of us turn to stare at Jay incredulously.

"So we'll simply walk in and ask for an alliance?" Fiona asks. Her words drip with more sarcasm than usual, even for her. "What a brilliant plan."

I listen in to Jay's thoughts. **If there was a way to coordinate with someone on the inside of the military, someone high ranking who would be more interested in seeing peace come about than stomping out any potential threats to the Council's rule . . .**

"You and General Austin are close, aren't you?" Jay asks me.

My back stiffens. I try not to think of the last time I saw my adoptive father—on the other side of prison bars. I try even harder not to think about his comforting smile or his hand ruffling my hair when I was a kid.

"I think *how* close is going to depend on what you're planning," I say.

"What if the Order worked with him?" Jay asks. "If we shared information, each organization could plan around the other. The general doesn't seem like the sort of person who would attack the Order out of spite. We could—secretly—work in tandem. The Order could supply Austin with information from its extensive network, and the military could handle the bulk of the fighting. If we work together, it could bring about the end of this war faster than if either group were to work alone."

"A nice idea, in theory," I say. Does my voice sound tight? I can't believe Jay is suggesting we work with the military. I know how angry and hurt he is at their betrayal. And with good reason. "But there's no guarantee Austin would agree or that he wouldn't eventually be forced to turn on us by the Council. Besides, I swore to never use my gift on him. Even if I was willing to break my promise, he probably has starlight protection from Nytes' gifts. We won't be able to communicate telepathically. Someone would have to sneak in and out of Central to talk with him—no easy task. Plus, our go-between would have to be someone Austin trusts or there'd be no point, and I don't have time for it."

"I'll do it." The words sound choked out, but Jay doesn't hesitate before saying them. His hands tighten into fists on the tabletop. **It wasn't on Austin's order that our arrest was issued. I have no reason to be angry with him. He tried to help us. He always has.** "My gift would make it easier to sneak in and out of Central, and Austin knows me. He'll trust me." He takes a deep breath. "I don't know the general as well as you do, but I don't think he would betray the Order to the Council. He would come up with something, or warn us. And I think stopping the rebels is his first priority. If the Order could help with that, he'll likely work with us."

Austin wasn't the one who betrayed us. It was entirely the High Council. But despite knowing this, the thought of trying to form an alliance with the military makes my stomach turn. It screams *bad idea*. How much could we *really* rely on the military when such an alliance would have to remain a secret between us and Austin? How long until the Council starts questioning where Austin's getting his info from? What if Austin isn't willing to work with us to begin with and Jay risks his neck for nothing? What if Jay gets caught?

"I like it," Fiona says after the silence has stretched on for an uncomfortably long time. "It's the best plan we've heard so far. The Order doesn't have to fight directly, but we'll still be helping to end the war. It comes with risks, of course, but any plan we go with will."

Trist and Syon nod along as she speaks. Even Peter looks like he's actually tuned in for once as his eyes flick between me, Jay, and Fiona.

A weight presses down on my chest. I don't like this. I can't deny it's the best option we've got, but there are so many risks. Not least of all Jay's safety.

"I don't like you being the one to do this," I say. "If you're caught—"

"A risk whoever did this would have to face," Jay says. "And of all the possible candidates, besides yourself, I have the highest chance of getting in and out without being detected. And of having Austin's trust." His gaze is steadier than before, unwavering. **I can do this, Lai. Let me. Please.**

I hate it when he looks at me like that. It makes it almost impossible to say no—especially when I'm the only one in the room who wants to. I sigh. "Okay. Let's do it. Just—be careful, okay? There's no guarantee he'll even hear you out."

A smile lifts the corners of Jay's lips, and I resist the urge to lean over and kiss him. My hands shake, but I lace my fingers through Jay's under the table until they still. It'll be okay. Jay will be safe. We have a plan, and if this alliance happens, the Order can start acting. We could potentially end this war. We can save lives.

Now I just have to hope that Austin comes through. Because without his help, the Order won't be able to do much of anything—no matter how badly our members want to fight.

7
JAY

FORTUNATELY FOR MY new mission, I'm already familiar with the secret underground tunnel leading into Central. Lai and I used it when we were still in the military to sneak out and visit the Order. When I emerge from the tunnel into the little-used meeting room in Central, I'm careful to shut the trapdoor behind me. The tile-covered door blends in perfectly. How Lai ever found it is a mystery to me. However, the military isn't aware of it, thus it isn't guarded. That's all I truly need to know.

I allow my internal grid to unfold behind my eyes. It's past curfew, so most everyone is asleep, but there are still the soldiers on patrol to watch out for. And the Watchers that patrol Central—small, spherical, hovering machines that record audio and video as they roam the halls at random. Much less easy to plan for and track, but so long as I'm cautious, I should be able to see them coming and avoid them. I can't afford to make a misstep.

When there's no one outside the meeting room, I slip into the hallway. It's easy to keep my steps light; the military trained me well and I was keen to learn. Something lodges in my throat as I recall just how eager I was to do whatever the military told me.

It's dark. The only light comes in from the high, narrow slits of windows at the top of the walls. It's a long, slow process getting from the meeting room on the first floor to Austin's office on the third. When I have to make a tight pass by two patrolling soldiers, the beams of their flashlights sweep out before me. I hold my breath as they approach. Waiting, calculating from the patrol paths I used to take myself to predict when and where they'll turn. So long as I don't make a sound, I'll be safe.

The footsteps come closer. Closer. My lungs are about to burst. Then they keep walking by me, and I release the quietest breath I can. I wait a few more heartbeats before slipping into the hall the soldiers were just in and heading the opposite way.

My nerves refuse to calm even when Austin's office is finally in sight. Between me and it is a large reception room. My heart thuds as I sense Austin's secretary, Noah, at the front desk. My back is pressed to the wall leading into the room, so I can't see him, but I hear the soft *tap tap* of clicking keys on a computer. From what I remember of the layout, the desk looks straight over the room, which has to be crossed in order to reach Austin's office.

Shouldn't Noah be in the barracks by now? Or on another of his many missions to a different sector?

Deep breaths. Calm down. Panicking won't solve this. Think. *Think.*

I scan the bit of room visible to me for anything I could use to my advantage, but it's a typical reception space: two couches face each other over a low coffee table, a few chairs line the walls, and a couple of paintings hang as decoration. I briefly wish I had a more useful gift for causing distractions like Erik or Al.

I finger the throwing knives strapped around my arms. No, I need something more subtle. I twist the MMA around my wrist to better see the face of it. I flick through the options on the tiny screen until I reach the electronic signal blocker. There should be an option that would shut down any electronic devices in the vicinity. My finger hovers over it. If Noah's computer were to suddenly crash, he might leave to get help from someone in tech. Or he could become suspicious of such a sudden malfunction and look around for the source. Still—it's my best chance.

I tap the screen on my MMA—then immediately retreat as quietly and quickly as I can in the direction opposite the tech office. It would've been nice to get some distance beforehand, but with Central's high-grade security, I needed to be as close as possible for the signal blocker to work when I activated it.

For agonizing breaths as I continue to backtrack, nothing happens. Then, on my internal grid, Noah's presence flickers with yellow surprise. He heads toward the hallway entrance. I nearly breathe a sigh of relief. But I still need to be quiet, and there's yet more work ahead.

I wait for Noah to start down the hallway that I know to be the quickest route to the tech office, but he passes the turn and keeps going straight. Straight down the path I took. At nearly every corner, he stops and pauses before continuing on. My heart pounds in my ears. He's searching for an intruder. He knows—or suspects, which is almost as bad.

I continue backtracking down hallways, wondering if he can hear my footsteps, my breaths, wishing I were as stealthy as Lai. Noah doesn't need to be silent, which lends him more speed. He's catching up to me.

And we have company. Two patrolling soldiers are making their rounds nearby. I can't go any farther without running into them.

I press myself back against a wall as Noah comes nearer and nearer, willing myself to blend into the shadows.

Noah's footsteps sound from the adjoining hall. He's close. Too close. I count my heartbeats in an attempt to calm myself, but it's little use. If he continues, he'll walk directly into me.

My lungs burn from not breathing.

The footsteps stop. The edges of Noah's cautious presence on my grid flicker with exhaustion, doubt. He doesn't continue forward.

It feels like nothing less than a miracle when his presence turns down the hall running perpendicular to mine. Noah resumes his previous stop-and-start search, but heading away from me now.

I allow myself to breathe normally once more. I can't believe what a close call that was. My knees shake so badly I don't want to move, but of course I have to. Now, while the coast is clear.

I head back to the reception room—now empty—and knock softly on Austin's office door in the code Lai and Austin set up between just the two of them when she was younger. She taught it to me before I left Regail Hall in hopes that it might help.

Nothing happens. I feel his presence on the other side of the door, dyed scarlet with wariness, but he doesn't move. My throat constricts as the seconds tick by. Should I knock again? What if he doesn't answer? What if Noah comes back?

The door opens. I nearly choke on my relief as Austin ushers me quickly inside, presence tinged with surprise as he does so. He locks the door as soon as I'm in.

I take long, deep breaths as I attempt to calm the adrenaline rushing through me. It's okay. I made it. Everything's all right now.

Austin's office is as messy as I remember it—which is actually a bit odd because usually when Noah is in Central, he organizes everything and keeps Austin in check. However, now, books sit in tottering piles around the room. Overstuffed folders spill off his desk onto the floor, where it appears some impromptu meeting was set up. Mugs with varying levels of liquid remaining in them sit scattered throughout the room on every surface—the windowsill, the edge of the desk, stacks of books, the two chairs across from Austin's desk. How does he even move through all this?

"I can't say I was expecting to see you here ever again," Austin says. There's a tinge of orange confusion to his presence, but no anger or caution.

"I'm here on business, I'm afraid. And limited on time if I want to leave unnoticed."

Austin sits with a sigh in his chair—the only empty surface in the office. His hair appears more gray than black now, and deeper lines than I remember run across his square face. Even his perpetually strict posture is slumped. Concern worms its way through me despite myself. "Are you all right, sir?"

Austin gestures to one of the chairs before his desk. "I'm fine, thank you. Your concern is appreciated, though, especially after all that's happened." He snorts. "Traitors indeed."

I hover by the chair, but between all the folders, mugs, and the spare parts of a radio occupying it, it's impossible to sit. I grip the back. "What happened with our arrests wasn't your fault. We're all aware of that."

"But I couldn't do anything to stop it, either." Austin closes his eyes and rubs the bridge of his nose between his forefinger and thumb. I've never seen him so exhausted. "However, that is beside the point. As you said, we will have to be quick." When he opens his eyes once more, his back straightens as well. "Why are you here?"

So I tell him about the Order, its intelligence network, and the alliance we wish to set up with him. I attempt to reveal only the most necessary details about the Order and try not to mention anything that could potentially hurt us. I practiced this speech with Lai before I left, but the words are still stiff on my tongue.

Some of the exhaustion leaves the lines of Austin's face as he listens. He looks more like the old him when he says, "From what you've said, it does sound like an alliance between the military and the Amaryllis Order could be beneficial for us both. It's true the military hasn't been able to make a move. The rebels have almost every advantage over us. We need help. But I know almost nothing about the Order, even if Lai is a part of them. Tell me, how do you feel about the group? Do you trust them?"

"You're asking my thoughts?"

"Do you see anyone else here?"

I wasn't expecting to be asked my own opinion on the Order. I don't have the experience that Austin or even Lai does in these matters, and my history is hardly shining, considering how I blindly trusted the Council. However, Austin appears serious, so I consider how best to give my honest answer.

"I think they can be trusted," I say slowly. "I have yet to see any behavior contradicting what they say their goals are, and every member I have met so far has appeared genuinely invested in seeing peace between the gifted and ungifted—nor have I sensed anyone lying about these things with my gift. I believe in them. More than that, I am truly happy to be working with the Order."

"I see," Austin says. His voice and presence both are neutral, so I'm not sure how to interpret that. Just when it looks as though he's about to speak again, there's a knock on the door.

My blood freezes. I check my grid: Noah. He's back. I look to Austin, frantic, but he appears unconcerned when he asks, "Who is it?"

"Noah, sir."

"Come in."

If I'd had more time, I might have attempted to hide. As it is, the door unlocks from the other side and Austin's secretary enters. His eyebrows lift slightly when he catches sight of me, though his presence doesn't convey much surprise. He locks the door once more. "I thought we might have a visitor," he says. "I guess you weren't an officer for nothing."

Noah's trimmed his dark brown hair since I last saw him some months ago, but it's still so long it nearly reaches his eyes. His copper skin appears darker as well; I wonder if his last job had him working outside. Despite the heavy half-moons under his eyes, his uniform is crisp and his posture upright.

I look to Austin, attempting, and failing, to bite back my panic.

"You don't need to worry about Noah," Austin says. Despite the fact that my heart is trying to jump out of my chest, Austin's presence is still as a statue. "I trust him. Besides, if I do agree to your proposal, it'll be less of a headache if he knows, too. You won't have to try sneaking past him every time we meet, and he'll be able to help me with providing assistance."

"You can trust me," Noah says. He places a hand over his chest. "I won't reveal that you were ever here."

There's no itch behind my eyes that would indicate he's lying. I still can't dispel my wariness, though. Truth be told, I don't know much about Noah. He's a Nyte, nearly twenty, so one of the first. He's been in the military for far longer than my four years; when I entered, he was already Austin's secretary and essentially his second shadow. Whenever Noah was in Central, he was with Austin. However, for some reason, the Council often sends him on missions to other sectors. It likely has something to do with his gift, but I'm completely unaware as to what it is. He's a noncombatant as far as I know. Perhaps something suited to negotiating with other sectors' ambassadors. In any case, he's always kept himself somewhat distant from everyone but Austin, and I've never attempted to learn more about him. I regret that slightly now. Austin, I trust. Noah is an unknown.

"Now then, where were we?" Austin says. "Ah yes. If you trust the Order, then I will tentatively agree to work in tandem with them."

I blink. "Just like that? That's it?"

"Do I need any more than that?"

"Well, I mean, I thought . . ."

Austin leans back in his chair. "After hearing Lai is involved, I was fairly certain I would agree to this alliance. However, Lai is deeply attached to this group from the sounds of it. I wanted to hear from someone with less personal bias. Someone clearheaded and able to make fair assessments—particularly someone who is good at seeing others' honest emotions and motives." At my stare, he raises an eyebrow. "You look surprised. You really think so little of your own ability to accurately judge others?"

"I . . ." However, I don't quite know what to say. Or how much, with Noah here listening. My eyes drop to the floor—or what very little I can see of it underneath all the clutter. "I don't know if I can trust my own judgment. I thought it was right to follow the Council and the military. But they only betrayed me repeatedly, in ways big and small."

"In all fairness, you didn't have many options," Austin says quietly. His presence swirls like a miniature storm. "I'm sorry. If I had never offered you a place in the military—"

"No." Before the team, before the military, I lived with my father, striving to be the perfect son. A useless attempt, since he despised me as both a Nyte and the cause of my mother's death in childbirth. And while there have been more difficulties than I can count in the military,

I have never regretted leaving my father. "You offered me a way out. For that, I can't thank you enough. No matter how poorly that way out may have ended."

Austin nearly smiles. He stands up. "Kitahara, you shouldn't let the Council's betrayal cast doubt over your insight. It's solid—more so than that of most people I've met. At the end of the day, when you have to make a decision, you have only yourself to trust. Never doubt that you know the correct answer and never regret choosing it."

"Thank you, sir." It's difficult to get the words out. My throat is tight. I nearly forget to add, "The Order and I look forward to working together with you. We will all give our best efforts to stop this war."

"I know you will." He gives a last, tired smile. "I'm sure we'll meet again soon to make more specific plans. Until then, be careful. Noah, would you mind seeing Kitahara out?"

"Of course, sir," Noah says.

I nod to Austin one final time before following his secretary.

After the bright light of Austin's office, the reception room feels much darker and more ominous than it did when I first passed through. The single light on Noah's desk hardly reaches beyond his workspace.

"Thank you for your help," I say to Noah as we stand by his desk, because I don't know what else to say and leaving without a word feels wrong. There is no door to act as a barrier between the reception room and the rest of Central's halls, so I keep my voice low.

"I didn't do anything, but thank you," Noah says. The corners of his mouth twitch in what I think might be a smile, but his expression abruptly shifts to one less easily recognizable. His presence on my grid turns toward unease. "Your team—are you all okay?"

His sudden shift in emotion hardens my guard despite the innocent nature of his question. "Yes. Everyone's well, thank you."

"I'm glad to hear it. You're all still together, then? You don't need anything?"

There's no itch behind my eyes after his first statement that would mean he's lying, but his unease is still there, and there's something distinctly off about the way he won't look at me as he speaks. And the halting way he's inquiring after us. There's something he wants to ask but feels he can't put forth directly.

"We're all together," I lie. "We don't need anything at the moment, either. Thank you for asking."

We both freeze as a sound echoes toward us from the hall, but when I check my grid, no one's there. It was likely some machine, maybe the air-conditioning system. Or a Watcher.

"I need to go." My voice couldn't possibly get any lower. "Thank you again."

Noah hesitates. "Take care, Kitahara. I'm sure I'll see you soon."

Somehow, as I stalk once more down the halls, those words don't bring the comfort they should. However, even my disquiet about Noah can't detract from the delayed elation of my success. Austin agreed to help the Order. With this, we might actually have a chance at stopping the war. We could win—the first time the thought has felt genuine since returning from that ambush. Finally, we have a way forward.

8
LAI

I'M STARTING TO get sick of the usual meeting room for core planning. It doesn't help that this is the same room we would always meet in when Paul was still alive and I keep catching myself glancing unconsciously at the doorway, waiting for him to walk in. Maybe I should suggest the five of us meet somewhere else next time. And every time after that.

Focus. "If we do this, we're not going to fight directly," I say. "Now that Austin's agreed to help us, there's no reason for the Order to have to face the rebels head-on. Although we have to be careful our alliance with the military doesn't slip out. That could cause more harm than good."

I pinch the bridge of my nose, trying to make my thoughts keep going. I haven't slept since Jay—now working out logistics with some of the captains—returned from his meeting with Austin almost twenty hours ago. As soon as he got back, the core Order leaders convened. With the military's support, I didn't have much reason to argue against the Order joining the war anymore. We won't take the full brunt of it. After that, it was a matter of meeting with all the captains and Helpers, and trying to rally as much support as we could with those we knew backed the Order going to war. We have to solidify our bases before we announce this to the rest of the organization.

"We need to mitigate the concerns of those who are currently reluctant to fight," I say. "Reassure them that this isn't as dangerous as it sounds—that we're not going to be sending everyone into battle just to get wiped out."

"And show that this is the best way to win peace," Trist adds. "We must fight for real peace. It will not come otherwise."

"We'll need to up our fighting instruction," Fiona says as she sifts through numerous sheets fanned across the table, looking for the one detailing our number of actual fighters and those signed up for the self-defense program. "Johann joining our teachers has helped a lot, but one person alone can only take on so much. We need more trained instructors."

Syon signs to her and she frowns. "No. I don't think we should allow anyone younger than fourteen to fight. And even that's pushing it."

"I think we should take anyone who's willing," Peter says. The words sound dragged out of him. I'm a little surprised he even came. I need to talk to him about Paul soon, but everything's been so busy and he's been so standoffish that I haven't had the chance. Maybe if he stays busy with Order responsibilities, the sheer amount of work will distract him enough from his grief that he can start to move on. "If someone wants to fight, we should let them."

Fiona glares at him across her scattered array of papers. "I will not allow *children* to fight in this war."

"What, and you think *we're* adults?" Peter asks with a humorless laugh that sends a chill down my spine. "We're kids ourselves. And if we're going to win this, we need all the help we can get."

"We could consider accepting those who are gifted," I say quietly. "They're stronger and would be better able to hold their own."

Fiona stares at me incredulously. "Do you even *hear* yourself right now? If we stoop to fighting this war with gifted children, we're no better than the military or even the rebels. If we're going to do this, we're going to do it with morals. We're not the same as them. We'll do this and we'll do it right."

No one argues the point, and internally, guilt crawls up my lungs. Do I really think it's okay to fight with children so long as they're strong? Is what Jay said about me a lifetime ago true—that I think the end justifies the means? I don't want to think about to what extent that's true.

But thinking about Jay reminds me of Al, and another kind of guilt replaces the first. I know she's reaching her limit with me, but I don't know what to do. Besides, I'm already stretched thin trying to help the Order without taking on the complicated problem of solving the tension between us. I need to focus right now.

Trist must sense the uneasiness in the air, as he tends to do, because he switches the topic. "We have Sakchai's Gate to get Outside at least, but we are short on weapons. And the ability to move many people at one time. Some members have bycs, but that will not be enough."

"And rallying the Order in the meantime?" Peter asks, still in that same lifeless voice. "We have to get everyone to agree on this before we can do anything. A two to one split isn't gonna cut it."

Silence meets his words. We all know that, of course. What we need to do more than anything is figure out a way to convince everyone that this is the right course to take. Not everyone has to participate—I don't *want* everyone to participate—but if there are doubts circulating when we go into this, not only will it hurt morale before we've even begun, but the feelings of negativity will only get worse as time goes on. Especially if things don't go well at first.

"We need a way to reassure everyone," Fiona says.

"Reassurance before going into battle will only sound like a naive lie," I say. "I've been in the military long enough to know that. We have to be honest and painfully blunt with everyone upfront."

"Doing it like that isn't exactly going to encourage support," Fiona says.

"Giving everyone a false sense of security will only backfire on us later when, surprise, surprise, we start losing people and money from spending what little funds we have on this." I cross my arms and dare her to contradict me. "What we *need* is to convince everyone it's worth the risk. To convince them that the outcome is worth the sacrifices." Again, Jay's words come back to me, hauntingly clear. *The end justifies the means. That's really what you believe?*

Stop that, I tell myself. This is different. This is war. Of course sacrifices will have to be made. Sacrifices have to be made to accomplish anything worth doing. And winning peace *is* worth it.

"I think what we *need*," Peter says quietly, "is for the Order to hear from Walker."

The assembled Order members—all 1,384 of them—still as Walker strides across the stage of the main hall. Silence descends, although it more closely resembles the calm in the eye of a storm than any real sense of peace.

"I want to thank everyone for coming tonight." Walker's lightly accented voice echoes through the huge hall even at a normal volume. "It has been a long, fraught few weeks. I'm sure you've all heard many things over the past few days about the Order's next move. I would like to clarify that for you now."

No one speaks. Waiting. Just as before.

"All of us in charge of running the Order have agreed that

joining the war against the rebels is our best chance of bringing true peace to the sector—to both gifted and ungifted."

A few raised voices, quickly hushed by their fellows. *Wait until the end. Let's hear what she has to say first.*

My heart hammers against my chest. This is our only chance to get things right. Everything has to be perfect.

"I know many of you have concerns about this direction," Walker continues. "And rightly so. We were founded on ideals of peace, and I have no intention of discarding them. However, ideals are only that. Without action, they remain an unattainable fantasy. To win true peace, we must defeat those who threaten our home. I am not suggesting a full-frontal attack of any kind. Our strikes will be quick, designed to hit hard in the most effective places with minimal risk to our members."

A pause to allow for anyone to speak up if they wish. Silence.

"It is perfectly acceptable if you do not wish to participate in this war. There will be deaths. There will be sacrifices in every way imaginable. We will certainly not force this onto anyone, and we will not accept anyone under the age of fourteen as part of our fighting forces. You can leave the Order if you so wish—although I hope you will stay and support those of us who choose to fight."

Walker's voice rises, filling every crevice and corner of the immense hall. "If our aim is truly peace and understanding, then we cannot sit idly by while others fight and risk their lives to protect this sector. Not when there is something we can do to help. If you wish to see a future where everyone can live freely together, then we *must* put an end to those who seek to destroy us and our homes. We must fight, and we must *win*."

The last words are barely out when a roar of cheers fills the hall. Most of it comes from those who already supported joining the

war—but a surprising amount comes from people who'd been hesi-
tant, now wrapped up in the energy of the people around them and
the sense that *this is right*.

Walker bows deeply to the sea of people, then disappears offstage
into the room where Fiona, Trist, Syon, and Peter are already
waiting.

"Well?" Fiona asks. "We have the Order's backing. What's our
next step?"

I release my hold over her power crystal, and with it, the illusion
of Walker falls away from me. Just as easily as I removed the illusion,
I shed the Sector Four accent I grew up with. "Those two rebel bases
our scouts found about a month ago," I say. "Pull all the information
we have on them."

9

ERIK

TWO WEEKS WITH the rebels, and it feels like I've been here for ages already. After the first few days, everyone stopped being so cautious around me. When I walk through the makeshift town, kids run up to me and start blabbering like I know who they are. I get dragged into games of ball, talks of the sector, and storytelling sessions about my past. It doesn't sound like I was close with any of the gifted in the town, but they tell me about raids we went on together, how everyone looked up to me—still looks up to me, by the sounds of it. It makes me uncomfortable. Especially when I know I'm betraying all these people looking at me with shining eyes.

I try to leave a gaggle of kids as politely as I can—"Sorry, I have to go; I'm going to be late meeting Gabriel"—but I barely make it fifteen steps before someone else pops up to chat. Seriously, how does anyone ever get to where they're going around here?

But eventually—finally—I make it to the spot I'm meeting Gabriel, where he's already waiting. Once he sees me, he lifts a hand and smiles slightly. My heart misses a beat. Whenever he smiles, the left side of his mouth always lifts a little higher than the right. It's way too disarming. "Good to see you," he says.

"You too," I say lamely. *Come on, idiot. Come up with something better than that.*

We start walking down the haphazard paths. Gabriel stopped using his cane earlier this week, but he's still pretty slow. Or deliberate, I guess. He might be one of those so-called limitless Nytes who can use their gifts without ever seeming to risk a fallout, but it still takes a toll on him. Little wonder. Everyone and their mom must want a power crystal that neutralizes other Nytes' gifts, and making so many must take a lot out of him. Lai told me about this other "limitless" Nyte, a guy in the Order called Syon. He has endless control over energy, but at the cost of his emotions. Any slight feeling could send his power spiraling out of control. Gabriel's price for unlimited power is his physical constitution. I don't know which sounds worse.

"You didn't have to come with me, you know," Gabriel says as we stroll along. Today he's delivering two of his power crystals to some rebels before our group meeting with Ellis later. I asked if I could tag along to get a better sense of the town's layout, and he said sure. But honestly, I just wanted an excuse to hang out with him. "You've actually already got a good sense of the area, don't you?" He's sharp. "I'm sure you have better things to do."

"I wanted to come," I say with a half shrug. "I'm happy you let me join you."

He raises an eyebrow. Was I too obvious? But the left side of his smile lifts a little higher, and he says, "Well, I'm glad you're here. Have you managed to settle in all right?"

I hold back a sigh of relief as I tell him about the woodshop in the main office, getting used to always being hungry, and training with Cal.

Cal is obviously my best bet for learning more about my past, and he's the easiest to talk to and be around, so I've been spending most of my time with him. Before I knew it, we were doing just about everything together. He's happy to tell me about the old days, but whenever he describes the past me, who genuinely hated the sectors, the ungifted, and maybe just about everything, it feels like he's talking about a total stranger. I like to think the current me has more of a passive-aggressiveness toward everything.

Other than Cal, the only person I hang out with is Gabriel—and I definitely don't mention how much I like being around him. He said we weren't close when I was with the rebels the first time, and it's obvious after a few questions he really doesn't know much about the me from back then. But even though talking to him won't help me, I still find myself drawn to him. I tell myself it's just because he's nice. Nice in a way that isn't because we used to be good friends. He doesn't look at me like he's waiting for the old me to return. With him, there're no expectations, no demands. I actually enjoy being with him. I find excuses to spend time together.

As far as I can tell, he isn't trying to decide whether or not I can be trusted, either, which is a huge improvement from all the other leaders except Cal. I can actually feel sort of normal around Gabriel. And forget that I'm stabbing him and everyone else in the back as I sit in my room at night and send telepathic reports on the rebels' plans to Lai. But of course, I don't actually say any of this to him as we walk through the streets, stopping every once in a while to say hi to the kids we pass.

When Gabriel gives his power crystal to the first rebel on our delivery route, she almost cries. The second guy won't stop hugging Gabriel and thanking him. I have to drag him away since he's too nice to say he needs to go himself.

"You really should take it easy on the power crystals," I say. "You're going to need that cane permanently at this rate." And the more neutralization crystals the rebels have, the harder it'll be for the Order and military to fight them.

"You, worried about someone?" Gabriel asks. "How rare."

Heat floods my face. "I worry about my friends. Doesn't everyone?"

It's the first time I've called anyone here a friend aloud other than Cal, but Gabriel doesn't mention it. "Even when you'd been with the rebels for years and you had your memories, you didn't show concern for others. If someone died, they were just a casualty of the cause. Everyone knew that about you."

Everyone knows this, everyone knows that, but no one knows anything that's actually important. I'm getting tired of the constant analysis of my past self—even if that's what I came here to learn. The more I hear about this former Erik, the more sick of him I get.

"Look, whoever that guy was, I'm not him anymore," I say. "I'd appreciate not having to hear any more comparisons from everyone."

Gabriel's slanted smile disappears. "I didn't mean to make you angry."

"I'm not angry."

We walk for a few steps in silence before Gabriel says, "I'm sorry. I knew you lost your memories, but I didn't think you'd be a different person. I guess I assumed your personality would be the same as before. I didn't mean to hurt you."

"You didn't." My heat is already fading. It's hard to stay annoyed when someone is being so genuinely apologetic. "Not really. Being here is just . . . a lot. Everyone expects me to be someone I'm not, and then they act all surprised when I'm myself. Plus, I'm not really a fan of this past Erik everyone apparently liked so much." My nose scrunches up. "I wish people here preferred the current me."

"I prefer the current you," Gabriel says. He says it without hesitation but not like he's just saying it to reassure me, either. He sounds like he means it. Which, okay, is how he always sounds, but it still throws me off. "If you acted like the old Erik, I wouldn't hang around with you so much. Probably not at all. I didn't really . . . agree with some of your past viewpoints."

"Like what?"

"Like wiping out all the ungifted."

I stop walking. Gabriel keeps going a few steps before he realizes I'm not beside him, then he stops, too.

"Are you sure you should say something like that?" I can't believe any rebel, let alone one of the top commanders here, would ever admit to not wanting to kill the ungifted. Isn't that the rebels' whole shtick? I am very, very aware of Ellis's butterfly in my shadow watching and listening to me and my surroundings at all times. "Isn't that the whole goal of the rebels?"

"Sara is aware of my opinions, if that's what you're worried about." He sounds amused. "We go further back than the rebels. When she first set out to start the group, I tried to talk her out of it. She didn't listen."

"So then you decided, what, if you can't beat 'em, join 'em?"

"No." Gabriel starts walking again, and since there's no point just standing around some temporarily deserted, slapped-together piles of wood, metal, and worn toys, I follow him. "Once the rebels became a formidable force, I was worried. I came to see what Sara had built and to try to get her to stop this before it was too late—but then I saw all the children." He sighs. "As it turned out, the rebels weren't just a fighting force but a place for homeless gifted children to take shelter."

He stops again, in a slightly more populated area. A few kids about as tall as my knees chase one another around a burning firepit.

A teenager sitting by the fire keeps a close eye on them, occasionally moving to stop the kids from getting too close to the flames.

"I was still against the rebels," Gabriel says. "But Sara wouldn't back down. And I knew if the military found or beat the rebels, they'd treat everyone here as a traitor. Even those too young to fight. Since I couldn't find what I was looking for in the sector anyway, I decided to stay here to help protect the kids." His eyes lock with mine. They send a chill down my arms. "And to keep trying to convince Sara to stop all this."

"And she's okay with that?" I ask. "She doesn't really strike me as the type to keep around someone who's constantly questioning her decisions."

"Like I said, we go back much further than the rebels' time," Gabriel says. His eyes drop to the ground. "She wasn't always like this. But grief over a close friend's death changed her and brought about her desire for revenge against the sector. I suspect she doesn't get angry with me because of our history." He almost smiles, but the expression looks painful. "Or maybe my gift is just so useful that she'll put up with me if it means she can use it for the rebels' sake."

I almost ask about the friend's death and Ellis's revenge, but I don't. It's obvious Gabriel's upset, and while I don't normally care that much about others' feelings if they're in the way of me finding out something important, I meant it when I said Gabriel's a friend. Maybe not a super-close one, especially since I've only known him for a couple of weeks, especially since I'm betraying him and everything he cares about here, but I like him. He's sincere and honestly cares about others. And he doesn't want war with the Etioles.

"I don't think Ellis is the kind of person who would keep someone around just because their gift is useful," I say. There's a weird sort of pressure when Gabriel looks up at me. Is he hoping I'll say something that'll set him at ease? My pulse beats in my ears. *Don't mess this up.* "She definitely wouldn't make you one of her top leaders if she didn't trust you or want you around. Yeah, you keep questioning her. But maybe she wants that. Maybe she thinks it's better to have someone who won't just agree with everything she says. Maybe there's even a part of her that hopes you will convince her to stop all this." *I* hope so, at least. That would make everything so much easier. But it all sounds nice anyway, and it has enough of a ring of truth that it could be possible.

Gabriel cracks the smallest lopsided smile in the world. "Maybe you're right. Even if you aren't, it doesn't change what I have to do."

Not the most optimistic response, but I'll take it.

"Come on," I say. "We should get to the meeting about that upcoming raid. We'll be late if we don't head there soon."

"Yeah." Gabriel's expression returns to its normal unreadable preset, but it feels like there's something different now. Or maybe the difference isn't in how he looks. My pulse still beats too loudly in my ears. "Let's go."

Other than digging around about my past—and finding out that no one knows about my time pre-rebels and quickly getting frustrated with that—my time here has involved a lot of meetings. I still don't know how the rebels get in and out of the home base, and I haven't asked in case it gets anyone wondering if there's a reason I want to leave. There isn't, other than wanting to see the sun again and taste the slightly fresher air of the Outside—but I don't need any unfounded suspicions when there are so many possible founded ones lying around. So I've been stuck underground. Which means attending planning meetings, scouting meetings, supply meetings, and every other type of meeting there could possibly be. Ellis asks me to come to all of them, and since there could be useful intel for Lai and the Order, I always accept. It's not like I have anything else to do, anyway. I'm starting to go stir-crazy down here.

We always convene in Ellis's office for these meetings. The rebel leader herself sits at her desk with a map in front of her. Ellis—who keeps insisting I call her Sara every time I see her—is probably my second-best bet for learning about my past, but I only go near her when I have to, so I haven't seen her much other than meetings. She gives me the creeps.

Cal waves as soon as I open the door and gestures for me to sit beside him on the dusty couch. Devin slumps against the wall behind Ellis's chair. He doesn't acknowledge my existence. We haven't talked since I returned. Joan stands straight as a beam in front of Ellis's desk, hands clasped behind her back. Her eyes flick to me and she nods in greeting. She's been distant and cold, but never outright mean. She'll answer just about any question I ask, but never in detail and always while giving me the feeling she really doesn't want to talk about it. Gabriel moves to the armchair across from the couch, and then we're all in our usual positions.

"Since everyone's here, let's get started," Ellis says. Unusually brusque for her. Her eyes don't leave the map. Her fingers trace a line drawn over it in thick black marker.

She goes over the plan to attack an armored supply truck on its route to another sector. Most of us have heard it three or four times by now, but she's changed a few details since last time, like which exact point we're going to strike based on the scouts' report on the terrain, and exactly how the team Joan is leading will make a coordinated attack with their gifts. I make mental notes to relay to Lai tonight.

"It should be relatively straightforward," Ellis says. "We haven't attacked this route since it changed course, so they shouldn't have any reason to expect we know the new course or that we'll be coming." Her eyes flick to Joan. "I'll be counting on you."

"I won't let you down," Joan says. The way she says it, there's no way I'd believe she could fail. That is, if not for the fact that I know the Order is going to launch their first counterstrike against the rebels during this raid.

"There's one last thing." Ellis's eyes move to me, and for a second, I'm terrified she heard my thoughts just now. "Erik. I want you to go with them."

"What?" It takes a moment to sink in through my paranoia. "Me? Why?"

"You must be going crazy stuck down here, right?" Ellis asks. She smiles at my expression, whatever it is, and knows she's right. "You came back to us. You should be allowed to fight with us. You want your chance for revenge against the sector that so ruthlessly discarded you, right?"

Desire for revenge? Maybe against the High Council, since they're the ones who accused me of being a traitor, but I don't have anything against some Etiole truck drivers who're just doing their jobs. They've never done anything to me. But I can't say that. So I force a smile that I hope matches hers. "You know me too well. I'm looking forward to it."

10

AL

AFTER TRAINING FINISHES, Trist tries to get me to talk to Lai—
again. But this time, he doesn't give me a choice, telling me I need to
report the trainees' progress to her.

"You're not good at being sneaky, Trist," I say. "I know what
you're trying to do."

"I never said I was trying for sneaky," he says.

"We haven't been able to hold an actual conversation in weeks.
Me reporting stats to her isn't going to change that."

"No," Trist says. He looks back over his shoulder at some of the
trainees who stayed behind to keep practicing drills. My chest swells
with pride at the sight of them. I've only been teaching for two weeks,
but I like it. More than I thought I would. "But it will give you at least
a chance. You two don't even try to speak with each other now."

I bite my tongue. How does this guy manage to pick up on so
much about other people when he's swamped with work for the Order?
"Fine." I try not to snap it. "I'll report how everyone's doing. Just
don't get your hopes up about anything else happening."

"I don't understand you two." Trist shakes his head. "You both know you would be happier if you made up, but you both continue this fight. Why?"

"It's not that simple." She's lied to me about way too much for way too long, even though it was obvious I trusted her. I was responsible for her friend's death. There's too much betrayal, too much hurt we both caused. A couple of words aren't going to fix that.

"Maybe. But it could help if you talked."

I don't say I doubt it, because he would just come up with another Trist-ism, so I say, "I'll keep it in mind."

But with the look he gives me, I know he gets what I'm thinking. "Take care, Al. Do not worry overly. There are enough worries as it is."

I find Lai with Jay and Seung in one of the strategy rooms the top brass usually meet in. Jay sees me first. He smiles and waves, and I wave back with relief. Lately, I feel more relaxed when he's around.

Lai and Seung don't look up from the map they're writing on. "It won't work if they come up from behind us," Lai is saying. She arcs a line across the paper. "It would destroy the whole formation, and we already know they have a Nyte with the gift of teleportation. That means anyone could have teleportation power crystals. It's too risky."

"*All* the plans are too risky," Seung says dryly. "Lai, there will never be a perfect foolproof plan. And certainly not for a fight against Nytes."

I watch as Lai's grip on her pen tightens so hard her knuckles go white. Her lips press together into a hard line. "Again. From the beginning."

I cough. Seung looks up, but Lai's eyes don't leave the map.

"I came to report on the combat training's progress." My voice sounds stiff even to me. *Come on. Just gotta get through this.*

"Can we talk about it later?" Lai still doesn't look at me. "I want to get our plan of attack finished first."

"It could help you plan your attack if you have a better idea of your fighters' abilities," I say.

"I can't imagine anyone has improved so much since Trist's report last week that it would alter how we plan our attack."

"You don't know that." Even though she's right, her impatient dismissal makes my blood boil. Why does she have to say it like that? Can't she just take two seconds to listen to me and then get back to her planning?

Finally, Lai spins around to glare at me. "I *do* know that, Al, and even if I didn't, I know you're only here because Trist asked you to come and not because you think you have information that could change the tide of our first fight. So just *wait*."

"Could you not just go into my head whenever you feel like it?" I snap. My boiling blood starts to catch fire. "You ever hear of something called privacy?"

"Why don't we just take a step back?" Jay asks. He comes to stand between me and Lai, hands raised in peace. "Everyone's on edge right now with how busy things have become since the Order decided to join the war. You're both tired. Let's just—"

"No," I say. "No, no more *let's just deal with this later*—I want to deal with it *now*. Fight me, Lai."

Seung's eyebrows shoot up and Jay's jaw drops, but Lai's eyes harden. "I thought you'd never say it. Let's go."

"Wait wait wait," Jay says. "This is a terrible idea. You both merely need some time to calm down—"

"Jay, this isn't going to be solved with time," Lai says. "We've *had* time."

"Took the words straight out of my mouth," I say.

Jay looks like he's going to keep protesting, but Seung comes around and puts a hand on his shoulder. "Don't bother, Kitahara. Some idiots only know how to speak with their fists."

Jay looks at all of us, but he's not going to find any allies. His shoulders slump. "I can't believe you're both doing this right now."

"No time like the present," I say. "Let's go."

None of us want to draw a crowd, so we head to a private practice room. There's plenty of space to move around for a fight. Better yet, no one else should stop by.

Even though I was tired from training the Order members, adrenaline replaces my exhaustion now. It only takes a glance at Lai to tell it's the same for her. She's looked dead on her feet for the last few weeks, but there's no sign of that now. Just a fire burning in her eyes that I haven't seen in a long time.

"You wanted the fight," she says while we stretch, "so what's your condition for winning?"

I could make it a first-hit-wins fight. That would make it easier, faster. But I don't want this to be fast. "Whoever falls to their knees first."

Her smile sharpens. "Don't regret that later."

"Are you really doing this?" Jay asks. I guess he couldn't stand to leave us alone because he and Seung ended up tagging along. "There are so many other things we need to be taking care of right now. And what if one of you gets hurt?"

He looks to Seung for support, but she just shrugs. "I only came to watch Lai get her ass handed to her."

"Thanks for the vote of confidence, Fiona," Lai says dryly.

"Anytime."

"Are we ready or what?" I ask.

Lai's eyes flick to me. Nothing about her changes in an obvious way, but it feels like she got sharper, angrier. *Good.* "Ready when you are."

That's all the invitation I need. I charge her, not caring about her never-strike-first rule or how she might've been expecting that from me. I just want to give her a solid punch to the face.

She sidesteps—of course—and I spin around to face her as soon as my punch misses, but she's ready. She swings at my head. I duck and her knee comes up to my face, but I block it with a cupped hand and aim a fist at her exposed stomach.

She jumps back and I follow. She tries another kick, but this time when I duck, she whips around for a punch. I deflect it off the side of my arm and try to aim my fist at her chest, but she slips away before it can connect.

It's a game of cat and mouse for a while. We both lunge and evade, but I can tell she gets tired of that real fast—just like me. Our swings become heavier and less controlled, and even though I know I'm flagging, I can't make myself focus enough to recover. *Get your shit together, Al. You're going to lose if you keep this up.*

And I would rather face an army of rebels alone than lose to Lai right now.

"You really care that much if you lose to me?" Lai asks as she blocks another of my punches. "It didn't used to matter which of us won or lost."

"That was before I wanted to beat the shit out of you."

She falters and my next hit *does* land, sending her stumbling back across the rough stone floor.

If it was the normal Lai, the girl who could keep her cool in a fight and was never so easily pushed off balance, it wouldn't have made any difference. But this angry, tired, reckless Lai? I'm able to land a fist to her stomach before she can recover.

I hear all the air leave her lungs in a rush as she gasps, trying to breathe. "You have *no* idea how much I've wanted to do that," I snarl as I land a kick on her ribcage, sending her staggering back. "How much I've wanted to wipe that conceited look off your face for the last three weeks. You always think you're right—that you know best, that whoever's trust you step on along the way is simply collateral damage. You never think about anyone but yourself."

She doesn't fall, just stands there clutching her stomach. Her dark eyes burn into me with a fire that's been smothered for a long, long time. Longer than we've known each other.

"You don't know *anything*," she hisses. Even though she's still struggling to catch her breath, she rushes at me with a series of quick punches. I block them, but they keep coming. "You think just because we've been friends for a couple months, I should trust you with everything about me? Even the things that could put the people I care about in danger? If you really trusted me like you say you did, you would've waited until I was ready to tell you about everything and been understanding—you would've been a *real* friend."

Now *I* falter. Her fist catches my jaw and sends me reeling back, but she follows after with a kick to my stomach before I can recover, similar to how I nailed her.

"Maybe if our whole friendship hadn't started with you *blackmailing me and reading my every thought*," I say, but the words come out as a wheeze. Pain rips through my stomach, but I ignore it as Lai keeps coming.

I throw my arms up to block her next hit as she says, "Funny how the blackmailing didn't bother you as much before you found out I learned your secret by using my gift. We weren't even friends then—why should I have held back? You use your gift to your advantage all the time—why shouldn't I?" There's no obvious opening in her hits. They keep coming faster, but also messier. "Why should I be judged for using my gift when other Nytes use theirs to help themselves all the time? What gives you the right to be angry at me for doing the same thing you do? I'm sorry my gift and methods aren't as *noble* as yours—"

Her voice cracks, and in the same instant, her next punch misses. I grab her arm and swing her around, letting go as I fling her at the ground. She throws an arm out to catch herself before she hits the floor, but I'm right behind her.

"You think this is just about your gift?" I aim an uppercut at her jaw, but she dodges. I keep pushing forward. "Your gift doesn't explain all your secrets—and you know what, fine, yeah, you didn't have to tell me everything up front, but after I opened up to you? After I told you *everything*? You couldn't even tell me a part of the truth?" I kick at her ankles in frustration, but she just jumps over my foot and aims a punch at my face. "What part of our friendship was real, Lai? Was any of it?"

"If it wasn't real, I wouldn't have been so afraid to tell you the truth." One of her punches slips through and strikes me full in the chest. I whip around to fend off her next blow. "I wouldn't have been so afraid you'd leave me if I told you everything. I wouldn't have spent so much time with you or laughed with you or genuinely wanted to fight together with you. I wouldn't have gone back for you that day. Paul wouldn't have died because of me."

Tears run down her face. I hesitate, but she keeps swinging, so I keep dodging and trying to find an opening of my own. It comes when she swings too far and I land my knee in her side. She falls back, breathing hard, but stays standing, fists still up.

But I can't bring myself to maintain my own stance. I just stare at her. "What do you mean Paul died because of you? You didn't do anything wrong."

"I'm the one who told Paul and Peter to follow me back for you," Lai says. Her breath is coming up short, and I can't tell if it's because of our fight or her crying. She wipes her arm angrily across her eyes, but the tears don't stop. "They didn't even know you, but I—" Her fists clench, and she races at me again.

This time, I can see that the anger in her eyes isn't for me. Was it ever? My own anger has disappeared like a fire doused by ice water all in one go, and now I wonder why I couldn't see before what I can see right now.

Lai's swings aren't just mad—they're desperate. She was so defensive about her gift. So clearly afraid of telling the truth—she admitted as much herself.

For the first time, it hits me that it wasn't that Lai didn't tell me about her gift or some of her other secrets because she didn't trust me, but because she felt too much self-loathing to do it.

But that just makes me angry again. I catch her fist and land a blow against her jaw. She falls back and I follow, both of us swinging and blocking and ducking. "That's what I mean when I say you didn't trust me," I half-shout. "You thought I'd leave once I knew the truth? You didn't trust me to stick around after that? Why do you get to decide that? And you really think Paul's death was your fault?" Lai hesitates, but I don't take advantage of the opening. "*I* was the one who went back for my own selfish reasons. You did what any good friend would've by trying to stay together. You even went back for me. His death was my fault—not yours."

We both stop moving, breathing hard and watching each other, but neither of us moves to continue the fight.

I have no idea what Lai is thinking. I know she knows exactly what *I'm* thinking, which is both infuriating and oddly relieving for once, because I don't have to try to put my feelings into words to get her to understand.

"Paul's death wasn't the fault of either of you," Seung says quietly, breaking the heavy silence. I forgot she and Jay were here. "He died at the hands of the rebels. You're both idiots for trying to take the blame for that instead of putting it where it rightfully belongs."

Neither of us look at her. Lai's still breathing heavily, but she isn't crying anymore, which is good, because I don't know how to handle crying.

She finally straightens and looks at me. The anger from before is gone, replaced by something duller. "I'm sorry, Al. For everything. I . . . I'm a terrible friend. I always have been. I don't trust people, and I definitely don't trust them to stick around once they know more about me. When we became friends, I knew you were good." She laughs. "And I'm definitely not. I thought our friendship wouldn't actually last, so I enjoyed it while I could, knowing it'd end once I told you the truth. Once you realized how awful I am."

"You're not awful, Lai."

She closes her eyes. "I am. I'm not saying that for your pity, but because it's true. There are still things I haven't told you, things that I've done. There are probably things I'll never tell you. That's who I am."

"It doesn't have to be. You can be whoever you want."

"That's the thing, though." She opens her eyes. "I don't hate being like this. I'm *okay* with who I am. I know I'm terrible in a lot of ways, but I don't want to change. I can survive like this. I can do the things I set out to—I can *thrive* because I'm like this. But that doesn't mean I'm blind to how it affects the people around me. I don't blame the people who choose to leave, but I don't want the people who remain to try to make me change, either."

I don't know what to say. This is probably the most honest Lai's ever been with me—probably the most honest she ever *will* be with me.

I let out a long, low sigh and straighten. She watches me. She doesn't give it away easily, but I know her well enough to tell she's nervous about what I'll say.

"Then I guess," I say, "I'll just have to learn to be friends with you as you are."

Lai blinks. Stares at me. Blinks again.

"Oh, thank gods," Jay says from behind me. His footsteps drum across the floor as he runs over to us. "Is this done now? Are we finished? Because you both look awful and exhausted. Well, more exhausted than before."

Lai laughs. She sounds more surprised than anything. "We're done, Jay." She holds out a hand to me with an uncertain smile. "Well, since neither of us got the other to her knees, call it a draw?"

I look at her hand and then at her with raised eyebrows. I grab her arm and pull her into a hug. "How about we say we both won?"

She tenses at first, but she's quick to hug me back. Tightly. I'm worried she's going to start crying again, but she just laughs. "Yeah, okay. Definitely a win."

11

JAY

SNEAKING INTO CENTRAL is much less excruciating after the first time. Now that Austin is aware of the fact I'm coming and we already have an alliance established between the Order and military, there's less dread weighing me down. Slipping past the patrolling soldiers and Watchers is still a careful process, and several times I feel as though it will give me a heart attack, but there is safety waiting for me at the end.

Noah looks up from his desk when I enter the reception room. He stands noiselessly, his presence a neutral, misty gray, and unlocks Austin's door for me to enter. "Please call me if there's anything I can help with," he says quietly. Then he closes the door and is gone.

I wait a few heartbeats before I say, "He's a diligent secretary, isn't he?"

"The best I've ever had," Austin says from behind his desk. Incredibly, the room is somehow messier and more cluttered than the last time I visited. The papers over the floor are now layered with new documents; in several places, its clear folders were stacked too precariously, tipped over, and were never righted. I step carefully to avoid dirtying anything as I approach Austin.

"Is he . . . okay with you working with the Order behind the Council and military's back?" I ask. Noah's presence didn't give any indication he was bothered to see me, but . . .

Several heartbeats pass before Austin answers. I can't easily identify the emotions coloring his presence. "Even if he objected, I don't think he'd ever say so."

"What do you mean?"

Austin sets a file folder on his desk with a swish of air that sounds like a sigh. "Noah's not a very . . . open person. Perhaps it comes from being brought up in the military since before he could walk and working directly under the Council since he could wield a weapon, but he never says what he's really thinking. I get the feeling he thinks his purpose in life is just to follow orders." Austin's eyes drift to the window. His presence on my grid flickers with night-black grief before fixing itself back into its usual neutrality. "I've been trying to break him out of that way of thinking for years, but given our positions and responsibilities, it's difficult. Especially now with the war."

"I'm sorry," I say. "I had no idea." I'd known Noah had been in the military for at least as long as Lai, but I never imagined he was actually born into the military. However . . . "But if he's worked directly under the Council for so long, why do you trust him so much? Is it really okay for him to know about you helping the Order?"

Austin merely chuckles. "Working for someone for a long time doesn't mean you're dutiful to them. Noah has more than enough reason to despise the Council. He follows their orders because he has to, but he's proved countless times that he is loyal to me over them. I trust him." There's no telltale itch behind my eyes that would indicate he's lying. At the very least, he believes what he says. And if he's known Noah and worked with him for so many years, I suppose he would know best. Still, an unknown party sharing knowledge in all this unsettles me. I should try to become better acquainted with Noah. Perhaps then I could ascertain whether or not he's truly trustworthy.

Austin's fingers flick through the random-seeming mess of papers on his desk. His presence is sharp with concentration. "I read the coded updates you sent. So, the Order has decided to join the war?"

I nod. "The idea is to make quick surprise strikes. The Order has found a way to somewhat accurately predict when the rebels will make their supply raids—which means we can counterstrike. We believe their next raid will take place tomorrow night. We'll attack then." I don't mention Erik has gone over to the rebels as a spy. Lai and I discussed it, and it feels safer to leave him out of these discussions. No one needs to know he's with the rebels. It could just complicate things when he returns to the sector.

"So what is the Order asking from me?" Austin's voice betrays no tension, but his presence gives away his wariness.

I pull a list from the pocket inside my jacket. I memorized its contents before coming here; however, it's always better to have a backup. "We would like to know the military's patrol schedule and location of security Watchers, especially Outside. Running into them would unnecessarily complicate matters."

Austin nods. "I'll have Noah pull the schedules up for you."

I hesitate because the next request is more difficult. "Lai would also like to request assistance in the way of weaponry. The Order has always been a peace organization up until now, so our arms are rather limited and basic. We're worried what little we have won't serve our members well enough. We also don't have enough to arm all our members." Hopefully mentioning that it's a request from Lai will soften Austin up a bit. He is her adoptive father, after all. Perhaps if he thinks of it as being for her rather than for an organization he knows little about, he'll be more inclined to acquiesce.

Austin leans back in his chair. His presence remains neutral, a fact that is typical but especially anxiety-inducing in this moment. We need him to agree at least partly to this. Otherwise we have all of about three dozen flimsy weapons for over a thousand people. Our members are working on other means of acquiring and developing weaponry, but Austin would be able to equip us the most effectively.

"That's a big request," Austin finally says. "I see what the Order gains from this arrangement, but for such a high price, what do I and the military gain?"

I launch into the answer Lai and I worked out beforehand. We can't offer something the Order can't deliver on, and it goes without saying that even though Austin agreed to help us, this has to be an arrangement that will benefit the military as well, or there would be no reason for him to maintain the alliance. "In return, the Order would share intel we've gained on the rebels' movement patterns, base locations, and expected strikes against the sector or supply routes. Our information network is excellent; you can trust our intel. I'm sure the military would benefit from having targets and advance warnings of attacks."

"And how does the Order acquire such useful information when even the military can't, with all our equipment and scouts?" Austin's voice is careful, but his presence burns with curiosity he can't hide.

"I'm afraid I can't disclose that, sir."

Austin's eyes bore into me, but I match his gaze evenly. I try to ignore my racing heart. If he says no . . .

"All right," Austin finally says. I nearly can't hold back my sigh of relief. He leans forward once more, elbows upon his disorganized desktop. "I'll see what I can do. It's going to be hard to place orders for weapons that don't make it to our soldiers, so you'll need to give me some time to work out a process."

"The Order intends to stop the rebel supply raid tomorrow night," I say. "The rebel team is small, and so ours shall be as well. Can you provide ten specific arms by tomorrow afternoon?" I hand him the list I'd been holding with the weapon requests written down. His eyes scan it, but he says nothing. My pulse picks up speed. "Of course I understand the need for time for such a large-scale endeavor as equipping most of the Order's members. But if it's about a dozen weapons . . ."

Austin's eyes lift to mine. "Cutting it close on time here, aren't you?"

"I apologize. Since you had so many duties to attend to and this was the earliest we could meet, we didn't have much choice. It was hardly the sort of thing we could ask in the written update, either." There's always a better chance of convincing someone to accept a difficult request in person.

"Why not give me the intel, and the military can strike instead of the Order?" Austin asks.

"The Order intends this to be our official declaration of entering the war. The rebels don't know about us or the amount of information we have on them—they won't be expecting a counterstrike. We will only have this element of surprise once. This is the best chance for the Order to have a successful entrance into the war and show that we are a considerable threat."

"I see. And if I can't supply the weapons by tomorrow?"

My heartbeat drums in my ears. "Then we will do our best tomorrow night."

Austin says nothing for several prolonged heartbeats. The Order does have some weaponry. It won't be impossible to succeed in tomorrow night's strike—just harder. And I know everyone wants to minimize the risks to our members going on the mission as much as possible.

"I'll see it done," Austin finally says. This time, my sigh of relief escapes. "I'll send one of my trusted lieutenants to Market with the weapons tomorrow at noon. She'll be looking for someone wearing . . ."

"A red scarf," I say. "A man wearing a red scarf."

Austin nods. "I'll come up with an excuse to tell her." His fingers tap a rhythm against the edge of the table. "In the meantime, I want places our soldiers can attack. The public has been anxious— we need to show them there's no reason to panic. That we're not losing this war."

"Yes," I say. "Of course. Thank you, sir. I'll have our information sent in another coded update tomorrow morning, so please keep an eye out for it. If you need more detailed—"

A knock on the door makes me jump nearly out of my skin. Noah's voice comes from the other side. "General Austin, a member of the High Council has arrived. He wishes to speak with you immediately."

My heart rattles inside my chest as my eyes connect with Austin's. He jerks his chin to his desk. I slide under it as he rolls his chair back to give me room.

As soon as I'm tucked under the desk, Austin says, "Please, show him in."

I close my eyes as the door creaks open and footsteps patter into the room. I focus on my internal grid to distract myself from the panic threatening to overwhelm me. The Councilor is protected by starlight, a metal that is the only material known to neutralize Nytes' gifts, so his presence doesn't appear. Noah's is tinged with worry.

"General," the stranger says. It's a man's nasal voice, strained with either impatience or anger. Perhaps both. It's odd not being able to tell definitively with my gift.

"Councilor Norman," Austin says. "I wasn't expecting any visitors at this hour."

An itch behind my eyes.

"This is the only time I *could* come," the Councilor says. "Do you have any idea how busy we've been since those damned rebels attacked us inside the sector? Running around trying to calm the people, telling them everything's fine—and just what has the military been doing? Why haven't you managed to make a single strike against them?"

Austin's presence glares scarlet, but his voice remains calm. "We don't yet have the necessary information to execute an attack. We have no locations and no guesses as to how or where the rebel Nytes will strike. Is this the only reason you've come?"

"Of course not," the Councilor scoffs. "Do you really think I'd come all the way here just for that?" A pause. "I would appreciate it if we could discuss what I've come for more . . . privately."

My heart jumps up my throat. He knows I'm here.

But no. I realize, belatedly, that he's speaking of Noah, still in the office.

"Of course," Austin says. He stands and I watch as his feet carry him out of my line of sight. "Why don't we change locations? It will be easier to show you what our scouts have found in one of the map rooms." Another pause. "And as to the matter of attack progress. One of our squads found something recently. It's likely a rebel base, but they're now confirming whether or not that is the case. We should have the answer soon." Another pause that feels so deliberate it's a wonder the Councilor doesn't pick up on it. "As soon as we have confirmation, we will strike."

My throat is dry. He's counting on the Order to get him that information.

"Oh, and Noah?" Austin says. "I want to double-check our soldiers' and Watchers' patrol schedules Outside to make sure there are no holes the rebels could slip through. Could you print that up and leave it on my desk for me before I get back?"

"Of course, sir," Noah says. "I'll see to it right away."

"Thank you."

Austin's presence leaves the room—with the Councilor alongside him, I assume—and makes its way down several hallways before coming to a stop in one of the meeting rooms. Noah's presence leaves as well but goes only so far as the reception room next door. He appears to be at his desk, likely pulling up the data Austin requested. Even once they're all long gone, it's a struggle to settle myself. That was far too close for comfort.

I unfurl myself out from under the desk and stretch. Should I remain until Austin returns or return to Regail Hall once Noah's finished pulling up the patrol schedules? I already discussed the two issues of biggest concern with him. The rest is nothing critical, and if I wait, I risk being discovered by that Councilor.

The fury that is becoming unsettlingly familiar rises to the surface. That Councilor is one of the people who wrongfully branded us traitors and made us wanted criminals. He threw our years of loyalty to the ground and trampled us underfoot.

No. Stop. I need to remain calm right now. Getting angry will only cause me to make a mistake. That isn't something I can afford in this situation. I still need to make it out of Central undetected.

The door opens, but with my focus still on my grid, I know it's Noah and thus no need for alarm. He holds up a folder. "I assume this is for you?"

"Yes," I say as I accept the file. "Thank you for your help. And for your warning with that Councilor. If you hadn't knocked and let us know someone was here, I would've been caught." If that Councilor had stormed straight into Austin's office, I'd be dead. I need to be more cautious in the future. Just because I've made it into Central doesn't mean I can afford to let my guard down at any point.

"It's nothing," Noah says. "Just my job." However, he lingers, and much like the last time we parted, I get the feeling there's something he wants to say but feels he can't. Austin's words from when I first arrived come back to me.

"Is there something bothering you?" I attempt to make my tone as disarming as possible. "If you've something you wish to say, please feel free. I'll listen."

His presence flashes yellow, then orange, and back to its original green so rapidly I have difficulty interpreting the emotional shift. "I wanted to ask how Erik is," Noah says after several heartbeats.

"Erik?" He's not lying. Why would he be curious about him in particular? The use of his first name surprises me as well. Were they close? I don't recall ever seeing them speak together.

Noah must notice my confusion because his eyes drop to the floor as his presence hums with embarrassment. And, strangely, guilt. "We were—friends. Sort of. A long time ago. Before he lost his memories. I just wanted to know if he was okay."

I stare at him. He's still not lying, but I can't help feeling even more suspicious than before. He mentioned Erik's amnesia so casually—but I'm sure Erik would've never told him about it, especially seeing as how he wouldn't remember his old acquaintance with Noah. Did Austin mention it to him? No, more than that, Erik was a rebel before the military took him in. How could he have been friends with Noah at that time?

"Erik doesn't know you were friends, does he?" I attempt to keep any suspicion out of my tone. "He's been searching for clues about his past all this time. Why didn't you tell him anything?"

Again, that strange guilt radiating from his presence. This time, it's so overwhelming it engulfs every other emotion. My hands clench reflexively. "I . . . it would've . . . complicated things," Noah says. "I thought it might be better if he didn't know."

He's still not lying. But complicated things can have any number of meanings.

As much as I want to push, to discover what's truly going on, I can't let on that I don't trust Noah. I need his help for the foreseeable future. I should retreat, reassess, and gain more information so I can come up with a plan.

However, Noah's looking at me expectantly and I realize he's waiting for me to tell him how Erik's been doing. I can't tell him the truth about Erik going back to the rebels as an Order spy. If I tell Noah, he'll surely tell Austin, and the fewer people who know about Erik's current situation, the better. Besides, I'd never tell him anything about my friends until I know whether or not he's trustworthy. I say, "Erik's doing well. Complaining about how the Order doesn't have a woodshop, but he's adjusting."

For the first time, Noah smiles. It's a small one, but a smile nonetheless. "I'm glad. Really. But—don't tell him about me? Or that I'm asking after him?"

Even more reason to be suspicious. "Of course," I say. "I don't know your circumstances, but your secret's safe with me." Not that I've been in touch with Erik since he left. Lai is the only one with the ability to speak with him now.

Relief rolls off Noah's presence in waves. "Thank you. I appreciate it." He nods to the door. "If you don't have anything else you want to discuss with the general, you might want to head out before the Councilor returns. General Austin didn't have much on his end to discuss with you tonight."

"That would likely be for the best," I say. "If there's anything else, we can discuss it next time."

"I'll let the general know."

As I exit Austin's office, a headache begins to press down on me. There are more than enough matters to worry over already, yet now I'm concerned about Noah as well. Something is off about him. Why does he feel guilty whenever Erik comes up? What exactly is their past relationship—if they truly were friends, why wouldn't Noah have spoken to Erik after his memory loss? Not to mention he's worked directly under the Council since he was a child. With Noah being at the heart of the Order and military's secret alliance, I *have* to ascertain whether or not he's a threat. It could be the Order's downfall otherwise.

12
ERIK

TO LEAVE THE rebels' underground headquarters, we take a tunnel that snakes up—turning into full-on stairs a few times—before ending at a thick metal door set in the ground amid a bunch of boulders. The place looks just like everywhere else Outside. Barren. Full of rocks. If you didn't know exactly where to look for the door, you'd never find it.

As nice as it is to be aboveground again, I don't get the chance to enjoy it. As soon as we're topside, we're moving.

Our team consists of five people. There's Joan, of course, plus Siobhan, Jared, and Lily. I don't know Siobhan that well, but Jared and Lily are a pair of siblings who've talked me through a few stories about my past life with the rebels. It's nice having some familiar faces around.

Joan leads the raid. I'm really only here to follow orders and provide support since Ellis didn't give me a specific role. Mostly, I just hope we don't have to kill anyone. I don't think I can slaughter a bunch of defenseless Etioles.

The rebels don't have a lot of technology, and what they do have, they save for more important missions. Which means our group moves out on foot.

The moon hangs overhead, a sliver of orange. We don't risk lights, so even though the thin moonlight sucks, it's all we've got. I stick to the back and make sure no one can get the jump on us.

It feels like we sneak around for hours before Joan finally holds up her hand for us to stop. We crouch in the cover of some boulders without speaking. With everyone dressed in all black, in the dead of night, even knowing where to look, I can barely see some of my teammates. They don't budge an inch.

And then we wait.

I watch the moon as I fiddle with the power crystals on the silver chain Ellis gave me. I've added a couple more since joining the rebels. Apparently it's pretty common to trade them. *It's like a wish*, Gabriel said as he gave me his own neutralization crystal before we left earlier. I felt guilty accepting it, adding more pressure to him, but as bad as I felt, I don't want to die. His hand lingered over mine. *A wish for someone to come back safely. Everyone has friends they want to return alive, so we're all trying to increase the odds of that however we can.*

A wish. I've gotten so many of those from strangers over the last two and a half weeks it doesn't feel worth counting them all. But looking at my string of crystals, it's weird to think of each one as someone wishing for me to make it back okay. I guess there're a lot of people watching out for me, but it doesn't really feel like it. If anything, they're weights dragging me down. A reminder. A curse. The person they really want to protect is the old Erik. The real Erik is selling all of them out. It'd be better for them if I *didn't* make it back alive.

A murky green one stares me down. Lai's. *Above all else, you have to live.*

I close my eyes. Don't think about it. Everything will be fine. Everything *is* fine.

No one says anything, but there's a shift. Everyone stiffens. The air hums. A buzzing crawls up my skin before it reaches my ears. They're here.

The actual appearance of the trucks follows after the rumblings of their engines. There're three total: one supply truck and two smaller armored trucks on either side of it, lights flashing over the dead, empty landscape.

We wait as they drive toward our hiding place. My muscles groan from crouching for so long. My heart is about to break some ribs as the trucks get closer, closer, almost on top of us.

They pass us.

Siobhan jumps out behind one of the armored trucks, and with an upward swipe of her hand, thick vines break through the ground to wrap around it. The wheels screech as the truck tries to keep going forward and fails. The vines tighten.

"Don't damage it too much," Joan orders crisply as Jared and Lily sprint to deal with the second armored truck. "If we get rid of its occupants, we can take it for ourselves."

"Understood."

Joan glances at me, but she doesn't say anything before taking off. I follow her.

It feels like a lifetime since I was on a battlefield. It's hard to keep my head on straight. Everything's happening too quickly—where's the Order? Lai definitely said they'd be here to counterattack, but there's no sign of them. Did I mess up when I sent her the location?

The other armored truck's driver must have realized what was happening and tried to fight back, but they can't do anything against a change in landscape. Lily's gift is making holes appear wherever she wants, and so the truck now sits in a pit as deep as the truck is tall.

Up ahead, the supply truck screeches as it twists and makes a break for it, but the field of boulders blocks its path. If the truck wasn't made of starlight metal, I could've stopped it with my gift. As it is, with a glance between me and Joan, I lift her through the air with my gift and send her flying into the back of the truck. She latches onto a door handle with one hand. With her sword gripped in the other, she jams the blade into the thin crack between the doors and tries to pry them open.

I can't lift myself through the air, so I have to run after the supply truck to catch up. Not that I have any chance if Joan doesn't stop it. Even with the heightened speed of a Nyte, the idea of outrunning a truck is ridiculous.

Shouts and screams break the air behind me, but I don't look back. Just keep running. Go.

I can't see what's happening ahead of me, but guessing by the ear-shattering crash that splits the air, Joan must've formed a wall of ice in front of the truck to force it to a stop.

I pick up the pace. Whether or not I actually want to get there any faster is another question.

After the crash and the screams just seconds before, the air feels dead as a graveyard now. The hairs on the back of my neck rise.

When I reach the truck, there really is a wall of ice, the fender smashed up against it like a crushed tin can. Faint moonlight plays over the shiny black shell of the truck, and without any movement or sound around me, it feels like I just stumbled across a long-abandoned piece of the sector rather than an until-recently running truck that I helped bring down. My stomach turns.

The back doors slam open and then Joan is there, beckoning me over.

I jog up to her. "The driver?"

Her pale, ice-blue eyes glitter in the shadows of the truck's cargo hold. They drop away. "She escaped."

"She *escaped*?" I repeat. "How in the gods' names does some Etiole in hulking Outside armor escape you of all Nytes?"

Joan's eyes snap back to mine. She lifts her chin. "She wasn't even armed."

"Since when has that ever mattered?" Haven't they *been* killing defenseless civilians? Isn't the rebels' sole goal to wipe out all Etioles—innocents included?

Joan scowls. "Shut up and get in here already."

I don't argue. I'm more relieved than anything—one less life on my conscience. There are already more than I want. But I wasn't expecting mercy from any rebel, let alone efficient, reliable, cool Joan. Maybe there's more to her than I thought.

Joan backs into the truck so I can join her inside. Soon, our teammates will be here, too. *Come on, Lai. Where are you?*

"Is this thing still operational?" I ask. "I noticed it had a small, ah, accident."

"If not, then we load everything into the armored trucks," Joan says. She kicks one of the crates lightly with the toe of her boot. They'd probably been stacked before, but with the chase and the crash, they lie randomly across the floor. At least it doesn't look like any broke open. "We don't need a slow, bulky vehicle like this. Better to abandon it and take back only what's useful. Start looking for the food and I'll see what else we can use."

"On it."

Distantly, a scream goes up.

Footsteps head toward us. Joan and I both look to the barely open doors, but neither of us move. There are a lot of footsteps. More than the number of our teammates.

My heart hammers. The Order. Do they know I'm on their side? Probably not. They're going to attack me the same as Joan, intending to kill. Lai warned me as much, but it really does suck being in the middle of two warring sides when you can't actually fight either of them.

Joan lifts her sword. I take out my compressed weapon, and with the click of a button, the cylinder unfolds and snaps out into my sword. The hilt is surprisingly reassuring in my hand considering how much I hated the thing when the military first issued it to me.

The footsteps stop outside the doors.

Joan lifts her hand toward them.

The door creaks open.

A blast of ice bursts through the doorway at the same time a wall of earth rips the doors off their hinges.

Joan runs straight into the chaos, probably because she's crazy, but after stopping just long enough to pick up some crates with my telekinesis, I follow. If I get separated from her, I'm dead.

As it turns out, Joan created a protective tunnel of ice leading out of the truck to shield us from whoever's waiting outside. When I make it out the other end, it's to find more chaos waiting. People shift through the darkness like demons, too difficult to make out in the faint moonlight. I find Joan by the glint of light off her ice as she sends it flying around her. The newcomers lift something up—shields?—and the ice bounces off. Siobhan fights back-to-back with Joan, blood running down the side of her face and dim moonlight bouncing off the metal claws on her hands, but I can't see Jared or Lily. Everything is strangely muted.

Something whistles through the air toward me and I push my telekinesis out. I feel whatever it is sent flying back once it hits my force. Arrows? Knives? How many people are there around us? Too many.

Joan must think the same. Our eyes meet. Does she suspect me? Then, "Retreat. Now."

She skips back as Siobhan races toward me, and with a wave of Joan's hand, a long, thick wall of ice separates us from our attackers. She says nothing as we run. None of us do. But triumphant cheers follow us in the dead air. I feel like I should be enjoying that victory, too, but all I can think about are Jared and Lily laughing over an old story as they tried to help me.

Ellis's palms slam onto her desk. The shadows around her office flicker, lengthen, sharpen with her anger. Joan and I stand before her, Joan with her hands grasped firmly behind her back, chin lowered, every inch a soldier reporting back from duty.

Cal stands by the window, wringing his hands in front of him and occasionally glancing outside. Gabriel sits in the armchair beside him; only his eyes move as he looks from Joan to me to Ellis and back again. Devin lounges against the wall behind Ellis, arms crossed, unusually quiet. Even the ever-present sneer on his face lacks its usual force.

"What do you mean some strangers showed up and intervened?" Ellis demands. Her voice is colder than Joan's ice. But she doesn't wait for an answer. "If it wasn't the military and they weren't with the trucks, who were these people? How did they find us?"

Devin's eyes drift to me. "I can think of one way."

I bristle instantly. Mostly to disguise my guilt. "If you're going to accuse someone of something that stupid, you should at least have some proof."

"You were on the sector's side. As soon as you 'returned' here, these bastards show up *exactly* where and when we're making a raid no one should've been able to predict. You think that looks like a coincidence?"

"I might have been with the military, but I don't know jack about these randos." I take a step forward and lift my chin, daring him to contradict me. Hoping my ability to lie is as good as I've always believed. "And even if I did, how exactly are you claiming I get information to them without anyone here noticing?"

Devin steps off from the wall. Hate burns in his soulless eyes. "I don't know how, but I know you did. This timing is way too convenient. You could've at least waited a little longer to make yourself look less suspicious."

"The timing doesn't coincide with Erik's arrival so much as with when we declared war," Gabriel says evenly. He watches Devin, who holds the look angrily. "It makes sense that any group other than the military who'd been planning to fight us would wait until we were at war to do it. And this was our first attack since the war officially began. Unless you have some evidence against Erik that you're not sharing with us, I suggest you keep your divisive views to yourself. The appearance of a new, completely unknown enemy force is bad enough without you instigating a fight amongst ourselves."

"Gabriel's right," Ellis says. "We can't start pointing fingers blindly. Besides, it's only thanks to Erik that we managed to recover any supplies at all from this disaster."

I throw a discreet, grateful glance to Gabriel, who nods slightly in return.

Ellis stares down at her hands, still splayed over her desk. "We managed to get some more food, but it's not enough. Especially since we don't know how we've been tracked or if it could happen again.

We have to figure out how they got their intel on us and put a stop to it. That's our new priority." She looks up at all of us. "We're going to have to send some of our Nytes into the sector to get food however they can. Cal, get Lesedi and tell her we need her and her teleportation gift to help us out. Assemble a team for gathering food."

"Roger."

"Joan, I want you to infiltrate Sector Eight and find out what you can about this mystery group. Listen for any rumors. Try to find out who they are, where they're located, their numbers, anything. Take whoever you need with you. Try to find a place we can strike if you can. Don't engage until we have a plan."

"Understood."

"Oh, and Joan?" Ellis's voice is sickly sweet.

Despite the fact that Joan *has* to know that whatever's coming next can only be bad, her expression doesn't change. "Yes?"

"Next time, I expect no mercy."

Joan's lips press together. It takes a minute for me to realize what's happening. Sure, I remember Joan not killing that truck driver, but how would Ellis know about that? It didn't come up in the report.

Then I remember Ellis's butterfly in my shadow and I try not to flinch. She really is constantly watching. And even though Joan did something I thought was great, I unintentionally betrayed her act of compassion. On top of all the intentional betrayal, I mean.

"Yes, Sara," Joan says.

"Devin," Ellis says, "I'm putting you in charge of examining the home base and seeing if there's anything that could've transmitted information to them, any bugs or cameras. Leave no stone unturned." Her eyes narrow. "And *don't* come to me with any claims of a traitor without definitive proof."

He smiles slowly, coldly. "Got it."

"Do you? Do you really?" Ellis continues to stare at him, her eyes suddenly, intensely empty of emotion. It feels more like I'm looking at the shadow of a person than an actual human being. I shudder. The smile slips off Devin's face. Without speaking, he nods.

"Good." Ellis retrains her gaze on me, but thankfully, there's life in her eyes again. Still, my shoulders are stiff and I know I won't be able to relax until I get the hell away from her. "Erik, I want to talk with you in private. The rest of you are dismissed."

My lungs sink to the bottom of my stomach. What could she possibly have to talk to me about? Despite what she said, does she actually suspect me of being a spy? If she starts interrogating me, I don't know how well my lies will hold up against her.

Gabriel looks like he might say something, but with his lips pursed in what might be disapproval, he just stands and heads out the door with the others. Cal glances over his shoulder at me, concerned, but I force a smile and wave him on. The door shuts behind all of them with a ridiculously loud click.

"So?" I ask as I turn back to Ellis. I try to sound casual. If I sound guilty, she'll think I have something to be guilty about.

She watches me. It's not that searing emptiness from before, but it's still piercing enough to unnerve me. She doesn't need to become a shade from hell to put me on edge.

"When you were in Sector Eight," she says finally, "did you hear anything about a group like this? One that was intending to go to war with us?"

"No. But I did spend most of my time looking for information about my past—I didn't really pay attention to anything outside of that. I could've easily missed something."

Ellis nods, but I can't tell if she's satisfied by my answer or not. "It's like they've popped up out of nowhere. Who are they? How could they have gotten their intel on us?"

I don't answer. I'm not sure she wants me to, and I don't know what I'd say if she did. I'm walking on rotting stairs here as it is.

Her eyes are locked on a point somewhere past me, and I wonder if she's communicating with someone through her shadow butterflies. She has that same look of half-concentration, half-distance.

I know I shouldn't, but I ask, "What happens if this place is ever found?"

Her eyes snap to me. Okay, probably not communicating with someone. "What are you talking about?"

"I just realized I never heard about an emergency plan, is all." I hold my hands behind my back the way Joan did earlier. "If tonight wasn't a fluke and this new group is somehow getting enough information on us to know about our raids, it's not impossible they could find this place eventually. It's just a 'what if.' But what if they attacked us here? All our supplies and everyone's homes—not to mention the children. There must be a backup plan in case that happens, right?"

It's not going to happen, but I still want to know. As soon as I told Lai about all the kids here, she ruled out any possibility of attacking the rebels' home base. She refused to get noncombatants involved—especially when they're so young. It made my respect for her go up. And made me more relieved than I want to admit. A successful surprise attack on the home base could stop the war. But not at the cost of all the children who call this place home.

Ellis considers me for a long time before she chooses to answer. Her words are slow, deliberate. "We evacuate the youngest children through the emergency tunnel. Half our fighters will stay and fight to buy them time, and the other half will go with the kids to protect them. Then we'll regroup." Her gaze is unnervingly intense as she talks. She doesn't even blink. "But there's no reason they should find this place."

I raise my hands in peace, but my heart is hammering through my chest. Does she suspect me? Does she think I asked so I could give the mystery group better intel? Because she thinks I'd give them this location? Man, I really shouldn't have said anything. *Idiot. You need to be more careful than ever now that the Order's moved. Just because you say something that doesn't have to do with you* actually *spying doesn't mean it won't be taken as you spying.* "I'm still learning how everything operates around here. You don't seem stupid enough not to have some kind of backup plan, and I wanted to know what it was. Doesn't everyone else know?"

She continues to watch me. I think that's what I find so unsettling about her. Her limitless patience. The way she just waits and watches you like she can see straight into your soul and she's taking her time picking it apart to determine the best way to utterly crush you.

"Thinking ahead is only natural," she finally says. When she's ready to speak. "It's reasonable you'd want to know. But I suggest that instead of pondering a worst-case scenario, you start thinking about how we can eliminate the threats in our way so we don't get to that point."

"Got it." I try not to show my nervousness. I need to be more careful from now on—the last thing I need is to be openly suspected as a spy. Ugh. This is going to be a long war. "Just tell me what you need me to do."

13

LAI

AS SOON AS the counterstrike team returns, Regail Hall bursts into celebration. Cheers echo through the stone tunnels as word spreads of the team's success. Some of the members sustained light injuries, but thanks to Austin supplying the weapons we asked for in time and the element of surprise we had over the rebels, we suffered no deaths or life-threatening injuries. Amal, the commander of the team, leads them through an unintentional sort of victory march through the halls as they head for where Fiona and Trist are waiting for their report. Just about everyone in the Order comes out to congratulate them on the way. I can't even get close to Amal to say welcome back.

"I'm glad everything went well," Jay says. He grips my hand as the counterstrike team marches proudly past where we stand among the crowd.

"Me too," I say, squeezing back. "But it's only going to get harder from here. The rebels know we exist now. We won't have surprise on our side anymore."

"No. But for the moment, isn't it enough to enjoy this victory while we can? We were able to save some of the civilians and escort them back to the sector, stop the rebels, and prevent them from gaining more supplies. It's good to look ahead and be cautious, but it's also important to remember what's been accomplished." Jay smiles softly like *he's* the mind reader. "Don't worry, Lai. Everyone's doing their best."

"Yeah. I know." I return the smile, but I just can't relax. Erik's position is going to be more precarious after this. I'm worried about his safety. Nothing will be as easy or seamless as this first strike, either, and as much as I want everyone to take confidence in this victory, I don't want them to think it'll always end this well. I have to keep everyone safe. I need to be better, make sure I lead perfectly. No matter what, I will see an end to this war.

TWO MONTHS
LATER

14

LAI

NIGHT COVERS EVERYTHING. Without the goggles Austin supplied
the Order, it'd be almost impossible to see anything Outside. I wait
with the Order's counterstrike team in a shallow depression overlook-
ing the location of the rebels' next supply truck ambush. They've gotten much more cautious now that we've intercepted them six
times—and more dangerous. They know to expect us now, though
they still haven't figured out how we've been nailing down their exact
battle plans. Tensions are running high over there, apparently. I ask
Erik if he's okay every day, but his responses are always short. I can
hear the thoughts he isn't trying to convey to me, the anxiety, the constant hunger, the fear, but I leave him alone. If he doesn't want to talk
about it, I won't force him. I just hope he's safe.

Our team tonight is small but powerful. Between me, Al, Jay, and
Peter, I feel like we could take anyone down. It was a serious debate
with Fiona, Trist, and Syon on whether or not to bring Peter along.
No matter how much time passes since Paul's death, he's still distant
and distracted. He glazes over in meetings. Trying to distract him
from his grief with more work just ends in mistakes the rest of us then
have to fix. He needs to be back out in the field—he needs to

remember what we're fighting for. And that people *are* fighting. Life is going on.

My grip tightens around my double-headed spear's shaft as the ground starts to shake. The truck is coming. Jay and Al tense on either side of me in preparation for the upcoming fight, but Peter is staring up at the stars. I give him a telepathic poke.

Focus, Peter.

Yeah. I know. He shakes his head and grips his daggers.

I don't have time to convey anything else. The armored truck passes our shallow hiding space. Rebels spring out in front of and behind it—six of them, just like Erik said. One of them lifts a hand. Vines break out of the ground to jam the tires. The truck screeches to a stop.

Then we're moving. Al heads our formation, sending her fire scattering in front of our charge, but the rebels are ready. They must all have Gabriel's neutralization crystal, because the fire doesn't affect anyone it touches. The three rebels in back turn to face us while the three in front start trying to break into the truck. Shouts sound from inside of it.

Of the three rebels coming to meet us, Al dispatches the first easily with her halberd and keeps running to take care of those in front. She makes it look so effortless, so graceful, I'm almost jealous. She doesn't even need her flames to dominate a battle. Jay and I tag-team the second rebel while the third goes for Peter.

Our opponent is thick with muscle and armed with a spear. She swings low, trying to trip up our footwork, but Jay throws one of his knives at her chest and she has to sidestep quickly to dodge it. I come in from her other side. She swings again, this time aiming for my stomach, and I fall back. Jay throws another knife and she deflects it with her spear shaft. But he'd already started running at her as soon as he'd thrown it. He gets in close and thrusts one of his knives just under her rib cage. When she lifts her spear to try to plunge it into his back, I run my spear through her heart. She chokes and falls to her knees with a muffled sob.

I hope her death was as painless as possible. My stomach still turns every time I kill someone, especially after hearing so much about the rebels from Erik. But I can't afford to hesitate. It could cost my friends' lives. At least there's no one Erik is close with on this raid.

I turn back to make sure Peter's okay—just in time to see the third rebel's sword narrowly miss his chest. Peter fumbles with his daggers. The rebel thrusts again. This time, he hits Peter's arm. Deep. Blood immediately falls as Peter drops one of his daggers with a gasp.

I'm behind the rebel before he can attack again. He spins around to block my spear, but I caught him off guard. He doesn't put enough strength behind it. My spear twists around his blade and sends it flying out of his grip before one of Jay's knives finds its mark in his throat.

"Jay, give Al some backup," I say. The words snap off my tongue. "I'll stay with Peter."

"You don't need to—" Peter starts.

"Understood," Jay says. He runs toward Al without another word.

I take the small first-aid kit out of the compartment on my tool belt. Pull out the bandages to try to stem Peter's bleeding.

"We're still in the middle of a battle," Peter protests, but I yank his arm toward me and apply pressure to the wound.

"Al and Jay can handle the rest," I say. "You're bleeding too much." There are other things I want to say, but I bite them back. Later. He's shaking under my touch. He knows he messed up. He needs time to calm down before I talk to him.

Once the bleeding seems to have stopped, I pull out clean

bandages and wrap them around the cut. I've just finished my hasty job when Al calls, "All clear!"

Peter and I go to join the others by the truck. I scan Jay and Al quickly, but neither of them look hurt. I'm sure the military-grade protective gear from Austin helped. Al is already burning the vines off the tires. Thankfully, the truck is still intact this time and the ungifted inside it shouldn't have any problem going on their way.

"The last three rebels retreated when I arrived to help Al," Jay says. "We were able to injure one of them, but not badly. He'll be on the battlefield again, I'm sure."

"As long as they're gone, that's fine for now." I glance to the driver's side door of the truck when the window starts to roll down.

The woman inside is covered head-to-toe in the protective gear the ungifted need to survive Outside, but even through her helmet, I can see her eyes shining with recognition. "You're the—the Order, aren't you? Thank you. Oh gods, thank you. I thought we were dead." A man leans around her other side to nod vigorously.

I can't help it. Pride swells in my chest. For the past two months, we've delivered all the civilians we've saved to a hospital in the sector, where they could recover. Each time, if they weren't too badly injured, we'd talk to the victims on our way back to Sector Eight. We'd tell them a bit about the Order, of how we want peace between the gifted and ungifted, how we want to help bring down the rebels. They were skeptical at first. But they spoke of us. And now, this seventh time, the people we saved recognized us. They know about us. And they'll tell others about how we saved them.

It feels wrong to use such awful events for our own advantage, but something good might as well come out of it.

"We are with the Order," I say. If the two recognize me, Jay, or Al from the Council's wanted list, they don't show it. Either that or they don't care since we just saved them. "We're glad you're both safe. Do you need any help from here?"

The two glance at each other. "Would you—mind coming with us on our way to Sector Eight?" the woman asks. "That's where you're from, right? If those rebels come back, there's no way we'll stand a chance."

I smile. "Of course. We'd be glad to see you safely home."

As much as I want to sleep in after a counterstrike mission, the Order waits for no one. The morning after the rebels' attempted raid, Peter and I follow Rowan as they lead us through their lab. Rowan is our tech geek and the head of the Order's research team. A fourteen-year-old Nyte with a gift that lets them understand how something works just by touching it and the endless curiosity of an inventor, they, and their research team, have been responsible for the Order's best inventions and tech improvements. Well, "research team" is glorifying it a bit. It's a group of about a dozen people who are inquisitive and like to figure things out. They're far from professionals, but they're passionate.

"Have you had any success making the Outside suits less vulnerable to tearing?" I ask as Rowan continues to lead us past rows of tables littered with tools and half-finished devices I can't make heads or tails of. We stop every few feet so Rowan can update us on all the current projects, but I think we're finally at the end.

"We're working on testing a new fabric one of our teammates came up with a few days ago," Rowan says. Their tightly curled black hair bobs with every step they take. Rowan tilts their head in greeting to a pair of researchers we pass, but the two are so engrossed in some kind of disassembled dashboard they don't notice. "I can't say anything for sure, but we have high hopes. With the new composition we're working on, the fabric should be lighter and stronger than that of even military-issued suits. Pretty neat, huh? Oh, and of course we've been working on strengthening the areas surrounding vital spots especially—that's been our main focus, and we've been making a ton of progress. In fact—"

Rowan enthusiastically continues on about some new discovery in the science community to do with reinforced fabrics or something. A sharp contrast to me and Peter, both of us only having enough energy to keep walking and ask the necessary check-in questions. When was the last time I was that excited about anything?

Then again, Rowan is and has always been full of energy. I don't know what we'd do without them. The Outside suits especially have been a big concern among our ungifted members; it only takes a tear as wide as a hair to kill them within minutes. Anything we can do to further protect our friends is a great help, and we have Rowan to thank for most of our gear's advancement. But at this exact moment, I wish they would calm down just a little. Watching them exhausts me even more.

"It sounds like you guys are making good headway," Peter cuts in during Rowan's monologue about some big-name Etiole inventor in Sector Three and her recent publication on . . . something.

"This is fantastic, Rowan," I agree, leaping on the chance to make an exit. "You and your team are doing great."

Rowan beams. "Thank you, Lai. It's only because you supported my motion to make this team that we've been able to get this far."

"I'm just grateful for how much you've all helped us." I check the notes on my clipboard. How is there always such an endless list of things to do? I barely manage to hold back a groan. Or maybe it's a yawn. "We have to go meet with a few other people, but thank you for showing us around today, Rowan."

Their smile widens. "No problem, Lai. You guys just let me know if you need anything else."

"Will do."

We part with a wave, and then Peter and I delve back into our notes as we walk past the tables of equipment on our way out.

Peter flips through his papers with the tired motion of someone who's sick of always looking for something. "Our next core meeting is tonight. What's up for discussion?"

"Concerns from Sakchai that she's falling under suspicion from the Council as a backer of the Order. She wants to lie low for a while, so we need to plan around that." Sakchai is probably our most important supporter—the head of a transport company that trades goods between sectors, she's one of the few people in the sector who has her own pair of Gates leading Outside for business use. Without her, we wouldn't even be able to consider participating in this war. "We need to figure out a way to get more medicine, too."

"Got it. Then for now, I'm going to go check in with the recruit team about our next screening for potential new members. They've been flooding in lately."

Peter's voice drags over the words. We've stopped at the entranceway of the lab, which is the obvious point of parting, but even though we both still have too much to get done today, I say, "Peter. We need to talk."

He waits but won't look at me.

He's thinner than I've ever seen him. His cheekiness and general easygoing air from when Paul was around haven't resurfaced once in the last three months. All of us have said multiple times that he can step down from his duties as a captain, take some time, but every time, he'd shake his head and say he needed something to focus on. We've all tried everything we can think of to comfort him or cheer him up, but nothing's worked.

I don't know what to say to console him. That's never been something I'm good at. Paul's death still drags at my heart every time I think of him or look at his brother, though I'm sure that's nothing compared to what Peter himself must be going through. But I have to at least try to say something.

"I'm worried about you," I say softly. "I'm sure if Paul were here, he would be, too. He wouldn't want you to be so consumed by grief that you put yourself in danger when you go out into battle."

Peter doesn't say anything for a long time. Then, "Lai, why did you assign me to last night's raid team? You're the one who made that decision, aren't you?"

I hesitate, but there's no reason not to say the truth. "I was hoping it'd remind you of what's happening and why we're here. What we've all spent years working on."

"So you think if you give me a goal and tell me to go for it, I'll forget about Paul?"

"That's not—"

"We're not all you, Lai," Peter says very, very quietly. "I can't just shut up my emotions for the greater good like you do." He still won't look me in the eye. "If that's it, I'm going."

He doesn't wait for a response before leaving.

I find Jay watching over the Order's budding farm plot. He sits on his heels at the edge of it, looking out over the fuzzy green tufts sprouting from the soil. His chin rests on his arms, eyes distant and thoughtful.

I sit beside him. "How goes it?"

"Me or the carrots?"

"Both."

"Fine, and looking a little wilted but still good."

"Well, hope you can perk up again soon."

He laughs and I feel a knot inside my chest loosen. "What about you?" he asks. "You look exhausted."

"Wow, thanks."

"Merely an observation."

"Well, it's a little too spot-on." Even as I sit here, fatigue pulls at my limbs. I'd go to sleep right here and now if I didn't crave conversation with Jay.

"Are you doing okay?" he asks.

"I've been worse."

Jay watches me quietly for a moment. Then he stands and holds out a hand to me. "Let's dance."

I laugh in surprise. "Dance? Why?"

"Do you need a reason to?"

"It's just really sudden. Besides, I've never danced before."

"Me either."

"But you think now is the time to try?"

"I think it might as well be."

I laugh again as I take his hand and let him pull me up. "Lead the way, Major."

He starts to hum as he pulls me back gently by the hands, away from the little plot of vegetables. I recognize the song. It's one of the last pieces we played together on the piano in Central. Something that might as well have been a million years ago already.

For someone who's never danced before, Jay's pretty good. I think. I don't really have any experience to go off of. But he leads me back and forth steadily, and lifts my hand in his to twirl me around.

I find myself laughing again. "You sure you've never danced before?"

He laughs, too. "I've only ever watched. My father would occasionally host parties involving dances, but I never wanted to join in. I did see enough to get the gist of it, though."

"Well, that's a shame for everyone else at those parties."

"You're a little awkward at giving compliments, you know."

I sigh dramatically. "I know. It's not in my nature."

We both laugh and keep moving back and forth, back and forth, and I think that I could stay like this forever. Being gently led by Jay, his eyes softening as they meet mine, his hands warm in my own. For just this moment, nothing else exists. There is no exhaustion, no war, no worry over a friend whose grief is inconsolable. Just the two of us, dancing to a hummed tune from another life.

15

ERIK

NOTE TO FUTURE self: I am *not* cut out for babysitting. Gabriel laughs as a bunch of five- and seven-year-old brats run around the small cluster of battered tents and leaning plywood homes we're playing tag in. They dart in and out of places easily. And I trip trying to catch up to them. Just when I think I've caught one of them, he darts out of range and slides into the space formed by a sheet of metal leaning against one of the wooden structures. An opening way too small for me to fit in.

"Why don't we play a new game?" I groan.

"Can't, can't!" one of the tinier brats says. She dances in place as she points at me, giggling. "You're it!"

"Yeah, but I've been 'it' for the last ten minutes. You guys are just too good at this."

"You should give Erik a break," Gabriel says to the little girl, who's clearly the leader of the group of about ten kids. Gabriel looks like he's trying not to laugh. Again. "He's old, you know. He can't keep up with you. Why don't you all play ball for a bit?"

"I wanna play ball!" one of the boys says. His hand shoots into the air like he's in class. "Playing with Erik is boring. He's no good at tag."

"Hey!" I say, feeling a little offended. "I was just going easy on you."

The boy sticks his tongue out at me. But then one of the girls scoops up a nearby ball with barely any air left in it and they all scamper off to play a different game. They make sure to stay in sight.

I sigh as I sit next to Gabriel on the ground. He's still trying not to laugh, but he's so obvious about it. He's doing that thing where he holds his hand over his mouth to hide his smile, as if I wouldn't see it in his eyes and the curve of his eyebrows. His cane rests in easy reach. He's gotten thinner these past few months. Hunger scrapes at my own stomach in a way I can't remember ever feeling. The Order's been successful in almost all of their raids so far, which is good for them and the sector, but means less supplies for the rebels. Including food. I can't remember the last time I ate and felt full after it. Or even just not hungry anymore.

"Is it really *that* funny?" I lie on my back with my hands propped behind my head so it's not resting on the solid rock ground.

"I can't help it," Gabriel says. His hand drops and I can see his smile full-on now. My chest lightens. "You, the formerly battle-hungry second-in-command of the rebels, then soldier, playing with little kids. And failing at it."

Normally I hate it when someone compares the current me to my past self, but I laugh. It *is* a funny contrast. "If I'm doing such a bad job at it, I'll just stop helping you babysit, then."

"As if. You know the kids love you."

"Yeah—love to *mock* me."

"That's basically the same thing for them."

"I guess you'd know as the standing full-time babysitter," I say. For the past few months, I've taken any excuse I can get to hang out with Gabriel. But a big part of his job as a noncombatant is to watch the younger kids while older rebels are out in the field. So if I want to be with him, it means I've got to spend time with the brats, too. Which isn't all bad. They can be annoying, but they're good kids. Most of the time.

Spending too much time with them just increases my guilt and anxiety, though. I'm selling out the people they think of as family—big brothers and sisters who've been taking care of them. When some of those rebels who I know often take care of the kids don't return from a raid, I have to keep my distance for a week or two. There's also the fact that I don't know what will happen to all these children once this war is finished. If the sector wins, what will the High Council do to them? I can't imagine they'd just let them go free. How can I protect them? And if the rebels win, what kind of world would they grow up in?

No. We'll figure something out. The sooner we finish this war, the sooner they can eat full meals, be actually safe, and have better lives. Lai could bring them into the Order. She's said so before. But I can't help them until this war is over. That's why I need to keep spying. The kids' safety is the most important—right? This will be better for them in the long run, won't it?

"Something on your mind?" Gabriel asks. He's looking at me curiously and I realize I don't know what kind of expression is on my face.

I hesitate. I don't like lying to him, but I say, "Some more of my memories returned last night. Well, pieces. Nothing clear." It started happening a month ago. Dreams that feel too real to be dreams. For the most part, it's been more like sensations than anything. The image of a dark back alley that didn't look like the architectural style of Sector Eight's buildings. The taste of a drink I didn't recognize, laughing with a dark-haired, copper-skinned someone who seemed somehow familiar. The smell of blood. It's honestly worse than when I didn't remember anything. All these little things with no context are driving me crazy. There isn't any way for me to figure out what they mean, and I don't know why they've suddenly started coming back, either. They hit at random, with no apparent connections between the memories. I hate it.

"Ah," Gabriel says softly. "I'm sorry."

"Don't be. It's not your fault." I've told Gabriel before how frustrating it is, so he gets what I mean without me having to explain.

"I'm still sorry you're going through that. It must be hard not remembering anything."

"I used to think that," I say. "But you know, recently, I've been thinking maybe it's a good thing I don't remember. I mean, I was able to become someone totally different, right? And better, I think. I'm definitely glad I'm not war-hungry anymore. It doesn't sound like I was exactly happy before, either."

"And now?"

"Huh?"

"Are you happy now?" Gabriel asks.

I watch him as I think about it. It's true that guilt and anxiety crush me every time I report to Lai or collect intel for her. But it's not like that stuff is constant. I also get to babysit with Gabriel and joke around with Cal. Yeah, this situation in general isn't great, but I mean it when I say, "Yeah. I think I am happy now. I mean, I've got you, don't I?" My face feels hot, so I quickly add, "And Cal and everyone else, too, I mean."

Smooth. I've been wanting to tell Gabriel about my crush on him, but between stabbing him and all his friends in the back, not being sure if he's interested in guys, and my not being sexually attracted to people or wanting physical intimacy, there are way too many obstacles. And as if that wasn't enough, he still remembers the old me. There's no way he'd be interested in being with someone like that.

I don't have the guts to look Gabriel in the face and see if he caught my slip. But his voice sounds the same as always when he says, "I'm happy when we're together, too. You're pretty bad at looking after kids, and you're bad at being honest, too—like, *really* bad." I grimace. "But you're an amazing artist. Your ability to create beautiful things is breathtaking. You genuinely care about others. You give your all to support your friends, and you try to do good by everyone. I like that about you. I like a lot of things about you."

I finally manage to meet his eyes. His slanted smile is softer than usual. It makes my heart pound painfully. I almost say something— I'm not sure what, maybe a confession of my feelings or that I'm not nearly as good as he thinks I am—but then the little ringleader of the kids calls, "Erik, Gabriel! We're gonna arm wrestle, come referee!"

The moment shatters. Gabriel laughs. His expression is back to usual, all private gentleness gone. "We better go join them, huh?"

"Guess you're right." I don't know if what I feel is disappointment or relief. I rock myself to my feet and offer Gabriel a hand up. Since he's been overdoing it so much with his gift lately, he needs all the help he can get. He takes it. His hand is so hot I think it'll burn me. Even once he lets go, I still feel where our skin touched.

I walk down a dark hall, totally sure of where I'm going and what I'm about to do—I just can't remember exactly what either of those things are right now. At the end of that hall, Cal and Joan wait for me.

"Come to see me off?" My voice echoes around us, weirdly hollow. "That was nice of you both."

"Don't get used to it," Joan says. When I walk closer to her, she holds out her hands and I take them. Her fingers twine through mine.

"It's our first raid—our first attack against the Etioles," Cal says. His eyes shine in the dark, solemn and maybe sad. "Of course we're worried about you."

"What, you think I can't handle it? This is me we're talking about."

"Which is exactly why we're worried, you arrogant show-off," Joan says. I roll my eyes and she squeezes my hands.

"It'll be fine," I say. "You'll see. Everything will go just as planned, and before long, we'll have wiped every damned Etiole out of existence."

My eyes snap open. It takes a while for them to adjust to the dark—and for my heart to slow down.

I've never had a full memory like that come back to me. It's only ever been snippets. But that was so *clear*. It felt like it was actually happening. What's going on? Why now, when I've just been getting scraps for the last month? Why that memory?

Well, no going back to sleep now. What time is it, anyway? It's hard to keep track when you're stuck underground.

Once my eyes adjust, I can pick out the details of my room. I haven't changed anything, so everything looks just like it did when I disappeared from the rebels. Drawings wallpaper every surface but the floor, everything from furniture to doodles to sketches of make-believe cities and grand, ambitious buildings that'll never exist. There are sketches, paintings, drawings in ink and charcoal—everything. Just like back at Central, wooden furniture and tiny models of buildings crowd the room. A miniature city is tucked underneath a large table in one corner.

The room is nice. It's everything I would've imagined my former room to be, complete with drawings and models in my own style. But I don't remember any of it. It feels like I'm sleeping in a stranger's room, in a stranger's bed. Seeing a stranger's memories.

I wonder for the millionth time what happened to all the furniture I left back in my and Jay's room. We were always talking about ways we could dump it all on other people, but we never did get around to it.

The thought of my old roommate makes my heart sink. I wish I could talk to him again—something I would've never imagined I'd think three months ago.

I need to get out.

It must be pretty late because no one's around when I walk through the main office's halls. I should go back. I'm already under suspicion, and probably from more people than just Devin at this point. If I'm caught wandering around at night, it'll only look bad. But I can't stand the thought of returning.

I stop in front of one of the meeting rooms and push the door open. I don't care about the actual room; I cross through it to get to the balcony. The air isn't that different from inside the building. All the air is stale down here. But it's nice being in such a big open space. From the balcony, I look out over the city sleeping in the darkness. It's only three stories down, but it feels so much farther away. Fires are lit in some parts of the town, either guards or early risers. I can't make out details from here with barely any light. The whole uneven collection of random furniture and makeshift shelters looks like a long, huge monster sleeping in the night, just waiting for the right moment to rear up and bare its fangs.

"What are you doing up at this hour?"

I turn to see Joan leaning against the open balcony door behind me, arms and legs both crossed, but not threateningly. I didn't even hear her come up behind me.

I face the town again. After that dream, I don't really know how to talk to her. "I couldn't sleep."

"Is that so?" She joins me at the balcony's twisting iron railing and rests her elbows against it, hands dangling over the empty air. Watchful, silent. I don't ask why she's awake.

"This reminds me of a dream I had," I say. "You and I were standing on a balcony just like this, and you said the night was approaching. I mean, I thought it was a dream. Hoped it was a memory. It came before you guys told me I'd been a rebel."

"Well, it wasn't just a dream."

I grip the railing and lean back. "I've been having a lot of not-just-dreams lately. You were in the last one, you know."

She doesn't say anything.

"Were we . . . ?"

"Sort of. Not really."

"Wow, that makes things a whole lot clearer. Thanks for the enlightenment."

A corner of her mouth quirks up. "It wasn't romance—not really. We were never physical, and there were never any feelings of love between us, either. We tried. I think we both wanted there to be something. But we were just two broken people trying to find comfort in being with someone else who was broken."

"Is there really something so wrong with that?" I can't remember ever being in a relationship. I don't actually know how it works. But that doesn't sound so terrible to me.

"There's nothing inherently wrong with it," Joan says. "But it wasn't real for us. When I met Paul, and you and I broke things off, neither of us were worse off for it."

"You left me for another man?" I ask with pretend insult. "That hurts, Joan."

She smirks. "Maybe you should've learned how to treat your partner better, Erik."

"Ouch, Joan. Ouch."

There's something different between us now. I've never tried to joke with her before tonight. She's definitely only ever used a brisk, businesslike tone with me until now.

"Hey, Joan," I say. "Will you tell me about how the rebels started? How did we all end up here?"

She hesitates. Cal's told me tons of stories, hopeful they'd spark something in my black hole of missing memories, and always patient when they didn't. But I never wanted to ask him how it all started. I was too afraid. But now that my memories seem to be coming back, I want to know. I *need* to know.

"Well," she says, and her hands clasp each other over the railing as she leans farther over it, "it was just you and Sara at first. The two of you picked me and Cal up off the streets, and for a while, it was just the four of us. We didn't know where to go from there. You and Sara were serious about wiping out the ungifted. Me and Cal, I think we both just wanted a place to go. I know I couldn't have cared less about making war against the sectors at the time. The four of us eventually left the sector to explore Outside, try to find a place we could live in peace. We found the underground tunnels by chance. When we went back to recruit more gifted, you and Sara helped Devin out of a fight, and he came along worshipping the both of you."

A laugh stumbles out of me. "Devin used to worship *me*? You can't be serious."

She shakes her head, eyes never leaving the city below us. "It's true. He used to idolize you, just like he does Sara now. When you and I sort of became a thing, he was disgusted. He said you'd become weak and started to resent you. After your disappearance and then reappearance on the sector's side, things only got worse."

It's too hard to imagine. All of it.

I don't know if Joan can pick up on my anxiety, but she keeps going. "Eventually, Gabriel, Sara's old friend, came to find us. And as word of us spread, more Nytes came to join us, trying to find a place to live without fear. Some of them wanted to fight. Some didn't. But we got to the point that we could finally organize actual resistance. We started with the raids and—well, you probably know the rest from there." Her eyes soften. "But the four of us—you, me, Sara, Cal—no matter how many people we gained, it was always *us*. We used to joke and spar together and talk about how one day, we'd make a world where the gifted could live freely."

Her eyes rise to meet the solid ground above us, hiding us, protecting us, crushing us. "But you know, Erik, I never wanted to kill all the Etioles." Her eyes fall again, and her voice with them. "If we weren't so dead-set on total elimination of the ungifted being the only way to gain peace for Nytes, would Paul have had to die? He was so kind. He never wanted to hurt anyone. He always told me he wished the rebels would try a more peaceful approach, but I ignored him. I thought he was just too much of an idealist to understand—I thought this war, at least, was necessary, if not killing every Etiole. But now I wonder. What if we had tried something different? What if instead of an ambush, we really had tried to negotiate peace at that meeting with your team?" Again, her eyes rise almost unconsciously upward, like she's looking for a light that she's forgotten isn't actually there. "Would Paul have lived?"

I follow Joan's gaze up to the underside of the ground way above us, too thick to let any light in—and yet, I feel better pretending that I can almost see it trickling through. "I don't know."

I go to Cal's room once the base starts actually waking up. He opens his door expectantly and we head to the small training room on the

168

second floor to spar, same as just about every morning I've been here.

Cal fights a lot like Lai—fast and light. Unlike Lai, his single hits aren't all that strong, but he's able to stack them until his opponent gives way. He beat me easily when we started this routine about a week after I rejoined the rebels, but always with surprise. "You've always been stronger than me," he said. "Always."

He didn't say it, but I knew he was disappointed. In my almost four months in the military, I didn't train a whole lot. Finding out about my memories was always my first priority, and practicing to fight felt like a waste of time when I could easily use my telekinesis to win. But with Gabriel's gift around on both sides, I can't rely on that anymore.

So Cal and I began training almost daily, for hours, to the point that I can now match him. It almost felt like my body *knew* it used to be stronger. I started leaning into patterns I didn't know I had. I moved more easily, more quickly, like I was falling into a rhythm. It made me feel better. Like I was settling back into my own skin.

In our second hour of sparring, Cal hits the ground laughing. "Glad to see you've got your old strength back."

A grin slips out as I help him stand. "Thanks. Want to take a break?"

"Oho, so you're giving up now, are you?"

I shove him and he laughs again. "Not a chance. I just thought you were looking pretty damn tired."

He throws a hand over his chest like he's offended. "Me? Of course not."

My smile widens. Of all the rebels, Cal is definitely my favorite. There's something about him that I can click with, like we've always been best friends. I mean, apparently we were. But it doesn't feel that way since I don't remember it. I wonder what he thinks when we're together. Is it like nothing's changed? Or am I a completely different person to him now? I can never bring myself to ask.

"And here I am giving you a good excuse for why you lost," I say. "I can't believe you didn't take it."

"Please," he says with a sniff. "I make my own excuses, thanks."

"I figured you were running out at this rate."

"Oh, I *never* run out of excuses, Erik."

We both laugh again, and it's the best I've felt in weeks. I'm glad Cal's always willing to give up his mornings for me even though Ellis constantly has him running around.

"So what are your plans for the day?" I ask as we sit on the ground. The training room is a small space with nothing in it except a few racks of sticks for makeshift weapons. We usually bring our own real ones.

"Well, let's see." Cal's hands grip his water bottle as he leans back, legs straight out in front of him. "I have to file a report for my last mission, update the troops on the upcoming raid I'm leading, run a few errands for Sara, and maybe eat or sleep at some point."

"Sleep is so overrated."

"Yeah, well." He knocks his shoulder against mine. "So what are you up to? Wait, let me guess. Building models?"

"Oh, you are good." I don't mention the meetings lined up with Ellis and some of the other rebels, or the tasks I've been assigned myself. Cal already knows about them. At least I'll get to meet with Gabriel again tonight. At the thought of him, my ears feel hot, but I try to ignore it.

"Intuition," Cal says. "My massive intellect knows no bounds, after all."

"Ah. How could I have forgotten?"

Cal's mood sobers instantly. I realize I accidentally touched on a bad subject, but there's no way to take it back.

"Hey, Erik," he says. "Have you remembered anything about me?"

I don't want to lie to Cal—especially when it'd be so easy for him to *realize* I was lying—so as much as I want to say yes, I shake my head. "Not anything big."

"Joan told me you started remembering some stuff," Cal says. I feel a twinge of anxiety—or maybe loneliness. When did they even have a chance to talk between my conversation with Joan late last night and my meeting up with Cal this morning? I wonder what else they've been saying about me when I'm not around. I feel bad even thinking it, as close as Cal was to me when I returned, and as much as I'm betraying all of them, but I can't help it. Being here in general makes me anxious.

"Just pieces," I say. "Brief sensations and scraps of images more than anything. A few things with Joan. You were there, too—just, not, you know, anything huge."

"I guess it's to be expected that you'd remember her before you remember me. You two were pretty close."

"I don't know. Joan says there was nothing like love between us. That we were both just looking for someone to make us feel whole."

"If you found that in each other, I'd say that makes you pretty close. Love or not."

With as much as Cal jokes around, sometimes I forget how insightful he can be.

"Maybe," I say. Cal's got a sad, far-off look on his face, so I nudge his side. "Don't worry so much. I'll remember eventually, and even if I don't, we're still friends now, right? What's it matter if I can't remember what we used to be like when we can hang out like this now?"

A smile slowly spreads across his face. "Yeah. You're right. And since you can't remember, I won't have to pay you back all the stuff I owe you."

"Hey now. A debt is still a debt."

"Debt? What debt? I don't remember any debt. Do you?"

We banter back and forth a little longer before Cal has to leave, saying, "Someone has to be responsible around here." He sticks his tongue out at me.

"Yeah, yeah," I say with a dismissive wave of my hand. Then I hesitate. "Be careful on that raid. You better make it back all in one piece."

His smile doesn't waver. "Oh, don't you worry about me. I'll be back before you know it."

I hope so. I really, really hope so.

The room darkens a few shades after he leaves, and my mood along with it. If I'm honest with myself, being friends with Cal is my favorite part of being here. He's cheerful, easy to talk to, and even though he's a rebel, he doesn't hate on Etioles all the time. He usually just shrugs and says something like, "I don't despise them, but I definitely don't want to defend them after everything they've done."

Actually, when I think about it, Gabriel and Joan are pretty much the same. The only ones in command I've heard talk about the ungifted with genuine hate are Ellis and Devin. I wonder if, out of all the people gathered here, they're the only ones who actually want to wipe out the Etioles. Well, that's a reach, but still. What if the rebels as a whole could be swayed to peace? Most of them seem to want that. If there was just a way to get them to agree to a real negotiations meeting . . .

But no. So long as Ellis is leading them, it doesn't matter. I've been here long enough to know she doesn't want peace. She'll accept nothing less than the annihilation of all the ungifted. Unless someone can change *her* mind, we'll just keep hurtling down this path till one side or the other is destroyed.

16
JAY

I OFTEN FIND myself drawn to the Order's underground crop fields when I have free time. There are two more now than when we started this venture some months ago. They're all relatively close to one another, so I take turns visiting each of them and confirming that everything is as it should be. I linger by the third and final plot of potatoes.

I sit on my heels and look out over the field, tiny compared to all the ones I used to watch over at Father's farm. Yet there's still that same feeling of ease when I take it all in. The comforting silence around me. The smell of wet dirt and greenery. If I weren't a Nyte, I wonder whether I truly would've taken over Father's company. The idea of being able to spend my life calmly tending to the growth of other things is a pleasant one.

If only things could stay just like this. Still. Peaceful.

Footsteps resound through one of the hallways behind me. I don't bother moving, sensing on my internal grid that they belong to Lai and Al. The sound of their banter follows soon after.

"Like I said, there's no way I'd lose in an all-out fight against Fiona." Lai.

"Like *I* said, Seung's strong—especially when she fights with her gift," Al retorts. "I can't count how many times she got me with that in our practice matches."

"I never said she wasn't strong. I just said I could take her."

"I'd like to see that."

"Ugh, she never spars with me anymore. She always says she has more important things to take care of than"—Lai's voice shifts to a high-pitched, smug imitation of Seung's—"*entertaining a bored child. Can you believe that?*"

"Actually, yes. I can."

They enter the space and I stand to greet them. Lai brightens when she sees me, a fact that makes me immensely happy.

"Hey," I say. "What are you two doing down here?"

"Looking for you," Al says with a raised eyebrow. "What else?"

"Has something happened?"

"What, we can't just want to talk?" Lai asks. However, even as she says it, her presence drips with guilt. The fact is, the three of us haven't spoken together merely for fun in a long time. We've all been busy with our duties for the Order. Even meeting for meals is difficult.

We sit by the edge of the field. At first, we merely maintain a pleasant quiet. Lai's gaze keeps drifting to the plants. Perhaps it's only my imagination, but her eyes soften each time they return from the growing roots.

I'm surprised she has time to come and simply sit here like this. She's been switched on for such an extended period of time, I thought she'd crash before she willingly took a break. She still looks fatigued, but at least she's taking a moment to rest.

"How's everything going?" I ask.

"Really well," Lai says. "The Order's counterstrikes have been successful, and thanks to Austin's help with the military's patrolling Watchers that caught the fights, videos of them have been spreading. Our scouts within the sector say almost everyone is talking about the Order these days, and we have more people trying to join us than ever. Of course, it means more work on our part to screen everyone. And the risk of spies trying to sneak in is higher than ever."

"Oh yeah, Peter mentioned the same thing," I say. "I'm going with him to screen some potential new recruits today."

"Thanks for helping with that."

"Of course."

"The trainees are coming along, too," Al says. She grins with a fierce pride of a different sort than I'm used to seeing her wear. "They're going to be kicking ass and taking names in the next battle."

"Let's just hope that isn't anytime soon," Lai murmurs.

"Always the pessimist," Al says with a roll of her eyes. "C'mon, the Order's been doing great for months. Have a little more confidence in your friends."

"It's not a lack of confidence in everyone that's making me worried." Lai's eyes find their way back to the field. "It's the knowledge of how capable and strong Ellis is. She isn't going to take all of this lying down. We had the element of surprise on our side in the beginning, but that's gone now. It's only a matter of time before she switches gears and comes at us seriously. Seriously enough to try and wipe us out."

"There's no use worrying about it until we either receive new information or something else happens," I say. "We'll pull through as best we can, just like always."

"That's right," Al says. "With all of us together, we're practically unstoppable."

"Almost all together," I say quietly. The image of Erik grinning and giving one of his flippant two-fingered salutes flashes in my mind.

I wish he was here with us. I wish I knew how he was doing or that he would be safe. It feels like a year has passed since we all parted.

"The sooner we end this war, the sooner Erik can come back," Lai says grimly. "And if his position over there becomes too risky, we'll *get* him back."

"He knows what he's doing." Al's voice is rough. "We just have to do what we can to support him from here."

Lai's smile returns, although in less force now. "You're right. I just can't help but worry."

"Well, try to keep that under control so it doesn't spread," Al says. "Because I do *not* want to catch it."

"Worry is an emotion, Al, not a sickness," Lai says with a roll of her eyes.

"Hey. Emotions are definitely contagious."

"I can attest to that," I say.

"Oh, not you, too, Jay."

"I'm merely stating my observations."

Lai gives me a playful shove. "Yeah, well, no one asked for them."

"As long as he's siding with me, I'll ask," Al says.

"Terrible. Just terrible, both of you." Lai shakes her head. But then she laughs, and it's the most relaxed I've seen her since before we returned from Ellis's ambush all those months ago. When I sense her presence on my grid, it isn't wrought with stress, fear, or doubt. For once, she's genuinely happy. And so am I.

I find Peter outside the small, rundown apartment we're to meet the potential recruits in. I'm still high on the military's wanted list, so though interest in our team has subsided significantly due to the war, I had to use Seung's power crystal to get here. Even with the crystal, I couldn't help wanting to look over my shoulder every ten steps to confirm no one was following me through the busy streets. I switch off the crystal's illusion once I'm safely in the shadows of the indoor hallway.

Peter holds a clipboard in one hand and flips through the numerous sheets attached to it with the other. He looks tired—who of the higher-ranked members doesn't anymore?—but I know his exhaustion comes from more than physical tasks. A large part of his presence is still dark and heavy with grief from the day we lost Paul.

But there's something more troubling him today. He frowns when he looks up at me, in the way one usually does when they have bad news they don't want to convey.

"What's wrong?" I ask.

"No, it's . . ." He sighs. "Well, I guess you'll see. We have an interested party today you might not be so . . . interested in seeing."

That gets my attention. "What are you talking about?"

"Do you want to take a break from today's screening? I really wouldn't mind." His ignoring my question merely makes me more concerned—and curious. Who could possibly be here that Peter doesn't even want to say their name?

"I won't shirk my responsibilities when everyone else in the Order is giving it their all," I say. "No matter who's standing on the other side of that door."

Peter watches me. Then he sighs once more. "You're way too good of a guy, Jay. I'll give you a heads-up before we go in, and then you can let me know if you change your mind." He meets my eyes. "It's your dad."

I don't register the words at first. Or rather, I *can't* register them. The idea is so preposterous it goes straight over my head. "My father? There's no way he'd be here. He's not interested in seeing peace between the gifted and ungifted. He hates"—it takes a heartbeat to control the words—"the gifted."

"Then maybe we do need you today to make sure he's not here for any unsavory reasons," Peter says. "But I get it if you want to sit this one out. Really."

The words are still swirling in my head without connecting to anything. It doesn't make sense. There must be a mistake.

However, I know the Order. And the Order doesn't make mistakes when it comes to researching newcomers.

I take a deep breath. It's shakier than I expected. But I think of Lai, doing a million things at once for the Order's success, running herself ragged. I think of Al and the pride with which she spoke of the Order members she's been training, even though she wore her weariness like a mask. Of Erik, risking his life amid the rebels to get us critical information. They're all doing so much to try to end this war at their own expense. If they can do that, I can at least face my father.

I lift my head high. "Thank you for your concern, but I'll be fine. Let's begin."

Peter watches me carefully for a heartbeat before something like a smile breaks his lips. It's the first time I've seen anything like it since Paul's death. He extends a second clipboard to me. "Well, all righty then. Let's get this show on the road."

He opens the door and steps inside without further ado. I follow without hesitation.

Inside waits a group of about ten people. It's the maximum number the Order will screen at a time, to ensure no one gets overlooked. Everyone looks up as we enter.

A few mutters spread at the sight of me—a gifted ex-officer wanted by the Council for turning traitor. But they quiet soon enough when Peter gives them an almost reproving look. I can't say how much I appreciate it.

Against my will, I seek Father instantly. He's seated on one of the folding chairs the same as everyone else, but his eyes lock on me as fast as mine do him. He appears older than I remember. Gray strands run through his messier-than-typical black hair, and the lines around his severe, sharp face are deep. I haven't seen him outside of a suit since I was a child; however, now he's wearing worn clothes stained by dirt as though he just came from working in the fields. When was the last time he did that himself? Not since he taught me the basics of farming when I was a child, surely.

I pull my eyes from him as Peter begins the usual rundown. "Afternoon, all. My name's Peter, and this is Jay." I nod in greeting to everyone and he goes on. "As you heard last time, we're going to do some simple checks on everyone today using our gifts to confirm you're here for genuine reasons and not to hurt the Order." He gestures to the four chairs separate from where everyone currently sits, two on each side of the room. "You need to get approval from both of us in order to pass. One at a time, in whatever order you like. We'll just be asking some easy questions, so no need to be nervous."

I survey the candidates, forcing Father out of my focus, and check their presences on my grid. Everyone's uneasy, but not suspiciously so. No. Wait. There's one light-haired boy in the back who's more unsettled than the others, though he doesn't show it visibly.

When I look at him, he meets my gaze almost defiantly. My fingers tap against my clipboard. Something's wrong. However, he isn't doing anything suspicious for the moment, and if anything's off, Peter or I will catch it. Everything will be fine.

"Any questions?" Peter asks. "No? None? Then let's get started."

We split off to our separate chairs and wait. At first, no one steps up to either of us. No one ever wants to be the first. However, soon enough, a middle-aged woman comes to sit in the seat across from me, and a young boy goes to Peter. I keep an eye on the light-haired boy, but he sticks to his seat and speaks to no one. Father doesn't so much as look at me. Why in the gods' names is he here?

Focus, focus. I smile at the nervous woman in front of me. "Good afternoon," I say. "Are you doing well?"

"What? Oh. Oh, yes." She seems thrown off by my casual question—or perhaps it's because of my wanted criminal status—so I attempt to make my posture more relaxed to appear less threatening. It's difficult with Father sitting not so far away.

"You don't need to worry," I say. "I'm just going to ask you a few questions."

"Of course. Please, go ahead."

"Why do you wish to join the Amaryllis Order?"

"Well, I . . ." The woman hesitates. Then she straightens and meets my gaze. Her presence beats anxiously but with sincerity when she says, "I just don't think it's right, the way Nytes are treated. I know the rumors about how the military's abusing Nytes—and I've seen it myself on the streets. Something's got to change, and if there's anything I can do to help, then I want to do it."

There's no itch behind my eyes to indicate she's lying. I smile. "Thank you. I truly appreciate hearing that."

She hesitates once more. "You're the same, aren't you? Everyone knows about the attempted peace meeting and your team's arrest. People saw it happen from their windows. I—I'm sorry."

That, I wasn't expecting. The people we screen often recognize me. However, they don't typically comment on my bad record with the sector. We always act as if that doesn't exist, as though I'm any other regular person. Her words give me warmth.

"It wasn't your fault," I say. "But thank you. Really."

Her presence relaxes a little, and I feel already that she'll be fine to join us. But I continue with the questions, and once we've finished and she comes up clear, I let her know and ask for the next person.

The potential recruits trickle through. Father approaches neither me nor Peter initially, but as more and more people finish, he eventually goes to Peter. I try not to let it bother me. I attempt to ignore him as I screen the others, and surprisingly, it isn't that difficult. *His being here doesn't change anything. I have a job to do, and I'm going to do it.*

And then Father comes to me. There are still a few people left, including the light-haired boy I got a strange feeling from earlier, but I wonder if Father decides it'd be better to get talking to me over with, because he sits himself down before me with all the self-purpose I remember him possessing.

Pretend he's just like everyone else. Merely a stranger I'm screening. "Good afternoon." I look straight at him. "I'm going to ask you a few simple questions. Please answer as truthfully as possible in order to avoid any confusion."

"You mean, or else your demonic power will activate." He says the statement with no true malice, which nearly makes it worse.

"I'll now begin. Why do you wish to join the Amaryllis Order?"

"Are we truly going to play this game?"

"You will answer my questions or I will be unable to clear you. If you do not wish to cooperate, you may leave at any time." I keep my voice calm, nonthreatening. I don't want him to think that anything he says has an effect on me.

He leans forward so his elbows rest on his knees and lowers his voice so no one else in the small room will hear. "I came because I thought you might be here."

I blink at him over the rims of my glasses. He's not lying. He was looking for me? "That seems an insufficient reason to join our organization," I say reflexively. "This is a commitment, not a lost and found. We're serious in our efforts for peace."

He leans back again, inscrutable as I remember. However, there's something in his expression that I can't place, even when I check his presence on my grid. The fact that I can't tell what he's feeling, something I often know intuitively about someone even without relying on my gift, is disconcerting.

"If you were to join, in what capacities would you be willing and able to assist the Order?" I ask.

Father doesn't say anything for an extended period of time. He merely watches me, a game of his I remember all too well. In the past, I would generally avoid his gaze or say whatever it was I knew he wanted to hear. Now, I return his stare, refusing to back down.

And the more I look at him, the more I wonder why I was ever so overwhelmed by him. He's nowhere near as intimidating as Al when she wants to be, nor as resolute, devoted, and hardworking as Lai, nor even as single-mindedly decisive about going after what he wants as Erik. He could never kill me like the many rebels I've faced in battle, and there's nothing he could possibly take from me anymore.

I can't believe this man once appeared so huge to me. At one time, he was the biggest problem in my life. Now, I worry about my friends dying, losing my own life, doing something that could put the Order in jeopardy. In comparison to all the life-ending fears I grapple with on a daily basis, any sort of worry to do with my father is nothing.

When I realize this, it feels as though a chain I hadn't known was locked around my chest suddenly snaps clean off. There's nothing this man can do to me anymore. There's no reason for me to be concerned about him. I no longer want his approval when he has so little for me to even respect about him, and that was the last thing he had over me. With that gone, I'm free.

Free.

I smile. The sudden gesture clearly takes Father by surprise. His lips purse together, and I can nearly see the gears turning behind his eyes. Finally, he says, "I would be able to supply food and funds. I heard from one of the other members that the Order is searching for those who can assist in such regards."

"That is correct," I say. "I take it you would not be participating in battle, nor would you have a need to live in the Order's home base?"

He smiles wryly. "No to both."

"Do you mean any harm to the Order?"

"No."

"Do you have any reason to betray the Order in the future?"

"No."

Still no lies. And that was the last of my questions. Besides, if Peter already cleared him, he's likely fine. "That's all," I say. "You have my clearance. I still think you might want to reconsider your reason for being interested in the Order, but other than that, there are no problems. Thank you for your time. You may return to your seat. We will discuss the next steps from here once everyone has been screened."

He doesn't move. "That's it?"

"That is all of my questions, yes."

He stares at me with the expression of one who doesn't recognize the person he's looking at. "You don't have anything to say to me?"

"As I said, I have finished my questions—"

"Not the questions," he hisses.

It's unusual for him to lose his composure. I watch him calmly. I won't let him decide the pace.

He realizes his slip and smooths down his shirt, taking a moment to regain himself.

"I don't know what you want from me," I say. "We have nothing more to discuss. We haven't had anything to discuss in years."

"You left and decided that was the end of things on your own."

"I don't recall you trying to stop me."

"So this is *my* fault now?"

"It was never anyone's fault." As the words leave my mouth, I realize I mean it. "Things were only going to get worse the longer we stayed near each other. You couldn't stand me. I couldn't stand living in a place I knew I wasn't wanted. It was for the best—for both of us."

He continues to look at me as though he has no idea who I am. "You can't be serious. After everything I've done for you—you wouldn't have *anything* without me." I hold his gaze without flinching. "I could've abandoned you when I discovered you were a Nyte, but I raised you. I gave you the best education, raised you to inherit the company I've worked my entire life for—but you threw it all away. And now that I've finally found you, you have nothing to say to me?"

Despite myself, despite knowing that staying calm would be the bigger victory here, I say, "If you truly wanted me around, then why did you never once try to contact me in the military? It would have been easy for you, but you never did, even though I sent you letters every year. Even when I was put on a frontline team, you remained silent."

He doesn't appear to have an answer for that.

My voice lowers. "I know you blame me for Mother's death." His head snaps up, but I keep going. "I understand why. But I can't live with someone who would rather I didn't exist."

I think of how much happier I've been since knowing my team. Getting to know them, their strengths and their flaws, becoming friends with them—it's made me feel more *real* than I can ever recall. I feel like I finally have a reason to live. Not for those people, but *because* of them. They taught me what it means to be true to myself and what I want. And I've come to realize that anything or anyone that makes me feel unhappy or unfulfilled is not something I want. I deserve better than that.

"There are still others I need to screen," I say. "Please return to your seat."

He stands, reluctantly, and I think he'll say something, but he merely rejoins the rest of the group. I wait until he's seated once more before I turn my attention to the light-haired boy from earlier. He's sitting very still with his eyes staring straight ahead and his chin slightly lifted, as though he's trying to portray confidence in having nothing to hide. However, people with nothing to hide are never that stiff or nervous.

"You," I say, and hold out a hand toward him. I attempt to sound oblivious. "We haven't spoken yet, have we? Please, come."

He walks over to me with a physical self-assuredness that his presence on my grid doesn't reflect.

When he sits across from me, I smile. "Nice to meet you. What's your name?"

"Alex Holt."

An itch behind my eyes. I flip through the pages on my clipboard until I get to his profile, using the motion to discreetly check the throwing knife tucked inside my sleeve. "Ah, here we are. Then I'll begin the questions. Why do you wish to join the Order?"

"I want to create a better world for the gifted."

That's not a lie, but it does make me think this boy is likely with the rebels. Ringing fills my ears. I want to alert Peter, but there's nothing I can do without signaling to "Holt" that I've caught on to him.

I force myself to smile once more. "I can understand that. In what capacities would you be willing and able to assist the Order?"

"I can fight," he says. "I'll fight with the Order against the rebels until we reach peace."

Another lie. "You're against the rebels, then?"

"Of course."

"And you've never been part of their organization?"

"Never."

Lies, lies, lies. There's no point keeping up this charade any longer. I ready the blade up my sleeve before I murmur, "You're not a very good liar, are you? Tell me, are you here to spy on the Order for the rebels?"

He stares at me dumbly for half a heartbeat. Then he lunges at me.

I duck underneath his outstretched arms and roll off my chair, landing in a crouch on my feet. He follows, thrusting a dagger toward my chest. Someone shouts. I dodge behind him and swing my leg at the backs of his knees. He isn't fast enough to react. He falls.

Before he has the chance to recover, I grab his arm and shove him face-first onto the floor, twisting the arm behind him and shoving my knee into his back to keep him down. As soon as he's incapacitated, I grab his other arm so he can't try anything. The dagger clatters out of his grip.

"You're slow," I say. A lot slower than Lai and Al, who I've been practicing with for the past several months. I didn't even need my knife. "Peter?"

"Already on it; he can't use his gift," Peter says as he walks toward us. He holds up a wrist, the bracelet strung with power crystals on it in clear display—including the neutralization crystal he received from Gabriel. A story Lai was sad to tell.

The potential recruits are talking, but I don't take the time to distinguish what's being said.

"It's the first time we've caught a rebel spy," Peter says.

"What should we do with him?" I ask.

"Let me go," the boy snarls. He struggles to get loose beneath me. I tighten my grip.

"Not a bad idea," Peter says thoughtfully.

I raise my eyebrows at him.

"Why don't you go back and report your failure to Ellis?" Peter asks the boy. He crouches by his head so they can see each other clearly. "Tell her we aren't going to let you or anyone else slip through our ranks. She can try as much as she wants, but she's going to fail. Consider this a warning. We'll let you live, but the next person isn't going to be so lucky." Peter's eyes narrow. "And if you try anything funny on your way out, this isn't going to end so well for you. We have a deal?"

The boy doesn't say anything. Despite his bravado, I can sense his fear on my grid. He doesn't want to die. Finally, he nods.

I reluctantly release my grip on him and get up so he can stand.

He does, hesitantly. He looks back at me and Peter, and for a heartbeat, I think he's going to attempt attacking again after all. However, he turns and races out the apartment door. I track his presence on my grid as he runs and runs, never once pausing. I keep an eye on him just in case he doubles back to attempt following us later.

Peter turns to our still-muttering assembly. They fall quiet when he speaks. "Sorry for the interruption, folks. But I would like to take this opportunity to remind everyone that we're in the middle of a war—one that the Order is actively participating in. One that *you* will soon be participating in if you decide to join us, however directly or indirectly. If you're afraid, you're free to leave."

When I look back at our small group, it's to see Father half-standing from his chair. At first, I think it's because he's preparing to leave. Then I realize from his posture that he's *been* standing and that his presence is a bright red-orange of alarm. Was he frightened by the spy? No, it's not quite fear he's feeling. Was he . . . worried about me?

He sits back down as I continue to watch him. He won't meet my eyes.

"All right, we're going to need to speed things up," Peter says with a clap of his hands. "Gotta finish up before any reinforcements can come. It's a shame, but we won't be able to use this place again. Okay, who's next?"

17
ERIK

IT WAS ELLIS'S idea to have a sparring contest while we wait for Cal's team to return from the latest raid. We *were* comparing scouts' reports on the military's patrol schedule in her office, but when none of us could focus, Ellis said we'd have a competition. See who was the strongest of the rebel leaders.

It sounded like a pain. I tried to get out of it, but since Ellis made Gabriel the ref, that left Ellis, Joan, Devin, and me; and Ellis insisted we needed an even number to make it a real contest. Of course Devin was all in. Joan wasn't excited about it, but she agreed. And since no one else was complaining, I pretty much had to join.

Ellis beat me easily in the first round, even with our no-gift rule, and after a long, grueling fight, Joan took down Devin. Her disgust for him was obvious as she sent him to the floor. Great. That means I have to fight the maniac next.

We're all taking a break now, though. I sit next to Gabriel by the wall while I take a huge pull of water. Luckily, that's one thing we've got plenty of, since there's an underground lake.

"I can't believe we're actually doing this right now." I wipe an arm across my forehead to get rid of the sweat. "Man, you're lucky. I call ref next."

Gabriel cracks a small smile. My heart stumbles. "I'm not envious of you. But you are doing well, you know."

"*Please*. It took Ellis all of, what, two minutes to take me down? That girl's a Feral."

"Really, Erik, give yourself a little more credit. It had to have been two and a half minutes at least."

I elbow him and he laughs. My heart jerks again. I want to hold his hand or lean my head against his shoulder. I've never been into kissing or the more physical stuff, but I want to be close to Gabriel. But then I remember the reports I send Lai every night. I think of Gabriel's friends who come back dead. Because of me.

Ellis stands and stretches her arms overhead. "All right, are we ready for—" Her expression drops abruptly. She gets that look that comes when she's speaking to someone through one of her butterflies.

Everyone freezes. My heart trips again—this time for a very different reason. The Order must've attacked. Is Cal okay? Did the Order win? What's happening? I nervously finger Lai's power crystal on my bracelet.

Finally, Ellis turns to us. Her face is weirdly blank. "Cal and his team are currently retreating. They weren't able to gain any supplies before the Order attacked them." She doesn't sound angry like she did all the other times the Order interfered. But she doesn't sound put off, either. Why does she have to be so hard to read?

The immediate tension is crushing. No one talks. Everyone just stares at Ellis.

"Is Cal okay?" I try not to wince when everyone looks at me. But hey, it's a valid question, isn't it? It's definitely not something that makes me sound like a spy. Right?

"He said he's fine, but we lost a friend and two others are injured," Ellis says. Her eyes switch to Gabriel. "He also said he fought someone with a neutralization power crystal—an Etiole, apparently."

Something passes between them that makes me think this is something they've talked about before. I forget sometimes just how far back they go. But Lai told me about how the both of them were originally part of the Order, when it was just some no-name group of friends. Ellis knows about the Order's origins. And she *should* know that Gabriel gave all the remaining core members his power crystals before he left them, too.

But Devin wouldn't know about any of that, and he's not good enough at reading people to realize this is something both Ellis and Gabriel were obviously already aware of. "Traitor," he snarls. He strides across the training room toward Gabriel, but I'm on my feet and between them in two seconds. Devin looks like he's going to try to shove me out of his way, but he stops when Ellis holds up a hand.

"Gabriel and I have discussed this already," she says. "The Order has roughly six neutralization power crystals."

Devin and Joan stare at her in shock. I barely remember to do the same.

"That's news to us," Joan says slowly.

"I'm sorry for not warning you," Ellis says. "We weren't certain before now that the group behind all these attacks was the same one we knew." She smiles ruefully. "It would appear they've changed quite a bit since the last time we saw them." She looks at each of us in turn. "You needn't fear. Gabriel hasn't betrayed us."

I hold back a sigh of relief. It'd be bad if the rebels suddenly turned on Gabriel. I don't know how well I'd be able to protect him, given my own shaky standing.

"It doesn't change the fact that someone had to have leaked our plans to the enemy," Devin says. My relief at Gabriel's clearance dies in my throat as Devin swings around to face me. "The six of us were the only ones who knew the details of tonight's raid ahead of time. Which means someone here is a traitor."

"*Or*," Ellis says, "we were bugged and we still haven't found the devices. Or a Nyte used their gift on us. Maybe someone has the ability to see into the future?"

The suggestion reminds me of Paul and my heart plummets. But I'm careful to keep my face totally neutral. *Don't give anything away. Don't give them any more reason to suspect you.*

"As I said before," Ellis continues, "do not make accusations against someone without first bringing me proof."

"How is this situation not proof enough?" Devin asks incredulously. It's the first time I've ever heard him question Ellis—which means this is bad. "Sara, I know you trust the people you've chosen, but can't you see how shady this is?"

"Do you think I'm blindly trusting?" Ellis asks, voice sharp as a starlight blade. She snaps her fingers, and from out of my shadow, a single black butterfly glides into the air and flies toward her. It lands on her raised index finger. Its wings flutter at the same rate as my pulse. "I've been watching Erik since the day he came back to us. If he'd been sending messages, I would have known about it instantly."

Stay calm. See? Ellis doesn't suspect me. Everything's fine.

Devin glares at me. Joan watches him, me, and Ellis, cautious, considering.

But it's Gabriel who says, "It's been a rough day. Yet another of our raids has failed, and we're going to keep going hungry because of it. Our friends are hurt. What we need to do right now is not point fingers but get ready for the wounded."

"I've already sent a shadow messenger to our healers," Ellis says. "They're preparing for when Cal's group returns. Our next step is to make a plan of attack without letting a single word of information out of these walls." The corners of her lips lift in an expression that is *definitely* unsettling. Whatever she's thinking right now, nothing good can come of it. "I think it may be time to switch tactics. Everyone, meet me back in my office in an hour."

We all watch her, but she doesn't offer any hints about her grand plan. Whatever it is, I have a bad feeling. Just what is she scheming— and how can I protect Lai and the others from it?

Ten minutes before we're all supposed to meet up again, I find Gabriel sitting on the steps of the main office. I take a seat next to him and stretch my legs out in front of me. I warned Lai about Ellis plotting something, but without anything to *actually* report, I haven't been able to do anything but pace back and forth in my room for the last hour.

Gabriel's staring straight ahead at a group of kids playing ball. Their giggles and high-pitched yells explode in the air.

"The meeting is starting soon," I say.

"I know." He doesn't look at me.

"Something on your mind?"

"No."

"Riiight."

He almost smiles but doesn't answer.

The longer I look at him, the harder it is to look away. Of all the rebels, he's the only one I've met who just radiates calm and kindness.

"I've been wondering this for a while," I say, "but what were you doing in the sector? Before you joined the rebels? You must've left a lot behind." I know from what Lai's told me that he was part of the original Order group, but even she doesn't know what he did outside of it. She said he'd always brush off questions like that.

Gabriel takes his time before answering. "I didn't really leave behind much. Like many Nytes in Sector Eight, I originally came from a different sector. There's someone I was—*am* looking for. I tracked him as far as Sector Eight's military, but then I couldn't get any further in my search."

"You were looking for someone?" It's the first I've heard about that. "Who?"

His mouth turns down in an expression of hate I *never* thought I'd see on him. "The person who murdered my parents. I'm going to kill him." A chill runs down my spine. He still isn't looking at me. "But I have no shot at that under normal circumstances. The kids weren't the only reason I joined Sara. I thought if I was with the rebels, I might eventually find my chance to kill him."

"And did you?"

He shakes his head stiffly. "He's a coward content to hide in the background. It's going to take a lot more than this to draw him out."

"I had no idea. I'm really sorry."

"Don't be. It's not your fault."

"Still. That's awful."

He shrugs with one shoulder. "It happened a long time ago. But it's not a lie that I wanted to convince Sara to stop this war. I thought if anyone could, I had a pretty good chance as her old friend."

"But didn't you want this war to draw out your parents' murderer?"

His eyes squeeze shut. "I know it doesn't make any sense. I want two very different things, and I can't have them both. But I can't choose one or the other. I'm just a hypocrite."

"You're not a hypocrite," I say. "Human nature is pretty contradictory, you know? It's not like you're the only person who has conflicting wants." Like me wanting to be close with Gabriel and Cal even though I'm sending information to their enemies that could get them or their friends killed. Guilt twists my gut.

"That doesn't make what I'm doing any better."

"I doubt what any of us are doing right now is all that great."

He finally, *finally* turns to look at me and smiles tiredly. "If that's your idea of a pep talk, it kind of sucks."

I shrug. "I never said I was good at it."

His smile gets a little bigger. Seeing it makes my heart stutter.

"Listen, Gabriel," I say quietly. "I think wanting contradictory things is fine. But you're going to have to make a decision sooner or later. Just make sure you don't regret whatever it is."

I can't read Gabriel's expression. He's good at that. I wonder if he taught Lai how to do it. But before he can answer, someone behind us on the stairs says, "It's time."

Gabriel and I twist around to see Joan. We share a glance, then follow her into the building and through the halls to Ellis's office, where she, Devin, and Cal—freshly bandaged but looking mostly unscathed, much to my relief—are already waiting. There's a weird, wired tension in the air as we take our usual places. Gabriel in his chair off to the side. Joan in front of Ellis's desk. Devin behind it. Cal and I on the couch. I give him a look that says, *I'm glad you're okay,* and he returns it with lifted eyebrows that mean, *You doubted me?*

Ellis sits at her desk, back straight, fingers laced together with her chin on top of them. "I have our next plan of action. This time, we move directly against Sector Eight."

Maybe it's the dark look in her eyes when she says it, but goose bumps crawl up my arms.

"Do tell," Devin says eagerly.

"Wait," Gabriel says before Ellis can go on. The room freezes. My eyes dart to Gabriel, but he won't meet them. "Trying to take the sector head-on could mean sacrificing many of our friends' lives." He and Ellis exchange a look. He takes a deep breath. "We don't *have* to fight them."

"What are you talking about?" Devin snaps.

"Why not try to negotiate peace with the sector?" Gabriel asks. My heart beats way too loudly in my ears. "We don't need to lose any more of our friends. We can negotiate rights for the gifted, make things better for everyone, and stop this war. The military can take out our aboveground bases all they want, but they haven't been able to do any major damage to us, and they must have realized that by now. If we offer a truce, they'll take it. And if we're no longer at war with the sector, I doubt the Order will continue attacking us."

If I thought the room was cold before, it's frigid now.

It's not like I'm against trying to change Ellis's mind. That's absolutely what I want. But there's definitely a time and place for that, and it definitely isn't right before she's about to announce our next big plan of attack, right in front of all her captains.

Ellis watches Gabriel silently for so long I start to sweat *for* him. Joan and Cal look at him with equal parts surprise and unease. Devin's just mad, like usual. Gabriel is deliberately expressionless. I wonder what I look like. I want to back him up, agree with him, put a stop to all this—but I can't just do what I want anymore. I'm already suspected as a spy. Suggesting we don't attack the sector, the rebels' main enemy, isn't exactly a great strategy for me.

"An idealistic suggestion," Ellis finally says. She leans back in her chair, eyes never leaving Gabriel. "If we tried to negotiate, they'd merely kill or imprison us as soon as we reentered the sector. The sector and military aren't to be trusted—the Council especially. How many of their citizens have we killed already? They would never just let us go. We're seeing this through to the end."

"You don't know that," Gabriel says. "We could—"

"That's all I'm going to hear on this," Ellis says. "I know you're against the war, but I don't have time to hear it right now. If you don't want to join us, then you can go."

Gabriel's lips press together into a thin line. Finally, he meets my eyes, but I have no idea what he's thinking. He looks away.

Is he disappointed in me for not backing him up? But he has to know I couldn't with my standing. Maybe he just didn't want me to see him fail. Maybe he's not thinking about me at all, other than wishing I'd stop trying to get him to look at me again. Ugh.

"A full-on, direct attack," Ellis says, returning her focus to everyone. We all snap to attention under her gaze. "Up till now, we've been concentrating on raids because we need supplies. But we're at war—and it's about time we reminded the sector of that. No more small teams sneaking around at night. We'll take a sizeable force no one will be able to easily block and that can take down anyone who stands in our way. Easy."

Something's wrong. There's something she isn't saying, and I don't know why or what it is. Ellis never says anything is easy. She never looks down on her enemies. What is she playing at?

"Sounds good to me," Devin says with a gleeful smile. I have to stop my face from scrunching up in disgust. It's harder to read the others' expressions.

"This is going to be a full-force strike," Ellis continues. "The more of our enemies we can take out, the better. Which means I want our strongest people there. I want all of *you* there." Her eyes land on me as she talks, and I fight not to show anything on my face. I'm not like everyone else—I haven't exactly been enthusiastic about the war, and the most I've done is provide backup on supply raids. That and the info leaks must have been too much. She's testing me.

I know what I'm supposed to do here. I'm supposed to smile and say that I would *love* to help her any way I can. I have no reason to refuse. And I know I look suspicious after all the Order's successful counterstrikes. I have to prove to Ellis that I'm innocent. So I smile and say, "I'd *love* to help you any way I can."

18

JAY

AT MY MEETING with Austin and Noah, I skim through the details of the Order's recent raid counterstrike and skip straight to the rebels' new plan to attack Sector Eight directly. Erik sent the word incredibly early this morning, and I came to meet with the general that same night. The attack is happening the day after tomorrow—apparently Ellis hopes to cut off any information leaks by putting everything in motion quickly.

Once I've finished, Austin taps his pen against the edge of the map on his desk. A flurry of dots soon pepper the area. "With that many rebel Nytes to face, we'll be at a disadvantage. Most of the gifted soldiers have already deserted us over the past few months."

I'm aware. Most of them have joined the Order. Austin's eyes flick up to me as though he knows this as well.

"We'll have to gather a fair number of troops to face the rebels in a direct fight like this," Austin continues. "But it will take time to mobilize that many and get them in place. And unless we want the High Council questioning how I knew about this attack, I won't be able to deploy anyone until the military's surveillance equipment picks up the rebels' advance Outside. I can adjust the patrols so our Watchers will find them faster than on their current schedule, but we'll still need time."

"What are you proposing?" I ask. The way Austin laid out his concerns gives me the feeling he already has something in mind to counteract the military's dilemma. Something I likely won't approve of.

"The Order could stall for time," Austin says. He watches for my reaction, his presence radiating caution. "You know the path the rebels will take to the sector. You could ambush them, hold them there until my forces arrive."

"The Order isn't a militarized group," I say at the same time Lai, listening in to my thoughts, chimes in with, *That's ridiculous.* Since tonight's discussion is such an important one, she's tuning in to make sure all goes well. *We're not an army. I'm not going to risk our members like that.*

"I'm aware," Austin says. For a heartbeat, I think he's responding to Lai, but then I realize he's speaking to me. Of course. Since Lai promised Austin she would never use her gift on him when he adopted her, she can't speak with him telepathically.

"If you know that, then why would you suggest we send our members to such a large-scale battle?" I ask. "I see no reason for us to risk our members' lives for this."

Small, efficient counterstrikes to stop the rebels' raids with our best fighters is one thing. Facing the rebels head-on is quite another. For the last two months, we've been trading info on the aboveground rebel bases' locations with Austin in exchange for weapons and equipment. The military—better equipped to deal with more serious battles—has been steadily taking them out, much to the general public's relief and Austin's credit. These are small victories, judging by what Lai heard from Erik about the rebels conducting their most important business underground. However, we haven't told Austin that. The aboveground base locations are an essential bargaining chip. We can't afford to lose the one thing we can offer the military, and Austin has never asked us for more—until now. Why is he suddenly changing things?

"Not even to protect the sector and the Order?" Austin asks. He raises a single eyebrow. Beside the general's messy desk, Noah glances between the two of us, his presence wavering with uncertainty. "If the military can't intercept the rebels in time, it could mean a terrible loss for the sector. Worst-case scenario, the rebels damage the dome and the air Outside would kill all Etioles in Sector Eight within minutes." I say nothing. "Or, if you prefer, I could have our troops ready to meet the rebels exactly on time. However, when the Council asks how I knew they'd be coming, I may have to reveal my source of information."

He doesn't have to spell it out. If the Councilors find out about the Order, there's not a doubt in either of our minds they'll attempt to either destroy or manipulate us. They're already angered by our presence, as the public's approval of us extends much further than for them. Austin is giving me an ultimatum.

Lai? Are you there?

I'm here. There's a long pause before she continues, but I know what she'll say. *Tell him we'll do it. But he better get his soldiers there fast. We'll buy him twenty minutes, max, and then we're pulling out.*

I relay her decision to Austin and he smiles thinly. "Twenty minutes will be more than enough," Austin says. "If you can exhaust their forces, there should be less loss on our side, too."

A plan that's much more advantageous for the military than the Order—especially since the Council will likely claim this victory as entirely its own. However, if this arrangement can protect the sector from harm and the Order from discovery, we don't have much choice in the matter.

"I'm sorry to say, but I do have a meeting to get to," Austin says. He stands from his desk, nearly toppling a stack of coffee-stained mugs that Noah just barely manages to catch in time. "I hadn't anticipated you coming tonight."

"A meeting this late?" I ask.

"War doesn't care about time, sadly."

He isn't the general of Sector Eight's military for nothing, I suppose. The exhaustion dripping from his presence reminds me of Lai. However, I say nothing of it. Everyone's doing their best right now.

"Thank you for tonight, General Austin," I say. "The Order appreciates your support, as always."

"And I appreciate their intel." Austin's presence is tinged with amusement. His hand rests on the doorknob. "Don't forget to collect the next order of supplies tomorrow, same place and time as usual. Tell Lai I say hi and that I hope she's doing well. Noah, if you could see Kitahara out?"

"Of course, sir."

With a final nod, Austin leaves the office and locks the door behind him. It's just me and Noah.

For the past two months, I've been searching for every scrap of information I can on Noah. Yet despite the Order's extensive intelligence network and my asking those in the Order who were in the military long before I was, there's nothing. I know more about him from what Austin told me than I do from my fruitless search. In some ways, it makes sense. If Noah was born into the military, then of course the military would have all his files—and they'd all be confidential, given his high-ranking position as the general's secretary and his role as a direct subordinate of the High Council.

Without more information, I can't trust him, and yet, nothing negative has come so far of his joining my and Austin's meetings. Nothing suspicious has occurred with our exchange of information or the supplies the military has given the Order. The Council appears no more knowledgeable about the Order than the rest of the sector. There's no indication he's done anything that would harm us. Yet.

I glance at Noah, but he's merely placing the mugs he caught earlier in an already-existing pile of dirty dishes in the corner of the room. Prior to the war, he was always the one who kept Austin's office organized and clean. Now, it appears even he doesn't have time to take care of such mundane tasks.

"Have you been doing well lately?" I ask. "You look exhausted."

"Who isn't these days?" Noah asks. His smile doesn't reach his eyes.

I need to take advantage of us being alone for once to learn more about him—which means we need to talk about something that will hit close to home for him. Erik and the High Council are clearly sore spots for him. We haven't talked one-on-one since those first couple of meetings, so I don't know the reason. However, I can find out. I don't like cornering others with my gift, but if it's a choice between that or potentially being betrayed, it's not truly a choice at all. Besides, I'm worried about his connection with my friend. What if he could hurt Erik?

"Erik's been complaining about all the work lately, too," I say. "He keeps saying he'd rather just build furniture."

As expected, Noah's presence spikes when I say Erik's name. But his smile becomes a real one. "That sounds like him," he says. "He's better suited to art than fighting, don't you think?"

"I do," I say. That, at least, isn't a lie. "So he was drawing and building even when you knew him?"

"Always."

"Really? How long ago did you two meet?"

Noah's presence abruptly withdraws into itself. Cautious. His smile drops. "A few years. I don't remember exactly when."

He's not lying, but that doesn't tell me much, either. "How did you two meet? You never said." It shouldn't have been possible with Erik having been a rebel and Noah being a soldier. How they met could say a lot about their relationship and who exactly Noah is. By this point in our alliance, I don't think he could possibly be a rebel, but that doesn't mean he's not suspicious for other reasons.

"No," Noah says slowly. "I didn't."

I hold up my hands placatingly. "I'm merely curious. The only Erik I know is the one right in front of me. I just wanted to learn more about him, if he was different before he lost his memories."

Noah looks me up and down, likely attempting to decide how sincere I am and whether or not I can be trusted. I smile; however, I don't know if that helps or hurts. I'm not very good at creating a fake impression of trustworthiness.

Finally, he says, "He was very different then. You wouldn't have even recognized him." He's not lying, but when he adds, "Sometimes, I think maybe it's better he forgot his past so he could get this new start," his presence plummets into a deep violet of guilt and anxiety. It overwhelms anything else he's feeling. But why?

"I didn't realize there was that much of a difference," I say. "Is the reason you never wanted to talk to Erik after he lost his memories because he wasn't like the friend you remembered?"

"No. That wasn't it."

Still not lying. But none of this is helpful. "Then why the secrecy? I don't understand."

"Like I said before, it would complicate—"

"That's not an answer. If I suddenly lost my memories, I would still want Lai, Al, Erik, and all my other friends to talk to me. I would want them to remind me of what I lost."

"What if it's better Erik doesn't remember what he lost?" Noah asks. His presence vacillates between sincerity and that guilt. "What if reminding him of all that just makes him miserable? He wasn't—content. Before. If I came back into his life or told him about his past, wouldn't that just ruin his chance to start over and be happy?"

"Is that really something for you to decide?" I ask.

Noah's presence switches into sudden, explosive anger, though his expression doesn't show it. His fingers twitch. I tense in case he attacks. "You don't know anything," he says.

"You're right," I say. "Like I said, the only Erik I know is the one who exists right now. And I'm worried about him." There's little point in being subtle anymore. Besides, from his presence, I can tell Noah truly is concerned about Erik. That relationship, whatever form it took, is important to him. So long as he understands that I'm speaking from a place of worry for Erik, I believe he might be more honest with me. At the very least, I don't think he'll turn on me. "You said you were friends, yet you don't want him to know about you. You're cagey about your history with him. You work directly for the Council—the ones who turned on Erik and the rest of us. Isn't it a given I would want to know more? To confirm whether or not I can trust you and whether you mean any harm to Erik?"

Noah glares daggers at me, but I hold his gaze. In the past two months I've spent meeting with him and Austin, there are things I've come to understand about Noah. Most importantly, that he doesn't seem like a bad person. I don't know where his loyalties lie or what he might do, but I don't believe he wishes to harm others.

Sure enough, his presence begins to dim. The fury fades out, replaced with his former exhaustion. It's heavier now, more solid than before.

"You can sense if someone is lying, right?" Noah eventually asks.

I hesitate. Nod.

"Then you'll know I'm telling the truth. I'd never deliberately hurt Erik. I've done what I have because I care about him deeply. I don't have any intention of betraying him, you, or the Order. Even if the Council finds out about all of you, I won't say or do anything to help them. I hate the Council." His hands crumple into fists. "It's true I follow their orders. The Council raised me to be . . . the perfect spy. My job is to get Nytes from other sectors over into Sector Eight's military. By any means. If I don't, they'll kill me. If I mess up, I'm punished." His thumb traces raised scars over his hands, and shock spikes through me. Kill him? The Council is terrible, but I never thought they'd have me killed if I didn't carry out my orders. Why would they take such extreme measures against Noah over recruiting other gifted? I can't ask before he continues. "I've never obeyed them because I wanted to. I have my reasons for not wanting Erik to know we were friends—but they have nothing to do with you or this war. Is that good enough for you? Can you stop prying now?"

He truly didn't lie at any point. Every word he said rang with truth, not only through my gift, but in the sincerity with which he spoke. There are still more things I don't know about him than things I do. However, I'm aware he won't tell me more than this, and he's already said what I need to know. He won't betray Erik or the Order.

"I'm sorry," I say. "I didn't mean to make you upset or push you. I didn't know about your circumstances, either. I just . . ."

Noah releases a slow stream of breath. "No. I understand. You want to protect the people important to you. I get that."

"Thank you. And thank you for being honest with me. I don't know what exactly you're going through, but I hope it gets better." An empty condolence. However, it's the only thing I can think to say.

"Thanks." Noah doesn't look at me. "You'd better go. It's getting late."

19

AL

I'M EXHAUSTED AFTER today's training session. We didn't go too hard because of the huge fight tomorrow, but my worry for everyone drained me. Fixing postures, testing their strength and reflexes, watching them spar—every small thing wore me out.

When practice finishes, I clap my hands to get everyone's attention. A few hundred people look to me. Something swells inside my chest as I take them all in. They've been working hard these last few months. They've come so far, and they've been so brave and dedicated. "Good work today, everyone. You've got a big day up ahead, so rest and make sure you've got everything ready. Remember what you learned. Try not to overstress. You're all going to do great."

They cheer even though I wasn't expecting them to. Maybe I should've tried to say something more motivational. But I'm not really good at that kind of stuff—that's more Walker's thing. I'm better at being straightforward and trying to give them advice on what to do to stay alive.

My students pick up their water and towels. Some hang around and chat. Most leave. If they're on the ambush team to stall the rebels' big attack, they've probably got a lot to do. Supplies to prepare, good-byes to say. Just in case.

As many students as I have now, there used to be more. I close my eyes as each face comes to mind. Sam, a redheaded woman with a good eye for throwing knives. Iljean, an older man who worked hard to make up for the fact that he wasn't as fit as everyone else. Arman, a boy around my age whose defense was always just a little too weak, his sword positioning too easy to break through. I wonder if that's what got him in the end.

I watch my remaining students. How many of them won't come back to me? Who won't I see again? I've done what I can, and they've all gotten stronger. But this is war. I'm not so naive as to think no one will die.

I join one of the chatting groups. Irina, Arman's older sister, stands with them. She's been a lot quieter since her brother's death, but she hasn't missed a single practice. "Irina," I say. "Mind if I talk to you for a minute?"

She nods and leaves her group with a wave. They don't say anything, but their eyes follow us. I make sure we're far enough away that no one can eavesdrop before I turn back to her. "Hey. Are you doing okay? I heard you volunteered for the battle."

"Yes." Irina looks at me like I just said something as obvious as "the Order's at war with the rebels."

I shake my head. "You're not being reckless, are you? Running off into a fight to avenge your brother? This isn't like the Order's other missions. This isn't a surprise raid on a small group of rebels. They're going to be attacking the sector with a huge strike force. If you rush in, you're not going to make it out. Arman wouldn't want that."

Irina tilts her head. Her eyes run me up and down, like she's reassessing me. I don't like it.

"I know it's different," she says. "And I know it's important. That's why I'm going. I love my brother. I miss him a lot, and I appreciate you remembering us and checking in on me. But I'm not fighting for something like revenge."

I narrow my eyes. "Really."

"Really." She says it so simply I almost have to believe her. "Even if I knew who killed my brother, it's not like killing that person would bring him back. Revenge wouldn't change anything."

Something jerks in my stomach. "It wouldn't bring Arman back, but you'd be delivering justice, wouldn't you?"

"What kind of justice would that be? Killing someone because they're fighting for what they believe in at the risk of their own life, just like we are? Whoever killed Arman probably had friends and family waiting for them to return. They fought so they could live. That's all. My brother knew the risk of fighting, and so do I. Is that it?"

She acts tough—a girl after my own heart—but I hear the hitch in her voice. She's trying not to cry.

"I just wanted to make sure you'd be okay," I say. "I'm sorry if I assumed something you don't like. You can go—be sure to get plenty of rest."

She nods tightly and goes back to her group. She barely stops to grab her stuff before leaving her friends and heading out.

I sigh. Did I really say something that bad? She seemed pretty upset. Was it just because I brought up Arman? Or is she that against the idea of revenge? Well, either way, I'm glad it doesn't sound like she's going into the fight to find her brother's killer.

What about you? a voice says in the back of my head. *If you're so relieved she's not looking for revenge, how come you're still going after it?*

211

Irina's situation is different. This is war—of course people are going to kill and be killed. Mother and Father didn't do anything wrong when my brother suddenly murdered them. And then he ran away like a coward. I'm going to deliver the justice they deserve. That's all.

But the doubt won't stop nagging me. Why did my brother kill our parents? We were a happy family. I always thought he loved them as much as I did. Our parents tried to do whatever they could to make us happy even though we didn't have money—they picked up odd jobs to buy us books, toys, sweets. They didn't even care that I was a Nyte. They never treated me any differently. If they knew my brother was a Nyte, they never showed it.

Something sticks in my throat, and I start straightening up the practice weapons rack so I can keep my hands busy. How could I not have known my own brother was a Nyte? What's his gift? When did he know he was a Nyte? Was it before he killed our parents or after? Was he hiding it from us? Does him being gifted have something to do with why he killed Mother and Father?

A headache pounds at the back of my head. Along with Irina's words. *Revenge wouldn't change anything.*

It's not like I ever expected our parents to come back. I'm not stupid. But for so long, revenge was all I had. And once I joined the military, there was no backing out. There was nothing else I even wanted to try doing.

But it's not like that anymore. I left the military. I'm free. I'm fighting for something I actually believe in, with friends I love and students I'm proud of. I have so much now. I don't need revenge to keep living anymore.

What about my brother—the choices he's made? I used to just be filled with anger and hate when I thought of him. Now, the hate is still there, but duller. Less urgent than the questions of *why*.

He's still a murderer. He's still a rebel. But for the first time, more than wanting to kill him, I want to talk to him. I want to know what he was thinking, how my kind, thoughtful older brother turned into a monster. I'll probably still have to kill him—he's a rebel, so we're enemies no matter what. But there are things I want to ask him before that.

"Al? You got a minute?"

I stop messing with the practice weapons and turn around to see Lai and Jay waiting. Lai's arms are crossed, and her heel taps against the floor like standing still for five seconds is going to kill her.

"Sure," I say. "What is it?"

"Not here." Lai jerks her chin toward the training room's entrance.

I look to Jay, but he shrugs like he doesn't know what's going on, either. I shrug back and we follow her out into the halls until we get to an empty room.

Lai doesn't talk until the door's closed. "With all the prep for tomorrow's battle, there's something I think you both should know," she says. "Just in case the worst happens." She talks briskly, like she's giving orders to troops. But she won't really meet our eyes, and her shoulders slump with exhaustion. She's making me worried.

"Hey, don't talk like that," I say. "Everything's going to be fine." I know I shouldn't say stuff like that right before a huge battle—but it's Lai. If anyone's going to come out alive and kicking at the end of all this, it's going to be her.

She shakes her head. "It's best to prepare for any possibility." When I try to argue, she waves me off. "Just listen, okay? This is important."

Jay's eyes flick between us, but he doesn't say anything, so I stay quiet, too.

"The truth is, I'm Walker," Lai says. Finally, she meets our eyes. "Luke entrusted the Order to me when he . . . passed. When the others and I decided to make the Order a more serious organization, I took on the identity of Walker to protect those around me. It's why I didn't tell you before now—especially with the war going on." She sighs. "But tomorrow I'll be leading the ambush against the rebels as Walker. So I wanted you to know."

I can tell by the way her eyes narrow as she watches us that she's trying to gauge our reactions. But I don't know what to feel. Lai being *Walker?* No wonder she's always so tired. It explains a lot, actually. If she'd said this a few months ago, I probably would've been mad. But she made it pretty clear after our fight that she has her secrets and she'd be keeping them. That that's who she is. It's not like I can really be angry with her when she warned us. And surprisingly, I actually *don't* feel angry. Okay, maybe a little irritated.

"I mean, I figured there was stuff you were still hiding from us," I say. "You said as much before. But whatever, you're telling us now, right? It's fine. Let's just focus on beating up some rebels tomorrow."

Jay smiles slightly. He's hard to read, but he's always patient, so I doubt he's taking the secrecy personally. I'm almost surprised he didn't already know, what with how much Lai tells him. "I'm glad you confided in us with this, Lai," he says. "Thank you."

"Yeah, well," Lai says. "I figured now was the time."

"Surprised you thought there *was* a time," I say. She elbows me in the ribs, and I grin at her as I shove back.

After that, as we head off to a strategy meeting together, we talk about what we'll eat for lunch when we make it back tomorrow—Lai and I arguing over every food the other suggests while Jay tries to mediate. For that one moment, I can almost pretend everything is normal. That my best friend isn't leading us into battle tomorrow, that I'm not going to lose anyone I care about, that I won't eventually have to make a decision about my brother and revenge.

20

LAI

"THE DEFENSE TEAM is ready," Trist says. He sits between Fiona and Amal, the other captains and Helpers spread out around the table as we go over everything one last time before the assault tomorrow morning. "If the rebels have found us somehow and are using this as a distraction to attack Regail Hall, we will not give them an easy time." He glances to Syon, sitting on the other side of Fiona—our trump card. None of us want him to have to fight, but if it comes down to it, he's the strongest Nyte in the Order. No one can win against him—unless they have a neutralization crystal. Which is highly possible. But not worth dwelling on.

In the accented tone I use only when I'm acting as Walker, I say, "Attack team, report?"

"Everyone's as prepared as they can be," Fiona says. She and I will be leading them into battle. Our biggest group yet. If the rebels are coming out in full force, we can't do anything less if we want to win. "The funds recently given to us by Akito Kitahara have helped tremendously in acquiring more weapons and armor. Everyone is sufficiently equipped."

"His contribution has truly been a gift," I murmur. I try not to think of Jay's dad. Jay himself has seemed surprisingly okay since he joined the Order, and it's true his dad's donations have helped us significantly. But I still don't think I could have a civil conversation with the man who treated Jay so poorly for all those years. "Scouting team?"

"Equipment's all set up and ready to go," Rowan says. They glance at Navarro, the captain in charge of scouting, who says, "My team is prepared to head out as soon as you give the word."

As soon as I give the word. It's a struggle to stop myself from looking down. I have the utmost confidence in the Order. We've been winning—we'll win this time, too. But Erik has a bad feeling about Ellis's plan, and for some reason, so do I. Yet we can't just let them attack Sector Eight directly. Plus, Ellis herself is going to be there, along with all the rebel leaders. This is too good a chance to pass up. If everything goes right, we could claim total victory tomorrow. We could end this war. But this won't be an easy battle by any means. Once I give the word, a lot of our friends are going to die, no matter the outcome of the fight.

"We move out early tomorrow," I finally say. "Tell everyone to rest well and steel themselves. This isn't going to be a fight like any we've had before. We can do this—we have to. We can't let the rebels reach the sector. It won't be easy, but if we do this right, it could cripple the rebels and potentially put an end to the war. Remind everyone what we're fighting for."

As everyone claps or nods or both, I try not to think of who here won't make it back after tomorrow's fight. Anxiety compresses my chest so badly I can barely breathe.

The packed, winding streets of Sector Eight are almost beautiful in their busyness. They glitter and reflect back against the dome overhead, creating two parallel labyrinth cities with no escape, no room to breathe, nothing outside of this single reality.

I watch the sector from the top of Regail Hall, my legs dangling over the side of the roof as I let my eyes lose focus until all the specks of light become blurs of color melding together, nonsensical, unimportant.

I don't turn around when I hear footsteps.

Fiona comes to stand beside me without a word. She reaches down to hand me a steaming mug of tea. Once I take it, she sits next to me with her own mug.

We don't say anything for a long time. Ever since the war started, right before a strike, this has been our routine. Roof. Tea. Silent company.

But Fiona breaks the routine when she says, "We'll be okay."

"How can you be so sure?"

"Because I know us. Even if any of us were to die, the Order would continue on. That's who we are."

"Reassuring."

She shrugs and sips her tea. "You find reassurance where you can these days. I find mine in knowing we're not risking everything on this. Half our leadership is staying behind. Our backers are all non-combatants, of course, which means the Order will still have the monetary and practical means to continue, no matter how many or which members we lose in this fight. And those who remain will push forward because they believe in our cause and won't want to see our group's sacrifices be in vain. That's the kind of organization we made."

I don't say anything for a while. "You know, you've gotten a lot better at pep talks recently. Or at least practical talks."

"I've always been good at practical talks."

I smile slightly and finally take a sip of my tea. "No one's necessary, huh. I kind of like that. It's a lot less pressure when you think about it that way."

I feel Fiona looking at me, but when I look back, her gaze is on the streets below us. "I wouldn't say *no one* is necessary."

"Isn't that exactly what you just said?"

She tips her head back and looks at the dome overhead or maybe the sky beyond it. "I can think of two exceptions."

I almost ask who they are but don't. I'd rather not know. "Well, let's hope those two are still alive by the end of tomorrow."

Fiona smiles quietly to herself and closes her eyes. "They will be."

I wish I could share her confidence. I look up, too, and try to see the stars past all the glitzy reflections of the sector. Will I be able to look for them tomorrow night, too? Even if I can, how much will be different? Who won't be by my side anymore? Because no matter how much I know that what we're doing is right and that we can win, I can't shake the feeling that this victory will come at too high a cost.

It takes long hours of careful, camouflaged trekking through the Outside before we reach the destination the rebels are supposed to pass through on their way to the sector. The scouts reported there was nothing suspicious so far. They found a handful of rebels in the area, presumably scouts.

With Fiona and Peter by my side, and the knowledge that Jay and Al are close by somewhere, I start to feel better about things. Everything is going like it's supposed to. We can do this.

We reach the dusty area littered with towering boulders and low-rise cliffs we need to launch a successful ambush against the rebels. I wave my hand and everyone disperses to their positions. Fiona and Peter each take their assigned squads, and I push down the urge to call them back where I can see them. It will be okay. Everything is fine.

We're barely in position when I get Erik's warning. **Lai, you need to run—it's a trap, Ellis gave us false info to lure you out and now she's—**

But then rebels burst out from the boulders surrounding us and I don't hear the rest.

21

AL

THERE'RE SO MANY damned rebels I can barely see the other Order members. Jay and I stand back-to-back against waves of them. I can see friends trying to fight their way toward us—maybe toward anything—but they're cut down one after another. Frustration and fury build in my throat as I swing my halberd at the rebel standing in my way. She falls. Someone else takes her place.

The Order separated to launch attacks on the incoming rebels from all angles. Now it's obvious they were expecting that.

"How'd they know we were coming and what we'd do?" I ask through gritted teeth.

"I don't know," Jay says.

I thrust my palm out, and flames envelop the rebels in front of me. Their screams ring in my ears, but not as loudly as my friends'. The people I've been training for the last three months. The good people I've gotten to know.

I swing my halberd out of fury and grief. My back leaves Jay's as I plunge forward into the crowd of enemies, and I hear him yell, "Al, come back!" but I don't want to. I don't want to hold back.

Flames explode out from me in every direction. The Order team in charge of this area is gone. I don't know if they were able to regroup with another squad or if everyone was taken down, but the thought that they might all be dead just adds fuel to my fire.

The rebels around me scramble back, and I let my flames die down. I want to kill them with my own hands.

I charge forward, halberd ready, but one of the rebels blocks my thunderous swing with his spear. I feel the shock reverberate through our weapons and push harder. At the same time, I bring my knee up in between our weapons and nail him in the stomach. He gasps and loosens his grip. My halberd finishes him off.

Two people run up behind me and swing, but I duck under their weapons. When I straighten, I bring my halberd down against one girl's axe. The other whirls around behind me and pulls back her spear for a hit. I sidestep and the spear nearly takes out the other rebel, but she jumps out of the way with a shouted "Hey, careful!" at her friend.

"Sorry!" the other girl says as they regroup, weapons raised.

I tighten my grip on my halberd. I charge.

They raise their weapons in defense, but this time when I swing, flames wrap around my weapon. One of the girls shrieks as the flames crawl up her arms. The other tries to run, but my fire catches her before she can make it.

White-hot pain splits my back. I stagger forward and whip around to face the newcomer who struck me, but as I do, two other rebels close in on my sides. They want to go? Let's go.

I release my flames again, murderous with rage, but the rebels don't back down. When my fire reaches them, it doesn't touch them at all. They must have neutralization power crystals.

Fine. We'll do this the old-fashioned way. I heft my halberd up. My back cries out against the movement. The attack from earlier caused some damage, but I've been through worse and made it out before. This time won't be any different.

The rebel on my left attacks first. He charges forward and swings his sword, but I easily block him with the shaft of my halberd. The other two race in to try to take advantage of my distraction, but I shove off from the rebel's sword to duck under the other two's weapons. One of them brings her bladed brass knuckles down and they graze my arm as I jerk back out of reach. The third rebel comes up behind me and I whip my halberd around. He blocks with his sword, and the other two rush at me from behind. *Shit.*

The air shifts beside me. Someone grabs my shoulder and then my stomach twists into a knot as all the air is sucked out from inside and around me. My vision blurs to black.

Then, just as fast as it happened, it stops, and the grip on my shoulder releases and I collapse to my knees, wheezing for air. What the fuck? Did I just die? Is that what death feels like?

But when my vision stops swimming, the pain in my back still registers. I look up and see the battle I'd just been in still raging on below. A sheer cliff face plunges down in front of me, not tall, but not short enough to easily scale.

I can't take my eyes from the scene. The rebels, all in their black uniforms, are obviously winning. The Order is scattered, small teams standing together in the face of overwhelming numbers. This is how bad it is? *This* is what we're fighting against? How did it get to this so quickly?

"Are you okay?" someone asks from behind me.

But it's not just someone. I know that voice. I whip around despite the pain in my back and raise my halberd.

My brother stands in front of me. He lifts his hands in peace, dark brown eyes heavy and sad as he watches me.

"You," I snarl. I swing my halberd around and catch him in the chest with the pole end of it. I hear the rush of air as he loses his breath. Then I've got on him his back, kneeling into his stomach to keep him from getting up, one of the blades of my halberd against his throat.

It takes every ounce of my willpower to not immediately kill him. The only thing that holds me back is my need for answers. "What did you do? What's happening?"

"Good to see you again, too," he croaks around his lost breath. He flicks one of his wrists out to indicate a bracelet. When I look closer, I see that it's not just any bracelet—it's strung with multi-colored power crystals. "One of our members," he says slowly, "has a gift of teleportation. It's very useful. We traded crystals."

"You—you saved me?" I can't believe it. "How did you even—?"

"Your flames are easy to recognize," he says with a small smile. I can't believe he's smiling right now. I want to punch it off his damn face. "You lose your temper as quickly as always. I've been watching the fight from here, but when I saw your fire, I was worried, so . . ." He looks away.

Every muscle in my body is telling me to bring down my weapon. *Attack. Kill. Now, finally.*

But I don't. All I can think about is Irina saying there's no point in revenge. Even if I kill him right now, nothing will change. He's an enemy—a rebel—and I need to kill him anyway. But there are things I want to know before that. "Why?"

He tilts his head. "Why?"

I don't even know where to start. Years of pent-up rage and grief and betrayal I hadn't even known I'd still been holding onto pour out as I shout at him. "Why did you kill our parents? Why didn't you explain yourself that night—why did you run?" I bite back tears of fury. "Why did you save me just now?"

He doesn't say anything for a long time, and I almost swing my halberd at his head. The longer he takes, the more my friends are suffering down there in that lost battle.

"I didn't kill them," he finally says, quietly.

"What do you mean, you didn't kill them?" I ask. "Their blood was on your hands! You *ran*."

"A Nyte killed them—someone in Sector Eight's military." He looks straight at me. "I don't know what he was after. I didn't know what to do. He escaped, and by the time you came home and saw everything, I'd already decided. I'd go after him, find out why he did it, and then kill him." His eyes are unwavering. It makes my stomach lurch. "But I panicked when I saw you. I ran away without saying anything, but by the time I realized how that looked and went back, you were already gone." He smiles wryly. "In some ways, I thought it might be for the best. I didn't want to get you involved in all this. I never imagined you'd join the military and come looking for me."

"Yeah, that's all a likely story," I say, but my stomach is plummeting. Because as stupid as it is, I actually believe him. Stupid, stupid, stupidly looking into the same eyes of the older brother who always comforted me and told me he'd never let anything hurt me and believing this dumb crap.

But I know him—or at least, I know who he used to be. I could never imagine why the kind, gentle brother I'd always known had suddenly turned into a murderer. And I know his tics. Whenever he lied, his hands would fidget and he could never look someone in the eyes.

He's not doing any of that now.

My heartbeat is so loud he has to be able to hear it. Could he actually be telling the truth? Or has he just gotten better at lying since then, gotten rid of his tics? I can't believe myself right now. Why is this even a debate?

He looks at me and doesn't say anything. He doesn't try to defend himself or explain. He said what he wanted, and that's it. Just like how he's always been.

"You never even told me you were a Nyte," I whisper.

"I didn't know. Not until after everything happened. You know I've never been physically strong like Nytes, and my gift isn't an obvious one. That Nyte—somehow he knew you and I were gifted. He knew about me even though I didn't." His jaw clenches. "I found out later what my gift was."

"And then you went and joined the rebels."

"There were a few steps before that."

"*Why?*" I demand, but I don't know what exactly I'm asking, and now tears are streaming down my face and that makes me even angrier because I'm not sad, he hasn't won, I'm just *pissed*. But I don't know what or who I'm mad at.

He watches me with that sad look again, and I scrub my arm across my eyes to get rid of the stupid tears. Suddenly it feels like the ground has been ripped out from under my feet. Everything I've done these last nine years has been to find my brother—to kill him—and now that I've finally caught him, it's to discover that everything I thought I knew might've been a lie. If what he's saying is actually true, I don't know where that leaves me.

I don't want to deal with this right now. I *can't* deal with this right now. I need time and facts—but more importantly, there's something else I need to be doing.

I stand up off of him. "Take me back."

"What?"

"Take me back down there. My friends need me."

His eyebrows crease together. He sits up slowly. "Alary, you're hurt. The Order—they're not going to win this one. You could die."

"I'm not going to abandon my friends. They're dying while we talk. If there's something I can do to save them, I will." I stare him down, remembering Paul, thinking of Jay, still fighting—hopefully—and of all the Order members I came to know who are trying to hang on right now.

He hesitates. "I don't want to put you back in the middle of danger."

"I'll go even if you don't. And if you try to stop me, I *will* kill you." I should kill him now—he's a rebel—but I still don't know what I want to do about that yet.

I glare at him, and he watches me with that damned unreadable expression he's always had. Finally, he sighs. "I won't be able to save you again."

"I wouldn't want you to."

"You're sure about this?"

"I won't die. I'm stronger than you think."

The corner of his mouth quirks. "I know. You've always been stronger than I think. Which is saying something, because I've always thought you were the strongest person I know."

Unexpected pleasure hits me. Which is *not* something I want to be feeling right now, from him, during this disaster.

He sighs. "All right. Tell me where you want to go, and I'll take you there. But that's all I can do."

"That's fine," I say. "But you better be ready. Because I won't hesitate to kill you if I see fit the next time we meet, Gabriel."

22

LAI

WE'RE LOSING. BADLY.

I tried to call a retreat, but there's nowhere to run. Rebels at our backs and pouring in from every side. It's all I can do to keep together the group of Order members I've managed to rally around me. The longer we fight, the more of us fall. My heart twists every time I see one of my friends on the ground, unmoving, no thoughts coming from them. From those who are still alive, panicked thoughts pound into my head, each one more frenzied than the last. When one of them abruptly disappears, my heart misses a beat and my breath catches and won't come back.

This is all my fault.

It's hard to breathe. I swing my spear and keep fighting, but I know we can't win. There are too many of them. They trapped us perfectly.

My fault.

I kill anyone standing in my way, fueled by guilt and uncontainable grief. If I just keep moving, I can hold it all off. If I just keep killing the people who are killing my friends, I can stave off everything.

A break in the crowd of rebels reveals exactly who I was both hoping and dreading to see. Ellis, plunging her way through our remaining numbers toward my group, her sword like a shadow of death.

My calls of retreat must've given me away as the Order's leader. Even from this distance, I can tell Ellis's eyes are locked on me. Everything moves in slow motion. Will she attack my group first or go straight for me? I won't lose anyone else. I refuse.

Ellis reaches us. Her eyes flash and I yell, "Fall back!" as I rush forward to meet her. I don't look to see whether my friends listened to me.

My helmet's visor hides my face. Ellis won't know it's me—just how I want it. How I *need* it.

We run at each other. Her sword connects with my spear, and the clang of metal on metal resounds around us. My arms shake with the force of both our swings.

"Thought you were clever, didn't you?" Ellis asks through our crossed weapons. Her voice is soft, deadly. "Sorry, but this is where your meddling stops."

I don't answer as we break apart. When she runs for me again, I remember when she first taught me how to fight with a spear, positioning my elbows so they weren't in so tight, fixing my footwork, smiling hugely when I was finally able to get it all right at the same time.

Now, her sword comes swinging at my side. I block with the shaft of my spear and try to aim a kick at her side, but she slips back and comes in for another strike.

Luke and Sara and I sitting in that old storage closet, ignoring the outside world, our responsibilities as soldiers, just talking. Just being friends.

I'm too slow to sidestep her sword. The blade nicks my side. She pursues the opening with an upward thrust of her sword, but I spin around behind her and bring my spear down on the back of her leg. She manages to dodge in time, but I feel my blade graze her.

Going to my and Sara's room after Luke's death, after we found the letters he left us, me crying. But not Sara. She just looked at me, blank as death, like she couldn't understand my grief. The fury that burned in her eyes when she left the military.

Our weapons cross, and we keep pushing and pulling, back and forth, streaks of flashing metal.

Sara telling me that fighting was like dancing, really. Stay light on your feet and strong. Remember your balance. "There, see? You can do it."

I shout as I thrust my spear toward her, blind with rage or pain or guilt—everything the same, everything overwhelming, pressing down on my chest, suffocating, dying—but I lunge too far.

Ellis ducks beneath my shaft, and when she comes up swinging her sword, the blade cuts straight through my right arm above the elbow.

I don't register it at first. I don't even feel it. I look at where the rest of my arm used to be, where empty space suddenly exists, and then it slams into me like a building's weight all at once. I scream as I fall to my knees, unable to stand it, everything converging, blurring and crushing in its intensity. Electrifying pain explodes over the remains of my arm. Black edges my vision.

Reflex takes over. Eight years of military training kick in as I rip my belt off and use my one good hand and teeth to wrap it around my arm. I pull the strap with my teeth until it's so tight it hurts before I manage to fasten it. It feels like watching a stranger apply the tourniquet.

Ellis stands in front of me; she doesn't even try to stop my attempt to save myself. Triumph radiates off her. "Well, well, well, looks like this is the end of my pest problems. Any last words, Ms. Leader?"

I choke on everything in me that doesn't have words. I failed. I led everyone into this trap, and I couldn't even beat Ellis. I couldn't do anything. Everyone is dying, and it's all my fault.

Ellis raises her arm for the final blow. I can barely keep my eyes open through the pain.

But as her sword falls, someone rushes in between us.

Ellis's eyes widen as her sword overpowers Fiona's and cuts through her instead of me.

"No!" someone screams. I realize, in the seconds that last forever as Fiona falls, that it was me.

I rip my helmet off before I grab Fiona with my one arm. I cradle her toward me, the tears already falling, maybe falling even before Fiona was struck. I'm dimly aware of Ellis still in front of me, but then someone else is there fighting her, people are fighting around me—but I don't have it in me to care about what's happening.

"No," I whisper, choking on the word. "No, no, *no*. Why? The Order needs you. You needed to lead them after this."

Fiona gasps for breath and coughs. She tries to smile, but it just comes out as a grimace. "Didn't I tell you already? I'm replaceable. You? You *are* the Order. It can't exist without you."

I can't stop crying. Everything is too much. It's all one huge nightmare as the blood flows from Fiona's chest into the dusty ground beneath us, flowing against my arm as I hold her to me. It's too deep. I know even without looking, because I know Ellis, and I know her blow was meant to kill.

Fiona reaches up and grabs my shoulder with such intensity I think maybe she'll live after all. "Lai, listen to me. No, *listen*. You can't die here. Everyone needs you. You have to make it out, no matter what."

"I need you, Fiona," I whisper. "You were always there. You've always kept everything together. The Order doesn't need me—I need it. All I ever did was support it from the shadows. I can't do this without you."

Her grip tightens on my shoulder and I wince. "You're wrong," she hisses. "You built everything the Order is—the foundation, the support—you're everything. Everyone needs you to lead them. Without you—" She coughs. Her hand falls away from me.

I cry even harder. "Don't go, Fiona. I can't do anything without you."

"That's a lie and you know it." Fiona tries to smile again, but all I can see is the blood. "But . . . I did enjoy being friends. You know I love you, right?"

"I love you, too, Fiona."

"Good. Sorry, Lai, but I'm going to meet Luke and Paul first. I'll tell them you said hi."

"No!" I yell. Even to me it's barely intelligible through my crying. The grief and guilt are crushing my heart to dust. I can't do this. This isn't real. We can still save Fiona, if we can just get her out of here, we can—

But Fiona's breath shudders out and nothing more follows.

23

ERIK

I SEE LAI fall. Everyone around her and Ellis's fight had stopped to watch. There was something mesmerizing in the way the two of them moved, twisting, strong, deadly graceful. They're so fast nobody tries to jump in to help either of them. They'd just get in the way.

Come on, Lai. Win. Live.

But she lost her cool and went too far. The balance broke. Ellis took her right arm and then it was over. She would've taken her life, too, if Seung hadn't jumped between them at the last minute. Ellis froze when Lai threw off her helmet and pulled her friend to her.

No. This isn't how everything was supposed to go down. This isn't happening.

I don't know what to do. My feet won't move. It's like my body forgot how to function.

But then Devin races toward the still-frozen Ellis and defeated Lai, sword pulled back and murder in his eyes, and I don't have to think. I run.

I barely make it in time to block Devin's sword as it comes swinging down on Lai. I push my way between them and dig my feet in, shoving against Devin with everything I've got. Panic and adrenaline give me extra strength. I manage to thrust Devin back, away from Lai. I glance behind me to check on her, but she's hunched over Seung, talking to her. I can't look at her arm.

"What are you doing?" Devin yells. His sword drips blood as he points it at me. "That's the Order's leader—we kill her, we've as good as destroyed them."

I don't answer. Just lift my sword in grim defense.

"I didn't want to believe it," Ellis says from behind Devin. She'd been staring emptily at the ground, but now she looks up at me with heavy eyes. "I was so relieved when my butterfly never caught you doing anything suspicious. But the information leaks—the timing was too much. Especially when I told so few people about our plans."

Cal and Joan have appeared from out of the crowd to stand behind Ellis. Gabriel materializes with Lesedi's teleportation crystal. They all stare at me. Confused.

I can't bring myself to look at any of them. Especially not Gabriel or Cal. I don't want to see the moment they realize.

Ellis laughs humorlessly. "I should've known. It really was you, wasn't it?" She jerks her chin toward Lai. "I forgot how useful Lai's gift can be for communicating secretly. You have a power crystal from her, don't you?"

My grip tightens around my sword hilt. "I tried to get you to stop." My voice comes out way more strained than I expected it to. More than I want it to. "To call for peace. We don't need to waste lives like this. There are other ways."

"You mean it's true?" Cal asks. He takes a step forward, but Joan catches his arm so he can't go any farther. The betrayal written all over his face crushes the air out of my lungs. "You've been selling us out this whole time? But I thought—we *welcomed* you back—we're *friends*—"

"I'm sorry, Cal," I whisper. Even though this place was a battle-field just seconds ago, everything is dead quiet now. Everyone's watching. "You *are* my friend. But I was never on your side." How hypocritical is that? It sounds stupid even to me—but it's true. Or at least, I want it to be.

Everything in his expression shuts down. Gabriel keeps staring at me like he can't figure out what I'm saying. Joan's eyes fall, but Ellis's harden and Devin just laughs. "I *told* you," he says. His voice rings in the air. "I *told* you he couldn't be trusted!"

And then he charges. My heart twists more than it should at everyone's reactions—I knew I was betraying them, I knew they'd find out eventually—but I hold my sword ready and steel myself. I won't let things end here like this. And I'm sure as hell not about to let myself get killed by Devin. Like I'd ever give him that satisfaction.

But before he can strike, a wall of fire blasts between us. He keeps running straight through it, untouched, but when he swings his sword, it hits the shaft of Johann's halberd. He shouts and tries to push through, but Jay comes up behind him and thrusts one of his knives at Devin's open back.

Devin whips around to strike at Jay, but Jay's fast enough to avoid Devin's angry swings. And as soon as his attention's on Jay, Johann comes up on his side for another attack.

Devin hisses in pain as her blade catches his arm. He retreats a few steps.

I don't think I've ever been so relieved to see two people in my life. When they turn to face me, my eyes burn. I didn't think I'd miss them so much, but now that they're here in front of me, it takes every-thing I have to hold back my exhaustion from the past few months' charade and not collapse against them. I can't even get the words out.

"Glad to finally have you back," Johann says. She looks tired, but the fire that's always burned in her eyes seems to grow brighter. "Now we all just need to get out of here."

Devin lifts his sword again with a sneer. "We'll see about that."

Joan and Cal step forward to back him up. Gabriel just watches, still looking lost, and I can't bring myself to meet his gaze even though he's trying so hard to get me to. Ellis closes her eyes, and when she looks up again, she's back to usual herself. Her sadness is already gone. She's hard as steel once more.

I tense. There's no way the three of us can beat the four of them—not while protecting Lai, too. More Order members are gathering around us, but they're beat. We all are. We're not going to make it.

Devin takes a step forward.

A girl materializes out of thin air in front of the rebels. Lesedi, the head scout. "Sara—the military is on its way."

Ellis freezes. "What?"

"A huge force—fully armed, headed straight here, maybe ten minutes away. There's enough of them that we'll take heavy losses if it turns into a fight—we wouldn't be able to escape without them following us back to base, either. We need to go."

Lesedi finally looks around and blinks. She has a bad habit of popping up in the middle of things without checking the situation first, but for the first time, I'm glad for it. Her attention stays on me, standing with the Order members, before she turns back to Ellis.

Everyone's watching the rebel leader. No one on our side moves, waiting for the trick.

Finally, Ellis looks up. Her eyes are on me when she says, "Fall back."

"What?" Devin demands. "Are you kidding? We can wipe out

the Order and a traitor right here and now! There's nothing stopping us from taking them out for good!"

"No. We've accomplished what we came to." Ellis has already turned her back on us as she walks away. "Our friends are injured, and we won't stand a chance against a fresh military attack force. Besides, the Order is already as good as dead. We're going."

"But—"

"Did you not understand?" Ellis's voice drips venom. "I *said*, we're retreating. If you choose to stay and fight alone, I won't mourn your death."

Devin hesitates, but not for long. He throws one last murderous glare at us before reluctantly joining Ellis, along with Cal and Joan. None of them look back. Gabriel is still trying to get me to meet his eyes, but I can't. Seeing the betrayal on his face might just break me. Finally, he goes, too. The rebels around us slowly follow after, others spreading word to those who're still fighting that they're retreating.

As soon as the immediate threat of danger passes, Jay kneels by Lai. "Lai, can you hear me?" He's already checking the improvised tourniquet and tightening it further.

She doesn't answer.

I look at Lai and Seung's body still in her lap, and at the massacre around us, and I wonder where I went wrong. I should've known this was a trap. I should've never told Lai about it—or I at least should've told her she shouldn't plan a counterattack. I was careless.

The looks of betrayal on Cal's face and confusion on Gabriel's flash behind my eyes, and I choke back something I can't put a name on.

Someone claps a hand on my shoulder, and I flinch before I see it's Johann. "Thanks for making it back to us, Erik."

At the sound of her voice, despite everything, I feel weirdly better. Anchored. Like I'm back where I'm supposed to be. "Thanks, Al."

We kneel by Lai's side as Jay tries to stanch the bleeding and get her to respond, and Peter and others come running toward us. But she remains as quiet as the dead.

24

JAY

LAI WEIGHS HEAVY in my arms. I'm not certain when she lost consciousness, but it makes me rush all the more. My heart hammers against my eardrums. *No. No. No.* I hold her closer to my chest as I sprint through the underground tunnels of Regail Hall with Al, Erik, and Peter close behind.

We're among the first members to return, but already, word of the Order's utter defeat is spreading. Shouts and cries echo off the stone walls. People race through the halls and disappear around corners. Is Lai getting colder, or is it my imagination? *Hold on, Lai. You're going to make it.*

We reach the infirmary. It's already a flurry of motion as everyone prepares for the incoming wounded. The whipping of sheets, the clatter of tools, and shouts of instruction fill the room. Doctors and nurses, some professionally trained, most merely volunteers, run from one end of the long room to the other.

"We need help," I manage to choke out. A few people stop. At the sight of Lai and all the blood, three of them immediately direct me to a nearby bed. I set her down gently, as if that'll prevent her from feeling any more pain. But then I'm whisked out the door with the others to make space for the incoming wounded and the busy doctors.

We all stand in the hallway uncertainly. I want to go back in. I want to stay by Lai's side and make sure she'll pull through. However, I'd merely be in the way. There are other things Lai would want me to do while she's out. I can nearly hear her scolding me now. *Come on, Major, you being there wouldn't change anything. Better to help out where you can, right?*

Al is the first to speak. "Erik, do you know what happened out there?"

It takes an agonizing amount of energy to look up at Erik. His presence is heavy with regret, guilt, exhaustion. Blood stains his clothes. I don't want to think about whose side it belongs to. He nods, a single, jerky movement.

"Ellis told me and the other rebel leaders that we'd be attacking the sector." Erik's presence flashes. "But then when we were marching over, Ellis changed everything. The plan, the positions, the people—she used teleportation crystals, and then we were suddenly ambushing the Order. The Order planned a counterattack based on fake information, believing it was the rebels' real plan. And Ellis knew they would, and exactly how to counter them."

Guilt radiates from him in waves as he closes his eyes. He's always been so careful to hide his emotions, but his pain is evident in the lines around his eyes.

"This wasn't your fault," I say softly. "You and Lai—you were both doing the best you could."

"Yeah, well, our best got a lot of people killed."

The memory of Lai the moment Ellis took her arm burns behind my eyes. How she knelt there on the ground, no longer fighting back even before Seung saved her.

I squeeze my eyes shut. I don't want to think about it.

"Damn it all," Al hisses. Her fist hits the stone wall. I'm surprised it doesn't crack with the force of her blow. But with the way she twists, I notice the blood running down her back that I hadn't before.

"Al, your back—you're hurt," I say. It's a struggle to get the words out. "We need to—"

"It's not as bad as it looks. My armor took most of the blow. There'll be more urgent wounds for the doctors to see to."

"Then at least let me clean and bandage it."

"It's fine. It can wait."

"That wasn't a request."

Her eyes snap to me as her presence flashes with irritation, but she must see something in my face, because she just sits down on the floor with her back to me. I take the first-aid kit from my equipment belt and start treating her injury. It's shallower than I initially suspected but still not something I want to leave as is.

Peter remains silent all the while, Seung's body cradled in his arms. His eyes are blank, and I'm suddenly transported to when it was his twin's body he was holding in his arms just the same way a few months ago. My heart wrenches for him. He hadn't even recovered from his brother's death, and now he's lost a close friend. Perhaps more than one.

No. Lai's going to make it. She's going to be all right.

Footsteps pound through the halls as more people rush into the infirmary, most of them supported by friends. So many people are crying. I have to shut off my grid, or else the devastating grief of everyone in Regail Hall will suffocate me. I can barely contain my own hurt as I finish treating Al's injury.

When more footsteps approach us, I assume it's more people heading to the infirmary. However, at a strangled cry, I look up to see Clemente and Syon.

They're staring at Seung. Peter opens his mouth but doesn't manage to get anything out before the tears finally start falling. Clemente rushes to wrap him and Seung's body in his arms.

Syon watches. Something flickers behind his eyes, something he's fighting, and when I reopen my internal grid, his typically calm presence is a swirling storm of disbelief shot with immeasurable pain. However, he's fighting it. Those feelings tremble at the edges of his presence like the bands of a storm, and whenever they come too close, he shoves them back. It's a battle he's losing.

The lanterns around us dim and flicker erratically. Al, Erik, and I share an uneasy glance, but Peter and Clemente immediately snap to Syon. Apprehension flashes over their presences. Peter transfers Seung to Clemente's arms and runs to Syon's side—just as all the lights burst out of existence and the halls are thrown into interminable darkness.

The shouts and cries of before heighten with the loss of light. Panic now swims through the sorrow of my grid, and I have to shut it off again before it can crush me. My hands lurch through the dark, searching, until I lock hands with Al and Erik. A tiny measure of calm enters me.

Lai told us once that all of Regail Hall is powered by Syon. However, his immeasurably strong gift comes at a cost. Even the tiniest amount of emotion affects his gift—anything could throw his power out of balance and cause it to go out of control. She said it'd be a catastrophe if that ever happened.

Electric energy crackles through the air, begging to be released. An explosion waiting to happen.

"Syon, it's going to be okay," Peter whispers. It's disconcerting hearing his soft voice emanate from the darkness amid hundreds of shouts. "I know this is hard. I know you're hurting, and you should be able to feel your grief without anyone telling you to stop. And I am so, so sorry to ask you this, but you have to stay strong. We need you right now. Without your gift, more people could die. Lai's barely alive. Without your light, she can't get the help she needs."

I know it's going to hurt, but I open the internal grid in my head once more. I watch as Syon's presence rages with uncontainable grief. But now, stronger than the sadness, fear pierces through. Fear for what else he could lose.

His presence keeps fighting back against the emotions circling around it, but it's just the same as before. You can't *not* feel your own emotions.

I drop Al and Erik's hands and find my way to Syon's side using my internal grid. I reach out and feel something warm under my hands. Whether it's Peter or Syon, I can't tell. I wrap my arms around whoever it is.

"Syon, listen," I murmur. "You can't try to fight how you feel. You can't repress your own emotions for long, and it'll only hurt you worse in the long run. The grief you're feeling right now—don't try to push it away. Acknowledge it. Accept it. Just don't let it consume you."

Hands press against my chest. Syon's presence doesn't change. I can nearly taste the electricity in the air.

I hug whoever I'm holding tighter as panic beats against the inside of my skull. "I know it's hard. I know you're sad. Afraid. But think of your happy memories with Seung. Find a moment you love and hold onto it. It might be painful right now—but focus on that love more than your grief."

For a few heartbeats, his presence continues its futile struggle. Then, he fights not to ignore his grief or shut it out—a fight he already lost—but to let it sink into him alongside his love for Seung, without letting it take over him. It's difficult. I wouldn't typically ask this of anyone, but Peter is right. We need him to be in control—for everyone's sake.

Long, painful heartbeats pass.

The lights flicker back into existence. They're dim at first but slowly strengthen. The shouts of panic subside. The light illuminates Peter, kneeling and hugging Syon to him, hands clasped against the younger boy's head and back, and my arms wrapped around both of them. It shows Clemente, staring down at Seung's face as his tears continue to stream down. It allows me to see Erik and Al still gripping hands, tethering each other. And on my grid, all of us connected by our grief.

The pounding of footsteps begins once more now that the hallways are again visible. A set detaches from the crowd and rushes in our direction. I stand up from Peter and Syon's sides to see who it is just as someone crushes me in a hug.

I can't see the man's face, but it doesn't matter—I push him off immediately. My nerves are still wired from the battle. Even if they weren't, I don't want to be touched.

I can't tell which of us is more surprised—me or my father. However, his surprise melts quickly into relief.

"You're okay," he says. "You made it back." He grips my shoulders as he examines me, and I nearly shove him off again. I can't recall him ever touching me before. Panic colors his presence. "You're covered in blood—we—you need to—"

"It's not mine." I don't have the energy to be polite. "I'm fine. You—what are you doing in Regail Hall?"

"I've been waiting here for everyone to return after I heard about the big battle," my father says after a pause, likely in which he's trying to determine whether or not I'm truly okay. "I wanted—I needed to know you made it back all right. When I heard about the ambush, I assumed the worst."

It's only now that I notice his eyes are shining. The lanterns' light flickers over his face, making his features appear sharper than usual. The light accentuates the dark smudges under his eyes. His fingers tremble where they dig into my shoulders.

Despite myself, despite all that's happened in the past several hours, my heart jerks. "It's all right." I put my hands over his and squeeze. "I'm okay. I'm right here."

His hands keep shaking. "I know."

"I thought you didn't care." My voice comes out so quietly I'm not certain he hears it.

However, he must, because he looks down at the space between us. Then he hugs me to him once more, and I try very hard not to flinch. When he speaks again, he's crying. "I'm sorry. I'm so sorry. I know I can't take back what I've done, but please—give me a second chance. I want to make things right between us. I want us to be a family, the way a father and son should be. Please, stop fighting and putting your life in danger. Let's go home—together."

I should be happy. If it was the me from before this war, from before I met my teammates, I would've been elated. Nothing in this world would have made me gladder than to hear my father say those words.

Now, I can't stop thinking about all the nights I was coldly brushed off by this man, so different a person now as he holds me closer, as though he's trying to make up for my whole childhood during which he wouldn't touch me. The four years after I joined the military, throughout which he never once contacted me. I think of Lai, who gave up everything for so many years to fight for what was important to her. Lai, kneeling, bleeding, dying.

Strangely, I remember too the time Lai and I walked back from the Order the night before we left for the rebels' "peace negotiations," the way she looked up at the sky far overhead, streetlights flickering softly over her face as her expression softened and she said she wanted to meet her mother again.

"Thank you," I say. "But I'm sorry. I can't go back with you." I gently hold him away from me, and now that I can see his tears, this man who I can never once remember crying, my heart twists. However, I say, "I can't run away from this fight. I *won't* run from it. We've already lost so much; I refuse to let those sacrifices be in vain. No matter what it takes, we'll end this war. Until that happens, I'll keep fighting."

Purpose swells within me and grows with every heartbeat as I look at my father. He watches me back. For the first time in my life, it doesn't feel like a match of wills.

Finally, he sighs. "I can see that I won't convince you otherwise. You're more stubborn than I thought—just like your mother." He smiles slightly to himself. "If that's the case, then all I ask is that you be safe." He looks me in the eyes and takes my hands in his. "I mean what I said about becoming a real family. After all this is over, I'll be waiting for you. So please, *please* come back."

"I will." A knot catches in my throat as I say the words, because I *know* better than to promise such a thing during a war.

My father reluctantly lets go of my hands. I glance at everyone still around us, and he understands. He gives me one last hug that I stiffly allow. Then he takes his leave.

People continue to rush by us into the infirmary, and I catch the whispers of those not too distracted by injuries or wounded friends. The Order's remaining leaders, all falling apart right here in the hall. Everyone knows by now that Lai is Walker and that she's critically injured, that Seung is dead—and now Clemente, Peter, and Syon, the last three core leaders, are struggling to keep themselves together. What would Lai say if she were here right now?

I take a deep breath as I turn to face my friends. Peter still holds Syon to him as though he'll never let go. Syon's face is buried in Peter's shoulder. My heart aches just watching them. I don't know if I can do this. I don't know if I have any right to.

I take a heartbeat to gather my resolve. I have to hold it all in a single point in my chest for fear it'll disperse and I'll lose what I need in order to keep moving forward. "We need to decide our next step."

They all look up at me—even Peter and Syon.

I force myself to continue. "The Order needs its leaders right now. Everyone needs to hear that this isn't the end, that we'll be able to recover despite our losses. If we don't do something soon, everything Lai and Seung worked so hard to build will fall apart. They wouldn't want this."

There's a feeling of rightness to the words. There's something we can be doing right now. The sorrow and pain are still there, but greater than that is my determination to keep going.

Everyone's presences are dark with pain, but a sense of resolve slowly begins trickling through them as well.

"We must keep moving," Clemente says quietly when our eyes catch. "I know this. I know it is what both Fiona and Lai would want."

Peter is silent for a heartbeat before he says, "We're not going to lose anyone else if we can help it. We need to regather and reorganize." He looks at Syon, still wrapped in his arms, and some wordless understanding passes between them. They stand. "It's time to get moving."

25

LAI

EVERYTHING IS DARK. Everything hurts. My right arm burns like it's caught fire, but I can't move. I fight against the heavy darkness trying to drag me down. What's going on—where am I? Fight. Run. *Go.*

I wake up gasping for air—I can't breathe—I can't escape—and almost slam my head into someone leaning over me.

Something pushes my shoulders down. I fight against it, screaming now, then sucking in air, and the force tightens, and when I try to kick back, something pins down my legs, too, and I'm twisting, trying to escape, but everything hurts and my shouts turn to cries of pain.

I dimly hear someone speaking, as if from the top of a pit far above me. "Lai—Lai, it's okay, you're okay, please, calm down. Everything is okay."

Someone brushes my hair back from my face with cool, gentle fingers. The words turn into soft murmuring I can't understand, but the familiarity of it makes me pause. I hesitate, then the fight leaves my body all at once. I sink into the ground—no, a bed. I'm on a bed.

My vision starts to clear. Jay is the one leaning over me, sitting beside me on the bed as his one hand holds my shoulder down and the other keeps stroking my hair back. He's still speaking softly, but I can't make out the words.

The pressure on my legs lifts. "Lai? You with us?" Al. Al is here.

I blink. I can see Jay, but everything is hazy. I keep blinking, trying to make everything come into focus. I want to see him clearly. I want to see him so badly.

"Come on, Lai." Another voice, softer. Erik. How is he here? Am I dreaming?

"I—" I try to speak, but the words won't come. My throat is so dry. I don't even know what I could say anyway.

Jay reaches over to somewhere I can't see and brings a glass to my lips. He lifts my head and supports me as I try to drink the water. I almost choke on it.

"Easy," he says gently, so, so gently. The kind of gentleness I've only ever heard from Jay.

I want to cry. I want to sink against him and hear him murmuring softly to me again and feel his touch against my face and disappear into nothingness.

But he lifts the glass back up and I try to drink again.

My senses slowly come back to me. We're in my room in Regail Hall. Al sits on the end of my bed while Erik stands at the head of it. They're all watching me with more concern than I could ever imagine any of them showing.

With the return of my senses comes more awareness of the pain. I gasp as I try to move, and fire ignites in my arm—no, what remains of it. The fight. Ellis. Fiona.

The force of the pain is almost too much. I can't differentiate the physical hurt from the emotional. I feel myself slipping back, but Jay's grip on my shoulder tightens almost painfully, and he says in a strained voice, "Lai, stay with us. Please. Please."

"My fault," I whisper, but I can't tell whether or not I actually said it or if I just thought it. By the stricken look on Jay's face, I must've said it. "I—"

"It wasn't your fault," Jay says forcefully. "You couldn't have known."

"Shouldn't've gone," I whisper. Jay's face is losing focus again. "Alvaro. Sierra. Markus. Hugh. Maya. Ori. Fiona." My breath catches in my throat. I didn't think I was crying, but Jay gently wipes tears from my cheeks. "Fiona. *Fiona.*"

I cry. I cry like I can't remember ever crying. Not even when Paul was killed. Not even when Luke died. The pain in what remains of my arm can't compete with the weight crushing my chest.

Everything is abruptly starker and more real than it's ever felt. Like everything up until this point was just a video I was watching, occasionally directing, but mostly keeping my distance from on the other side of a monitor.

I can't stop crying. For once, I don't try. There's too much. Everything washes over me, and I struggle to keep my head above it all, to keep breathing, because each gasp for air is a thousand pieces of shattered glass scraping against the inside of my throat down into my lungs, piercing through my chest.

Jay holds me close to him. The warmth of his body is too much, too hot, burning me, but I don't pull away. Then Al is hugging us, too, and Erik's arms wrap around us all.

As I dissolve into my grief and pain, it feels like they're the only things keeping me anchored in this world.

26

JAY

IT TAKES SOME time for Lai to calm down. Once she does, she looks so exhausted I'm somewhat surprised she doesn't go straight back to sleep. But she sits up and leans against the wall. Her eyes watch us, but they're flat. "How long?"

"Three days," I say. I still can't believe she's awake—she's okay. She's alive. It pushes away my exhaustion better than sleep could. "Things are keeping together relatively well. Clemente and Peter have taken over with reorganizing and getting supplies from around the sector for those who were injured. Everyone's doing what they can."

"And Ellis?"

"The rebels haven't moved since they ambushed us."

"They might've dealt us a heavy blow, but we took down a good number of them, too," Al says. "It'll probably take some time for them to recover before their next attack."

Lai doesn't say anything.

"So?" Erik asks. "What now?"

Lai blinks at him like she doesn't understand.

"I mean, what's the Order's next move?" he clarifies.

"Erik," I say in soft warning. "She just woke up."

"No," Lai says. "This is important. The Order can't wait for me. It shouldn't have to." She takes a moment. I wonder if talking so much is hard for her right now. She looked like she was in a lot of pain earlier. My gut twists at the memory of her screaming, struggling to breathe, crying uncontrollably. Most of her minor injuries have already healed into scars, adding to her extensive collection, but even with a Nyte's extraordinarily fast healing, her arm must be in agony. I wish there was something I could do to take away her pain.

"I'm resigning as leader of the Order," Lai says.

We all stare at her. No one speaks right away.

"What?" I finally croak.

"It deserves someone better than me." Lai's eyes are on her hand, her fingers twisted into the sheets of her bed. "Someone who won't lead them into the ground."

"Lai, that's nonsense—"

"I can't fight like this anyway."

"Lai!" I shout. Erik and Al both flinch, but Lai doesn't so much as glance at me. That she refuses to do even that cuts at me. "Lai, you can't take all of the blame for this on yourself. And even if it was your fault—so what? You're just going to give up and walk away because the Order suffered its first defeat?"

She doesn't reply.

"This is war." I feel my voice getting hotter the more I speak, but I can't stop it. I don't want to. "You knew what this would be like going in. Did you think the Order could get by without a single loss? Were you really that conceited? And now that things didn't go exactly as you planned, you're just going to quit? Abandon all the people who are still relying on you?"

"What am I supposed to do?" Lai snaps. Finally, something like life returns to her eyes. Even though I'm angry, that spark pushes relief through me. "Who's going to follow me after I led everyone straight into a trap? I couldn't even take down Ellis. They all lost friends; so many of them were there—they're not going to believe in someone so weak. This is for the best for everyone."

"You truly think losing their leader on top of everything else is *for the best*?" I demand. "You're merely wallowing in your own self-pity. You're blaming yourself for everything that went wrong because it's an easy out. I thought you were the kind of person to see something through to the end—but you're only running away."

"*Jay*," Al hisses.

It's not as though I don't understand. Lai's lost her arm and one of her oldest friends, has been unconscious for three days, and has barely been awake for ten minutes. However, I can't just ignore this. If I don't speak my mind now, what if this new resignation sets in? What if she truly begins to believe what she said and steps down?

This isn't the Lai I know. The Lai I know would never give up so easily. She'd already be asking for details on what the Order's been doing to recover and giving new orders to help it move forward. She'd push herself despite her injuries until we all *forced* her to rest. That's who she is. That's what I love about her.

But now, Lai won't even acknowledge me. She keeps staring down and remains silent.

I've been holding everything inside me together these last few days for her—for the hope that she'd wake up, that we could keep moving. Now, something inside me breaks.

I stand up. "Clemente and Peter told me they wanted my help when I was available. I'd better go see them."

When Lai still doesn't speak, I leave without looking back.

I don't make it far down the hall before Al's voice follows me, asking me to stop, and then her hand catches my upper arm and *makes* me stop.

"Jay," she says. "Look. I get it. But right now, we need to stick together. Lai needs us. She needs you most of all—you're one of her biggest supporters. She could use some support right now."

"Yeah." It's only one word, but it's hard to get out. All I can think of is how easily Lai just gave up—how she wouldn't even look at me.

"So?" Al asks.

"I don't think I can do this right now, Al."

"Of course you can. I know you can."

I meet Al's eyes, but it feels like a mistake as soon as I see the trust burning there. I have to look away. "It's just—Lai is how I always wished I *could* be. Strong. Confident. Determined. I . . . I thought she was invincible. Not that she couldn't be defeated by anyone but that she'd keep going no matter how many times she lost. Seeing her just give up . . ."

"She's only human, Jay," Al says gently. I've never heard her speak that way before. "We all have our moments when we want to give up. And she just lost a lot at once. *Of course* she's hurting. *Of course* she thinks it'd be better to stop now before she loses anymore." She puts a hand on my shoulder. "That's why she needs us to remind her there's still plenty to keep fighting for."

It takes several heartbeats for me to corral everything inside me under control. Finally, I sigh. "I need to apologize to her."

"Nah," Al says. "I think it'd mean more to her if you explained why you were so upset. C'mon. Let's go back."

27

AL

I DRAG JAY back into Lai's room, but only about a minute has passed, so everything's the same. Erik's head snaps up when we walk back in, and relief practically rolls off him like smoke. Jay doesn't say anything as he stands by the door, but at least he's here. The last thing we need is for our team to fall apart as soon as it's together again. Especially when Lai needs us so much right now.

"Lai," I say. She doesn't look up at me. I need to get her back on her feet—or at least stumbling on them. "What do you think the Order's next move should be?"

"I don't know." Her voice sounds as tired as she looks, but there's a hard, mean edge to it: "I don't know anything anymore."

"Because of one loss?" I ask. "Don't get me wrong, it was a terrible loss—you lost your arm, your friends. That's *hard*. I get that. But you lose badly once, and suddenly you don't know anything? Come on, Lai. You're tougher than that. You've been through a lot of shit and never given up. Why is this time different?"

She doesn't answer right away, but I don't get the feeling she's *not* going to reply, so I wait. Finally, she says, "It feels like I've gotten this far by just ignoring all my shortcomings. I could pretend they didn't exist and keep going. But I can't pretend not to see them anymore. I can't stop *feeling* them."

"That sounds like a good thing to me. Trying to ignore your weaknesses never leads to anything good. Now that you know, you can work on them and try to fix them."

She shakes her head. "There's too much," she says quietly. "There are too many things I'm lacking in. I've never thought Luke made the right choice in asking me to lead the Order. I took the position because I wanted to fulfill his last wish, not because I thought I was good enough, and now I have to face the fact that I'm not. I can't just keep leading everyone to their deaths because of my selfishness. That's not fair to anyone."

"Lai," I say, "you really think everyone would've come this far with you if they didn't believe in you as a leader? It takes a lot to convince someone to follow you—especially into a war. But everyone here—they really look up to you. They love you. They believe in you. *I* believe in you. That's not something a person can get just by being selfish."

She finally, *finally* looks up at me, and her expression is so vulnerable my voice softens reflexively. "Besides, if selfishness is really all that got you here, I don't think you would've made it this far. I don't know what it is that drives you to do so much for the Order or what got you here in the first place, but I don't think that's all that's moving you forward now. You might not've noticed it yet, but you're fighting for a lot more than you think. There's no other way you could've made the Order into what it is today."

I jump when Lai starts crying again. She looks down. Then, so quietly I can barely hear her, she says, "Thank you, Al."

I really am bad with crying people. But I sit next to her on the bed and wrap my arm around her shoulders, pulling her into me until she's crying into my shoulder. Erik and Jay come to stand beside us. "Anytime, Lai."

The next couple of days crawl by. Lai barely leaves her room. She doesn't ask how things are going in the Order, but I can tell she wants to. She hasn't brought up quitting being leader again, but she hasn't taken it back, either.

Peter, Trist, and Syon rushed over to see her as soon as they heard she was awake. I felt like I was intruding when the three of them burst into the room and ambushed Lai in tearful hugs—and I could tell Erik and Jay did, too. We made up an excuse to leave before they started talking.

Jay's keeping busy. Peter has pretty much replaced Fiona as the Order's co-second-in-command with Trist, and Jay's basically filling the captain position Peter left behind. The three of them and Syon are always talking to people, trying to calm everyone and arrange for more medicine, more food, more everything.

The mood of the Order itself is weird. Everyone's in a state of mourning, but maybe thanks to Jay and everyone's early intervention, there's this sort of understanding that they need to keep moving, too. Trist and Peter called a huge meeting of the Order soon after we all got back from the ambush, to relay news and try to rally morale, but since then, nothing big has happened. I think they're waiting for Lai. I think we all are.

But Trist and Peter's waiting feels different. When I talk to them, they're so *sure* Lai will come back around. "You'll see," Peter says one time when I ask him about it. He's obviously beyond tired, but he actually smiles. "Lai always pulls through. She just fell down a little harder than usual and needs more time to get back up. But she'll come 'round."

I wish I could be that confident. I believe in Lai. I know she can pull through. I just don't know if she *wants* to—and that's the biggest thing.

When I get exhausted doing the few things I can right now—which mostly involve running things from place to place and asking people if I can help and then running some more for the errands they give me—I go find Jay. I need him right now.

He's not with Trist or Peter, so I go down to the Order's vegetable plots. Sure enough, he's there, squatting at the edge of one of the small fields and looking out over the sprouting greenery. From the blank look in his eyes, I doubt he even sees it. I'm surprised that Erik's sitting with him.

They both look up as I walk in. "Hey," I say. "Thanks for inviting me to the party."

"It's a pretty lame party if you ask me," Erik says. He tries to give his old carefree grin, but it looks so fake it hurts. "But you're obviously welcome to join us."

I sit on the other side of Jay, and no one says anything for a long time. For some reason, that feels better. I thought I wanted to talk, but sitting here, I realize I just wanted company. I don't want to think about whether Lai will pull through or not, because I don't want to think about what'll happen if she doesn't. I don't want to try to talk because whatever comes out would just feel fake. So I stay with my teammates, and we support one another the only way we can right now. By being there.

28
ERIK

IT'S AGES BEFORE I can see Lai without any of her other friends around. Okay, so a couple days. But it feels like forever with everyone rushing around while I have nothing to do. I offer what info I can about the rebels, but it's nothing I haven't already told Lai at some point in the last three months.

Being here in Regail Hall for the first time ever is weird. Lai described it to me before, but it's nothing like actually being in the underground tunnels myself. It's hard to get used to. Having Jay and Al around helps. But the rebels' underground base was one huge open space—none of these maze-like halls. And all the strangers walking around. I feel like an outsider. I'd mostly gotten used to the rebels' faces. Guess now I have to start over from scratch again.

At least I don't have to worry about Ellis spying on us. I'd wondered how it'd work with her butterfly snooping around in my shadow, but I forgot that that part of her gift only works if she has the person's permission. When I retreated with the Order a few days ago—definitely thinking I did not want the butterfly around—I saw it shoot out of my shadow like it was ejected. So that's something good, at least.

Jay was also telling me about some guy named Noah in the military. Apparently we used to be friends before I lost my memories. But for the first time, I'm sick of faces from the past I can't remember. Right now, I don't want to know anything about him or what he knows about me. There's enough crap going on in the now.

Once I finally get to see Lai, just the two of us in her room, I don't know what to say. She looks way better than she did when she first woke up. But the dark smudges under her eyes are even worse than before, and I have a hard time ignoring her missing arm. The last time I met Lai in good shape was when we all said goodbye and I went off to the rebels. She was a hell of a lot more confident then. I used to always be annoyed by that confidence and her stubbornness, but right now, I'd give just about anything to see some of that come back.

"So," I say. "How're you feeling?"

"Better."

"Really? 'Cause I kind of have my doubts."

"Don't you always?"

"Only when they're warranted." I smile.

After the smallest pause, she returns it. "I'm sorry I dragged you into all this, Erik. I shouldn't have put you in such a hard, dangerous position. Especially when I knew you'd be betraying your friends over there. But I'm glad you're okay. And back with us."

Cal and Gabriel's faces flash in my memory. The smile takes more effort this time. "It's good to be back. But I knew what I was getting into when you made that offer. It was my choice. And I don't regret it." I hesitate. My voice lowers. "Except at the end. I should've told you not to plan a counterattack. I *knew* Ellis was plotting something, but I—"

"You had no way of knowing she'd trick you and most of her

other trusted friends," Lai says. "That she would lie to all of you is what threw everything off. You couldn't have known."

"And neither could you," I say. "So stop blaming yourself for it already."

She just stares down at her hand.

"Everyone's waiting for you, you know. It doesn't matter if you can't fight or whatever right now. Everyone just wants to see you up and at 'em and spewing your usual arrogance again." I roll my eyes. "Even *I* can't believe how much I want to hear your spiel of invincibility."

Lai cracks a grin, but it doesn't reach her eyes. "Things must be really bad if you of all people are saying that, Erik."

"Yeah, well. I want you back. So does everyone else. If it helps get your ass in gear, I'll admit to it."

She laughs. But it's not out of agreement.

"C'mon, Lai. We all make mistakes. No one's going to hold it against you."

"I know," she says quietly. "It's just—what if I fail again? What if I can only lead the Order to failure? If everything falls apart because of me, I don't know what I'd be living for anymore."

"Even if you fail again, you have plenty to live for. We're all here for you, you know. You don't have to take on everything by yourself. Me, Jay, Al—all your Order friends. You don't have to do this alone." I laugh. "No one here would *let* you do it alone."

Finally, Lai's smile is genuine. It's still not really her usual self, but it's the closest I've seen in a while. "Thanks, Erik. I appreciate it."

"You know I've got your back, Lai."

I'm about to try getting her to come to the leaders' meeting that's happening a few twisty, turning halls away—I sure as hell don't want to go since I hardly belong here and barely know anyone, but it'd be good for Lai—but before I can say anything, the screen in the corner of the room flickers on. Lai and I share a frown.

"Does it usually do that?" I ask.

"Never."

There's not a whole lot of time to work it out, because then Ellis's face is on the screen, and she's smiling that too-familiar sharp smile that makes my skin crawl. "Good afternoon, Sector Eight. My name is Sara Ellis, leader of the rebels, and I have a message for you."

29

LAI

MY STOMACH LURCHES at the sight of Ellis. Everything around her is dark, but she and the desk she sits at are in clear view. If she sustained any injuries in that last battle, there's no sign of them now. She took so much from me and I couldn't even give her a wound serious enough to last a week. Have I always been this weak? She looks tired, though. Much more so than I remember her looking during our fight.

"What's going on?" Erik asks.

I can't take my eyes from the screen. "I don't know. Ellis has probably hijacked the broadcasting network—likely every monitor in the sector, if even we're getting this." If Ellis could hack even us . . .

"I do apologize for forcing your attention like this," Ellis continues. Her eyes glint like a Feral's about to pounce. "But I think everyone will find what I have to say very . . . enlightening."

This can't be good. Is there a way to shut down the broadcast? If I could get Rowan—no. I can't give anyone orders anymore. I only ruin everything.

"I'm here today to talk to you about Nytes and Sector Eight's precious High Council." Ellis's voice is so sickly sweet it makes me want to throw up. "Mainly, how the gifted were created from the Council's experiments to make the perfect super-soldiers."

Wait. What? Erik and I exchange a glance, but even without reading his thoughts, I know he doesn't have any clue what she's talking about, either.

"I'm sure you heard about our attack inside the sector a few months back. It was to put an end to the Councilors' experiments and get the proof we needed of their guilt." Ellis's face is replaced by some kind of security camera footage. For some reason, my first thought is that it's surprisingly high quality. The video shows a large warehouse interior-turned-lab with a handful of people in very distinct black starlight robes talking to one another—and in the bottom right corner of the video, there's a date from almost twenty years ago, right next to the seal of the High Council.

The conversation of the Councilors is clear. "Sample pool? Can't we just get some orphans and homeless off the street?" At the sound of his voice, my fist tightens. I recognize it from when I eavesdropped on two Councilors back in Central months ago. I never actually saw the Councilor's face, but I'd recognize that nasal, self-important voice anywhere. Does this have to do with that conversation back then—the experiment and prototype they talked about?

"Tests indicate the results would be exponentially better if we could inject the serum while the child is still developing in the womb," another Councilor says—the second Councilor I heard that day. Just like back then, her silky smooth voice gives me chills. Something instinctively saying not to trust her. "We'll need pregnant mothers in order to get the best super-soldiers."

The third Councilor, who I don't know, sighs impatiently. "Just have some of our doctors enter the hospitals and slip it in like it's normal medication. Best to try it on people in other sectors as well to prevent too much focus on Sector Eight alone. We can't let the other sectors know about this. Everyone waged war on Sector Five just for *suspecting* they were breaking the treaty by developing guns. We'll just need to keep careful records of all test subjects who receive the serum."

"Understood," the one doctor-looking person with the three Councilors says. "But, sir, are you sure about this? These are innocent mothers and unborn children—"

"Who are supporting Sector Eight and assisting in the advancement of protective measures against other sectors. Their contributions will be remembered."

I can't breathe. This can't be real. It just can't be. The Council is terrible, but there's no way they would stoop to human experimentation. There's no way they could've kept it secret for so long—no way they could've gotten enough people to agree to work on something like this. No. It's impossible.

But it's also impossible to *not* remember those two Councilors' conversation I overhead all those months ago about getting the "demons" under their control.

The video cuts abruptly and shifts to another. The place is the same, but the date in the corner has skipped ahead about four years.

There's chaos in the room as people scramble, checking computers and doing tests. The Councilors are back, storming down the aisle nearest the camera.

"What do you mean several of the test subjects have died?" Nasal demands of a different doctor-looking person than the one from the last recording.

"Sir, many of the subjects' bodies couldn't handle the strain of the serum's effects as their bodies continued to grow—dozens, maybe hundreds have died already."

"And the rest?"

"No obvious signs of change yet."

"Keep an eye on them," Don't-Trust says. "Have our doctors announce that some new kind of degenerative disease that only afflicts children has appeared. We *cannot* let them know about the experiments."

"Yes, ma'am."

My stomach drops to the bottom of my feet. The epidemic from sixteen years ago—the "disease" that even now still affects kids. The one everyone thought *caused* Nytes. The reason everyone called Nytes demons. It was all because of the Councilors' experiments failed.

Too many thoughts run through my head for me to keep up with any of them. Is this a joke? Just another trick by the rebels? But that Council seal—it's authentic. That was definitely the warehouse we broke into months ago to investigate. And those were definitely the Councilors I eavesdropped on before. The same Councilors who're ruling the sector now. That kind of video couldn't have been faked so easily—could it?

What if it's real? What if the reason the gifted are like this—the reason *I'm* like this—is just because the High Council wanted stronger soldiers? My mom's life was ruined because of me. I ran away from her so I would stop bringing her heartache. I joined the military because I had nowhere else to go. For most of my life, I've done nothing but fight and scheme and learn how to get better at both those things. I've manipulated countless people to the point I don't even feel bad about it anymore. I've watched my friends die. All because I was gifted. All because of the Council.

Ellis returns to the screen. Her hands are folded in front of her on the desk, the shadows over her face darker than before. "We destroyed all the serums located in the warehouse. The latest 'prototype' was designed to make Nytes obedient to whatever orders they were given." Her mouth twists into a snarl. I have to hold back my own revulsion. "I've released the footage we stole from the warehouse to the sector's network. You'll also find the list of names of every *test subject*"—she says this with such scorn it almost cuts—"that was experimented on. You're free to access these and analyze them however much you like, but I can assure you this: They're real. Nytes are merely the results of the High Council's whimsical experiments to strengthen the military." She smiles grimly, like she knows a lot more that she's not saying. It feels like my thoughts go blank as I suddenly realize what she's doing. "That is all. I hope you have a pleasant day."

The screen flickers and goes dark.

"That can't be true," Erik says. His voice is weak. "This is just one of Ellis's plots—right?"

"Yes," I whisper.

"How do we prove it's not real?"

"I don't know if we can—the videos might be real. That might all be true."

"Wait—what? You just said—"

"It's a trap." Seconds ago, it's like my thoughts were wiped clean away by shock. Now, they're running one another over so fast I can barely keep up. "The broadcast is just a distraction. Trist and the others—where are they?"

Okay, a little explanation would be nice right about now. "They should still be in a meeting with all the other leadership."

"I'll explain once we've got everyone together. We don't have time to waste." I swing my legs over the bed, but before my feet hit the floor, I hesitate. Am I really going to do this? What if I'm wrong? Even if I managed to get everyone to believe me, what if I'm just making another mistake?

268

But what if I'm right and I choose not to do anything?

My fingernails dig into my palm. If I don't act now, what else could I lose? It'd be better to fight to protect what's important to me than to not even try and lose everything left that I love. Jay was right. I can't just sit here and indulge in my own self-pity anymore. I can't stop here. Not yet.

I take a steadying breath. *I can do this.* I stand. It takes a few seconds to steady myself. Losing my arm was my only serious injury; the rest of my body has mostly healed, but I still *feel* like it hasn't. Standing is disorienting—and makes me immediately irritated. The disconnect between remembering how easily, how thoughtlessly I've always moved clashing with how I feel in this moment cuts deep.

Then Erik is there beside me, holding out his arm for support. I take it.

We head into the hall, and I try my best to block out the panicked thoughts of everyone nearby rushing into my head. The questions, the fury—I can't handle it right now. I have to stay focused.

As soon as Erik opens the door to the meeting room, loud conversation bursts out. Everyone still crowds around a now-dark monitor, talking over one another, trying to figure out what to take care of first. I spot Jay and Al standing next to each other, then find Trist and Peter, near the front, trying to gain calm, with Syon nearby.

I let out a long, steadying breath before I raise my voice. "Quiet."

When everyone immediately falls silent and turns to me, I realize how uninspiring I must appear as a leader. I just rolled out of bed and I'm sure I *look* it. My bandaged stump of an arm is in clear view for everyone to see. But I straighten my back. I try to emanate the feeling of control I'd always felt prior to our huge loss. It doesn't come as easily now, but I find it.

"I think Ellis's broadcast is a distraction," I say, pushing past my nerves. "It'll throw the sector into chaos and confusion. People accusing each other. No one trusting those in charge. No one knowing what to do. It's the perfect chance to deal Sector Eight a death blow."

"But why would she—if she knew all this from the beginning, why didn't she reveal it right away?" Erik asks. His question reflects everyone's confusion. "She never even told me about all this." **I didn't get the feeling Gabriel or the others knew, either.** "Why would she even want this war on the sector when she could've just tried to overthrow the Council from the start? She could've done so much more to get peace for the gifted with this. She didn't *need* war."

"I have no idea what she's thinking," I say. "Maybe it's because she's more interested in wiping out the ungifted than getting them to live with us peacefully. But this is just like the negotiations meeting she staged. Why else wait until now to reveal such important information? This is nothing but a distraction for a bigger goal. We can't fall for it again."

The mood in the room shifts. The uncertain thoughts from when I first entered are still there, but sharpened with new purpose.

"Rowan, Navarro, find the files Ellis released and check their authenticity," I say. I don't leave myself time to question whether or not anyone will listen to me. "See if you can trace them back to their source—not the rebels, but to the cameras they were originally taken from."

"Roger," Rowan says with a salute. Navarro nods.

"Amal, you and the other captains gather everyone in the Order for an emergency assembly. We need to talk about Ellis's broadcast before panic spreads." I pause. "Along with some other important things moving forward."

"Understood," Amal says.

I open my mouth, close it. When my voice comes out again, it sounds less steady. "The rest of you, stay. We need to talk."

Everyone rushes out of the room to follow my orders. I try to meet their eyes as they pass me by—I owe them that much, at least, having abandoned them after that last battle—but they're all focused on setting out to accomplish their tasks.

Once it's only the seven of us left, I look to Trist and Peter and Syon. I'm at a loss for words. All the times they came to visit me over the past few days, I didn't know how to face them. I didn't know how to talk about Fiona. But somehow, it was like they understood. They were quiet in their encouragement but strong. They really believed in me, even when I didn't. Up until I saw Ellis's broadcast and *knew* what she was going to do, I didn't think I'd get back up. But somehow, they did.

"Good to have you back, Lai," Peter says with a grin. Trist smiles as warmly as ever at me. Syon is more subdued, as always, but he gives me a small nod. I know he's still mourning. Fiona was as close to family as he'd ever had. But he's still moving forward despite that.

"It's good to be back." I take a deep, shuddering breath. When I speak again, my voice sounds stronger in my ears. "We need to plan a counterattack. I doubt Ellis will try to be sneaky; there's no need for her to be since the sector will be in a state of chaos after that broadcast. We need to talk to Austin and coordinate with him and the military, but—I think we're going to have to face the rebels head-on." I hesitate for the first time since I started talking this out. "If anyone is willing to go back into battle."

It's a lot to ask of people who've already lost so much. Too much. Will any of them believe me about Ellis's imminent attack? Will any of them even be willing to follow me into battle again? I doubt it. I don't know if I would. But at the meeting, if it looks like everyone would rather have a new, better leader, I'll step aside and let them choose someone else. The Order is more than me. It should be led by someone who has everyone's trust.

You were wrong about me, Fiona. The Order doesn't need me. It'll continue on no matter who's leading it, so long as that person has everyone's confidence.

"I'm sure there are people who still want to fight," Al says. She's grinning fiercely. She's been quiet but supportive the last few days, but this is the first time I've seen the fire back in her since our lost battle. "The Order's made up of a bunch of survivors and fighters. I think you'll have more takers than you think. Besides, it beats the alternative. I'm sure they all know that."

Her confidence sinks into me, grounds me. How is she so good at that? "You're right," I say. "We'll need a plan before we can convince everyone, so we'll concentrate on that for now and go from there after the meeting. Jay—" I turn to him without thinking, but as soon as I see him, I flinch. We've spoken since our fight after I first woke up, but it wasn't really ever quite right. Is he sick of me by now? Is he tired of my indecisiveness?

But when I lock gazes with Jay, his eyes are soft. His hands are clasped in front of him as he awaits orders.

I swallow. "Jay, I need you to meet with Austin as soon as we figure out details here. If we're going to have any chance of pulling this off, we'll need the military's help. The Order alone can't win this."

"Of course," he says. "Just say the word." **I'm . . . sorry for getting angry at you before. You were hurting. Of course you were. You needed time, not me exploding on you.**

No, I answer back in his thoughts. *No, I needed that. I needed you to tell me I was wrong. I need that a lot more in my life, actually. Thank you.*

He smiles slightly. **Always.**

I turn to address everyone again. When I do, I see all of them, all these people I care so much about, all these people who kept believing in me, watching me expectantly. Waiting for orders. *Believing* in what I'm going to say.

My chest wells up with something I'm not sure I've ever felt before. Gratitude? Happiness? Whatever it is, I hold it close. I don't ever want to forget this moment, this sensation. This sense of responsibility.

I won't run away anymore. I'll stand by my friends and do whatever I can to protect them. No matter what else I might lose, I'm going to keep going. Even if I lose everything, I'm going to keep fighting with the scraps I have left.

30

JAY

I WEAVE THROUGH Central's rushing halls without attempting to hide myself. It hardly feels as though there's a need to at the moment. Most of the soldiers run past me without giving me a second glance; everything is chaos as orders are shouted through halls and everyone scrambles to carry them out. Squads head out to prevent the protests from turning violent. Others are sent to gather and confirm information. Presences converge on my internal grid in flurries of bright reds and purples. No one has time to pay me any mind. Those who do notice me either choose to ignore me or else gape openly. But no one attempts to stop me.

I manage to make it to Austin's reception room without incident, but the space is stuffed so full of officers I have to elbow my way to Noah's desk. Conversation rises in an overwhelming deluge around me. It crashes over me in vicious waves, suffocating me nearly as much as the bodies pressed around me. Noah is speaking rapidly on the phone, but as soon as he sees me, without breaking his stream of conversation, he presses a few keys on his keyboard and jerks his chin for me to head into Austin's office.

I attempt to make my way there, but officers block my path and refuse to move. Three of them stand in a line before the door, arms crossed or hands on the compressed weapons on their equipment belts.

"Whatever it is you want with the general, now's not the time," one of them says. I recognize her. She's the officer who came to get a piece of furniture Erik made, back when we were more actively trying to rid ourselves of his too-many creations. She struck me as sympathetic then, and even now, the lines around her eyes are understanding. "I know you've been through a lot, but—"

"I'm not here about the Council's experiments," I say. For perhaps the first time when speaking to another officer, there's no deference in my voice. I have a purpose here—and I *will* see it through. "General Austin is expecting me. Move aside."

The officer's eyebrows lift as surprise flashes through her presence. Yet she doesn't budge, and the two officers behind her draw their compressed weapons. Around us, others have noticed the commotion. They wall me in like a trapped Feral. Yet I don't feel any fear—only urgency. If I have to fight everyone here to get to Austin, I will.

However, before it can get to that point, Noah says clearly behind me, "All of you, stand down. The general is expecting ex-Major Kitahara. We don't have time."

"Of course a Nyte would try to let another Nyte through," a different officer, one in the crowd, says. "What if you're both just trying to take out your anger against the Council on the general? Like hell we'll let anything happen to him."

A Nyte-versus-Etiole fight right now? *Really?*

The door behind the three officers in front of me slams open. They startle and turn to find Austin standing in the doorway of his office. His eyes sweep over the scene once before he jerks his thumb for me to come inside. "Kitahara, hurry. We have much to discuss."

I push past the officers previously blocking my path. They no longer attempt to stop me.

Austin slams the door closed once I'm inside. "The rebels are planning to attack the sector," he says. "That broadcast—I'm sure of it."

"Lai suspects the same. She wants the Order and military to work together to stop them."

Austin shakes his head. For the first time, it occurs to me that he could refuse to help us. I forget how to breathe.

"I want to stop the rebel attack," Austin says at the look on my face. "But there's something I need to take care of first. Something that must be dealt with right away."

I can't comprehend what he means for a heartbeat. What could possibly be more urgent than stopping a force of Nytes from attacking Sector Eight? Then it occurs to me. "You mean to confront the High Council."

He nods. "Even if we beat the rebels, we won't be able to do anything with those Councilors in charge. If we wait, there's a chance they could escape or gather their allies together or else spread more of their lies. In all the current confusion, we have to take them down—now."

"But there won't be any point if the dome takes damage. It would only take a crack—"

"I don't think Ellis will necessarily aim for the dome," Austin says. He begins pacing back and forth, thumbnail between his teeth. "We'll need a sizeable force to take down the Council. I'm sure they won't go down without a fight. There will likely also be those who support their decisions, so they're going to be gathering their forces right now. We must deal with them first. But if the Order could hold off the rebels until we can come to back you up—we might just be able to take down our two biggest problems in one day."

My thoughts race faster than my heart. "How long do you think we'd have to hold out? We don't even know how many of them will be coming, and the Order is still recovering from its last loss."

"I know. I know it's a lot to ask. But it's the only way."

I take a deep, steadying breath. This isn't what Lai was hoping for. However, if it's all we can get, it's still better than the Order going out there to face the rebels alone.

"Can you spare any soldiers, weapons, or armor?" I ask. "Anything at all."

Austin's pacing pauses. "I'll have Noah arrange as much as we can spare." He calls for his secretary, who appears almost immediately.

"Yes, sir?" Noah asks. His eyes are wild—more so than the other soldiers' or even Order members'. Earlier, I assumed it was because of the rebels' announcement along with all the subsequent chaos he's had to deal with as the general's secretary, but when I take a closer look at his presence, I realize whatever is afflicting him is something else. Deep-rooted fear chokes on red-hot rage. Regret and grief tangle their fingers through the embers.

"I need you to get whatever support you can to the Order," Austin says. "They're going to hold off the rebels' attack for as long as they can until we can get there to help. Whatever we can spare, make sure it gets to them."

"Yes, sir."

"When you can join us, the Order members will be wearing red strips of cloth," I say. "As a way for the military to differentiate between us and the rebels." It was Erik's idea—it hadn't even occurred to me that there could be confusion over who's a rebel and who's an Order member. But especially with gifted on both sides, we don't want our own attacked.

"I'll make sure everyone knows," Austin says. "I'll leave you both to plan the details of the military and Order's coordination. I need to get the officers together and start moving."

"Understood," Noah and I say simultaneously. Then Austin is out the door, shouting orders, and I'm attempting to get everything straight in my head. It's going to be okay. We just have to hold the rebels off long enough for the military to arrive. The Council shouldn't pose much problem—they've always relied on the military for their primary firepower, and now that Austin will be leading the military against them, they'll have little to defend themselves with. We can do this. Deep breaths. Focus on what you can do right now. Worrying over everything else won't help.

"I'm coming with you," Noah says.

I blink. "What?"

"The Order—I'm going to fight with you," he says. "You're going to need however many spare soldiers you can get, aren't you? I'll help hold off the rebels."

"What? You can't—it's too dangerous." Even as the words leave my mouth, I don't know why I'm saying them. What he said is true, after all, and Noah is a gifted soldier. He could help the Order tremendously, even if his gift—whatever it is—isn't suited to battle. "You're too important to the military. Once all this is over, Austin is going to need you more than ever. You have to be there to help him."

However, Noah is shaking his head before I've even finished. "You don't understand. I *need* to be there. I . . . I have to make up for everything I've done on the Council's orders. Please. I need this as much as the Order does."

I hesitate, but his presence is solid with resolve. His earlier conflicting emotions are still there, but they're secondary now to his determination. Why am I hesitating? There should be no reason for me to say no. The Order needs all the help it can get. He's proven countless times he's on our side. Yet I recall the last time he spoke about the things he'd done on the Council's orders. The fear, the regret.

I grab his hand. "Noah. If you come, you have to promise you'll try to survive."

He opens his mouth, closes it again. Stares at me.

The anxiety beating against my chest strengthens. "You said you wanted to make up for what you've done, right? I don't know the details or what you think you have to make up for, but you can't do it if you're dead, right? That's why, if you want to repent for whatever wrongs you feel you've done on behalf of the Council, the best way you can do that is by helping Austin correct their mistakes. Only you can do that. If you understand, I'll gladly welcome you into the Order's ranks. If not, I'll have to refuse your assistance."

Noah's eyes drop to the floor. He takes a deep breath. Several heartbeats pass before he looks back up at me. This time, the resolve of his presence is a different shade. "I understand. Now come with me and we'll get together everything and everyone we can to help the Order."

31

LAI

I'M NERVOUS ABOUT standing in front of the Order again. It'll be my first time talking from the stage as Lai, the cover of Walker dead with Fiona. I know how I must look, one-armed and tired. As much as I clean myself up, and even after I've changed into more formal clothes to address everyone, I'm not blind. I can see the exhaustion in my face. In the way I move when I'm not careful.

But Trist, Peter, and Syon stick close to me. Before I have to walk out onstage, they hug me so close their heartbeats pound against my ears.

"All will be well, Lai," Trist murmurs.

"And if for some reason it's not, we'll be right there with you," Peter says. When he lets go, he takes my shoulders and, smiling, squeezes them. It's such a different smile from the easy one he wore before Paul's death. But it's a more resilient one. A fiercer one. "Go get 'em, Lai."

Syon solemnly signs encouragement to me before squeezing my hand.

"Way to almost make me cry right before I have to go talk to the entire Order, you guys."

Trist laughs as he pounds me on the back. "That is why we are here."

I smile. Even if I lose the Order, I know these three will still be here for me. No matter how this goes, I won't be alone.

"Well," I say, "let's get this show on the road."

I walk out onstage with Trist and Peter close behind. Their presence alone makes me calmer than I would've thought possible with everything going on.

The room stills and quiets as I take my place on the stage. Unlike when I hid behind the illusion of Walker, everyone sees me as I am. I'm overly conscious of my missing arm, and how it feels like a physical reminder of everything we've lost. Of how I let everyone down.

But even so, I'm still fighting. Still going. In spite of it all.

I lift my chin proudly before the room of a thousand people watching me. Even though the illusion of Walker is gone, I adopt my old accent from Sector Four to speak in the voice everyone recognizes as hers. "I would first like to apologize for my absence this past week. When everyone needed me most, I wasn't here as I should have been." I hesitate and drop the accent. And, unintentionally, my volume. "I also want to say I'm sorry for deceiving everyone for so long. I thought it would be better for everyone if I hid who I really was. I don't know whether that choice was right or wrong. But I am sorry for hiding it."

I take a deep breath and keep going, back at my original volume, in my normal voice, knowing I won't need Walker's anymore. Probably never again. My pulse hammers against my skin. "I'm also sorry for our recent loss. I led us straight into a trap and we suffered greatly for it. You all have every right to blame me."

There's no sound in the room. When I try to meet as many gazes as I can, I don't know what it is I'm seeing. For once, I don't lean in to anyone's minds. Maybe I'm actually respecting their privacy. Maybe

I'm just too afraid to know what everyone's actually thinking. Maybe knowing would make it impossible for me to go on.

Keep going. You can do this—you have *to do this.*

Another deep breath. "I want us to be able to properly mourn those we've lost. I owe them that much, at least. However, I'm sure you all saw the rebels' broadcast. I don't think there's anyone who isn't aware of what they revealed by this point. And we—" I hesitate. "*I* believe the rebels intend to use this broadcast as a diversion. While the sector is thrown into chaos, I think the rebels will attack in deadly force. I can think of no other reason for this timing or why else the rebels would have withheld this information for so long."

At this—finally—there's talk. Mutters and concerned whispers spread through the room like a rush of wind. I give everyone a few moments to process this and decide how they feel about it—or maybe I'm just putting off what I have to say next.

"I wish to fight back," I say and cringe when my voice comes out louder than I meant it to. My nerves crash against my chest. *Don't worry about it don't worry don't worry.* "We've already received reports of massive protests and riots going on throughout the sector. We've been in touch with the military for help regarding the likely upcoming attack, but they must deal with the protests as well as the Council. They won't be able to defend the sector from an outside attack in time."

My hand is shaking. I ball it into a fist at my side. I hope the gesture looks more like righteous anger than me trying to hide how nervous I am to tell all these people I want to put them back in death's way. All their eyes on me are like daggers. "The general has made an agreement with us. If we can buy enough time for the military to arrest the High Councilors and calm the riots, they'll join us in the fight and back us up. With the military there, we could finish this war for good." I raise my voice above the outbreak of conversation. "We're the only thing that could potentially stop the rebels from destroying the sector. I know we've just suffered a major loss. I know you have no reason to follow me back into battle—nor will I force anyone to. But if we don't fight back now, we could lose everything. If they break the dome or invade the sector in full force, there won't be a second chance. I'm going to fight. And I would ask everyone who is willing and able to join me."

I wait. Or maybe I just don't know what to say next. When it must become clear to everyone that I'm not going to say any more, the mutterings start up again. I can't make out the words through the blood pounding in my ears. What if they say no? What if they say yes, but they want a different leader? I wouldn't blame them. I'd be okay with stepping down and giving the role to someone more capable. Just so long as everyone doesn't give up. Just so long as we can all keep fighting together.

Someone shouts, "I'm in!" from near the back of the room. I blink and see Jay—Jay, who never shouts—standing tall, shoulders back, confident even when everyone turns to look at him.

Al, next to him, grins wickedly and shouts even louder, "I'm always down for kicking rebel ass!"

And Erik, on Jay's other side, shakes his head with amusement before he too yells, "I'll be right there beside you!"

My heart swells with something I don't have a name for when I look at the three of them. Even from a distance, they look so confident and resolute. Despite all the things I've lied to them about and all the trouble I've put them through, they're still defending me. I want to be worthy of them. I want to be able to do the same for them.

"I'm not about to let our friends' deaths be in vain!" someone else shouts, and I see Amal on a different side of the room, just as strong as always, head held high. "I'll keep fighting—for them! For everything they fought with us to protect!"

The room starts to stir again, differently from any of the times before. All the captains, and then the Helpers, shout their support. And then it seems everyone from every part of the room is shouting or cheering or maybe crying—but raising their fists and yelling words that get lost in the noise but that all resound into one firm answer: *We will fight. And this time, we will win.*

32

JAY

EVERYONE IS ASSEMBLED inside Sakchai's Gate. The garage it leads out from is a huge space with running conveyor belts and large crates stacked neatly around the room. A few transport vehicles crouch against one of the walls. The business owner herself stands resolutely with us—not a fighter intending to go with us, but prepared to see us off. She's even turned the wide-open space around the Gate into a makeshift infirmary to treat anyone injured in the battle as quickly as possible.

This means, of course, that she's thrown off any public pretense of not being an ally of the Order. Her workers bustle around the room, preparing beds, medicine, and tools for the doctors Sakchai hired just for this. They all watch us, but the looks seem more tinged with curiosity and admiration than anything—looks I'm unfamiliar with. Several of them break off to speak with members of the Order.

I catch Lai surveying our troops once more. Everyone wears a red strip of cloth in some way or another to differentiate themselves from the rebels; some with it tied around their upper arm; others, their leg; others still, around their waist. Many of our comrades are still injured from the last fight. However, most of the people here with us now are the ones who were left behind at Regail Hall during the last attack. People who are filled with a vengeance for their friends as well as fear at the prospect of facing the rebels who hurt them in the first place. Those who were injured in any way that would inhibit their ability to fight were left behind, no matter how much they wanted to come.

All except Lai. Even with her major injury, she refused to remain in Regail Hall. No one could tell her no, much as we attempted. The only thing left was for us to resolve that we'd have her back in this upcoming fight. I won't let anything happen to her again. We *are* going to make it out of this, victorious and alive.

I stand by Lai's side as a messenger reports on the arrival of what backup the military could provide. Behind her, a group of about a hundred soldiers stand uncertainly but at the ready. Since only Austin and Noah knew of the military and Order's alliance, it's little surprise they're confused. Yet I feel no suspicion from them. They know why they're here and what we're all attempting to do.

Once Lai has greeted them—most of their presences shifting to shock at the sight of the ex-lieutenant—and assigned them to their respective groups, I say, "You're doing a great job. I'm sure Fiona would be proud."

Lai closes her eyes as she leans her forehead into my shoulder. "I hope so. I keep trying to figure out if I overlooked something, but I'm out of ideas. This is the best I can do."

"Your best got the Order in motion again," I say softly. "Because of you, we have this huge defense team and the promise of help from the military once the Council's been taken care of."

"No," Lai says. "I might've helped, but all of this isn't because of me. It's because of everyone fighting together." She looks up at me and smiles. I've never seen her expression so gentle. "Thank you for everything, Jay. You've always helped me, even when you knew I was keeping things from you."

My heart scrapes up my throat. "That sounds too much like a goodbye."

"It's not," she says. "But, well. Just in case. I wanted you to know how much I—"

"No." I put my fingers over her lips. "Tell me after all this is over."

Her mouth rises into a smile under my fingers. "Yeah. Sure thing."

"Lai, you got a minute?" Peter calls from some distance away. He's with Clemente, Syon, and some of the captains. Syon's and Clemente's presences radiate discontent. The two of them are very reluctantly remaining behind to watch over the rest of the Order. They've made it clear they're unhappy about the situation, but Syon is too young, and one of the leaders had to stay. Since no one could convince Lai to stand down, the responsibility fell to Clemente.

Lai and I share a glance. "I'll be right back," she says.

"Yeah." It's difficult to get the single word out and even more so to watch her leave. Everything is going to be okay. We'll both make it out of this.

When I finally force myself to look away from her, I catch sight of Father nearby. He's lingering, waiting for me to notice him.

I hesitate. His previous burst of concern surprised me. I don't particularly want to talk to him right now, when there's so much going on and I'm still uncertain how to deal with him. However, there's every chance this could be our last opportunity to speak. If anything were to happen to me during this battle, would I really want his last memory of me to be me walking away from him? I can at least give him some peace of mind. I can do that much.

He barely waits until I've reached him before he says, "Are you sure you're going back out there? So soon—after what happened last time?"

"This could be the only chance we have," I say. "If we can't stop the rebels here, now, the sector will be lost. If they decide to aim for the dome and manage to crack it, all the ungifted will die within minutes. You know that."

"I do. But I would rather it wasn't *you* who was going out to fight."

"Doesn't everyone wish it were someone else?"

"Sometimes, I'm not so sure you do."

His comment takes me aback. However, when I think about it, I realize he's right. I don't want to transfer this responsibility to anyone else. I want to do this myself. I want to fight for what I believe in— and protect the people important to me. Lai. Al, Erik. My friends in the Order. Even Father.

"I'll be as safe as I can," I say when I can find no other answer. "I don't have a death wish."

"I know."

I hesitate. I still haven't fully decided what I want to do about Father yet. I don't know if I want any kind of relationship with him. I haven't forgotten everything he did when I was a child. I still recall the exhilarating sense of *freedom* when I realized I no longer needed anything from him during that Order screening. I'm not sure I want to give that up. However, this all seems like something I can decide if—*when* I return. I can at least part with him on good terms.

"I'll see you when I get back," I say. That feels safe.

He also hesitates before answering. "Yes. I'll see you soon."

We hug, awkwardly and briefly, before I pull away.

I don't look back as I head to where Al and Erik are checking their equipment. They're both in their old officer combat uniforms with their red strips of cloth tied over their armor, the same as Lai and me. Whereas Lai's is tied around her upper left arm and mine above my right knee, Al wears hers around her neck and Erik around his right wrist.

Al's eyes lock on me immediately. "Everything okay?"

Her concern makes me oddly relaxed as I join them in double-checking my equipment. "As good as it could be, I suppose."

"Glad to hear you're as optimistic as ever," Erik says. "You're going to have to fill me in on the details with all that once we get back, by the way."

I laugh. Over the course of the past few days, I've realized just how much I missed Erik—in some heartbeats, it feels as though he never left at all. I forget there are things he missed in his absence. Things *we* missed in his absence. "We'll all have to catch up after this is done. I still haven't had the chance to ask about your memories. Any luck?"

Erik smiles ruefully. "Some. Still missing too much to say the risk paid off."

"I'm sure everything'll come back someday," Al says. She grips Erik's shoulder, and he offers a tired smile in return.

"It doesn't really matter if they do or not," he says. "I don't need them anymore."

Al and I exchange a look of surprise; however, Erik doesn't seem particularly perturbed by his statement. He looks over at Lai as she hugs Peter, Syon, and Clemente for a long moment before breaking off to come join us.

Her presence on my grid settles and grows calmer as she nears us. I take her hand in mine and smile at her. She smiles back, and despite her obvious exhaustion, it's genuine.

"Remember," Lai says, turning to all of us, "the goal is to buy as much time as possible. We'll start with trying to negotiate. Assuming that fails, we go after the rebels' leaders. If they fall, it should cause enough confusion in their ranks to buy us the time we need."

Erik's presence wavers. Lai looks to him, and I have a feeling they trade some sort of telepathic communication, because his presence settles once more. He's still upset but more resolved somehow.

"I'll go after Ellis," Lai says. "She's probably going to be coming for me anyway, so I'll have to face her one way or another." Before any of us can protest, she holds up her hand. "I know the risks. But this is something I have to do. Besides, I won't be alone. I've asked several of the captains to help me. We don't *need* to win against her, either—so long as we can hold her off until the military arrives, it'll be our victory."

"I'll take Cal," Erik says after a heartbeat of hesitation. "I think he—I want to try to convince him to stop. I think I can do it."

Lai's gaze is hard when it locks with his. "If you can't, are you prepared to kill him?"

It's an extended period of time before Erik answers. "I'll do what I have to."

He's not lying, but his words don't put me at ease, either. I'll have to ask later who this Cal is to him.

"Dibs on my stupid brother," Al says. She doesn't look at any of us when she says it, and my heart goes out to her. She told us of her confrontation with her older brother a few days ago, once things had calmed down a bit, and of the things he said. Erik's shock at their relation might have been the biggest surprise of all. After that, he spoke a lot about Gabriel and why he was with the rebels. From the way he talked, I gather they were close.

"So that leaves Joan and Devin?" I ask. I'm not sure which of the two I'd be less eager to face. However, I've realized a problem with this plan. I have no intention of leaving Lai's side during this battle—but that leaves two rebel leaders unaccounted for, and both of them formidable enemies.

For the first time, Lai hesitates. "Peter volunteered to go after Devin, but I don't like it. I know he wants revenge for Paul after what that rebel did to him. But Devin is strong, and I'm worried Peter might not be able to stay calm. I don't think he can do it alone." She looks me in the eye. I know what she's going to ask of me even before she says it. "Jay. Will you help him?"

I don't want to leave you, I think to her.

I know, she responds in my head. *But this is important. We have to make sure all the rebel leaders go down. And if anything happened to Peter and I didn't try to prevent it somehow, I'd never forgive myself. Please, Jay. This means everything to me. There's no one else I'd trust this to.*

My jaw clamps shut. I don't want to say yes. I want to say there's no way I'll leave her to fight the rebels' leader alone—especially after their last confrontation and her current state. But her presence is solid, sure. She knows what she wants. If I say no, I don't know if she'd ever forgive me. "Of course," I say. "I'll do everything I can to make sure he's safe. I promise."

Her shoulders slump as though a weight has been lifted from them. "Thank you. And be careful. As for Joan, with her gift, she's going to be tricky to deal with. I've asked two of our gifted captains to take care of her." She takes a shaky breath. "If any of us fail, we'll have to cover for whoever's fallen."

A heavy silence follows her words. Her meaning is clear. If any of us die, we'll have to try to kill that person's target as well as our own—with the knowledge that they killed one of our teammates.

"We've made it through a lot together," I say. "In worse situations than this, with much lower numbers on our side. We'll make it through this, too."

"We'll do more than make it through," Lai says. "We're going to win." Her eyes flash as she thrusts her hand forward.

Al slowly grins as she throws her own hand on top, then me, then Erik. I don't know who initiates it, but we're suddenly crushed together in a group hug, all of us hanging tightly onto one another.

"Just you watch," Al says. "All of us together? Nothing can beat us."

"Well, that's a given," Erik says with a half-laugh.

An extended period of time passes before Lai draws back first. I follow her gaze to see one of the scouts standing just off to the side.

His hands are shaking. "They're almost here."

33

LAI

WHEN THE REBELS reach Sector Eight, a mass of Order members and soldiers borrowed from the military stand between them and the domed city. They came out in full force—this must be most of their members. Some of the rebels still show signs of injuries from our last fight. They're all so young. Too young.

Ellis stands at their head. When only several dozen yards separate us, she waves her hand for everyone to hold. With her eyes on me, she keeps marching forward.

I feel surprisingly calm as I walk out to meet her. I'd thought my heart would be about to explode. I'd thought I wouldn't be able to look at Ellis without seeing Sara and feeling sick. Just like the last times we met. But now when I look at her, I don't see the girl who taught me to fight. I don't feel any of the warmth I used to when I'd catch sight of her. Despite how I try to search for it, I can't find any of the kindness I remember from our days together. This isn't the Sara I love. Not anymore. And it's about time I stop thinking of this person as her.

We both halt when there are only a few strides separating us. I still can't read her thoughts. I can't read the thoughts of anyone immediately behind her, either, which means Gabriel must be here somewhere. I vaguely wonder how he's changed over the years. Has he become cold and cruel like Ellis? Secretive and manipulative like me? Somehow, I can't imagine that.

"We're asking you to stop here." My voice carries to both armies in the dead air. There's no wind, nothing to help abate the oppressive heat. It must be unbearable for the ungifted who have to wear the Outside armor. But they still came to fight with us.

"I'm afraid I have to decline," Ellis says. Her expression is inscrutable. "We've come too far to stop now. We will have victory today."

"Victory doesn't come only when you've killed all your enemies. There are protests against the Councilors' experiments throughout the sector—just as I'm sure you knew there would be. People are speaking up for us. They're outraged for us."

"And you think that will last?" Ellis spits on the ground. "They didn't hesitate to stab us in the back before, but now that they've been handed someone different to hate, suddenly they're our allies? Ridiculous. They're just reveling in their temporary feelings of self-righteousness."

"And if they're not?" I ask. "If they really want to help the gifted? You're not even going to give them a chance?"

"There's no need. An Etiole is an Etiole through and through."

"You're such a hypocrite," I say, finally unable to hold back the outburst. Surprise colors Ellis's expression. "What gives you the right to stand there and judge an entire sector of people? You're no better than the people who abuse Nytes. It'd be one thing if you said you wanted to bring people to justice for what they've done, but you just want to indiscriminately kill everyone—even the people who've helped the gifted."

I wave my hand behind me at all the Order members, gifted and ungifted, who've saved me countless times in immeasurable ways, the people who are risking their lives and everything they love to stand here and fight. "What about the ungifted who fight *with* the gifted? What about the people who've protected Nytes? You're just going to kill them all because of how *they* were born? How does that make you any better than the Etioles who hurt us?"

The surprise is still on Ellis's face, and I realize it's because I've stopped talking so formally. I started to talk the way I did when we were friends and it was just the two of us and Luke. My throat tightens, but Ellis's expression returns to its former blankness, and that somehow makes everything easier.

"How is it those sympathetic Etioles you speak so highly of are never anywhere to be found when the gifted need them most?" she demands. Now she gestures to her own assembled army. "Where were they when our friends were beaten or chased out or killed? Why haven't there been protests before? Why are they only acting now that they've found out it's their own damn kind's fault we exist to begin with? So ready to turn the blame on someone else at the drop of a word—those kinds of people aren't to be trusted." Ellis's hands ball into fists. "And what about after the outrage dies down? Once the High Council's creation of Nytes is old news? People will act in the heat of the moment, but give it another few weeks, and they'll be tired of this already. No one will be trying to help us anymore. That's why we're going to fight for ourselves."

She says that, but when I look at the gifted behind her, it's to find their expressions much less certain than their leader's. Their grips are loose on their weapons, a fact I can see even from here. Their faces are less resolute than the last time we met in battle, their shoulders hunched over. Erik didn't know about the tapes and Council experiments when he was supposedly one of Ellis's high-commanding officers. I doubt most rebels knew. How do they feel about all this? Do they really still want this war? Just from a glance, I wouldn't be so sure. Even Ellis's officers look less hardened than usual—other than Devin, who always looks ready and happy to kill. My stomach twists at the sight of him, and I remember the moment his dagger came down on Paul's back, once, then again, the blood—

"What about all of you?" I ask in a raised voice to the rebel army. Some of them startle at being addressed. "Is this really what you want, even after seeing those videos? Even knowing the ungifted in the sector are protesting for you? You still think they deserve to die?"

No one answers. Several of them shift their weight and won't look in my direction. But for all their fidgeting, no one responds. No one throws down their weapon or says they refuse to fight. They might be unsure about this war, but from what I gather from the thoughts I *can* hear, no one is going to betray Ellis or their friends. Not after coming this far. I won't get any help from them.

I shift my focus back to Ellis. "Don't do this."

In a low, harsh whisper meant only for me, she says, "You shouldn't be here. You're hurt. You lost a fucking arm, for gods' sakes."

"You, invoking the gods?" I ask quietly, unable to help my amusement. It always seems to come out at the worst times. "You don't even believe in them."

"I'm serious, Lai."

"So am I."

"You could die." Her voice is oddly strained.

"As could you. I know what I'm fighting for. That's why I'm here."

"It's not too late. It doesn't have to be like this—you can still join us." A desperation I've never seen in Sara *or* Ellis fills her eyes. "The sectors are wrong, Lai—why can't you see that?"

"Why can you only see the parts that are wrong?" I ask. "What about our friends? What about Trist and his dad, who were only ever kind to us? What about Austin, the man who took us both in?" Something feels stuck in my throat. "What about what Luke wanted—peace for everyone? That's how everything started, isn't it?"

"Luke is dead!" Ellis hisses. Her voice cracks on the last word. "The Council killed him."

My breath catches in my throat. "You know how he died," I manage to say. "It wasn't murder."

"He found out about the Nyte experiments, Lai," Ellis says. "He was trying to find better proof of it before bringing it to the public—but the Council discovered what he was trying to do. They hunted him and he became paranoid. He was too afraid of getting us killed to share it with us, so he kept trying to fix it on his own. But he couldn't win. The Council set up his suicide."

My skin is ice-cold despite the heat. I don't understand. That can't be right. "But the letters he left us—"

"Yours was coded, too, wasn't it?" Ellis asks. "I'm guessing he asked you to take over the Order in yours."

I don't answer.

She laughs, but it sounds strangled. "He told me the truth about what happened in mine. How funny that he left us such different letters and yet we each raised an army in response." Her eyes roam over the Order members assembled behind me, prepared to fight. "I have a feeling he never guessed what you intended to do with the Order once you took over."

"I never intended for this to happen. I never *wanted* this to happen.

If you hadn't started the rebels, I—" But I don't know what I would've done. It's true I would've kept the Order going, would've tried to make it the best it could be to fulfill Luke's last wish, but I never would've steered it in the direction of war. That's not what Luke would have wanted. None of this is what Luke would have wanted. The truth of his death weighs heavy in my chest—but it doesn't change the present.

"No matter what the Council did to Luke, that's no excuse for wiping out the ungifted." My voice lowers. "The Sara I knew was kind, compassionate—she never would've wished anyone dead, let alone an entire sector full of innocent people." I can only look at her, willing her to understand. "You let them warp you, Sara. But it doesn't have to be like this. *Please*. All you have to do is call off this attack."

Ellis stares at me for an endless moment. Against the odds, hope sputters in my chest. Maybe she'll change her mind. Maybe she'll realize how wrong what she's doing is and we can stop meaninglessly shedding blood. But she shakes her head.

"I thought once you knew what they did to Luke, you'd realize I was right," she says. "I thought you'd finally see sense. But I guess the time for trying to reason with you is over, Lai." She raises her hand in signal to attack. The rebels surge forward, with the Order following suit, and the two sides crash together around me.

34

ERIK

I KNEW I'D have to fight people I *really* didn't want to—I just didn't think it'd happen so soon. Everyone I cross weapons with is a face I recognize. I grit my teeth and see them do the same as we go at each other. But I can't kill them. Even though it feels like a betrayal to the Order, I leave them alone as soon as they're on the ground or they retreat. We just have to stall for time until the military gets here, right? It's not like I have to kill for us to win. Once the rebels see the military, they'll surrender, right? Just like that last terrible battle. They will. They'll have to.

But the worst comes way sooner than I'm ready for. I'm racing through the crowd, dodging and alternately lashing out, when I run into the one person I want to avoid the most. The same person I need to take down for Lai's plan to work.

Cal stands in front of me, sword raised, breathing heavily from the battle as we both see each other and freeze.

"Cal," I start, but he rushes in before I can say anything else. I lift my sword to block his. Sparks fly off the metal.

"I don't want to hear it." His eyes are shining, but I can't tell if it's from rage or tears. Either way, it rips through my chest like a freshly sharpened saw. "Whatever excuses you have, I don't care."

"Cal, *please*, just listen to me."

He puts more strength behind his sword until I have to fall back. He follows after me and swings for another attack. I duck, recognizing from all our practices together the posture he uses when he's about to feint a hit. I come up on his side and aim a blow that would only graze him if it connects, but he jumps back and avoids it.

"I understood when you lost your memories," Cal says. He rushes at me again. "But *this*? You tricked us—you were betraying us the whole time!" I can only defend against his onslaught of blows as I feel myself getting pushed farther and farther back. "We took you in, gave you a place to call home, *trusted* you—and all along, you were telling our enemies exactly how to beat us. How many of my friends did you get killed? How many people have suffered because of you?"

"You think I *wanted* it to turn out like this?" I finally manage to get the advantage when I twist my sword around his and thrust it down. He barely raises it back up in time to block my next attack. "I only wanted you all to stop this stupid war—but Ellis is so bent on killing everyone she can't even listen to reason, and you and everyone else just follow along even when you *know* this is wrong. You think I enjoyed selling everyone out? You think guilt wasn't eating me alive the whole time I was there? You think I didn't come to care about everyone and think of you guys as my friends?" My voice cracks on the last word, and Cal's next swing strikes me across the chest.

I gasp as warm blood trickles down my skin, over my armor—but I know it isn't deep enough to be serious. It takes Cal by surprise as much as me, though. He hesitates, staring at the injury he made with something caught between horror and grief. But he runs at me again.

"If you really thought of us as friends, you wouldn't have sold us out," he says. I duck beneath his swing, chest stinging, and lift my sword to block a hit from the side. "You wouldn't have gotten our comrades killed."

"I thought if I could end the war sooner, it'd save more lives on both sides." I shove his sword back with my own and aim a kick at his knees. He jumps over my leg. "I hoped if it looked like you guys couldn't win, you'd be willing to call a truce."

"You thought we'd give up?" Cal demands. "You really thought we'd abandon everything we've worked so hard for all these years just because we were at a disadvantage? You don't know anything. You don't understand us at all."

I say nothing. He charges again.

We keep at it without talking anymore. Before I went back to the rebels, I relied on my telekinesis to save my ass and barely knew how to use my sword. It was Cal who helped me relearn. He made me *want* to get better; his belief in me made me want to live up to his expectations. When I finally managed to beat him for the first time in one of our practice spars, his eyes were gleaming with pride—with confidence in me. When was the last time anyone looked at me like that?

But in the end, all I gave him in return was a knife in the back. I can see it in his eyes as he swings his sword, the tension in his muscles that was never there when we practiced together. He's fighting for more than this war right now. I wonder if he's even thinking of the rebels' cause.

He has every right to want to kill me. But I am *not* going to die here.

We keep trading blows. My arms start to feel like lead, but I continue pushing back. If I mess up even for a second, I'm going to die. This isn't the time to be careless.

My chance comes when Cal lunges too far forward. I swing my blade near the hilt of his sword, putting all the strength I have in the blow, and it flies out of his hands with a harsh *clang*.

He stares at his empty hands, then back at me. Since I still have Gabriel's power crystal and he somehow miraculously hasn't taken back its power, Cal's gift of manipulating the wind won't work on me. And he knows it.

Slowly, his hands fall to his sides. "It's your win, Erik."

I can't move. I hadn't actually thought about what I'd do if I won. I can't just let Cal go like I did with the other rebels. He's one of their top leaders and a crazy-good fighter. He's not even really hurt. If I let him go, he'll just pick up his sword and keep fighting—and I can't let the possibility of him hurting my friends exist.

But I don't want to kill him. And the longer I stare at him, the more I realize I *can't* kill him. Not Cal. Not the person who accepted me as I was and taught me the things I was supposed to know but didn't. Not the person who laughed with me and helped me and believed in me. Not my best friend.

The tip of my sword falls. My eyes start to burn, and I blink back whatever's trying to come out. "I can't," I say quietly. "Not you."

He looks at me with such surprise that guilt stabs my stomach worse than a blade. Of course he must think I don't care after everything I did. Of course he wouldn't believe me if I said how much I cared about him, about our friendship.

"Cal," I say. "Do you really believe the only way to finish this is to destroy the sectors? That it's best to kill all those tens of thousands of people? I never for a second thought you were a heartless murderer. But is that really what you're fighting to become?"

He doesn't say anything. I can feel people around us watching—a lot like when Ellis and Lai fought each other last time. I realize they're waiting to see what Cal will do. He's one of the rebels' leaders—and the most outgoing, friendliest one. It didn't take me long after I joined the rebels to realize how much they love Cal for his kindness and good humor. Whatever he chooses to do right now could have a huge impact on them. It could buy the Order the time it needs without Cal having to die for it.

Please, Cal. Please make the choice you know is right.

Cal sighs, long and low, and finally lifts his head to look at me. He almost smiles. "You've gotten soft," he says. I stiffen. "But you know, I kind of like that. You always were too distant before. I . . . was really happy when you came back, Erik. Not just because I could be with my best friend again. But because you were even better than before."

A heavy weight crushes my chest, but I don't know what to say. The tears from before are threatening again, and I blink them back, hard.

Cal almost laughs. But it disappears right away, and exhaustion as heavy as Lai's replaces it. "I'm . . . so tired of this fight, Erik."

"Then let's end it. Together. We don't need to lose anyone else, Cal."

He looks at me for a long time. I think he's going to say it's already impossible or that he'd rather die than give up here. But then he raises his voice and says for everyone around us to hear, "I'm surrendering. I have no reason to continue fighting for this war."

When I run to hug him, the tears finally fall.

35

AL

THERE'RE SO MANY people I can barely see in front of me. I stick close to Jay and a few others. We've managed to form a tight group, watching out for one another and teaming up to take on anyone too strong for just one of us to fight. It's the first time I've ever fought back-to-back like this in a real fight for so long. Usually I go off on my own once I get impatient trying to match everyone else's pace. But when my halberd misses its mark, Jay's there to cover for me. His knives flash in the light, tracing his movements better than my eyes can. He's gotten a lot faster than when we first met. And stronger.

We tag-team a huge, broad-shouldered girl. I act as the distraction and pull her attention toward me, swinging and thrusting my halberd at any opening I can. Jay circles and strikes as soon as she's too focused on me, diving in with his blades before she can block, then backing out again to safety. Together, it doesn't take us long to beat her.

We regroup with our other allies, forming an outward-facing ring with weapons bared. Anyone who's dumb enough to approach us quickly realizes their mistake.

At one point as I swing my halberd, feeling a rush of adrenaline as I let loose, I catch sight of my brother in the distance. I don't know what made me notice him, especially when he's so far out and not even in the battle itself—just watching from the top of a shaky-looking pillar of boulders—but I recognize him instantly. His eyes scan the battle, and even from here I can see the look of worry on his face. I remember how he just watched during the last fight, too. Of course. Gabriel's always been physically weak—it's why I never suspected him of being a Nyte. It'd be suicide for him to join.

He's my target—and if I take him out like I said I would, not only would it be a punch in the face to the rebels since he's one of their leaders, but it means his neutralization gift would disappear, too. This fight would be a lot easier for our side. It'd be so simple to cut a path through to him. To stand at the bottom of that pillar and shove it over.

But I don't. Taking him out would be a huge help for the Order, and *maybe* it would even make me feel satisfied about successfully carrying out my revenge. But he's so far away. To go after him would mean abandoning Jay and the others. Right now, my friends need me to fight by their sides. And I still don't even know if I actually want to kill him or not anymore. I've had time to think about what he said in that last battle. I think I believe him. But I want to talk to him more first.

I keep my back to Jay's, and we steadily, calmly take down another rebel. And then another. And another. I know Jay senses my mood change by the way he's tensed up, but when I don't make any move to run away, he loosens up again.

Guilt flares through my stomach. What have I been doing? Abandoning my friends in battle. Leaving them to chase after pointless revenge. Paul died because I acted like that. Jay could've died in that last fight. Maybe he would've if he hadn't gotten so much stronger. I'm not about to throw anything else away for the past. Never again.

"Doing okay?" Jay calls over the clang and shouts of battle. His arm is bleeding, but it doesn't look deep. He has one eye on me, the other on Lai, where she's fighting with Peter and Amal against a trio of rebels. Erik took off a while ago, but I'm not as worried about him. He can hold his own.

"Okay, enough," I say as I ward off a blow that would've otherwise hit my collarbone.

I see him nod slightly out of the corner of my eye, more to himself than me. "All right."

"Stick close to me," I say. My attention is on Lai now, too, as she thrusts her spear through one of the rebels' shoulders and flings him to the ground. Even though she's still figuring out how to fight one-armed, she's a terror on the battlefield. "We're going to make it out of this alive. All of us, together."

Another nod. "That goes without saying." But I can hear the relief in his voice.

We keep fighting when my eye catches Gabriel again—much, much closer than last time. Way closer than he should be. He's actually in the fight, swinging a sword he obviously knows how to use and just as obviously doesn't have enough strength to wield with any serious threat. In his other arm he holds a shield—something he actually *is* using well. He's relying on it a lot more than his weapon.

"What is that idiot doing?" I mutter. "He's going to get himself killed."

"Who?" Jay's voice spikes with alarm as he follows my line of sight. When he doesn't recognize the person I'm looking at, he frowns. "Is that your brother?"

But I don't really hear Jay's question. Gabriel's close. Close enough that I should go take care of him as my target.

No. I need to stay here. What if something happens to Lai or Jay or the others? I refuse to lose any of them.

But he's going to die like that. I have to do something.

Why do I care? I don't. Let that dumbass get himself killed. It doesn't concern me. In fact, he can take care of my job *for* me.

"Al," Jay says. "It's okay. Go. We'll be all right here."

I hesitate. But Jay's voice is certain, and I know I'll regret it later if I don't. "I'll be quick," I say. "Just shout if you need me and I'll be back before you can blink."

"I know you will."

I take off running.

An Order member is attacking my brother. He shuffles back awkwardly under the weight of the blows he's taking on his shield. When I get closer, I recognize the Order member. "Hey, Irina," I shout. "I've got this—can you go help Jay and the others?"

She looks up at the sound of my voice. Maybe because she's used to following my orders during training, she doesn't question me before running in the direction I came from.

Gabriel looks more surprised than she did. "Alary?"

I swing my halberd, but I aim for his shield and do it slowly, without a lot of power so it's easy to block. He still staggers back. "What are you doing here?" I hiss. "You can't fight—your body's never been strong enough for something like this!"

"I can't just watch my friends put their lives on the line and not do anything." Even though he's so weak, his eyes are hard. "If there's something I can do to help, I . . ."

I cut my halberd toward his side, giving him plenty of time to block it. This time, he realizes I'm not seriously attacking him and looks at me warily. "What are *you* doing? I thought you said next time you saw me, you were going to kill me."

"I *said* I was going to kill you if I saw fit," I say. "I haven't decided just yet, so don't go counting your blessings." But as I aim another careful hit, I have a feeling I already know what my decision is. I could easily kill him. He'd deserve it, if not for killing our parents, then for running away when we were kids, and again for joining the rebels. I'd be totally justified if I killed him right here and now. He's an enemy leader on the battlefield. This is war.

But he came out here and risked his life because he didn't want to just sit back and watch his friends die. Even though he knew he wasn't a fighter, he was still willing to fight beside them. Would a terrible person really do that?

I don't know whether I accidentally put too much power into my next hit or if Gabriel's grip came loose, but his shield goes flying into the crowd of people battling around us. He watches it go sadly. "You always did beat me, even when we were kids."

"Sorry to break it to you, Brother, but you've never been hard to beat."

He cracks a small grin and lifts his sword. But not high. Not really. He knows he'd lose in a second if I was being serious. He's just waiting for me.

I have to decide. I can't keep wasting time here play-attacking him when my friends are fighting for their lives all over the battlefield. I can't keep putting this off forever. *Come on, Al. Choose.*

I point my halberd at him. His expression doesn't change.

"I'm asking for your surrender," I say loudly, so anyone around us who might be listening can hear. To my surprise, a few people *do* turn around—mostly rebels, but once the Order members fighting them realize what's happening, they pause, too. "Put down your weapon and I'll let you live."

Gabriel watches me with something between amusement and confusion. But then his eyes flick around us and take in the people watching, and something must occur to him, because his expression suddenly sharpens. He looks at me again and straightens. His sword clatters to the ground as he raises his hands. "I surrender," he says. "This isn't a war I can stand behind any longer. Not after learning the truth about the Council and knowing of the riots on Nytes' behalf. I can't believe in this fight."

The metallic clash of battle around us stops.

"Gabriel's surrendered!"

"He . . . he doesn't believe in this war?"

"If Gabriel stops using his gift, we're—"

"They're saying Cal's surrendered, too—"

"If Cal and Gabriel both gave up, then—"

"Gabriel gave up?"

All of a sudden, the rebels around us start dropping their weapons. They lift their hands and announce their surrender. Some of them even kneel.

Ha. How's *that* for buying time?

The Order members around us look to me, and I realize I need to take control of the situation—quickly.

I raise my halberd above me and shout as loud as I can, "Rebels who are surrendering, drop your weapons and gather around me. So long as you don't try anything funny, I'll guarantee your lives."

As a bunch of rebels head toward me, their friends who haven't stopped fighting watch and go pale. More and more drop their weapons to join their yielding friends.

I can't believe how well this is working. I look to Gabriel, thinking he'll be put out by the rebels' loss here, but he just looks relieved. And then I get it.

"So this is your way of trying to protect them," I say quietly. "Can't say I disapprove."

He cracks a tired grin. "Well, I'm glad to have your approval, Alary."

"Al," I say as word spreads through the fighting crowds that my brother and dozens of other rebels are surrendering. "I go by Al now."

36
JAY

SOMETHING HAS HAPPENED. Some message is spreading through the rebels, and more and more of them are throwing down their weapons in surrender. Their presences ripple with defeat.

Pride swells within me as I hear that Cal and Gabriel have surrendered. Erik and Al did it. They managed to defeat their targets, and even without having to kill them—and it's having exactly the effect we hoped it would: panic, confusion, and surrender are spreading throughout the rebels' ranks. Of those on their knees, no one appears as though they're about to get back up. Their spines are bent in defeat. Their weapons are too far from them to easily retrieve. They've truly given up.

But not all of them. The fighting continues, and as I risk taking my attention from what's directly in front of me and our group, my eyes catch on Peter fighting, alone, some distance away. My heart races when I can't find Lai anywhere near him. Weren't they together? What happened? Where is she?

More immediate alarm presses in when I identify who it is Peter's fighting. Devin. The murder-hungry rebel who killed Paul.

Time feels as though it slows. I don't know where Lai is. I need to find her—but she told me to help Peter, to protect him. And I promised I would. *Please, Jay. This means everything to me. There's no one else I'd trust this to.*

When I made that promise, I didn't think it'd involve choosing between going to her side and staying by his. I thought we'd all be able to stick together. I thought I could protect them both. But I can't. I don't even know where Lai is right now, and the longer I hesitate, the farther Peter is pushed back.

Choose. You have to choose.

My grip tightens on my throwing knives.

Peter trips over a fallen rebel as he's dodging Devin's blows. He hits the ground, hard.

"I'll be back!" I shout to the others around me, but I don't have time to wait for their response.

I reach Peter and Devin just as Devin starts to bring his curved blade down on Peter.

I throw one of my knives at the dead center of Devin's chest.

He swats my knife out of the air with his sword.

Peter takes the chance to gain a little distance. His breaths fall heavy. We share a look and nod. No going back now. I'll have to hope we can finish this quickly and then find Lai.

I begin to circle Devin as Peter comes around his other side.

The rebel laughs, a sound that lives on the other side of sanity. "You think you can win against me if there're two of you? Fine. Bring it on!" The glee in his eyes makes me sick.

I charge, a knife ready in each hand. I feint to his left, and when he dodges, I drop and aim a kick to his ankles. He easily dodges the blow, but Peter comes up behind him with his daggers.

Devin laughs as he alternately dodges each of our attacks with ease, even when we're both going at him. "That's all you've got?" he asks. "Weak." He evades another hit. "Weak!" Another. "Let me show you how it's done."

As I dodge his strike, he grabs my upper arm with his free hand. Sudden pain shoots through my whole body. It's so unexpected and sharp I can't hold back my scream. Peter rushes in to try to help, slashing at Devin's side, but the rebel merely whirls around and throws me into Peter. Peter quickly changes his attack into a motion to catch me, then backs up so we're out of immediate range.

However, Devin doesn't wait for either of us to recover. Pain continues to course through my body like electricity. I can barely stand, let alone help as Peter dives in to cover me. What happened? Is this his gift? It hurts. I can't breathe. Make it stop.

And above it all, Devin keeps laughing.

Peter is too slow and sustains a long gash along the length of his arm. He shouts in pain and backs away, toward me, but Devin is right after him. I grit my teeth against the effects of Devin's gift as I run in to cover Peter. My whole body still hums with electric hurt. But I can't stand the thought of seeing Peter killed right in front of me, of watching another friend fall—and after I told Lai I'd do my best to protect him. I *won't* fail either of them.

Peter's ragged breaths ring in my ears as I match Devin blow for blow. But he's faster than I am and quick to overpower me. I'm on the ground before I'm even fully aware of it. Pain burns through my leg—but it's a different pain from before. A gash cuts across my calf, deep and burning. When I try to stand, I fall right back down.

Devin stands in front of me. I swing my knife at him, but he kicks it out of my hand with a laugh.

I clench my fists. *I'm sorry, Lai. I couldn't follow you to the end of this war after all.*

With a fire in his eyes, Devin lifts his sword to deal the final blow, but Peter rushes in to block the rebel's blade with his dagger. It looks like a toy in comparison.

"Peter, don't!" I shout. He won't be able to hold off Devin for long. He needs to get out of here, not try to protect me. If I can't stand, I'm already dead. There's no reason for both of us to die.

"No!" Peter shouts right back. His eyes burn more fiercely than Al's as he pushes against Devin, even as the rebel's blade gets closer and closer to Peter's collarbone. "I'm not going to watch any more of the people I care about die right in front of me!"

"Then I'll just have to kill you first." Devin laughs again, and I know his sword is about to toss Peter's small blade aside.

But then he stops laughing. The sound turns into a gasp, then a choking cough as he looks down at the sword suddenly sprouting through his chest from behind. In an incredibly strange moment that seems to last a year, we all look behind him.

I expect to see one of the Order members, maybe even Lai herself, appearing to save her old friend. Instead, one of the rebels' leaders stands there holding the blade piercing through Devin. The one with the gift over ice, Joan.

We all stare at her in shocked silence.

"The hell have you done?" Devin asks, but his voice comes out sputtering and wet.

"You have long been a disgrace to us," Joan says. Her voice is tinged with disgust. "Your love of violence, of pain—you've never fought for peace for the gifted. Only for yourself and the chance to kill. You should have been judged a long time ago."

Devin tries to twist around and slash at Joan, but the sword impaling him keeps him stuck in place.

Joan twists her sword and Devin screams. I think I'm going to be sick. "And that," she says quietly, "was for killing Paul."

Recognition flashes across Peter's face at the same time I remember the rebels' first ambush, back when we were still with the military. She was the rebel Paul had been head over heels for before everything fell apart.

As Joan rips her sword out of Devin and lets him fall to the ground, Peter snaps out of his shock and attempts to help me up. We back away as Joan watches Devin's last breaths contemptuously. I think he spits what sounds like a threat or an insult at her, but whatever he says, it doesn't matter. I see the moment the light leaves his eyes for good.

Peter and I watch Joan cautiously. Peter holds one of my arms over his shoulder—the sole reason I can stand right now as I leave any weight off my injured leg. Even if this rebel didn't have a powerful gift, even if she wasn't incredibly strong according to Erik, she'd have no problem killing both of us so long as Peter refuses to abandon me. I almost tell him he needs to leave me and run for it, but when I recall the look in his eyes as he attempted to hold back Devin, I know the words would fall on deaf ears. I say nothing.

"This isn't how it was supposed to be," Joan says quietly. She looks to the hilt of her sword, fingers gripped tight around it. Blood drips down them. "This isn't the war I wanted to fight."

She looks at us and I ready my knife, knowing it will be impossible to fend off any incoming attack but refusing to go down without a fight.

Joan tosses her sword on the ground between us. "I surrender."

37
LAI

IT DOESN'T TAKE long for me and Ellis to find each other again. We separated when our two armies came together, but I knew we would have to face off eventually as the leaders of our groups. And because of our history. She had to know, too.

It's not like the ambush, when she didn't know it was me and I was too consumed by my emotions to face her properly. This time is different. This time is the last—and we both know it.

I swing my spear around the blade of her sword, but it doesn't have the same force the move used to contain since I can only use one arm to maneuver it. The strength and precision of it is half what I intended. Ellis easily slides her blade out of the way.

She ducks under my spear and brings her sword around at my side, but I jump back. At least I didn't lose a leg. My ability to move freely and dodge are still the same. And since I only need to stall until the military gets here, it doesn't matter if my hits can't connect. So long as I can keep this going, it'll be our win in the end.

Ellis keeps coming and I keep dodging. Around us, though, things have started changing. The shouts of battle have shifted to ones of surrender and questions.

"Cal and Joan gave up?"

"Gabriel's finished—his gift—are the effects gone?"

"Is it true Devin is dead?"

"Over half the east side has surrendered!"

I take these in as best I can while fighting Ellis. I can tell she's listening, too.

"You should give up," I say as I bring the shaft of my spear up to block her next hit. "You can't win. Your allies are already surrendering."

"I don't give up." True to her word, nothing about her has dimmed since news started spreading about her closest friends' surrender. If anything, her hurt at their apparent betrayal has only made her fiercer. "Even if I have to fight alone, I *will* fight."

I have to give way under the pressure of her sword and fall back. She follows.

I feel the gazes of the two captains I asked to back me up in this fight. But they won't move unless I signal for them to, or it looks like I'm going to be killed. Ellis is too strong—I don't want to put them in harm's way if I don't need to. There's at least a chance she'll hesitate before finishing me off. My friends? None. And I don't want to lose anyone else if I can help it.

Her blade scrapes off the shaft of my spear as I deflect another attack, but it nearly makes me lose my grip. Fear lights my chest for a moment before I manage to get myself back under control.

I need to stall. If I can distract her, it could make an opening—or at least make her lose focus enough that she won't find an opening against me.

"This brings me back," I say as I thrust my spear at her chest. She easily sidesteps it and comes swinging at me, but I spin out of the way, to her side. "It's just like when you taught me how to fight."

"You've certainly improved since then."

I catch her sword along my shaft. "I remember I originally wanted to learn how to use a sword—I thought it was the coolest weapon. You're the one who convinced me the double-headed spear would suit me better. And you were right."

"Obviously." Almost despite herself, a half-smile twitches on Ellis's lips. Good. Keep going, just like this. "I knew you'd be better with a versatile weapon. It's just like you."

I nearly falter. But I tilt my shaft so her blade slides away from me. I swing one of the spearheads at her neck, but she shifts her sword up to block it.

"Do you know why I thought the sword was the coolest weapon?" I'm only supposed to be stalling for time, but the words catch in my throat. "Because you use it."

Now Ellis is the one who hesitates—but not enough for my strike to connect with her side. She skips back a few steps.

We assess each other, looking for a weakness. The calls of surrender are getting closer. The longer we go, the more of her side is realizing how pointless this fight is. The military's main force should be here anytime now. Once they're here, they can put an end to everything. Just a little longer. Just a little more. Yet my limbs are heavy. All I want to do is lie down. My vision blurs from the sweat dripping into my eyes, and I try to blink it away quickly. *Not now. Not yet. I can do this.*

"If you're getting tired, Lai, you can always give up," Ellis says. "I won't hold it against you."

"In your dreams."

We come together again with a clash of metal on metal. We twist and turn back and forth, none of our blows managing to hit, every swing taking more and more effort. It feels like we go on forever. But finally, the thing I've been waiting for comes—cheers from the Order members as they shout that the military has arrived. Renewed shouts of battle fill the air as fresh soldiers pour in.

I skip back out of Ellis's range. "Just give up," I say. "The military is here—you can't win anymore. But if you surrender right now, so will your friends. They don't have to die meaninglessly here."

"That's naive, Lai." She tries to smile but falters. "Where would they go? The sectors will never let us rejoin them. Not after this. And frankly, I don't want to."

"Things are changing. There are people fighting for us in the sector right now and people who are fighting for us right here. The sector doesn't know the identities of most of the rebels. Your friends, the people you're trying to protect, they can all just slip back in. The Order can help them."

"You're an idealist as ever, Lai." Ellis's eyes stay locked with mine. "And what about me? What about our other leaders? Should I just throw away all our lives? The sector knows us—and they will never forgive us for what we've done. I wouldn't, either, if I were them."

"You can either die here for no reason or let yourself be arrested and live to see another day," I say. "Is it that hard of a choice?"

Ellis just stares at me. "You really think I won't be killed for everything I've done once I'm taken in? The question isn't whether to live or die, Lai. It's whether I'm going to die fighting or lying down. And that is a very easy choice."

I don't know what to say. I can't tell her she's wrong—because she probably isn't. But why can't she see that giving herself up might mean saving more of her friends? What is she even fighting for at this point?

It doesn't matter. I don't care what she wants anymore. Dying is the easy way out. Dying means she doesn't have to take responsibility for everything she's done. Dying means everything will be more complicated once all this ends because there's so much only she knows. That knowledge could make a huge difference in how everything plays out after this. If she was being smart, she could even try to use that knowledge to broker a deal and save her friends.

I swing my spear at her ankles. She jumps over it easily, but I use the momentum to keep swinging around in a circle and slam the other end of my shaft into her side. She blocks it with her blade, but she stumbles back.

I have to find a way to immobilize her. If I can hold her down until a soldier arrives and restrains her with starlight . . .

Restraints. That's it.

Al, Erik, Jay? Where are you? I need your help.

Ellis and I keep at it for interminable moments. Even as the fighting stalls out around us with the military's swing through the rebels' decimated forces, that only seems to fuel Ellis's strength. Her blows come harder, faster, but more haphazard, too.

"You can still choose to stop." I block her swing with my spear shaft. She keeps putting force into it, trying to break through, but I don't let her. "They might be more lenient if you surrender."

"Not a chance."

I figured. Still, I wanted to give her the option. I send the telepathic signal to everyone.

Ellis pulls her sword back to swing again, but in the time it takes me to blink, she's on the ground, crushed against the earth by an invisible force. Behind her, Al stands with Gabriel in tow, a somber expression on his face as he watches Ellis struggle and snarl on the ground, having taken away the portion of his gift residing in Ellis's power crystal. Running up to us, Erik, hand extended forward, pinning Ellis down with his gift, Cal keeping pace behind him. And Jay, arm slung over Peter's shoulder for support, the two of them accompanied by Joan and a military officer I asked Jay to find and bring—one equipped with near-indestructible starlight restraints.

The officer looks among all of us quickly, but he doesn't stop to ask questions. As soon as he sees Ellis pinned down, he removes intricately connected pieces of starlight metal from his equipment bag and claps them around Ellis's wrists, legs, and upper arms. He has to act fast, because as soon as he puts the restraints on, Erik's gift stops working in reaction to the starlight and Ellis thrashes against the bindings. To no avail.

She looks up at her old officers, her friends, now all staring at their feet. "You would all betray me like this?" She doesn't cry. But the hollowness in her eyes is almost worse. "I thought we were in this together."

"It was time to stop, Sara," Joan says quietly. She meets Ellis's gaze with an expression caught somewhere between pity and regret. "I'm sorry. It had to end."

Ellis won't look at her. As the officer hauls the rebel leader to her feet, other soldiers racing over to help him, I say, "I wish things had been different."

"So do I," Ellis says. And then she's gone.

38

ERIK

SOLDIERS FIGHT WITH the last few rebels who refuse to give up.
They don't attack those who already surrendered—thank the gods—
but they do circle around and keep an eye on them. Word's spread
that all the rebels' leaders are down. Can't say I'm sad to hear Devin's
dead. One less lunatic in the world. I'm just happy everyone I care
about is alive and safe, from Cal and Gabriel to my old reliable team.
My relief at seeing them all okay after Ellis is hauled away is so strong
I can't breathe for a second.

But I don't want the military to catch Cal or Gabriel. If the soldiers find out the two of them were rebel leaders, they might kill them.
There's already a chance they might be recognized. We've all barely
reunited when more soldiers start coming over, starlight cuffs in hand.
I step in front of Cal reflexively and notice Al do the same to Gabriel.

But Lai is the one who steps forward to face the soldiers. Even
with dirt, sweat, and blood smeared over her face, she looks like a
queen. Acts like one, too. "The Order will be taking custody of the
remaining rebel leaders," she says. It's not a request.

Most of the soldiers hesitate and glance at one another—which is honestly kind of reassuring since I thought they'd just laugh and push Lai out of the way. Not that she'd let them, but they could try.

One of them, with more badges decorating her uniform than the others, steps forward to meet Lai. My muscles tense. If she tries anything . . .

"We were told by General Austin that any orders given by former Lieutenant Lorelai Cathwell on the field were to be followed," she says. "But even so, I can't let enemy commanders escape arrest without reason. Why does the Order want them?"

"There are things we'd like to learn from them," Lai says. If she's surprised by the general's order like I am, she doesn't show it. "Intel gathering. There are also other rebels back at their home base. With the leaders' help, the Order would like to—peacefully—bring them in." Lai cocks an eyebrow at the officer. "I doubt they would willingly surrender to the oppressive military. But if it's the Order, a group they *know* seeks equality between gifted and ungifted, they may come quietly."

Lai glances at me and suddenly I get it. All the kids back in the underground headquarters. She wants to make sure the Order gets to them before the sector can. The Order couldn't convince the kids to leave by themselves, but if Joan, Cal, and Gabriel tell them it's okay, that the Order can be trusted? We might be able to save them.

The officer doesn't answer right away, which, I mean, fair. Lai's excuse is pretty flimsy. But Austin did say the soldiers had to follow Lai's orders. Just how far does that go?

Finally, the officer says, "I understand. I will report this to General Austin. He can decide whether or not to allow you to keep custody of the rebel leaders after that." The officer's hand moves obviously to the starlight handcuffs clipped to her equipment belt. "If they were to suddenly disappear or otherwise cause trouble, you and the Order's other officers will be taking their place."

"My thanks," Lai says, totally ignoring the last part of the officer's conditional acceptance. She holds out her hand. "We don't need your assistance, but we could use those starlight restraints if you'd be so kind."

The officer's nose wrinkles, but she tosses the handcuffs to Lai and waves for the others to do the same. I hate to do it, but I snap the cuffs around Cal's wrists. I don't think he or the others would try to run, but I get what Lai's thinking. We have to make it look like the Order's in total control. Otherwise that officer might just change her mind and bring Cal, Gabriel, and Joan in herself after all.

Other soldiers start running over and calling the officers for help. Soon, the group is gone, though with a lot of backward glances. I hope this works out.

I'm just about to ask Lai what's next when one of the soldiers running over calls *my* name. I sort of recognize the guy as he gets closer. He's the general's secretary—what was it, Noah? He stops a few feet away, breathing heavily. His uniform is spattered with blood and dust, but it doesn't look like he took any bad injuries. Even though he's obviously exhausted, his eyes light up when he sees me. But why? Then I remember what Jay said about me and Noah apparently having been friends back before I lost my memories. And about him being pretty shady.

"Noah, right?" I ask.

He nods and straightens.

Weird silence stretches between us, and I don't know what to say—especially not with everyone right here. I can feel all of them watching me.

"Can we talk?" Noah asks. He gestures vaguely behind him, not quite looking at me. "There are things I need to tell you."

I glance to Lai and the others, who each nod. "All right." As I reluctantly follow Noah away from my friends, I hear Lai giving out orders, getting everything moving again. It kind of sucks not to be there with them and be a part of it.

I do get the chance to see the battle's damage, though. Lots of people are down, but not as many as I expected—on either side. With the military swarming everything now, though, it's hard to really tell.

Noah doesn't stop until we're pretty far from anyone else. When he does, his fingers pull at one another. He doesn't talk right away.

"I can guess what this is about," I say. "We used to know each other, didn't we?"

He nods and takes a deep breath before he starts talking so fast I can barely process the words. Like he's trying to get it all out before he loses the guts to say any of it. "You—I really looked up to you. We met when you were on recon in the sector for the rebels. You didn't say as much, but I could guess. I'd been a spy for the military and the Council for a long time by then, after all." He smiles grimly to himself. "I didn't tell you I was from the military, just that I was a Nyte. You tried to convince me to leave the sector a few times, but I turned you down every time. I've always just dutifully done whatever the Council ordered me to. If I don't . . ." He trails off and I don't ask. "We became close. Really close. You were the only friend I'd ever had. I respected you a lot. I wanted to be like you—independent and free. But at the same time, I felt bad for you."

"Bad for me? Why?"

His hands twist together again. "You hated everything in the world. You just wanted to watch the sectors burn for what they did to your brother."

"My brother?" The words rush out before I can stop them. Cal mentioned him before, but he didn't know anything. If Noah could tell me what happened, if there's a chance my brother's still alive—

"He was killed by Etioles when you were both young. You told me you'd hated the ungifted ever since."

I might be sick. In the same second hope flooded me, it was immediately replaced by grief for someone I can't even remember. I should've known better. Cal wouldn't've lied to me, and I doubt I would've ended up with the rebels if my brother was still alive—or at least that I would've ended up there alone.

A cold chill that I can't shake seeps into my bones. Suddenly, I don't want to have this conversation. I don't want to hear whatever Noah has to say.

Noah must see it on my face, because he sighs. "You were so bitter. So hateful. Even though you seemed free, it felt like you were chained down by your past. You were miserable because of it, and I knew even if you succeeded in destroying the sectors like you wanted, you'd never be happy." His eyes meet mine. "But that wasn't why I took your memories."

"What?" For a minute, I seriously have no idea what he's talking about. Then it slams into me like a byc at full throttle. No. There's no way.

"I didn't—it wasn't—" Noah's hands wring each other so hard I think he's going to tear one of them off. "The Council already knew you were a rebel, and then they found out we were meeting up. At first they were going to kill you—they ordered *me* to kill you. I . . . I refused." His left thumb rubs over several laced scars on his other hand, almost unconsciously. I flinch at the sight of the raised welts.

"Then they got the idea that they could use my gift to wipe your memories and enlist you in the military. The Council knew you were strong—they thought they could use you. They said if I agreed to make you forget your past, they wouldn't kill you." His eyes squeeze shut, then reluctantly open again. "So I did. I tricked you into telling me when you'd be doing a raid with the rebels, and the military set up an ambush to catch you. After that, I kept my distance—I knew if you found out who you'd been, the Council would kill you. I'm sorry, Erik. I'm so, so sorry."

I hear what he's saying, but I can't process it. It's too much. I thought he was going to say we knew each other—but all this? Him being the one who took my memories? The reason he did? I can't take it.

"But—pieces of my memory have been returning the last couple months. Why?" It's the only thing I can manage to put into words.

"My gift's effects start to wear off the farther away a person is from me." He sounds relieved to be able to give a straightforward answer. "The longer the time away, the more they wear off." Noah suddenly shrinks in on himself. He won't meet my eyes. "I've never been able to stand up to the Council. But now that all this is happening—now that the Council's been taken down—I . . . I don't know what I'll do anymore. Except this." His voice falls. "I'm sorry. I came to tell you that. And to say I'll return your memories if you want."

At that, my head snaps up. Of course. If he's the one who sealed my memories in the first place, he'd be able to unseal them. But I hadn't thought that far ahead yet. Or maybe I just didn't let myself think that far ahead. The possibility I could get my past back— everything I wanted to know, right at my fingertips. All I have to do is ask.

But I'm suddenly terrified. The past few months, everyone who knew me before I lost my memories said how full of hate I was—even Noah. If my memories come back, will I go back to being that person? Even if I don't, will I be able to handle the things that turned me into that person to begin with?

I already know I don't have a family waiting for me. And even though I know I *should* want to remember my brother, that I should honor his life by remembering him, I can't bring myself to want to. It's only going to hurt.

What if remembering my past just makes me miserable? As soon as I think that, I realize how happy I actually am right now. Well, not *right* now. But I have friends—my team, Cal, Gabriel. I know what I want to do. I know what I've been fighting for and what I want to continue fighting for. What if remembering changes all that?

For the first time since I woke up an amnesiac almost half a year ago, I don't want my memories back.

"No." I don't realize I said the word out loud until Noah looks up at me. "No," I say again, more firmly this time. "I don't want my memories back. I mean, not now. Someday, maybe. But not right now. I don't . . ."

Noah's eyes soften and I get the feeling he's sad. I can't imagine why until I remember we were apparently close friends. His only friend, he said. He sold me out, but still. It sounds like he only did it so I wouldn't get killed instead. "I get it," he says. "You know if you change your mind, you can always come find me. But . . ."

"But?"

"But if I die, your memories *will* come back to you. You won't have a choice in the matter."

"Then I guess you're just gonna have to keep living."

Noah laughs. "Right. Noted."

I hesitate. "Noah. Thank you. I mean, you kind of stabbed me in the back, but—I know you were trying to protect me. And maybe it all ended up for the better. Who knows? If you hadn't wiped my memories, maybe I'd be dead by now. But—I want to say thank you. I wouldn't have a lot of the things that make me happy right now if it wasn't for you. However messed up the process was."

He smiles reluctantly, and it strikes me that even though I have all these new and renewed friendships, I don't have his. He might have accidentally saved me from a life of misery, and I don't even know who he is.

Noah holds out his hand to me. "Good luck, Erik. I wish you all the best."

I clasp his hand tightly, in what I hope he can tell is gratitude. "Thank you, Noah. For everything. I hope you find your own happiness—one that's free from the Council. You deserve it."

His eyes fall to the ground. "Erik, I know you can't remember, but I . . . I've done too many awful things for the Council. I've killed innocent people for them. I chose my own life over others'. I don't deserve happiness."

I choke back a laugh. "You think *I'm* going to judge you? I know you probably didn't have a lot of choice with the Council watching your every move. I don't even have a good excuse for the things I did. I just think . . . everyone deserves to be happy. Especially someone who's never had the chance to be." I grip his hand tighter and look him in the eye. "I might not remember you, but I know I want you to be free, too. I hope you get that chance. I really do."

Noah's grip loosens, then tightens on my hand. "Thank you, Erik."

Before I can reply, he leans in and kisses my cheek. Then he runs away, back into the crowd on the still battlefield.

39

JAY

IT'S OVER. THOUGH it doesn't feel like it. Everything is surreal, like walking through a foggy dream that's pulled pieces from reality but distorted them. Fallen bodies, soldiers taking custody of the rebels who surrendered, medics attending to the injured, crying friends and trampled-over weapons. Word hisses through everyone that the last of the resisting rebels have fallen.

It's difficult to focus as Lai treats my leg. Everything is hazy around the edges. Everything except Lai. Her ponytail has come mostly undone; loose strands hang around her face. Dirt and blood are smudged across her armor; however, she sustained no serious injuries, thank the gods. Her presence glows with somber triumph and grief. She struggles to wrap the bandage with one hand, so I reach out to help her.

"Gods, I'm so glad you're okay," I whisper. I managed to hold everything in as we assessed casualties and everyone else dispersed to carry out their respective tasks, but now that I'm sitting and have nothing to actively take care of, everything catches up to me all at once. The fear, the shock, the fact that I nearly lost my life and could've lost many, if not every one, of my friends. "I lost sight of you during the fight and I thought—I didn't know what to—"

"It's okay now." We tie the bandage together and she hugs me close. Her warmth is an anchor, a reassurance. Her heart beats against mine. *We're alive, we're alive, we're alive.* "We're okay. Everyone's all right. We won. It's over."

"It's over," I repeat numbly. I can barely register the words. The gash in my calf burns.

"Yeah." Lai's hand shakes where it rests against the back of my neck. "Jay—thank you. Thank you for protecting Peter. Thank you for worrying about me. Thank you for being okay."

"Those aren't things you have to thank me for."

"I'm doing it anyway."

For some reason, I begin to cry. Lai leans her forehead against mine as tears start to streak her own cheeks. I close my eyes and we stay like that for a long time.

Eventually, Erik returns and rests a hand on both our shoulders. When Al rejoins us, she scoffs once, then wraps us all in a hug. Despite my shakiness and everything that's happened, a laugh actually chokes its way out of me. I lean into my friends, soaking in their presences, the fact that we're all here, that it's over.

We set up a temporary home base in Sakchai's Gate. Everything is a blur of motion as doctors and nurses rush through the beds already filled with wounded. Shouts for medicine and tools pierce the air. The fighters who've already returned but aren't terribly hurt attempt to help as best they can, assisting with moving the injured, carrying boxes of new medicine, bringing over buckets of water. Cal, Gabriel, and Joan keep together in a corner, under watch and restrained with starlight handcuffs until the immediate aftermath of the battle has been dealt with.

Lai runs back and forth dispensing orders, helping where she can, Peter and Clemente rushing around to do the same. There's little I can do with my leg but sit and wait with Al and Erik. The aftershock of the battle still hums through me, and I'm grateful for their company.

Messengers from Austin trickle in slowly over the next few hours. Amid riots and protests all over the sector, the military successfully pulled a coup d'état against the High Council. All Councilors have been arrested and taken in for questioning. General Austin and a few hastily chosen elected officials with clean records have been appointed temporarily in charge of the sector and matters regarding the investigation. They're promising justice—and immediate protection laws for all Nytes affected by the Councilors' experiments.

You can feel it in the air, even down in the Gate's hangar, so far removed from everything going on in the city. Cheers rend the air. Strangers hug one another. Some of the Order members throw their red cloths up in the air, and before long, everyone is doing it. When they drift down, people just keep tossing them back up, crying through their triumphant shouts.

40
LAI

THIS MORNING, THE new protection laws for the gifted were officially announced and put into effect. Our team of representatives, which has been working with the Legislators in the creation of the laws, has been out all day at official events, meetings, and press junkets—but none of us have been looking forward to anything so much as celebrating with all our friends. The main hall in the Order's underground tunnels is filled with bright lights, loud laughter and cheers, and a general air of happiness so thick you could choke on it.

We've barely had time to eat between all the hectic events of the day, so Jay, Al, Erik, and I claim a corner in the hall and fill it with loaded plates of food—the most we've had to eat in months. Trist, Peter, and Syon drift in and out, but for the most part, they're off enjoying themselves.

"Gods, I thought that last interview would never end," Erik groans as he stuffs a whole bread roll in his mouth. He's still adjusting to being able to eat full meals after the rebels' months-long shortage of food, and we all have to remind him to take it slow. At least his and Peter's giddy food fight from earlier is over. I had to put my foot down and send Peter away after he nailed Erik with a tomato and gleefully shouted, "Tomato surprise!" But I have to admit, it was nice seeing Peter joking around again. I haven't seen that side of him since Paul died.

"Why were we even chosen to represent the gifted in the military, anyway?" Al asks. "Weren't we kicked out?"

"Likely as a way to restore our credibility and reputation within the sector," Jay says thoughtfully. He blows on his soup. "Otherwise we'd still be traitors. Besides, we were closest to the action in the end."

"As long as they don't ask us to actually come *back* to the military," Al snorts. "Like hell I'm fighting for them again."

"Idiot, the war's over," Erik says around another bread roll. "There's no need for you to fight again *period*."

His words hit heavier than I think he meant them to. We all sit there in silence. It feels unreal. This is really it. We *won*. We don't have to fight anymore. We were able to help negotiate real laws for protecting the gifted.

I can't imagine living a life in which I don't have to fight. I fought on the streets as a kid. I fought in the military as a soldier. I fought as the leader of the Order. I have been fighting every day of my life for as long as I can remember, and now, all of a sudden, that's all over. I don't know how to live *without* fighting. What am I supposed to do now?

I look down at where my right arm used to be and brush my fingers against the edges of the bandaging. I wish Luke could have seen this day. It's everything he ever wanted. And Paul and Fiona—did they die thinking this future we have so close at hand would never come? Did Fiona think it'd be impossible for the Order to recover after that ambush she lost her life in?

No. No, she always knew we'd pull through. That's why she saved me. Her belief saved us all.

And I won't let it be in vain.

"We're going to be fighting in different ways now," I say. "There's still a lot to do, after all. New laws aren't going to erase discrimination overnight. The Order still needs to spread peace."

Not to mention the matter of the ex-rebels. Ellis is still being interrogated, but the death sentence has already been decided. All the rebels who surrendered at the final battle were arrested. They're currently being questioned while Austin and the new Legislators, who've replaced the Councilors, decide what to do with them. It's a tricky situation because the Legislators are trying to create a sense of peace in the sector, especially with the wronged gifted. Many rebels only became rebels because they had nowhere else to go. But they still killed. They still waged war with the goal of genocide.

And then there's the children. With the help of Joan, Cal, and Gabriel, the Order was able to sneak all the rebel kids out of the underground home base and into Regail Hall. Our members are looking after them, and though the kids are obviously suspicious of us, they're safe. They keep their grief and confusion close. I can't imagine they'll ever trust us completely after our major role in the death and imprisonment of their friends. But at least they won't get wrapped up in all the politics taking place.

The older rebels who'd remained at the underground base peacefully surrendered to the military. There was no point trying to resist. After that, we had to hand custody of the remaining rebel leaders over to the military. Due to their significant parts in ending the final battle and their leading the peaceful surrender of all the remaining rebels, I don't think the Legislators will kill them. At least, I'm hoping they won't. I'm arguing their cases, but it's going to be a long fight.

One good thing is that Gabriel's been returned to us. Not only did I ask it as a personal favor to Austin, but apparently Cal and Joan teamed up to try to get him cleared. They told their questioners that the only reason Gabriel joined the rebels was to try to stop them from the inside. He's never killed anyone. He's even the reason we were able to capture Ellis in the end. Between their determined insistence on his innocence and Austin's influence, Gabriel's been cleared of all charges.

I catch sight of him across the hall, surrounded by former rebel children. They cling to his arms as he laughs and swings them gently around. I have a feeling he'll find an excuse to come over and pull Erik away soon. Things were tense between them for a while, and Erik kept avoiding him, but they must've resolved things, because they're nearly inseparable now.

"I can't believe it's really over," Al says. "I mean, I know there's still work to do and not everything's going to be fixed right away. But still. No more war. Crazy, huh?"

"Pretty sure you mean *relieving*," Erik says. He elbows her side. She retaliates by shoving a chicken bone in his face, and he swats it away.

I can't help but laugh watching them. I'm so glad they're here. I'm so happy we're all together.

On the stage, an impromptu band is starting to form. It's an odd collection of trumpets, trombones, a few saxes, and an oboe. The musicians have no conductor, but they start playing, and all of a sudden, everyone is pulling one another into the center of the floor, twirling around to mismatched melodies that sound purer than centuries-old classical pieces.

When Jay stands, grinning, and offers me his hand, I take it. "I hope you've practiced since last time," he says.

"Of course," I say. "Every waking hour of every day since. I had to fill my time *somehow*."

We laugh as he leads me spinning into a dance. Al and Erik tease us from the sidelines. At least until Gabriel comes over and asks Erik for a dance, and then it's his turn to be teased, with Al saying, "Hold on, I don't remember giving you permission to date my brother." When Trist, Peter, and Syon come over to join us, we all take turns leading one another around in ridiculous pretenses of dancing.

Eventually, I have to take a break from it all. Jay and I sit on a bench together, residual laughter still on my lips as we kiss. I can't remember how many times this makes it, but neither of us can seem to stop trying to sneak them in today. I can't get over the feeling of victory surging through me—in ending the war, in getting rights for Nytes, in being surrounded by my friends. There's still a long way to go, but for now? I couldn't ask for anything more.

"So how's it feel?" Jay asks when we pull away. He leans his forehead against mine, peering at me over the rims of his glasses with eyes that reflect my own giddiness. "Achieving all you set out to?"

"Pretty damn good, I have to say."

"And now? Now that you've conquered the world, what do you want to do next?"

It's something I'd been thinking about a lot lately. Ever since the war ended, I kept wondering what I'd do from now on. Obviously there's still a lot of work to be done before discrimination between the gifted and ungifted is completely gone. Just because the Council was exposed doesn't mean the people who hate us will suddenly become understanding. There are still people who fear us or want to use us. I'll continue to lead the Order so long as they'll have me—this time, truly with the intent of spreading peace. But there's something else I want to do, too. Something just for me.

"I want to find my mom," I say. "I'm . . . not afraid anymore. I want to find her and tell her everything I've done. I want her to know me, and I want to get to know her. Is that weird?"

Jay's eyes drift back toward the crowd of dancers, and I follow his gaze to see his dad and Sakchai dancing back and forth—just as his dad steps on her foot and she jokingly reprimands him.

"It's not weird," Jay says. His voice falls softly. "I think it's normal."

I squeeze his hands. "Not wanting to get to know your dad with everything that's happened between you two is just as normal, you know."

"No. I want—I mean, I think I want to at least try. We'll see how it goes."

"Well, you better keep me updated on that."

"Oh, don't you worry." Jay kisses my forehead. "I will."

"Wow, get a room," Erik says. I hadn't even noticed him come over, but he stands not far from us with Al at his side.

"No one wants to see you two being all disgusting," Al chips in.

Jay's face is red as he pulls back, but I say, "I just won us a war— I'm going to do whatever the hell I want."

Al laughs. "Won't argue with you there."

"Well, *sorry* to interrupt, but at least spare us a little time," Erik says. Al grins. "Get over here and dance with us."

Al grabs my hand and pulls me back into the crowd. I can only laugh as she awkwardly twirls me around and I see Erik giving Jay the same treatment. There's still a lot to be done to win true peace. We all have a long way to go from here. But for now, everything is perfect.

ACKNOWLEDGMENTS

IT FEELS SURREAL to have finished this journey that I started eight years ago with Lai, Jay, Al, and Erik. Their story has taken various shapes over too many drafts to count, these characters constantly demanding that I get it right, and now here I am writing The End. Somehow I thought the acknowledgments would be easier to write for the second book, but it feels like even more people have joined me on this journey and offered me more support than I can put into words.

It goes without saying that I owe so much to the Swoon team responsible for bringing this book I love so much into existence. My amazing editor Holly West, my kickass cover designer Katie K., the wonderful director Lauren Scobell, and the absolutely legendary Jean Feiwel. My sweet and supportive agent, Kerry D'Agostino, who's been nothing but encouraging and has done a truly applaudable job of speaking reason to me when I'm freaking out (seriously, thank you). There are so many more people whose names I don't know who did more behind-the-scenes work than I can probably fathom, but who I want to thank nonetheless. None of this could've happened without everyone on this wonderful team, and my thanks for you all are endless. And of course, the Swoon Squad. I've never met such an absolutely lovely, supportive group of authors, and I can't say how much

I appreciate all the advice, encouragement, and support you've all given me over the last several years.

I want to thank my mom (always) for showing me to love reading from childhood and always encouraging me to follow my dreams, and my stepdad for helping and teaching me in too many ways to name. I love you both so much. To my sister, brother-in-law, and little nephew, Nicholas (congratulations on turning one!): You're an inspiration in being happy and I wish you all the brightest of futures.

I would never be where I am today if not for Kristin Dodson, who first made me think I could actually be a for-real writer and has been the most amazing, supportive friend anyone could ever ask for these last eleven years. Thank you for all the car talks, sleepovers, trading chapters and entire novels back and forth, writing *Warriors* fanfiction together, and telling me words I really needed to hear last fall. You're amazing and I love you (except for when you break my heart with your characters, damn it).

To all my incredible friends who have helped me through many a dilemma, writing and otherwise, over the last many, *many* years: Sydney Catlin, Paris Powers, Megen Nelson, Natalia Bravo, Maria Dones, Jasmine Tsunoda, Elena Nielsen, and Roger Zhao. I don't know what I'd do without you all, but I know my world would be a much dimmer place. You've all changed my life for the better.

To my amazing UCF writing family—*wow*, you all have helped me learn and grow so much over these past two years. My brilliant and supportive thesis director, Brenda Peynado, who blew my mind about how novels work and has taught me more than I'm probably even aware of. My wonderful professors, Terry Thaxton, Micah Dean Hicks, Jamie Poissant, Chrissy Kolaya, and Rochelle Hurt, who've taught me so much about both writing and the writer's life. My fellow classmates who constantly push me to do better and also make me laugh so hard I cry. Laura Mundell, Adam Byko, Lauren Gagnon, Kyle Kubik, Jessica Pinkley, Alicia Pipkin, Josh Des, Rebecca Fox, Nicole Balsamo, Madison Brake, and Becca Rowell, I don't know how I would've made it to graduation without your constant encouragement. And this tomato surprise is dedicated to you, Josh.

And finally, the biggest of thanks to my readers. Thank you so much for caring about this story I love and following these characters as they grew and stumbled and learned. It's been the greatest happiness of my life to be able to bring this story into existence, and I could only do it because of all of you. Thank you.

Check out more books chosen for publication by readers like you.

DID YOU KNOW...

readers like you helped to get this book published?

Join our book-obsessed community and help us discover awesome new writing talent.

1 Write it.
Share your original YA manuscript.

2 Read it.
Discover bright new bookish talent.

3 Share it.
Discuss, rate, and share your faves.

4 Love it.
Help us publish the books you love.

Share your own manuscript or dive between the pages at **swoonreads.com** or by downloading the **Swoon Reads app**.